The Sky Slayer

Joel Cornah

www.kristell-ink.com

Paperback ISBN 978-1-911497-10-3
EPUB ISBN 978-1-911497-11-0

Cover art by Evelinn Enoksen
Cover design by Ken Dawson
Typesetting by Book Polishers

Kristell Ink

An Imprint of Grimbold Books

4 Woodhall Drive
Banbury
Oxon
OX16 9TY
United Kingdom

www.kristell-ink.com

For the Barrow Downers
And especially my Friends of Finn
Including the original Lomi Thinlomine

Isles of Cath
Khamas
Red Docks
Har Yam
Iron Mines
Sea of Ice
Bád Inis
Port
Mountains of Cumhacht
Penguve
Glasoghear
Sea of Ice
Teach Iasc
Mountains of Treash
Bron'Halla
Pengover
Pits of Meabh
South of South

Chapter One

A Stranger Comes to Town

THE SEA HAD BROKEN HIM. ROB SARDAN HAD LOOKED INTO the waters and had seen his reflection. In the storms, the red winds, and the cold, he had learned what he was. He had wanted to be a hero, but what had he turned into?

King-killer. Sky-slayer. Sword-breaker.

A squawk distracted him, and he looked into a snow speckled tree. Nestled in the needles was a lizard-bird, its silver and white wings making it difficult to discern. Rob gave it a smile, and it chattered its toothy beak. It was the first living thing besides his captors and fellow prisoners that he had seen in two years. The thought sent a hollow feeling into him, and he felt the chasm of the future; a void of snow and isolation at the end of the world.

"She won't give you time off," a voice snapped. Rob sunk back into his hiding place.

"I know, but I'm still going to try," a higher voice said.

They were pengs. Short, feathery and coated in armour. One was carrying her helmet under one arm, her wide fingers tapping the pearl and gold patterns that ran through the metal.

The other peng was still wearing hers, the visor pulled down so that it extended into a spike that ran over her beak.

"Commander," the peng holding her helmet said. "You think I could get transferred to the north some time?"

"You'll have to be a bit more specific, Aisling," her commander replied. "Literally everywhere is north from here."

Even though he couldn't see her, Rob was sure she was glowering. This was Kerrok, the commander of guards. How did she always manage to find him?

"I mean Penguve," Aisling sniffed. "Need to check on my sisters and see if mother needs more food sending her way. Got connections now, don't I?"

"Loads," Kerrok snorted. "We're connected to everyone. That's if you ignore that giant wasteland surrounding us. Get through fifty miles of snow, ice and maybe a mountain or two, and then you can use those connections."

"I'd get a proper escort; I'm not stupid. Next time the supplies come, you know? I'd hop on one of them new snow ships they got."

"Well, good luck to you. I've been bothering Lomi about a transfer for ages."

"I heard you'd *asked* to be here!"

"I did." Kerrok prodded Aisling until she put her helmet on. "Didn't meet my expectations."

A hollow sound rang above their heads. Rob looked beyond the trees to the snow-capped ice cliffs that loomed overhead. A battalion was standing atop them, waving banners that showed a white peng crowned with laurels. Kerrok and Aisling rummaged in their packs and produced another banner. This one showed a dark blue snowflake surrounded by a chain of white links on a black field. The same banner flew all around the prison, and Rob was all too familiar with it.

"Don't be shy, Sardan," Kerrok said, waving at her companions. "I'm sure the new arrivals won't be intimidated by the sight of you."

Aisling looked around, crouching as if ready to strike. Her hands tightened into fists, and her head was poised, beak thrust forward in a typical pengish battle stance.

Rob scrambled from the bushes he'd been hiding in and brushed snow off his thick woollen tunic before pulling his cloak around him. Though the pengs barely reached his breast, they struck a wide stance and fingered the knives on their low hips, the razor edges glinting in the cold light.

"I thought you were the nice one, Aisling," he said with a slight shiver. The moisture of the snow had him soaked to the skin.

"It doesn't work like that," Aisling said. "Nobody's nice to you, King-killer."

A jolt went through Rob's spine, and he put a hand on his chest, feeling the warm pendant that rested against his skin. In his mind, red flashed and a howl of nightmarish wind blasted into his ears.

Coming back to reality, he tried to shrug but caught sight of a glimmer in Kerrok's eyes.

"What?" he demanded.

"Keep a civil tongue, prisoner," Kerrok chuckled. "I could have your rations reduced again."

"Oh no, less rice and gruel, what a tragedy," Rob leaned against a tree.

"Don't talk to the commander like that." Aisling strode forward, haughty and her eyes suddenly beaming with pride. "She's done more good for the world than you have, yeah? She's not a pirate friend; she's not a killer or a monster. Wouldn't catch any peng doing stuff like what you did."

"Yeah, and that whole empire you've got going; really just happiness and flowers all day, isn't it?"

"Son of Morven," Aisling hissed. "You think having a famous mother makes you special, right? Well, it doesn't! Not around here! Maybe Kenna Iron Helm and the Pirate Lord were impressed, but we're not! Don't you dare think we are!"

"I am not my mother," Rob said, calmly. "And you were the one talking about running home to your mother."

"At least mine is still alive!"

"Serving the Empress, yeah? Sounds like a wonderful life."

"He's goading you, soldier," Kerrok said. "I'll have him dealt with. Don't raise your hand or Lomi will have your feathers off."

"I obey," Aisling nodded to her superior and marched towards the cliff, ducking under the branches that leaned over the path.

"Mark this, Sardan," Kerrok said with a sharp jab of a feathery finger into his stomach. "Out in the world, you might be a famous vagabond, you might be the great Sword-breaker, but this is Bron'Halla. This is the Pengish Empire. You are human. You will always be on the lower rung. Understand?"

"Can't say that I do," he shrugged. "Maybe I'm just not as clever as you lot."

Kerrok licked her beak and shifted her eyes away. The procession was moving down a set of zigzagging stairs that skirted the cliff face, tall human shapes being prodded along by the halberds of small pengs.

"Why are you here, Sardan?" Kerrok asked. "Want to make an impression on the newcomers?"

"Didn't actually know they were coming today," Rob shrugged. "Just wanted some air."

"There's air in your cell. There's air on the balconies. Why were you hiding in the bushes? Waiting for someone else, perhaps?"

"Gorm," he admitted. "She thinks she can help me with my . . ." he hesitated.

"Yes, the screaming," Kerrok laughed. "You wake the whole cell block with that racket. Well, tell Gorm to make an official statement to the guards. We do not appreciate undocumented prisoner activities."

"It was my idea," he said. "I basically made her do it."

"Don't start," she groaned. "You're not a hero, Sardan. You are not your mother, you say. Well, you're right there. *You* can't protect people; *you* can't save people. You can't do anything so stop trying."

"Old habits."

The prisoners had reached the woods and Kerrok shouted a greeting in one of the pengish languages. Rob caught a few words he recognised; ceremonial nonsense, he realised, and soon stopped paying attention.

His eyes went to the prisoners; one was short and gangly despite layers of cloaks and a thick hood. The light dappling through the trees illuminated his gaunt features, lighting his gold nose ring and the deep-set eyes in a bronze face. His jaw line was smooth, rounded and framed his soft lips; Rob's stomach clenched, but he ignored it.

The other captive stood a little apart; arms crossed and hood back, yet her hair was covered by a scarf of blue silk that framed her passive features. Her nose was rounded and looked to have been broken at some point recently, but her eyes were sharp and were now glaring at Rob directly. He returned the stare with defiance, and she lowered her eyebrows before looking distractedly at something in the trees.

"You have been brought to the Final Prison," Kerrok said to the prisoners in a theatrical fashion. "Your crimes have earned you the spite of civilisation, but by the grace of the Pengish Empire you have been spared death. You will live your days in the Mourning Hall, where you shall learn a new life and die a more fulfilled person."

The tendency of the imperial pengs to use flowery language was something Rob had found quaint at first, but the years had worn him down. In the early days he had been awed and impressed; he missed that sense of wonder, which had become buried under monotony and time.

"Here, you," Kerrok approached the gangly man who cringed from her.

"Yes?" the man said with his eyes downcast.

"What is your name?"

"My name? Well, my name is . . . you know it's not important really."

"Your name. Now."

"My name is Gethin of Gwasgar." He stood a little straighter, his eyes looking over the trees and into the sky.

"Liar." Kerrok took a halberd from one of the new pengs and thrust the blunt end of it into the man's stomach. "You will learn not to lie to the Pengish Empire!" She cracked the flat of the blade across his arm. The prisoner howled in pain and curled on the ground as Kerrok raised her weapon again. "Vann is your name, Vann from Geata."

As she struck him again and again, Rob flinched, his heart beating hard in his ears. '*Don't do it*,' he thought. '*Kerrok wants you to step in. Don't.*'

Vann screamed, another crack of blunt wood sounding through the trees. The years of imprisonment had eaten through Rob like maggots, but they had never found the core of his old dreams. Despite everything he had been through it still flickered there, and Kerrok knew it.

'*There are no heroes*,' he reminded himself. '*Only villains who win.*'

He tightened a fist and ground his teeth, but stayed still. The sounds of the beating got louder as steps came closer. He opened his eyes just as Vann was shoved into him, knocking them both to the ground. Rob pushed the man off and stood over him. Kerrok rushed at Vann, but Rob knocked the halberd aside with a swift arm.

"That's enough," he said. "You wanted me to step in, well, fine then. I'll stop this if that's what you want?"

"No, don't," Vann coughed and got shakily to his feet. "Really, I'm fine. Feel right as rain in a moment. Just . . ." he shivered and hunched over, gagging.

Kerrok made a sound that was somewhere between a whistle

and a snort. She nodded to the pengs around her, and they sped forward, feathery hands taking Rob's arms and dragging him back.

"Steady on," Vann said, weakly.

"Speak again," Kerrok taunted. "Please, we are waiting to hear your words of wisdom." She lifted the halberd and Vann flinched. The blade was almost upon the prisoner when Rob shouted a wordless cry that distracted her enough to miss.

"I always said you were going blind," he jeered. "Can't hit a stationary target without complete silence and concentration, is that it?"

"So," Kerrok turned to face him. "Is this your show of bravery? Trying to save this filth from his due?"

"I'm just pointing out that you're lazy, and you keep missing your mark."

"My aim is precise and unyielding."

"That's not what the other officers were saying. Is it true you tried to hurl a stone at a trasati-bird and missed by more than an arm's length? They said the bird was just sitting still on an open branch for all the world to see."

Kerrok stepped closer to Rob. She looked up into his eyes. "What do you think you will achieve here, Sardan? You think these people will like you if you make a show of being on their side? Perhaps you think that by banding together you humans can mount a resistance? If you think you can fight us, you will learn better."

"I'm not interested in fighting; I've had enough of it."

"So melodramatic." She turned to the prisoners. "This fellow who wanted you to admire him for his bravery is no hero. He is a murderer, a betrayer of friends, and a thief. He is Rob Sardan. Why don't you tell them who you are, Sword-breaker?"

The title was a jab to his heart, and he spotted Vann stir and eye him with something that might have been admiration. That made his insides squirm with delight, but he pushed it away. The other prisoner shifted and gave him a glance before going back to looking at the trees, disinterested.

"I am here to pay for my past," Rob said through gritted teeth. "You can't use it as a weapon to beat me."

"Tell them what other titles you have," Kerrok prodded. "Go on; let them know what you are."

Rob shook his head, his long dreadlocks catching his eye as they swung from underneath his hat. He'd been in this cold, isolated prison for too long. He decided to play along, but he wouldn't let Kerrok see her taunts were getting to him, so he stood straight, squared his shoulders and spoke clearly.

"I am the son of Morven the dread," he said, defiantly. "They call me King-killer, Sky-slayer, and Sword-breaker," he was glad his voice didn't shake as he spoke. Vann looked awed, but the other prisoner seemed not to have been listening, her attention focused on a whirl of snow.

"Lovely titles," Kerrok mocked. "A hero in his own mind. But look at where you are. Even the mightiest humans succumb to the Pengish Empire."

"I came here by my own choice," Rob objected, a little more defensively than he'd intended.

"So you keep saying." Kerrok twirled her halberd and tossed it from hand to hand. "Son of Morven the dread, hah! She defied the Empire, but you sit here in our prison, a slave to our will. If she were alive, what would she think of you?"

Rob had seen similar behaviour before from bullies intent on showing off. '*Let her*,' he thought bitterly. '*Let her have her fun*.'

"Right."Vann shuffled forward, wringing his hands. "Shall we be off to that tower now?"

"We could do that," Kerrok nodded. "But I'm not quite finished here. Aisling, please knock Master Sardan to his knees."

Aisling saluted and took a halberd from one of her companions. Her eyes met Rob's briefly with a cold light. She ducked behind him, and he heard the whip of wood through air before it slammed against the backs of his knees.

He let his limbs go loose, and he relaxed his stomach muscles before the next blows came. Impact after impact drove harder into his body from every angle. With his eyes closed he fell to the ground, snow splashing across his limbs, but the peng continued her assault. The physical pain was dulled by the cold, but his mind played over the horrible title. Sword-breaker. Sword-breaker.

King-killer.

Sky-slayer.

Sword-breaker.

But he had made a promise. To live and to change.

"He won't break," Aisling hissed. "I told you so."

"Pengs are stronger than humans, remember. We must show them this."

"Ten on one doesn't seem fair," Vann said, muttering.

"You pengs," Rob spat before they could turn on the new prisoner, "outnumber everyone, that's your tactic. You can't win on your own. You're too weak." He lifted his head and tried to open his eyes, but one of them was swollen shut already. Kerrok now towered over him, halberd in one hand while the other reached to grasp his collar.

"Question *me* all you like," she said. "I am above your petty jibes. But the Empire will sweep across Diyngard until you and all your kind are under the rule of ice." She pushed her hand under his clothes.

"No!" he cried as she yanked the chain from around his neck, snapping the pendant free. She held it up, letting the light settle around the red disk on its gold chain. Etched on the pendant was the pale gold skeleton of a pterosaur. "Please, give it back! I need it!"

"Sky-slayer," she said in disgust. "You know, head-warden Lomi was once a follower of the Sky Sages. Our illustrious leader has told us all about it often enough. She swam in gold and red winds, seeking the slayers of the Air-keepers. And you're one, aren't you, Sardan? You killed an Air-keeper. How does it feel?"

"Please," Rob spat blood. "You know what happens to people who kill those things."

"Oh yes, I have heard stories," she turned to the new prisoners. "Cursed with nightmares so intense that they can never sleep. I have endured his screaming; now all of you will have to do so." She turned back to Rob. "Enjoy your nightmares, perhaps they will teach you the consequences of defying the Empire. Perhaps you will learn and change your life." Kerrok dangled the pendant in front of Rob. "Say again what you think of pengs."

He hissed and then lowered his head, hoping she would take it as a sign of defeat, that she would move on and stop this blatant display. It was just an act, he supposed. It was all to intimidate the prisoners; it was all a show of power.

As the silence crept on, he recalled an old friend who had relished silence, had made it her cloak and her friend. He kept his mouth shut and waited. They'd leave him, eventually, if the silence did its work.

"I told you to say it again," Kerrok insisted.

Rob kept his silence.

"Very well." She dropped the pendant in front of him. It lay in the snow; the dulled gold stark against the white. The cracked glass across its circle was too dirty to glimmer, but the ice around it did. He reached out to take it.

The blunt end of the halberd crashed on the pendant. The gold shattered, the glass splintered, and red mist flittered from the broken centre. Rob's ears rang, his bones ran cold, and his eye strained to stay open. He couldn't breathe. The whole world seemed distant and unintelligible.

"Come, let us leave him," Kerrok said, gathering up the shards. "Aisling, finish him off."

Aisling approached, stern and straight backed. Her eyes met Rob's, and she lifted her halberd with only a slight hesitation. As consciousness left him, Rob heard the echoes again.

King-killer.

Sky-slayer.

Sword-breaker.

Chapter Two

Lomi Thinlomine

He screamed. He screamed so loud and so hard that his lungs felt as if they would collapse. Voices hammered his skull, dying breaths and a horrifying laughter rang across the world.

Light seared his eyes as he opened them. Coughing, he rolled, shivering and convulsing as his left eye demanded to be closed. The swelling had gone down, but it was still bleeding, reddening the snow in drops.

The little trasati-bird landed beside his head and snapped its toothy beak. He gave a pained smile and reached to stroke the bird, but it nipped at his finger. Recoiling, Rob sat up, cradling the cut as the creature took flight, its talons curling in the cold.

It took his mind back to when he had been a child in the desert living amongst the lizard people, the saurai. They had tended the gigantic trasati, the scaly creatures that seemed to come in every size and shape. Some were feathered, others slimy, all were impressive. His mother had been there, too; Morven, who had been a legend, who had defeated the Pirate Lord Mothar, and then left Rob eternally in her shadow.

He had gone on to make his own stories, to become a legend in his own right, and yet he still saw her influence in everything he did. Rob had fled to this prison to get away from her shadow, and to get away from the pain.

Footsteps crunched, and a shadow stretched over him, hiding the diminished sun. Turning he looked up at the tall woman who stood there, loose robes were tied about her waist with rope while a cloak was fastened to her broad shoulders. She pulled back her hood and let her braids run down towards the small of her back, revealing her round face.

"I saw the trasati-bird," she said quietly, which was difficult as she had a voice that rumbled as if it came from the depths of the earth. "I have seen birds and others turn towards you when you pass. It is strange to me; in my time I have only seen those who obtained inner peace commune with trasati."

"Hello to you, too, Gorm," Rob tried to smile, but his face ached. "Sorry I'm late for our session."

"It is no matter." She bowed and sat with her head still above his.

They sat for a while, the throbbing in Rob's face growing every time he tried to move. He wanted to talk, but also wanted his lips to heal.

"The pain is unpleasant," Gorm observed.

"Yeah," Rob winced. "You said you had ways of getting around pain and suffering. I will need it more than ever."

"I suffered many hurts at sea." Gorm cupped her hands in her lap while closing her eyes. "To be apart from pain is a dangerous exercise. I advise against it."

"Kerrok broke my pendant." Rob focused on a patch of snow that had been stained red. "You know what that means?"

Gorm remained still, her eyes closed and her breathing steady. Rob looked around and spotted his hat a yard or so away, crumpled and trodden on. Reaching out, he took it and pulled it over his flailing hair.

"Lomi has spoken of the Sky Sages," Gorm said at last. "Seekers of dark things, it is said. But others say they reward the slaying of pterosaurs because they truly believe that it is the right thing to do."

"Well, condemning someone to a life of horrific nightmares doesn't seem like the *right* thing to do." Rob snorted.

"Tell me how you discovered your ability to commune with trasati?" She opened her eyes, and Rob frowned at her.

"You're changing the subject."

"As I said, only those who have discovered peace may do it, or so I had heard. I had heard that the trasati can read our intents better than we can know our own. Within you is anger and pain, I see it in you every day. Do not let it be your guide."

"Gorm, I just need to get past the nightmares."

"The trasati feel your anger, loneliness and isolation, that is my guess."

"Thanks," he huffed and resigned himself to another lecture. "It's complicated. Trasati are creatures of emotion, of unbridled feeling. We humans keep our feelings shrouded and under control. To commune with the trasati means letting go of self-control."

"To control one's self is to conquer one's emotions," she retorted. "To be at peace with the self is to accept your emotions as real and to live with their meaning. Your anger has deep roots. I fear that the trasati, too, are angry about something."

"What would they be angry about?"

"I am not the one who communes with them," she stood, smiling. "My words may be wasted if you do not act upon them. And these past two years have seen very little action from you."

"Gorm, I'm tired," he breathed a slow breath. "Thanks for being concerned, I do appreciate it." He decided not to tell her that he found her advice contradictory and fuzzy. "Please, teach me the technique."

"Not now," she shook her head. "The hour is darkening. We should return to our cells."

"The cells," Rob said. "Day in and day out. Well, can you call them days if the sun never properly sets half the year, and never rises the other half?"

"What would you do if you were out in the world again?"

"I can think of a few things I need to do." He touched the spot on his chest where the pendant had hung. "Escaping from this place might be worth a song or two one day."

"I thought you regretted your acts that have led to songs," Gorm chastised. "Do not so eagerly seek glory for its own sake."

Disappointed, Rob staggered to his feet, light-headed and sick. His toes were tingling, and a pulse of fear rippled through him. His heart beat with ferocity and the echoes of screams tolled in his skull; final breaths and stolen lives.

He was a Sky-slayer, and so he was cursed. Any who killed an Air-keeper, the great pterosaurs of the Spill Mountains, were cursed. But Rob had gone further, he had killed their king. It was an act his younger self might have been proud of, but now he looked back on it, killing the Air King had been one of the worst things he had done.

The more he tried to justify it, the more it hurt. The Air King had killed Rob's friends, had tried to take the Sea-Stone Sword, had ruined the lives of countless people across Diyngard, and yet . . .

He shook his head and staggered out of the trees. There before him was the prison, Bron'Halla. Blinking up at the colossal tower, he craned his neck as far back as it would go. Even if he had lain on his back to look, he would not have been able to see the top, but he still felt inclined to try.

Vast did not begin to describe it; its peaks and jagged spikes cast everything into shadow for miles around. Frozen fire reached from the earth jabbing towards the sky ever higher, ever sharper, until it vanished beyond the clouds. Its many barbs melded to a point that pierced the firmament beyond sight; it was as if a furnace had solidified in a single moment; blue and white crystallised and set to stand as a monument.

Around it were other fortresses, diminished by its enormity; those closest to the tower had tried to imitate it in stone and stained glass, but those further took new forms as the pengs had diversified and challenged the ancient tower.

Rob came to a boulevard lined with iron lampposts, from which hung glittering baubles that refracted the dim sunlight in shards. Rob missed a step as he gained the pathway, it was not thick with snow but paved with glimmering white marble. The pengs went to a lot of trouble to recreate the white landscape of their home when they conquered distant lands but to do so here, at the southernmost tip of the world, seemed ridiculous.

At the end of the boulevard was a door four times the height of the tallest human Rob had ever seen. Yet the door seemed insignificant in its crystalline setting, almost swallowed by overhanging spikes of blue fire.

"Glory is like a circle in the water," Gorm said, making Rob jump. He had forgotten she was following him, "It never ceases to enlarge itself until by broad spreading it disperses to naught."

"I beg your pardon?"

"Nobody knows the names of the hands that built this tower, so their glory is lost. Remember that, my friend. Glory is nothing to seek after." She brushed snow from her front and nodded. "I shall see you later."

"Oh, yes, good," he nodded and looked around. "Did you see where the new prisoners were taken?"

"I did not. If I were you, I would seek Ilma and have your wounds tended. Even if you learned to separate your mind from your pain, the wounds would still need dressing and healing."

Rob frowned. He'd still been a child when he had come to this prison, and some of those childish ways had stuck. Waving, he left Gorm and headed into the tower.

The entrance to Bron'Halla opened with a sound like an avalanche. Ice and snow trickled from the doorframe creating a white curtain. Beyond was a crystallised hall with a spiked ceiling and a sweeping floor of sapphire. A series of passages sprung from the wall opposite, and he went through absently. He passed pengs in regimental armour and nodded at the familiar faces; this was rarely reciprocated, but when it was it gave him a sense of victory.

He came to a long corridor of blue glass that rose and splintered into new passages. Every wall was a gleaming pattern of blue, silver and white shards of light splitting and bending all around until Rob thought he'd go blind.

At the top of a spiral staircase he found an ornate door; carvings of pengs and sea creatures wound their way across its face, spiralling from the centre where the handle shone pale. Rob pushed his way in.

Chattering stopped, and faces turned to him; four humans sat cross-legged before a table that held a steaming teapot and five cups. Behind was Lomi Thinlomine, a peng, old and frazzled, draped with cloaks and holding a walking-stick across her lap. Her eyes were closed, but her beak was moving with whispered words.

"You may drink now," Lomi said, and the humans reached for their cups. The older peng picked up her own, which was curved to fit her beak.

Her eyes flicked to Rob, and she nodded to the corner; he bowed and went to stand while she continued her lesson. The students were prisoners, one of whom had arrived at the same time Rob had; Ilma of Ramas, a bony, shallow-faced woman twice his age. She had a shine to her eyes, and she winked at him over the rim of her cup.

Ilma had been made the unofficial medic for many prisoners; the pengish doctors had a tendency to be rough, unkind, and insistent that everyone endures pain. Ilma gave prisoners strong drinks to numb them. Where she got them from was a mystery.

"A theory espoused by Blath the unbridled," Lomi said, handing a scroll to Ilma. "It will answer your questions regarding the venoms of the sea serpents."

"I don't understand," said another prisoner. "They're all dead; the venom is gone."

"Learning for its own sake," said Ilma defensively.

Lomi struggled to her feet and leaned on her walking stick. "I would like your essays on The Legacy of Aodhamir prepared by the ninth day. And you must write in Old High Penguvian. No excuses."

Ilma was engrossed in her scroll as she left but gave Rob a cursory wave. Lomi pointed to the floor in front of her table. Rob felt his spine tingle as the warden made her way to a dresser at the end of the room, her walking stick tapping.

There was a glass teapot over a flickering candle, the light of which was broken into rainbows by the crystal walls. Within the teapot was a flower that was sending clouds of colour through the water; Lomi poured some of this tea into two cups.

"How is your Geatish? You have not written in it for some time."

"I'm not too good," he diverted his eyes. "The alphabet is weird."

"It is different," she nodded. "But you learned the letters of Shenish and your skill with it is excellent."

"I learned those from birth. Galoti is so close to Shen as to make no difference."

"And yet you speak Concaedian fluently."

"I still call it sea-speak"

"*Concaedian* is spoken by but a fraction of the world. It spread with the Sea-King's empire. The only reason it is spoken in so many realms is that it was put there by the edge of a sword. By one sword in particular . . ."

Their eyes met. "The Sea-Stone Sword."

"Indeed. The new prisoners have heard of you, Rob Sardan. Are you prepared for their questions?"

"I've avoided them for two years; I can avoid them again."

"But should you?" she asked, handing him one of the cups. "I cannot command you in this matter, but I will advise you. It is not healthy to keep your past as a spectre, haunting your mind."

"I don't want to be thought of in that way," he protested. "King-killer, Sky-slayer, Sword-breaker! That's how they'll see me. Death, violence, breaking things. That's not who I want to be."

"But perhaps it *is* who you are."

"If that is who I am then maybe I should have died on the Teeth."

"I cannot tell you what you should have done." She pressed her feathery fingers together and closed her eyes. "I am no seer, and I am not able to leap into the past to change things. But those acts brought you to this place; you have blood on your hands, how does it make you feel?"

"You know how it makes me feel! We've had this conversation a hundred times, and it never changes anything."

"You refuse to change. You told me you wanted to change, to be a different person, but then you do ill-advised things like attack one of my officers."

So they had come to it at last. Rob met her glare defiantly.

"Kerrok was out of order!" he protested. "I couldn't let her bully that new prisoner."

Lomi poured tea into her beak and swallowed. "It is not your place to act against a peng, let alone one of high rank." She gave a heavy sigh and leaned forward. "You told me you did not want to be the same person, that you were determined to become something new."

"I meant that I didn't want to fall into the same traps as before," he ground his teeth. "I was immature, and I stopped caring about the people; I only cared about actions that looked good."

"You wanted fame, and you wanted to be remembered. You wanted your actions to inspire others, and you wanted glory. You still want that."

"If someone stands up to bullies then others will too!"

"What did you do in your confrontation with my officer? Was it an act of defence, of heroism, or was it your desire to be *seen* as such? You wanted the new prisoners to see you as an ally, as one who would defend them."

"It's not like that," he tried to protest, but she raised a hand, wide and feathery.

"Commander Kerrok has confiscated your Sky-slayer's pendant, I hear, and I, for one, think she is in the right to do so."

"She didn't confiscate it; she broke it!"

Lomi looked up sharply, her eyes blazing before returning their attention to her tea. The sound of bubbling water took over; Rob ignored the sound, focusing on the leaves dancing in the broth.

"You were a Sky Sage," Rob ventured. "You must know how to fix it."

"It was a long time ago. Their ancient healing scrolls were interesting, I recall. Ilma would have enjoyed them. But I would never be welcomed back. I took treasures and secrets, but I shall not disseminate them."

"Why not?"

"I choose not to. You will sleep, and that will be your punishment. Your sleep shall be haunted by the Air King's breath. That is the curse of the Sky-slayers. Until you are given a new pendant, I suggest you learn to live with what you have done."

"I can't!" His eyes were hot with fear and pain. "The screams, the blood! I can't live like that! You can't be so heartless!"

"Rob Sardan, you must live with who you are and you must find a way to survive. That is how you will change. When you are no longer the person who gloried in blood and death, then the dreams will no longer harm you."

"That's not how it works, and you know it. The screams will follow me until I die, they'll never leave, never dim, and they'll always be there!"

"But they will not always have power over you."

"Just you try it! Try having someone scream in your ear every night, have them dying in your dreams, weeping and crying as they're torn to pieces. I can't live with it! Nobody can!" He slammed his fist into the table and trembled. His back ached, and a sickly jab went through his chest.

Lomi was watching him through narrowed eyes. She shook her head and poured more tea into her beak before setting her cup down and standing.

"Go to the hot springs. Now. I will send a medic. Tomorrow you will be taken to the glass houses where you will aid the potting and care of my teas."

Rob left, irritated but frightened. His bones burned, and his insides squirmed like a sea serpent trying to escape his ribcage. The prospect of facing the rest of his life without the protection of his pendant was like crossing a volcanic chasm. He stared into the depths, wondering if one day he would simply jump in.

Chapter Three

Healing Heat

Beneath the immeasurable tower, Rob roamed the catacombs, steam and vapour clinging to his clothes. White wooden pillars supported the barrel vaulted ceiling and stood between bubbling pools, some frothing more vigorously than others. Above each was a vent that vanished into the tower, taking heat to cells and corridors.

He followed the dim lantern light, eyes on the white stone, which reflected the flickering fires with star-like twinkles. He stumbled on a hook sticking up from the floor; he growled and kicked it. There was a hollow sound and he knelt to brush the dirt from a trapdoor. His arms ached, and he couldn't lift it, besides which there were locks holding it.

The locks on the trapdoor were large and shined brighter than the rusted hinges. He traced a finger along the wood and wondered if he could break it with brute force but decided against this as his arms were sore and his head swam with exhaustion.

Coming to the side of one of the pools, he dipped a hand in. The bubbles were murmuring, and the temperature was warm enough for him. Stripping layers of clothing off, he shuddered until he slid into the warm water. Scars were streaked across him, white lines against brown skin. Some were from swords, others from the teeth and talons of the Air King. Lightning had scorched the red sky that night; rain had been pummelling him, and the ocean had sung at his command.

His shoulders ached at the memory of the weight they had once carried; the sword carved from the stone of the sea and imbibed with the heart of a god. It was *the* Sword, the only one that mattered; The Sea-Stone Sword. He thought it had been the answer to his questions, and his dream fulfilled, but now he hated the thing.

"Squirm a little more, I'm sure it will help," the voice was sharp and tinged with sarcasm. "I thought you were supposed to know a thing or two about healing."

Ilma leaned into view, her coat rattling with vials and instruments. Her white hair was tied in braids slung across her shoulders. A thick cotton tunic and layers of clothing coated her, and her deep eyes were bright green, lighting her rounded face.

"Bless," she said, putting a hand to his forehead. "You've got a bit of a fever. I thought as much. Heard you'd got into a fight with Kerrok, silly boy. You know I don't trust her."

"Well, she does like making me bleed."

"It's not that," she said as she worked, pulling vials out of her coat. "She talks too much about how much she loves the empire."

"She's a peng; that's what they do."

"She goes on about it too much, if you ask me. More than the others. Mind you, not much else to talk about here in the south, eh? What else would they say to each other? 'Nice snow we have today'?"

"She's not been promoted in ages," Rob said with a snort. "So she's probably trying to get another stripe on her armour."

"If she beats you to within an inch of your life they'll give her a reward?"

"Well, I've got you to bring me back from the brink every time."

"What would you do without me, eh?"

"Die horribly," he sighed and sank into the water a little.

"Don't you dare. I couldn't bear it. You're about my daughter's age, and looking at you makes me think about her. She was on a crew, you see?"

"So was I, back in the day."

"Back in the day? You're not old. When you get to be my age, you can say things like 'back in the day'."

"Well, it feels like a long time ago. It feels like it was someone else who had those adventures."

"Oh, stop being so glum!" She pushed a phial of a horrific smelling ointment under his nose. "Sniff it as hard as you can. I'm your medic; you have to do as I say."

"What happens if I don't?"

"Pain. And an earful from the warden."

"And what happens to *me*?" he grinned, and she slapped the back of his head. "Yes, you make a compelling argument."

She smiled and set about giving him more medicine, making him smell herbs and then poking and prodding various parts of his body. She examined his toes for a long while, her brow creased.

"Ever thought of trying to escape?" he mused.

"What would I do that for?"

"Lomi said the Sky Sages had ancient healing scrolls."

"Scrolls that heal people? I doubt that."

"You know what I mean! Old healing knowledge."

"Yes, plenty of ancient societies like that have their healing knowledge locked where nobody can find it. What's the point? If I got my hands on that kind of knowledge, I'd do something useful with it."

"I'm sure you would."

"Ah, but what am I saying? The open ocean is just a dream now, healing scrolls or no." She set about drying her hands on her robes. "You're okay," she said. "Just don't go running. And keep your feet well wrapped. I may need to bandage some of those wounds on your chest, and one more thing, smell this."

Her fingers clamped around his nose and jerked it violently from left to right. Pain blinded him and he sprang back screaming as water splashed everywhere. Blood poured and turned his vision red, as his head became a wasp's nest.

"Your nose was broken," she explained. "I fixed it."

"Yes, thanks!" he shouted, hands clamped to his face. "You're a legend."

"Well, it'll feel better in the long run." She looked satisfied and held her chin high. "Get some rest and come to dinner."

"I'd rather not," he breathed slower though the wasps were still mulling about in his head. "I'm not in the mood for an interrogation."

"Yes, because the world revolves around you and your adventures. Come on, Rob, stop acting like you're the only person who's got any guilt in the world. You'd be the only one here if you were."

"I don't think I'm the only one." He knew it sounded childish, but he carried on. "I just feel *my* pain more than other people feel it."

"Other people can't feel *your* pain; that's not how it works. Stop expecting them to." She threw a towel at his head. "Do what you want, I'm hungry."

"I'll try not to die of starvation. I don't fancy a watery grave."

"Just a snowy one. Live in chains and die in snow, that's what we're here for."

"What happened to the new prisoners?" he asked. "The man with the nose ring; Vann I think he was called."

"Library, I think," Ilma smirked. "Now you just behave yourself there!"

She left, and the closing door echoed across the cavern. Rob fumbled with his hair, tying his dreadlocks as tightly as he could while the water bubbled against his skin. The prospect of hours in his cell with screaming dreams hung over him. He had tried to remind himself that the screams were not *his* victims; they were the Air-King's. This rarely consoled him; he had killed people, too. He had suffered their screams, as well. Not even a Sky-slayer's pendant could save him from them.

He decided to find a distraction. Vann had seemed friendly when they'd met in the woods, and he hoped that there wouldn't be questions about his old life fired at him. Yet, he deeply wanted news of the outside.

During his two-year imprisonment, hearing what was happening beyond the ice was rare. The pengs talked to one another of pengish business, the empire and expansion of powers. He had once heard a whisper of pirates and a hushed gasp at the name Mothar.

He sat on the humming ground beside the spring, letting the water drip from him in rivers. The chamber was warm and the air heavy, making him feel as if he would fall asleep if he stayed much longer. Pulling on his clothes, he tried to shake off his anxiety, wondering whether he would have made this choice if he still had his pendant.

The tower's labyrinthine corridors, rising and falling in a cascade of confusion, had etched in his memory. Though he took detours, wandered aimlessly for a while and stopped to examine a balcony, he eventually found his way to the entrance to the library.

It was another ornate door, carved with the images of pengs of various houses reading scrolls or tomes. Some pengs had bushy eyebrows; others had tufts of feathers that stuck up around their necks. There were symbols in each corner: a fish on a trident, a mammoth's face, a pine tree in flames, and the crowned peng; then in the centre was the snowflake surrounded by chains. He pushed the doors, splitting the crest of Bron'Halla in two. He got a small joy out of that act.

The library's light dazzled him, and he blinked in the glimmering sheen that hit him. Tall windows let the moon or the sun illuminate the circular chamber. It danced and flickered through crystalline bookcases and polished white floors. Even the books were starched where they could be, and the few of darker hues seemed to scream for attention.

The bookshelves were arranged in increasing circles, like ripples in a lake, taller in the centre and diminishing towards the walls. There were breaks making pathways through in a twisting course that took the visitor through the ranks of tomes.

He was passing a set of scrolls covered in blue writing when he saw Vann hunched over a book, shivering and pulling cloaks over his shoulders with one hand, the other held over his bald head. With a jerk, he spotted Rob.

"Oh," he said. "They sent you to check on me? I'm doing what I was asked, but some of these books are hard, you know? How am I supposed to know if *Dissections of Draigs* goes under biology or warfare? There's loads of stuff about fighting, but there're these horrible diagrams. Look!"

He held the book up, straining at the weight. Etched in red was a dual heart system exposed in a chest filled with bone.

"*The two hearts of the draigs give them their longer life, it is said,*" Rob read. "*Puncture one and the other still beats, giving the subject a half-life. Even if killed, a draig's hearts will continue to beat until the fire of their blood is quelled.*"

"What?" Vann said with a nervous laugh. "You can read that stuff? Draigish?"

"Cendylic," Rob smiled and took the book. "It's a bit confusing; the language recognises multiple genders, and I get mixed up. I'm learning, though. Love draigs, always have done. Don't tell the pengs, mind."

"Too right," Vann sniffed and stretched, cracking his back. "You're a big one, aren't you?" he said, beaming. "Didn't notice it before, but blimey you've got some muscles."

"Oh, right . . ." Rob felt blood rush into his face.

"Ah, mate, nothing like seeing some humans around here, let me tell you. These pengs are mental cases."

"They're what?"

"Mental cases. Got weird customs and barmy ideas."

"I'm sure they think the same of us." He put the book on a shelf of writings about draigs. "And don't call people 'mental cases'."

"Right." Vann looked away. "Might make them angry? They already got us locked up, biggie, they ain't gonna do much worse." Vann tugged the collar of his robes aside and revealed a bandaged wound on his shoulder.

"They did that to you?"

"Yeah, nasty little blighters on the road accosted us while they were bringing us in, didn't they? No provocation; just attacked us."

Rob frowned. The pengs were harsh, even violent, but they usually had a reason for it. They had their sense of honour and law, of course, and often it was at odds with other peoples' customs, but he could usually see the sense they were making. Then he thought of Kerrok.

"Someone said you could talk to birds," Vann ventured.

Rob shook his head, smiling as his hair flopped over his face. "I can understand them, and make my intent known. You can too, if you know how. I'm not the best at it."

Vann leaned against the table and tapped it with his fingers. "Why would you want to talk to birds?"

"Not just birds, it's any other animals, too." He shrugged defensively. "Can be interesting; you can make allies. I heard a story when I was little about . . ." he stopped and turned away.

The story was one of his mother's favourites. It was a tale of Uallas the young; before she had fought the monsters, she had befriended them. Stories like that haunted him; they'd been the fuel that had driven him towards his hopeless quest.

"What's the point of animal allies?" Vann went back to the books stacked on the table. "Unless they know a way out of here; they keep saying it's impossible."

"It isn't. I knew someone who escaped a long time ago. Her name was Jareth."

"Rings a bell. She a pirate or something?" Vann sniffed and rubbed his nose.

"She was, but then she wasn't. You interested in pirates?"

"Me? No, can't bloody stand them. You heard about that Skagra?"

Rob searched his memories. "Might have crossed paths."

"And you're still alive? Lucky. She went bonkers after that stuff with the Sword of whatsit. That sea-stone thing."

"The Sea-Stone Sword?"

"Yeah." Vann shuddered. "She came to my homeland and burned things. Nailed people to trees, and took prisoners. I got away, see? Nicked some treasure, too." He grinned. "Then I came south, heard pengs were looking for folk to work. Biggest mistake of my life."

"Why was Skagra doing that?"

"Eh? How should I know? Anyways, what are you here for?"

"That's a long story," Rob laughed. He looked away, hiding the guilt that flooded his mind and made his back tense in hot knots. Vann shoved a series of books into shelves at random.

"I'm hungry," he said. "They said I could eat when I'd finished, how about you show me to where the food's at?"

"I'm *not* hungry," Rob frowned. "And I'm not eager for more company."

"I am, though." He pulled Rob's arm. "Come on, mate, it'll be fun. Big lad like you needs fattening up."

"All right," he laughed despite himself. "I'll show you."

THE COMMON ROOM was cramped, but its walls and floor were dazzling. A series of benches had been set up, and people were sat at them, plates on their laps and tankards in their hands.

There were pengs at the doors and in each of the corners, their beady eyes glowering from behind visors.

Vann rubbed his hands as a peng brought them a bowl of cooked mushrooms and steaming carrots in a swimming broth. Rob thanked the peng in her language, and she nodded her approval.

"Blimey, you speak *their* language too?" Vann asked.

"I've been here for two years, and some of the finer details are still beyond me. It's simpler than Cendylic as pengs only have one gender. But then there are all the different dialects and the fact that they mix languages from all over the world."

"Yeah, well, they been conquering, haven't they? Flaming feather folk." Vann took a sip of his broth. "Is this the best soup they got? Suppose it's just the sort of thing to save your life in this place. I'm not cut out for prison life."

"You're not cut out for much," said another prisoner who had been standing by the door, her arms folded and face turned away from them. She wore a black headscarf, and her robes were white and purple though tattered and worn.

"Exactly! I don't see why they're so interested in putting me in this place. I'd be better off on one of them ships they were pushing."

"Those ships were heading to the colonies," the woman said, her eyes glancing past Rob before she continued. "The empire is trying to suppress a rebellion; you of all people should know that. Who do you think attacked us on the road? Those were not imperial pengs, they were renegades."

"I've heard of them," Rob said. "They want to change the system. No more empire. No more conquest. No more prisoners."

"Can't say I'm completely against them, then." Vann grinned.

"When they say 'no more prisoners'," the woman took a step into the room, "They mean no more prisoners left alive."

"If you were a renegade," Vann countered, "wouldn't you get the prisoners on your side first?"

"They do not believe that non-pengs are worthy of their consideration. They desire complete isolation and removal of all other forms of life from their territories."

"What's your name?" Rob asked.

"Let's not try to make friends," she said.

"Alya here's been pulling me down whenever I get a decent idea," Vann grumbled.

"That is not true, I have never discouraged good ideas; you are simply incapable of having one."

"See what I mean?"

"So your name is Alya?" Rob pressed. She maintained eye contact as if daring him to break it. He kept it as long as he could, but Vann tugged on his arm.

"So, what you were saying before, about the rebellion?"

"The pengs keep it quiet," Alya said. "Most people think all pengs are the same, so what difference do a few factions make? There are countless groups and communities in human lands, and don't get us started on dr- on, well, you know?"

"No, I don't."

Rob shuffled closer and whispered, "Draigs."

The pengs turned simultaneously to glare with deep, sharp eyes, their hands grasping their weapons as a reflex. Vann cringed, his face contorted; Rob shifted his weight, hoping to disrupt the uncomfortable silence.

"Well," Vann said. "We're not likely to be bothered by any renegade pengs while we're in here, are we?"

"Even if they did come we would have ample warning." Rob agreed.

"Good to know. I don't like surprises; they give me stomach ache, and I'm not cut out for illness. My parents always told me 'never get ill, or you'll be sick' and you know what, they were right . . ."

"Vann, you are babbling more than usual." Alya sniffed.

"All right, you don't need to treat me like a prisoner."

"You are a prisoner, or had you forgotten?"

Vann lowered his head. Rob frowned at Alya and was about to shout an objection, but three pengs entered and snatched their empty food plates. In the confusion, he forgot what he had intended to say and settled for simply glaring at her as she maintained her place at the door.

"So, what're you here for?" Vann asked. "I was caught stealing from a big old pengish dynasty. They weren't too pleased I can tell you. The House of Fearghal was right at the top of the ladder, you know? Next in line to the throne, they said. They were the richest pengs west of the mountains, see? How could I resist?"

"They *were* the richest," one of the pengs said. "They were traitors."

"Well, stealing from pengs is frowned upon," Vann went on, "traitors or no. Turned out this big old family were plotting against the empress, and I bet if the plot hadn't been discovered they might have killed me."

"What a shame," said Alya. "We would have been deprived of your wonderful company and intelligent conversation."

"Exactly!" Vann smiled. "What about you, then? What they get you for?"

"Information," she replied.

"Care to expand on that?" Rob said.

"No."

"Fair play," Vann turned back to Rob. "So come on, we've all coughed up. What are you here for, Rob?"

"I'm sure you've heard the stories," Rob said.

"Not me, squire. Don't hold with many stories. I hear loads off me sister, though. She lives in Leoht with my mam; they work at that old Tomb, you know? The Tomb of the Dead God; oldest religion in Diyngard, so they say. The great god of the earth who was killed by Razal."

"So why do they worship this god if it's dead?"

"I . . ." Vann frowned. "I never thought to ask."

"You didn't think?" Alya snorted. "What a surprise."

"Don't you have some milk to curdle with your sour attitude?" Rob snapped.

"Ignore her," Vann advised. "Here, if we ever get out of here, I could show you the old business. I always wanted to start it again. See, my ma had a trade before she got religious. Trasati shows!" He spread his hands theatrically. "Performing beasts! Oh, I love that stuff. They got one of them ones with the spiked backs, you know, the big old plates going down its back and the spikes on its tail. Well, they got one of them, and it can whistle a tune like nobody's business."

Rob stared in horror. "You keep trasati as entertainment?"

"Not me," he sighed heavily. "Wish it was, though, but I never had the knack, see? All them big scaly creatures just wanted to eat me, I think."

"Why?" Rob's arms were tense, his spine tingling with building fury.

His childhood had been filled with the trasati, watching them across the desert plains, listening to their songs as they called to one another. They could be dangerous, but they were their own creatures, beings with thoughts and feelings.

"Maybe I'm delicious?" Vann laughed.

"I think that you are upsetting your new friend," Alya observed.

"Eh? What're you on about now?"

"Best you stop talking before Master Sardan decides to break *you*."

"What did I do to deserve that?"

"How long a list would you like?" She smiled sardonically.

"Rob, you're not seriously angry, are you?" Vann said.

"Don't talk to me," Rob stood. "You think it's funny to make trasati dance for your amusement?"

"Well, if it's for my amusement then, by definition, it's funny. I thought you liked animals and trasati! Why you being so weird?"

"Don't say another word." Rob stepped dangerously close, his heart an inferno. "If you knew who I was you would back away right now."

"Oh yeah, and who are you?"

Rob glowered, his eyes narrowing as his mouth contorted; his features folding into the old ferocity that had struck fear into the Pirate Lord himself. Vann took a step back, eyes wide and legs trembling.

Rob turned to go, but he caught a last glimpse of Vann's terrified face. The expression latched onto his mind and etched into his memory. He felt a stab of pity break through his anger, and he almost turned back. Almost.

Chapter Four

Tea Leaves and Torture

THE GLASSHOUSES WERE ROOMS THAT JUTTED FROM THE TOWER in shards. The floor was uneven, but each potting station was at an angle to accommodate such. Steam from a vent was wafting across the room, and the glass walls magnified what little sunlight was coming from the sky.

"Sit," commanded a peng in thick gloves. "I warn you, I will not tolerate back talk."

Rob sat in front of a set of gold leaves. The peng instructed him to prune the flowers and collect pollen. He spent hours going from station to station, pruning, potting, watering and keeping tabs on the tea and herbs. His pengish companion remained silent; her head bowed over ledgers and scrolls, a wooden pen switching between hands as she wrote furiously.

A tapping noise accompanied by wheezing and faint whistles echoed from the corridor outside. Moments later Lomi reached around the door. The prison warden gave the herb master a nod, and she bustled out, vanishing down the stairs in a stream of mud and leaves.

"Perhaps you misunderstood," the warden said. "You are here to learn, change, and become a better person, not start fights in the common room."

"I didn't fight." He prodded the soil around a set of flowers. "He kept provoking me."

"In my years, many have tried to provoke me; a prisoner once knocked over my tea."

"Oh, how awful for you," Rob growled.

"It was! The tea was especially good, full of flavour and a heart of gold. My sister had brought it to me from the colonies, and it meant a lot to me."

"I can see why it would be upsetting, then."

"It was not the tea alone that upset me, but the act." Sitting she let out a sigh. "I am charged with keeping prisoners in this fortress; it is a charge against my wishes, against who I am."

"You do it very well." He hoped it sounded kind.

"Thank you. I have had many evenings of fearful contemplation; of desperate searching and hopelessness. My duty to the Empire, my people, my country; this is in conflict with my image of myself, and I feel at war within my own mind."

"You left the Sky Sages. It seems you made your choice."

"A choice once made can still haunt the mind. It is important we recognise that it *is* a choice, that it was in our hands, and then we can see it clearer."

"Did you not like the Sky Sages?"

"I loved them, and I regret some of my words to them, and my theft. There were things in their stores the Empire desired, and yet I have since felt that many of those items should not see the light of day. So I locked them in the vaults. I meditate on my choice, and I try to make peace with who I am." She pointed her walking stick at him. "You have done things and have become things that are greatly incongruent with your inner self."

"Have I?"

"Sword-breaker," when she said it he flinched. Images flashed in his memory, the stone-wrought hilt, the craggy grip and coral-encrusted blade.

"You see?" she went on. "You hate that person, the one who did all of those great and terrible things. You feel that this person is someone else, you want to break away from your past and pretend it did not happen."

She was pressing wounds that he did not want to be opened. He was suffering enough, so to press the point was gratuitous.

"If *you* had done it," he said, slowly, "you wouldn't want to be that person."

"But you *are* that person, you did those things, and you need to come to terms with that."

"I know what I did!" he shouted and kicked his stool aside. "I have come to terms with it. That's why I'm here!"

"No! You are still angry, you froth with rage whenever it is mentioned, you flinch at the name Sword-breaker, and you cower and scream when the dreams come. You must find your true self and stop hiding from it."

"Oh, is that so?" He stepped away, brows knitting. "And what if my true self is terrible? What if my true self is a villain? What if that is what I am? A killer, a breaker, a betrayer of friends and one who leads everyone he loves unto death. What if that is who I truly am?"

"I do not believe that," she said. "There is kindness in you; there is a fierce desire for peace and life. But if this villain is your true self, you must face it. You must look it in the eye and know it to be a true reflection. Only then will you be able to change. Only when we accept who we are can we *change* who we are."

Her words were poison in his chest, cutting like thorns. "And how many people will I hurt on this quest?"

"Your past is a weapon, a sword you are trying to grasp," Lomi hobbled towards him, "but you are trying to grasp its blade and not its hilt. Once you take the hilt and hold it firm, you can use it."

"Swords kill people."

"But swords can be broken. You should know this. Either that or my metaphors could use some work. Or Empire uses swords to defend the weak, to push back those who would harm us. It is by the sword that people are able to live."

"Keep telling yourself that," he snorted.

"I shall," Lomi chirped. "Such things calm my dreams."

"What about the pendant?" he shot. It had been bubbling in his throat, and he couldn't contain it. "I can't dream without one. Where can I get a new pendant?"

"The Sky Sages should have delivered a new one to you," Lomi hummed. "It is strange that they have not."

"I had my uncle's pendant, though."

"It was not engraved with your name, nor were there spells of curse-breaking specific to you. That pendant would never have worked as well as one made specially. The fact that they have not come to you is worrying."

"I could go to them," he muttered.

"You know that I cannot allow that." Lomi shook her head. "Let us say that you manage to escape the tower, scale the cliff, and traverse the wastelands beyond. Let us say that you came to the coast and fashioned a raft to take you to Penguve, and then found a ship to take you on. Let us say you sailed the Farraige Sea, then into Ginnungagap. What then? How would you find the Sages?"

"You know where they are."

"I will not tell you. Better folk have tried and failed. Not even Skagra succeeded, and she is said to devour the flesh of her victims."

"How would anyone find them?"

"It is a secret only the Dead God could tell, and the dead do not speak much in my experience."

"So it's hopeless?"

"No." She put a hand on his arm. "Learn my lessons; escape the dreams through your own will."

"Has it been done before?"

"I believe it is possible. I have to." She pointed to the flower Rob had been tending. "This is called the Ayumu; it induces dreams of potency. You may walk in memories and see them anew. I can make you a tea that will give you the ability to sleep. However, you will face your past in ways you may not like."

"Can you be more specific?" Rob took in the flower's heady scent.

"I fear it is something you must experience." She tapped his shin with her staff. "Now, tell me why you fought with Vann?"

"He thinks it's funny to keep trasati imprisoned and makes them dance."

"Have you seen him do this?"

"He told me. His mother used to keep them, and he said he thought it was amusing. I don't suppose you'd understand. You pengs eat flesh and keep fish penned up for your tables."

"Though less so here in Bron'Halla."

"Only because it's hard to get your food here."

"You are quite right. However, I would ask you to be civil with your fellow prisoners. I would prefer a peaceful tower."

"Why not try one of the upper chambers? You know most of this tower is empty, don't you?"

"Is it? I've lived here my whole life and never noticed," she shook her head. "I hope my attempt at sarcasm has not offended you."

"No. But, you can't ask me to condone what he did!"

"I am not asking that." She put a feathery hand on his elbow. "You came here with the intent of changing. Here is a chance. If you can adapt, you will be a stronger person, you will endure and gain the power to drive towards whatever you wish."

"Power isn't a good thing." He narrowed his eyes. "I speak from experience."

"You are thinking of having power over others; I was talking about having power over yourself. You think you are a dangerous person? You believe you have so much power over others that they cannot make their own choices without you ruining it for them? Is that how you see yourself?"

"No, well . . ." he bit his lip. "I can be a bad influence."

"We all have that within us. But do you think you have made any progress while you have been here? I think you have made a lot. That you consented to come here of your own free will represents a great leap." She plunged a hand into her robes and pulled out a scroll. "Our next supply shipment will be arriving soon. The pengs often take a prisoner; the prisoner helps unload and pack supplies and sells the prison's wares. This year, I would like that prisoner to be you."

He twisted his jaw. "Very amusing."

"I am not being sarcastic."

Suspicion flooded as if he were under a waterfall. And yet, in the pool of his chest, a swirl of anticipation and longing bubbled. He imagined breathing free air, seeing the pengish cities, the ocean, new faces; he imagined the sounds of crowds, the roar of the sea and he wanted to leap.

The sea was like a magnet, its wide and everlasting noise singing in his ears. It was where he had been with his crew, it was where he had heard about his mother's adventures, and it was where he'd seen so many new things. Terrible things.

"I could see the ocean," he whispered. "Smell the salt and . . ." His former crew swam before his mind's eye, blood-soaked and broken. It had been his fault; Rob had found the Sea-Stone Sword, and the Air King had come after them. They'd died. He lowered his head and met Lomi's eyes. "It will hurt to see it again."

"That is why you *must* see it," she nodded, satisfied. "Pain is something you must feel; you cannot hope to move on, to break the mould of who you once were if you do not go through that pain."

"You make it sound like torture," he shuddered.

"You overestimate. You have been in this tower for two years, and apart from Ilma and Gorm, you don't seem to have many friends."

"There are only a few dozen here, and two out of twenty-odd isn't bad."

"Perhaps if you were close to them, but you are acquaintances at best. Ilma tends your wounds, shares your jokes and makes you laugh. However, I do not think she would speak to you of deep matters. She would not tell you of her daughter's life, nor will she as long as you remain at arm's length."

"Gorm told me about her mother's death," he pointed out. "She said she'd been killed by the Pirate Lord Mothar and that the whole village had been disgusted."

"Did she tell you how she felt?"

"No . . ." Rob sunk into a slouch. "I can't go around asking people to confide in me about personal things."

"You don't have to, but when people trust you, they will give you their thoughts. Nobody trusts you, Rob."

"And they shouldn't."

"As long as you believe that, you will not change." She hobbled to the door. "Go to your cell and awake at first toll. Join the others in the yard. And if you quarrel again, I shall have more than words for you."

Rob struggled down the stairs, his legs heavier than the whole world. He staggered into the wall as he reached the landing, eyes blurred, arms aching and neck throbbing. The night had not been kind and the screams were still echoing.

He wandered the empty halls, the morning still hours away. The vastness of the fortress was such that it was easy to get lost for as long as you liked. Peering into empty chambers and cells he took in the musty air, blinking as the light hit him through blue windows.

A balcony overlooked the lands around; the horizon was a shroud of wind-whipped snow and short-lived tornados. Across the expanse, the white ball of light that he used to mistake for the moon sailed; even in the height of summer the sun was a dim shape fighting the twilight as it refused to set.

A movement sent an echo through the ice and glass; Rob turned and clenched his hands. There was a shape haunting the corners of sight, distorted by the reflective walls and ceilings. A rattling breath snarled and cracked like the wind.

It was a human, draped in a cloak and hood, carrying a bundle and whispering to it. There was a fluttering and a piercing squawk and something burst out of the bundle.

"Come back!" The figure threw back his hood. It was Vann, wide-eyed and desperate. "We need to learn the basics, stupid bird! I've got corn!"

The trasati-bird fluttered into the room and landed on the balcony. It's black eyes found Rob, and it gave a chirrup, opening its wings to greet him. He whistled to it, imitating the noises he had heard it make in the woods. The bird whistled back.

"There you are!" Vann stumbled into the room, missing Rob and heading straight for the balcony. The bird snapped. "No, bad bird! I am a friend! I have corn; see? Corn means friends." The bird looked at the corn suspiciously.

Vann's cloak billowed in the wind revealing his sweat soaked tunic; to be wearing so few layers in this weather could not have been comfortable and Rob felt another pang of pity. The sweat had made the shirt cling close to Vann's back, revealing the form of his lithe body. Rob's eyes trailed to his legs, which were bowed but sturdy and clamped in canvas boots that reached to his calves.

"Now," Vann was saying. "I'll teach you the dance of feathers and scales. You'd like that one; it's just for half lizards like you.

Are you half lizard? I don't remember what the rules are about half-this and half-that." The trasati nibbled the corn and chirruped. "When you've learnt, we'll show the others. Rob will understand when he sees how good you are at it."

"Will I?" Rob asked, standing.

Vann jerked away from the window. The bird leapt and fluttered to Rob and whistled. Smiling, Rob whistled back, hoping to convey his condolences for the bird's inconvenience. It seemed placated and took to circling them, fluttering its wings.

"What are you doing there?" Vann asked with his hand against his chest as if to stop his heart from escaping.

"Enjoying the view. A bit of a coincidence you coming here, isn't it? I'd almost think you'd been following me."

"No, I wasn't." He eyed the trasati-bird and gulped. "Little Hari here's been leading me up and down for hours."

"Hari?" He looked at the bird, and it twittered. "I don't think she likes it."

"She?" Vann frowned. "Sorry, I don't know how to tell."

"How about Hildr," Rob suggested. "That's a name from your land, isn't it? I don't know much Geatish."

"Where'd you learn?"

"Library. Lomi likes us to learn as many languages as we can."

"You seem to be able to talk to this little lady." He reached out to pet Hildr, but she hopped away.

"It's not a language," Rob laughed. "You have to convey feelings through sounds. You have to be honest and maintain a constant string of emotion, you pour it through your throat or nose, or whatever you're using, and make the sounds. Takes some getting used to."

Vann grinned. "Maybe the little lass would understand what I was trying to get her to do."

"She won't do it if she doesn't want to."

"Yeah, but you can sweet talk anyone."

"Trasati rely on emotion; it is impossible to lie to them."

"Ah, that's boring." Vann stood and went to the balcony. "Listen, mate, I never wanted to get on your wrong side. Didn't know you was close with trasati and the like. I thought you was from Khamas, by your accent."

He sighed. "I was in Khamas for three years, but I grew up in Galot."

"In Galot? What you go there for?"

"I didn't *go* there; I was born there."

"Oh, right. Why'd your parents go there, then?"

"I don't know. My mother was involved in things I don't fully understand. It's not important," he shrugged. "How about you? They said you were from Geata, that's in the Ginnungagap, right?"

"Aye, right in the middle of it; we get pirates and all sorts down our way. That's why we got trasati shows, ain't it? The pirates are all for them, give us loads of money just to watch them."

"So you're blaming the pirates?" Rob tried to keep his temper, but it was rising. "Listen, Vann, don't get me wrong, I understand you were brought up with it, but please, it's not right."

"I suppose I never thought about it . . ." Vann tried to smile.

"The warden doesn't want me quarrelling," Rob went on. "But you have to realise that it's not right to be cruel like that."

"Look, I can't change what happened in the past, and maybe it was all wrong. I can't be the only one who's done bad stuff."

"No," Rob relented and smiled at him. "You are not."

The look on Vann's face was hopeful, and Rob recalled the fear that had haunted him after their argument previously. The struggle to let go the topic was real, and he wasn't sure Vann had truly relented on it, but he was willing to allow peace.

Chapter Five

A Ship of a Thousand Words

THE YARD WAS LITTLE MORE THAN A CLEARING BETWEEN THE smaller fortresses. Kerrok was standing in the centre surrounded by a gaggle of subordinate pengs dressed in white silks and thick cloaks. She eyed Rob and followed him as he and Vann joined a group of prisoners by a pile of wood.

"Your projects are to be continued," she announced. "New prisoners are to be instructed by the old. I would like three carved by fifth toll."

The prisoners set about pulling the wood from the pile and carving tools were handed around. Vann examined the saw he had been given and looked sidelong at Alya, who was holding an axe.

"If you're thinking about attacking, don't," Rob warned.

"Why not?" Vann whispered. "We could take them."

"Even if we could, what then? You fancy walking all the way across the ice?"

"Not really, but we could take them."

"Is that so?" Alya mused, swinging the axe into a log. It bounced and made only a dent in the wood. "These tools are badly made, look at the grooves on the blade. They're misaligned. And that saw is too flexible. Even with fully sharpened and solid tools, these pengs wear plate armour and chain mail. We would not even bruise them."

"They're trained fighters, too," Rob agreed. "You must have seen them; you said you were attacked on the road."

"Nah, most of them were just standing like lemons. Why didn't I do that?"

"If I recall," Alya chided, "you were doing exactly that before the captain forced you to fight. Can't say you did much better."

"I resent that!"

"And I resent you." Alya chopped the log, with her brows furrowed.

"Well," Vann muttered, "who cares about pengs and their civil wars, eh?"

"The empire represents a considerable amount of power and influence across four continents," Alya said. "To attack them would be incredibly dangerous. For us to be attacked on one of their secret roads was interesting."

"You think it was premeditated?" Rob whispered, leaning closer. "Maybe one of these pengs was in on it?"

"What, and get themselves killed in the attack?" Vann snorted.

"Some people might prefer death to prison," Alya said.

"Some people?" Rob turned on her slowly. "Would you be one?"

"I happen to prefer life. What interests me is the fact that no change seems to have come over the pengs, they are going about their business as if this was normal."

"You think the rebellion is getting stronger?"

Alya's face was stony, unreadable, but slowly she opened her mouth. "I think lots of things."

"Aye, don't we all?"

"Sardan, I don't see you working," Kerrok shouted. "If you haven't got three frames cut by fifth toll I'll have you on the Lightning Roof."

He went back to his impossible task.

"What's the Lightning Roof?" asked Vann.

"It's over there." Rob pointed to a blackened fortress some way into the woodland. Its spire was twisted with dark iron, and a shimmer of heat was rising from it; the trees about its base were greener than the rest. "Whenever a storm hits, the lightning tends to strike there, the heat is directed underground into pipes, which the pengs feed into the other towers."

"Why not just use the hot springs?" Vann asked.

"They're only accessible under that thing," he pointed at Bron'Halla.

"Why not just dig more tunnels?"

Rob heaved a heavy breath as he pulled a log towards him. "The ground is sacred. They believe that the tower was the dying breath of a gigantic drakan."

"A drakan?" Vann whispered.

"You should know about them," said Alya, suspiciously. "If you are from Geata then you live near Draig Cendyl."

"Never went there; family might have been, but I never did. Too warm for my liking. So what's a drakan, then?"

"It's a kind of trasati," Rob was unsure of the legends, having read them only recently. "There are fragments in the library, but I gather that in the peng-draig war, the drakans were the gigantic winged trasati."

"Like a pterosaur?"

"No, these were different; they had long necks, four legs, and spiked tails. You must have seen the trasati of Shen, right? Well, think of one of them but with wings."

"Blimey, that's not a pleasant thought!"

Rob frowned. "They were all killed in the war. Except for this gigantic one; they say it breathed ice-flames, blue fire that froze the air. According to the legend, it was a friend of the pengs and came here in its final days. With one last breath, it created that tower and died."

"What? And its body is supposed to be underground?"

"It's just a story," Rob shrugged. "But I like it."

"I bet my sister would love to see a drakan!"

"Well, she can't, they're all gone."

The cold buffeted him, and he caught the scent of the pengs around him, the must and feathers, the fish and salt. It reminded him where he was; trapped. His hand reached under his shirt to the spot where his pendant was supposed to hang. Sick cramps clenched inside his abdomen as he faced the prospect of another sleepless night. With a crease to his brow, he looked to the horizon above the tall cliff ring.

Escape may have been considered impossible, but he knew it wasn't. Jareth the pirate had done it, long ago. Perhaps they had changed their security since then, but the principal stood. One could walk the endless tundra. It was possible. That thought kept him going. It kept him alive.

Hours passed, and there was still only one frame ready; Rob gave the second his furious attention, ignoring the jibes and put-downs Alya was issuing under her breath. Vann was complaining about a headache, and she had suggested he try removing his head as a cure.

"Focus on what you are doing," Alya advised. "You are letting the far side get too thin, compensate by shaving here, and here. Make sure you go with the grain, I noticed you were not doing so before. Who taught you ship-craft? A rock, perhaps?"

"I only spent a few days learning and it was two years ago," Rob moaned, but he followed her instructions. "Where did you learn?"

"From the best teacher there is."

"And who's that?"

"Myself."

Kerrok sidled over with her entourage and inspected the work as the bells tolled from the enormous tower. With only two frames completed, Rob felt resigned to a night atop the Lightning Tower.

"This work is better than previously," Kerrok said, taking Rob off guard. "There is a fine curve to the bow and you three seem to have made significant progress towards perfecting the design."

Rob looked sidelong at Alya, who was examining the work with a frown, disappointed. Kerrok, on the other hand, gave a nod to her subordinates, and they lifted the frame and took it away.

"Good work, Sardan," she said, making him stare. "But given who you were working with this should come as no surprise."

"Oh?" He looked at Alya again, but she was packing tools, deep in thought.

"Too obsessed with your own fame, that's your problem," Kerrok laughed. "You're not the only famous person here, you know?"

"Yeah, I'm a famous actor!" Vann declared theatrically.

"Sardan, you have splinters," Kerrok waved a hand. "Go and see the medic. You, too, Kadir."

Alya raised her head, frowning with eyes like pits.

"Alya Kadir," Kerrok said. "Ship Master. A little less violent than Sword-breaker, eh?"

Rob scowled, and Alya did the same. Together with Vann, who insisted he had suffered a sprained wrist; they made their way across the clearing to where the medics were. Ilma and her friends were sitting at a bench, sipping from steaming cups and shivering.

Gorm was there too, her dark eyes resting on Alya. When they approached, Gorm reached a hand to Rob, displaying bandages on her palms and fingers.

"Hard work is its own reward," she said, more cheerful than usual. "Yet the body suffers even as the mind fills with knowledge."

"You and Lomi need to spend less time together," Rob teased.

"The world is full of wonders," she shrugged. "Even pengish wisdom is worth seeking."

Ilma nudged her and looked at Rob and the others with a shudder and a smile.

"We have specialities for everyone," she said. "Step right this way."

"Are theatrics necessary?" Alya asked. "No? Then please spare us."

"My people have long held that a cheerful medic makes a cheerful patient."

"Your people sound remarkable," Alya said, sardonically.

"Oh, stop being so cynical, Alya. You've got years to get used to my humour."

"I shall endeavour to stay as healthy as I can."

"Good." She produced a handkerchief and wrapped it around Alya's hand. "I've put a little concoction into the fabric; it should stop infections and keep swelling to a minimum."

"I will assume, for the time being, that you have done your job well."

"How kind of you," Ilma smiled, pleasantly. "I was watching your work, you're good, but from the look of your hands, I'd say . . ."

"I can talk, or I can heal, which would you prefer?"

"Fine, fine, be off with you," she waved, and Alya sauntered away.

Rob held out his hand, Ilma took it and plucked splinters from his palm. The jabs were like nettle stings, but he bore them. Vann stood to the side, awkward and unsure while one of the other medics tugged at his arm.

"Your friend has a temper," Ilma said, dabbing Rob with a cloth.

He looked over at Alya. "I'd hesitate to call her a friend."

"Oh, I think she'll like you eventually. We all have to get along here, it's not as if we can leave."

"It's not impossible to escape . . ." he thought about saying more, but she glowered at him.

"Right, you're fine, off with you, and no fighting!" She prodded him, and he waved as he walked away.

Vann caught up, frowning at the marks on his hands which had been dabbed with medicine. "Why don't I get bandages? I worked hard, just like everyone else!"

"Maybe they think you're able to take the pain?" Rob suggested with a grin. "Doesn't look too bad."

"But what if I get something in my hand? There was a plague in Yesh one time; someone got a little cut, and then a bug got in them and soon hundreds of people were dead!"

"Thankfully, there are only a few dozen here," said Alya joining them. "So no need to worry about that."

"But I'm one of those dozens and that's what concerns me."

"How noble of you." Alya nodded towards a group of pengs heading towards them. "I suspect they have come to scold you for your lack of perfection, Sardan. Can't say I blame them, famous people need scolding from time to time."

"I've had enough of that to last me a lifetime, thanks," Rob grumbled.

"You're going to the Lightning Tower, Sardan," Commander Kerrok called from the middle of the pengish group.

"Oh, come on, this isn't fair!" Vann objected. "You said these frames were better than any others, so why can't you let him off?"

"The task was to build three; you only finished two. Complain again, human, and I will not hesitate to punish you all."

"Vann, leave it," Rob held him back.

"Yes, Master Sword-breaker knows his place." Kerrok moved her entourage, chirruping happily. "Learn from him and you will live well here."

"If you can call this living," Rob sighed.

"If I recall correctly," Kerrok lifted her halberd and pointed it at Rob's face, "you came here voluntarily."

"What?" Vann's mouth fell open. "That's ridiculous."

"He asked for this, so it must be what he wants." Kerrok slid her blade towards Rob's neck. "The Sword-breaker, Sky-slayer, King-killer; all the titles in the world and here you're just a prisoner. You need to remember that."

"Stop this." Vann pushed the halberd away, making the pengs turn on him. "Listen, it's just a bit of woodwork, why does he need to be punished, eh? It doesn't make sense."

"I don't expect you to understand, human." Kerrok nodded to her companions and their weapons turned towards him. "Are you asking to join him?"

"I . . ." Vann looked at Rob and then gulped. "Maybe I am."

THE SUMMIT OF the Lightning Tower was cramped with two occupants and Rob shifted against Vann. The sun had sunk to its lowest point, leaving them in semi-darkness; whirls and storm clouds crawled across the horizon, edging their way closer.

"Alya was right about you," Rob said, frustrated, "you're a complete idiot."

"Yeah, well, look who's talking," Vann flashed his teeth as the wind buffeted his nose ring. "Does the sun never set?"

"Not in summer, no."

"Good, then we won't be stuck in the pitch-black all night."

"You're afraid of the dark?"

"It's a legitimate fear! You never know what's going to jump at you or steal your face."

Rob laughed and tapped the side of the balcony with his boot. The wilderness seemed to engulf the world; his eyes strained for the horizon, but it was lost behind storming clouds. He wanted to push his vision, to drag distant lands into his sight and to see, just one last time, the ocean.

Even though it had cost him so much, even after everything he had lost, everyone he had loved, even after the curse that haunted his dreams, and even after discovering the truth behind the reason for it all . . . he wanted to sail again.

He'd tasted salt air; he'd felt the rising waves and breathed with his crew. He'd done so much, seen so much, and the desire was more powerful than his guilt.

"Thinking of trying to walk it?" Vann asked. "Me too."

"I might not have to," Rob shuddered. "The supply run is due in a few days, and they're taking me with them."

"Really? Well, take me with you! We can both escape!"

"I'd like that," he smiled, "but I don't think you'd thank me."

"Eh? What're you talking about? Of course I would."

"I came here voluntarily, Vann. When I was free, there were things that happened, and they were my fault. Well, I was manipulated a bit, but at the end, I was unstable, I was susceptible to it because, deep down, I wanted it. I wanted fame, power, and glory. But when I finally had it, people got hurt."

"You can't put yourself in a pengish prison for all that, though. I mean, these little beggars would just tell you to throw yourself into the sea."

"Well, it's interesting," he suppressed a laugh. "They put me in here on the crime of stealing a pengish gem, a White-Ice Star."

"Bloody Razal's beard, Rob! How'd you get hold of one of them?"

"I didn't, well, that's a very long story, a friend helped forge some evidence. It doesn't matter." He put his head against his palm and tried to still the pain that throbbed behind his eyes. "I came here because I wanted to change, the person that went to sea was dangerous. I don't want to be like that. So I came here."

"You think it worked? You think you're ready to go back?"

"I can't be sure."

"You won't be sure until you're out there. And this is your chance to get out, go back and find everything the world has to offer. I could take you to see my home! You'd love it."

"Would I?" he snorted a laugh. "Thing is, I have a quest in mind. I have a reason to go, a reason to keep going. I need a pendant."

"Like that one Kerrok broke?"

"It's a Sky-slayer's pendant. I need one or I'll never be able to sleep again. Well, not properly."

"Why not?"

"When you kill a pterosaur, one that's an Air-keeper, they curse you. The dying breath of everyone they ever killed is echoed in your mind every time you sleep. The pendant cancels it out."

"They sell them somewhere?"

"No, we'd need to find the Sky Sages, ever heard of them?"

"Rings a bell," he shrugged. "Then what? After you've got the pendant, what's next?"

Rob thought, his eyes wandering the sky. "I want to see the fire lands of Draig Cendyl. I want to see the golden mountains in the Tohu Desert. I want to wander the oceans for years, from island to island, and then I want to go north."

"North? How far?"

"As far as it goes, into the legends that my mother searched for. You know, she was the only person to have sailed beyond Draig Cendyl, and returned? Well, there was also . . ." he stopped.

"Who?"

"The Pirate Lord, Mothar," the voice came from the trapdoor they had used to get onto the roof. Alya was leaning against the ladder.

"How long you been there?" asked Vann.

"Since you came here."

"Why didn't you say anything?"

"Nothing in particular came to mind." Her eyes scanned them, piercing and threatening. "And it seems you were talking about things you did not want others to hear, so I kept my silence."

"You remind me of an old friend," Rob growled. "So are you going to report us? Get us into more trouble for talking about escaping?"

"Gaining a little favour from one's captors can be advantageous. But in this instance, I think not."

"Why, you want in on the plan?" Vann frowned.

"You don't have a plan."

"I don't need a plan," Rob said, folding his arms. "As soon as I get a chance, I'll break away from the supply run and get on the first ship that'll take me. And Vann, if he can come."

"I see." Alya clambered up and stood, her robes fluttering as she loomed over them. "Assuming you can get away from the pengs, where will you go? The coast? It's thousands of miles of treacherous ice that's likely to crack under your weight and drag you into freezing water. A town or port, perhaps, full of pengs and pengish allies, all of whom would spot humans without an escort in a second. They'd have you chained and back here in moments."

"So where would you suggest we go, eh?" Vann growled.

"Let's say," she ignored him, "you find a ship; pengs won't sail for you and stowing away would get you nowhere, they check their holds hourly, and trespassers are thrown overboard. Allies would rather sell their teeth than get caught with escaped prisoners."

"So no ship," Rob bobbed his head, miserable. "Unless we sail ourselves."

"Good," she nodded. "However, can you outpace a longship? They can sometimes even catch galleys if the wind is good."

"Let's steal a longship, then!" Vann suggested, grinning.

"Do you have thirty pairs of arms that you have been hiding?" Alya raised an eyebrow, grimly.

"No, but it wouldn't surprise me if you had."

Alya beamed a malicious smile.

"All right, so we swim," Vann suggested.

"Four hundred miles to Penguve? You'd freeze before you'd gone five feet."

"How far is it to the Teeth?" asked Rob.

"Three times that!"

"So what you're saying is it's impossible to escape, and we shouldn't even try?" Vann sounded ready to throw Alya from the roof.

"I'm saying you have no plan," she retorted.

"So how would we escape?"

"In a ship faster than a longship, stronger than a galley, and small enough to be sailed by a skeleton crew; seven ideally, five at least."

"And how many of those are hanging around Penguve?"

"Just one." She knelt. "*My* ship."

Chapter Six

Hidden History

Alya spent more time alone than Rob did, and he was growing concerned. If they were to build a plan of escape, this level of secrecy could prove problematic. Yet allowing her privacy had meant she had been more willing to help. Any intrusion into her business had been met either with stony silence or cutting remarks.

"People!" Lomi called, clapping. "If I may interrupt, we are expecting a visitation from the supply run before first toll tomorrow. Food and clothing aplenty!"

There was a spattering of applause and cheers though Vann grumbled into his mug of ale.

"Along with the supplies, a guest is coming, my sister, Fleet Admiral Orna." The pengs' chattering became louder and soon Lomi had to wave to get them to stop. "She is going to assess our situation and decide whether we are worthy of an increase in supplies next moon."

"More slime soup and threadbare blankets, I'll bet," Rob muttered.

"I trust you will all dress well," Lomi went on. "If we impress them with your progress towards civilisation, then we may have good times in our future."

"Fat chance," Vann groaned as the prisoners went back to talking and the pengs settled into their patrols.

Alya was standing by the exit, her face a mask. Rob was about to go to her when she turned and left. He slumped on the bench and looked at Vann, who was fiddling with his nose ring.

Ilma shuffled to them and handed Rob, a bundle of cloths. "Some fresh bandages for your sulky friend," she said. "I tried to get to her, but she bolted."

"Scared of doctors, I expect," Vann said, happily. "Good to know she's actually human. Does she treat everyone like dirt or is it just me?"

"She's not all bad," Ilma sighed. "Come on, I saw your heads together all day, you up to something I shouldn't know about?" A mischievous grin split her face, and she pulled her legs onto the bench so that her chin rested on her knees. "Come on, spill it. Are you two, you know . . . ?"

"I don't know," Rob raised an eyebrow.

"Oh, come on, you and Vann have been hanging around every day for the past week. Something special?" She gave a wink and smiled, if possible, even wider.

"Nothing special about me," Vann said, sulkily. "Can't even hold a sword to save my life."

"Swords aren't all they're cracked up to be," Rob patted his arm.

"Oh, you two are just precious," Ilma teased. "Listen, you need to find some good dresses for the feast. I don't want you showing up covered in mud, Rob."

"When do I ever do that?" he objected.

"Whenever you get into an argument with Kerrok. Don't give her a reason. I'd love to have you look nice for a change;

you have such a handsome face." She patted his cheek. "Ah, and you could have ribbons in your hair and a nice new hat."

"I am keeping my hat," he frowned.

"Of course!" She bounced to her feet. "I'll show you where the clothes are."

"Yeah, I could do with a dress up," Vann said, standing. "I've not felt good clothes for a long time. Used to sell dresses and stuff; love me some silks and cotton. We once had this batch from near Tsayad and by Razal's beard, you wouldn't believe what kinds of patterns they'd made."

"I don't like them complicated," Ilma said. "Nice and simple is my way."

"Oh, but if you'd seen them you'd change your mind!"

"I've seen plenty in my time," she laughed and led them through the corridors.

They passed the time discussing various styles they had seen; Ilma was fascinated by the saurosi styles and pressed Rob for everything he could remember about them.

"I was only thirteen when I left and was more interested in getting my clothes dirty than anything else. I was a bit of a stupid kid."

"I heard the toharim have hair, is it true?" Ilma's old eyes sparkled, and she sighed with a long lost hope. "I wanted to see the saurosi lands when I was young. My daughter did. Now I'm here, and so there's not much else to be said."

"What are you here for?" Vann asked.

"It's Rob's fault," she huffed.

"Oi, I wasn't the one who lit a fire in the middle of the ship!" he protested.

"I needed to treat your wounds! Honestly, you'd think you had a death wish."

"Well, at the time, I did," he stopped, and the others looked at him. "It's nothing, ignore me."

"No, listen, mate, don't be like that." Vann put a hand on his shoulder. "That's a serious thing. You can't want to die, can you? You're so . . ." he sighed and released him. "You shouldn't go around saying things like that."

Rob took a breath and heaved his shoulders; the others resigned themselves to his silence.

Their feet echoed across the walls in ricocheting taps that magnified the tension in Rob's back. His spine ached, remembering old hurts. It was like the weight was still there as if he was still dragging that sword like a dead creature.

They came to a dim corridor, and the air grew humid. The hot springs were near and the promised warmth enveloped Rob with tingling anticipation. Vann and Ilma went on with their conversation, but he kept his eyes on the walls as they went deeper.

He stopped where the crystal turned to stark black stone. The frozen fire had knitted into the earth; there were streaks of white, silver and blue, twisted with black and grey rock that progressed downwards until the darker hues took over. Vann sniffed at the sight.

"Weird, isn't it?" he said.

"I sometimes forget why Eimhir wanted to come here. Every now and again I remember; it's for things like this. You don't see this anywhere else in the world."

"Yeah, well, gives me the shivers. Who's Eimhir?"

"Old friend."

"*Friend* is a very loose term," Ilma pointed out. "When Rob was found by the pengish ship, they were stranded in a little boat in the middle of the sea. No food, no drinking water, and Master Sardan here covered in blood."

"What did she do to you?"

"She didn't." Rob closed his eyes. "I did."

He marched down the tunnel, pulling his cloak around his chest. The walls shimmered as light trickled from crystals along the ceiling. Rob stared, distracted from his prickly thoughts. Whatever else might be said of the pengs, they had plenty of mystery and grace to their designs.

"Here, what's this?" Vann asked.

There was a mural spiralling on the walls. Words in ancient Penguvian were scrawled in circles around the heads of pengs in armour. There was an army of warriors, some with flowing manes pouring from helmets, others with diamonds on their brows, and all dressed in gold and pearl. They were charging, weapons raised, arms pointing towards shadows in the sky. Winged shapes, red flickering from toothy maws, drakans ridden by draigs.

The drakans were monstrous, bloody, and clad in fearsome armour, all four of their legs bearing gigantic claws while their bat-like wings blotted out the sun. On their backs were draigs, humanoid, red-scaled with horned heads and jutting mouths, they too wore armour and held axes, swords and javelins.

"This is the most ridiculous battle scene I have ever seen," Vann scoffed. "How in the name of Razal's buttocks do these birds think they can fight fire-breathing drakans? Or the draigs with their swords and what-not?"

"They managed it," Ilma said. "Most of pengish healing lore is built on their experiences in the War of Frost and Flame."

Vann frowned at the images as they passed, each more gruesome than the last.

"They lost a lot of people, a lot of land, and a lot of history," Ilma went on. "The draigs burned one of the great libraries. That's why they keep many of their most secret documents locked in deep vaults. Still, like I said, the pengs know how to treat burns better than anyone else."

"As for knife wounds, they leave a lot to be desired," Rob snorted.

But some of her words were sending ripples through his mind. They kept their secret records in deep vaults. He had seen a trapdoor in the underground springs, locked and concealed beneath dirt, but certainly there, and certainly used.

"I need to check something," his voice seemed vacant. He walked away from them and headed into the catacombs.

Rob wound his way in and out of pools, bending and kneeling, trying to work out where it was he had seen the trapdoor. He had never come in this way before and was disorientated.

The pengs would keep records of prisoners. He'd looked in the library, searching for names, but there hadn't been much of anything regarding Bron'Halla, besides its mythic history and political uses by various dynasties.

If there were secret vaults where they could keep prisoner records, they would have something on Jareth. She had walked the endless tundra and broken into the prison. She had stayed for years with Faolan. They had fallen in love, and they had wanted to stay together, but Jareth had led them both out so they could go on a quest.

Rob smiled to remember Faolan, the forager who had taught him the basics. Though her sarcasm had sometimes stung, he had liked her. She had been a Sky-slayer. She had born a pendant like his.

Escape was burning in his mind. He needed to get a new pendant, and he needed to find Mothar and make him pay for what he had done to Jareth, and Faolan, and all of Rob's old crew.

He stopped. Mothar was one man. Powerful, and immortal, it seemed. But did Rob want his life orchestrated by that beast again? There were other ills in the world. Ills like Skagra, the chaotic and bloodthirsty monster, overran Vann's home.

If he'd known what Skagra had intended, he might have killed her. But that was the old Rob. His younger self relished death and had slaughtered whenever it seemed apt. His stomach turned at the thought now. Perhaps he *was* making progress.

He found the trapdoor handle. It clanged and jerked when he pulled, but a padlock kept it securely closed.

When he got up, his insides squirmed. Vann was watching him with a glimmer in his eyes. He looked from Rob to the door and then sauntered over, cracking his knuckles.

"Yeah, remember what I said about robbing from that pengish family?" he said, grinning so wide his dimples deepened. "I'm quite handy with locks, see."

Rob turned to the door. "Do you think you can get it open?"

"Most likely." Vann knelt. "Open anything, me."

He pulled a set of forks from his pocket. Rob recognised the pengish seals on their handles, and he supposed Vann had lifted them from the common room. The tines on one fork had been artfully bent; the other was missing several of them.

While Vann worked, Rob sat on the edge of one of the pools and stared at the man who had become a friend very quickly. He smiled as he watched his shoulders move and his arms pulse with effort. Rob's throat closed as a horrible scene flashed before his mind's eye.

Niall. The boy he'd loved, cherished and defended. They were supposed to go to sea together. The plan had been to see the world, as co-captains, and to spend every night together until the end of the world. But it had all ended in poison and betrayal.

"You look upset," Vann said, pulling a fork from between his teeth. "Something the matter?"

"Just remembering something that happened a long time ago." Rob shrugged.

"You do that a lot. Maybe Gorm's right, you should let that stuff go. If I kept thinking about all the stuff Skagra did to my home I'd be permanently depressed; all that blood and all those people taken for her sick experiments."

"Experiments?"

Vann shrugged. "They said she experimented on people. Pumped them full of silver stuff and tried to make them into monsters like what she'd seen in some mines."

A haunting horror crept over him. The more he heard about Skagra, the more guilt he felt. She'd been beside him in the mines he'd lived in for years. Why had he not seen this? She'd hidden her identity, going by some nonsensical name.

The thing that got to Rob was how easily he'd been distracted. For all the time he'd been in the mines, sailed, and sat in this prison, his concerns had been about the Pirate Lord Mothar. The other dangers had barely registered in his mind.

A grinding and grumbling interrupted his thoughts as the trapdoor finally opened. Vann stepped back with a flourish and bowed. Rob held back a laugh and bowed back before peering into the deep, dark cavern below.

"What's down there?" Vann said.

"Records," Rob said. "Proper prison records, you know? Not the history and gloating they've got in the library. Stuff about who's been here, for how long, and what happened to them."

"And why's that interesting?"

"Some people escaped." Rob grinned and stepped through the door, beckoning Vann to follow. A winding staircase dug into the earth with small, shallow steps. The walk was a struggle for humans with large feet, but they kept going, the light from above dimming as they went.

The stair spilled onto a narrow corridor that got lower and lower until they were on their knees, scuffing their way through a cramped passage.

"I knew someone," Rob said. "A pirate named Jareth. She got out of here and survived. Well, for a few years anyway."

"The pengs catch up with her?"

"No," Rob looked resolutely forwards. "It was the Air-keepers."

"So, you killed one of them?" Vann ventured, sounding nervous. "I got that you need the pendant. So, you tried to save her?"

Rob wanted to say something, but nothing came out. The truth was he hadn't. Jareth had died of her own accord, had faced the Air-keepers alone while he'd cowered in a cave, cradling his dying captain. Shame and fury ran up his spine, blooming across the top of his head.

At the end of the passage a door opened onto a vault. Its metal walls were lit by glowing globes in each corner and rang as their feet touched the floor. The air shimmered with heat, and their clothes were soon sticking to their backs and arms. It was tall enough for them to stand, but they were closed in by banks of wooden chests, many of which looked to have buckled under the stress of the heat.

"This doesn't look efficient," Rob mused. "Why would you keep records in this place? The parchment would be ruined in minutes."

"It's not parchment," Vann opened one of the chests and lifted up a steel tablet. It boomed as he laid it on the floor, the weight sending vibrations through their feet.

Rob looked it over, spotting lists of names with various date notations that changed depending on the dynasty in charge of the empire at the time.

They opened chest after chest, scouring the tablets for any sign of Jareth's name. Occasionally, their eyes would go to the doors, thinking they'd heard a voice, or footsteps.

Opening one of the chests, Rob was almost blinded by a dazzling reflection. Gold glinted, and he had to kneel to get a better look at what was in there. On a red blanket were two bracelets and a long gold broadsword.

Its hilt was shaped with two entwined drakans, their snake-like necks bending in an s-shape while their mouths opened towards one another and spewed fire that reached up the blade. The drakan wings shaped the guard, and their winding bodies made the grip; the pommel was a ruby.

Rob reached out a hand and held it over the hilt, his head a haze of misty thoughts. Nothing fell into place; every moment seemed to slide away as his eyes fixed on the sword. He could not pinpoint why he was so mesmerised by it, but then Alya's voice broke him out of this moment of confusion.

"It is a Llafn Gwaed," she said, "a Blood Blade."

She was standing in the doorway, leaning against it and

smiling. Rob stood and glowered at her. "What are you doing here?"

"I was taking a bath," she said, flicking her damp hair from her face and tucking it back under her headscarf. "I saw the two of you enter the trapdoor. Perhaps it would be prudent for you to practice whispering."

"We would have if we'd known you were listening in," Vann said.

"If I did not wish it known that I was listening in, and I didn't, I would find it easy to spy on you. And I did." She strode in, her bare feet pattering the floor.

"What's your game, Alya Kadir?" Rob asked.

"To escape, to find my ship, and to take it back."

"What then?"

"Freedom!" She put her hand on top of the chest holding the sword and closed it. "You are looking for records on the exploits of Jareth Sea-Splitter. How exactly do you think it will help? Read her exploits, read them twice if you want, it will result in the same; a waste of time."

"You don't want us to escape on our own," Vann said.

"You cannot escape on your own," she retorted.

"Jareth did," Rob said.

"She came here alone, but she did not escape alone. You must know that much. Faolan and Armun helped her, or so the story goes."

"You know how they did it?" Rob looked at her hopefully.

"Of course I do."

"How long have you known this?"

"Several days," she grinned.

"Why didn't you tell us?"

"You didn't ask me. In future, perhaps you will."

"How did she do it?" Rob pressed.

Alya looked up at the ceiling. "It is said that she flew. Nothing else is written, so her plan, whatever it was, is useless for us."

"So what's *your* plan?" Rob stalked after her as she turned to leave. "We should know as much as we can, surely?"

"I am working on the details," she said. "I shall let you know in good time. For now, I advise you to continue as you were. Ilma is no doubt worrying where you have gone."

Rob watched her go and struggled with whether or not he should chase her down. Vann looked relieved that she was gone, his posture suddenly much more relaxed. They heard her leave the tunnel, the echoes muted.

"You want to go after her?" Vann ventured, uncertain.

"Not now." He shook his head and Vann sighed in relief.

Chapter Seven

Old Cloaks

"Oh, so now you join me," Ilma said, sulking. "Run off while I'm in the middle of things, why don't you? Honestly, you two are the worst."

They had come to a cave-like room, its doors like twisted stalactites winding down from the ceiling to curve at the floor. They all had to duck to enter, but it was lofty within the room, the ceiling upheld by pillars of crystal. There were piles and piles of clothes, some in hampers, some folded on shelves; there were coats, dresses, skirts, tails, boots, and sandals.

"Where'd they get all this stuff?" Vann asked, picking a pair of trousers several sizes too large for him.

"Old prisoners," Rob said. "They leave clothes behind when they die."

"They can have mine now if they like," he huffed.

"I'd like to see that," Rob teased, tugging at his shirt.

Ilma found a tunic and belt that fit her and she added a flowing skirt of many layers. Vann tried a similar one, but it did not go lower than his ankles, so he sulkily put it back.

Rob found a kilt of thick, tartan cotton, with a sash and a wide canvas belt. He pulled off his trousers but left his silk britches. Vann gazed over at him, and Ilma smiled at the pair of them; Rob found a tight black shirt to go with his attire. There was a loop for a scabbard in his belt, and Rob moved it to his right hip though the lack of a real sword made it a hollow gesture.

"Doesn't it go over the left?" Vann said. "You know, so you can draw a proper sword and get fighting!"

"He favours the left hand," Ilma said.

"Tends to put others off balance," Rob said, miming a fighting stance.

As Vann admired his physique, Rob's innards warmed. The more the feeling spread, the more it itched at his mind. His throat went dry, and his eyes burned; he was back in that cell on the day of reckoning, hearing the breath slow to a stop, feeling Niall's body fall limp, and smelling the reek.

"Everything okay?" Ilma asked, putting her arm around him. "You look very handsome in that, you know?"

"I'm fine," he smiled weakly. "Come on, I need a coat, it's too cold."

Vann decided on a set of robes that slashed across his chest in tight circles, surrounding his torso with streams of colour. Over this, he wore a cloak of silver, which he fastened with an emerald brooch. Ilma, meanwhile, chose a frilly shirt and a thick cardigan with stripes of red and white.

Rob was searching through a pile of coats when a visitor interrupted them.

"Might I suggest the red one," Lomi hobbled in. "You all look very nice."

"No need to sound so surprised," Vann said.

"At my age, there is only one surprise left." She shambled in and gestured to Rob. "May I speak with this young man in private for a few moments?"

"Of course, he's the important one, after all," Ilma chortled.

"I also need to speak with you, doctor," Lomi added pointedly. "Come to my office at next toll and Vann, I would like to see you at the toll after that. Bring your work on the history of the Iasg Rebellion."

"I haven't finished it yet!" he moaned.

"Then finish it, you will feel all the better for it once it is done. A task that hangs over you is a heavier weight than holding the sea on your shoulders."

"Nonsense," he muttered as he left.

"I have some patients," Ilma sighed. "And I have to wash before the feast."

Once she had gone, Lomi nodded, and her cheeks bulged in a pengish smile as Rob pulled the red coat she had indicated from the pile. It was a double-breasted frock coat with wide cuffs and collars, the stitching was black, and it had brass buttons down the front. The material was damaged in places, but it was good.

"It belonged to a prisoner who left us," Lomi touched the material, her eyes closed. "Her name was Jareth, called by some the Sea-Splitter."

Rob stared at the coat. Jareth had been the first mate on his ship; she had been his friend, his guardian, and so much more. She had let him borrow a coat once before, and he had never been able to return it. The blue raincoat had been reduced to shreds while he had been on his way to Bron'Halla. It made his stomach drop to think of it.

"You do not wish to wear it?" Lomi enquired. "Is it because she is dead? Do you think she would not have wanted you to wear her clothes? Or do you think it would be an act of disrespect?"

"She was brave, fiercely loyal and a good person. She knew what the Sea-Stone Sword was and never touched it. I should have followed her example; I don't deserve to wear her clothes."

"That coat will be here for many years, and countless prisoners may wear it. How many will be worthy of your friend's memory? Would you wish someone who never knew her, never respected her, to wear it?"

"It's only a coat," he stroked a finger across the buttons and sighed.

"That is true, it is only a coat, to most people. But to you it is the friend you lost, it is a symbol of the love that was between you. A first mate and an apprentice, you respected her, and she knew you for who you are. I do not think that coat would be suited to anyone but one who knew and loved her."

Argument felt like a weary prospect, so Rob submitted. Sweeping the coat over his shoulders, he fastened it, made a twirl and felt its tails whirl behind him. It sent a thrill through him, and he could not stop the grin plastering his face.

"Very dashing," Lomi said. "Come, I have other things to say."

She led him through the cave, past rows upon rows of human apparel and even some saurosi robes. Soon the clothing gave way to armour and weaponry, but it was dulled compared to what he had expected.

He picked up a crossbow, its hinges rusted and its string loose. Lomi nodded and snatched a bolt from the shelf next to it.

"These weapons were old when I took my seat here," she said. "My sisters and I used them for games."

"A dangerous way to pass the time." He lifted the crossbow and pretended to aim it at the far wall. "How many sisters did you lose in those 'games'?"

"None at all!" she laughed. "These weapons are near useless. We used to fire bolts and catch them in our bare hands."

"Sounds impressive."

"It looks impressive if you don't know how it is done. Anyone who has never fired a crossbow would think you're a magician, but even the slightest inkling and you'd see it as a fun trick." She plucked a vial from another shelf. "Speaking of tricks, here's a pretty thing. Smoke pellets; we used to anger our mother so much with these. Break the glass they fill the room with smoke!" she chortled, almost sadly. "Alas, they have lost their potency, you'll be lucky to get a wisp of white from them today."

"Why are you showing me these?"

"I know you are thinking of escaping." She drew a heavy breath and leaned against the shelving, her walking stick propped under her arm. "To do so you would require weapons, and as you can see, we have none that you could use."

Rob averted his gaze, focusing on a vial of smoke, wondering if the pressure of his hands alone could break the glass. When he had held the Sea-Stone Sword, white vapour had surrounded his body, rising in waves from his parched skin. He looked down at the pengish warden, her face drawn in concern.

"You found the vaults I hear," she said softly. "You found the chest of my shame. The trinkets I took from the Sky Sages when I left them. Golden toys, and little more."

"That sword looked pretty deadly." Rob frowned at her.

"The Llafn Gwaed. It is a sign of the peaceful ways of the Sky Sages. It stays gold until it touches blood, and then changes colour, a different colour for the kind of blood. So long as it remains gold, it is a sign that you have never killed anyone."

"At least not with that blade."

"The Sky Sages never killed," Lomi went on. "The pendants are made of the gold of the Dead God's body, and so they combat the Slayer's Curse. They oppose the Air-keepers, but do not kill them."

"They contract us retroactively," Rob snorted. "They won't get involved, but they'll reward us nonetheless."

"So long as the Air-keepers fear that people can slay them and avoid the Curse, they will not make greater inroads into destroying Diyngard."

He could hear the Air King's breath in his head. The rattling noise that had forced its way into his dreams became immediate and present.

"I had those kinds of ideas," Rob said. "Stopping the Air King from taking the Sea-Stone Sword was the reason I killed him. He'd killed my crew; he was threatening my friends, the world, and made it seem easy. I didn't have to think about it. I wanted him dead. If I ever went back to sea, what would I find? Mothar the Pirate Lord, Skagra the bloodthirsty, and who knows what else?" Shame was boiling in his chest. "I can't give in to those wishes. Last time I tried to be a hero I lost my friends. I did terrible things because I wanted to be remembered as a legend."

"You wanted to be a hero, but when it happened, your whole world fell apart," Lomi said sadly. "How long do legends last? The heroes who fought in the War of Frost and Flame are shadows now. Their names are like dust, their glory melted into water. Glory is like a circle in the water which never ceases to enlarge itself until by broad spreading it disperses to nought."

"Gorm told me that." Rob smiled.

"It is true enough," Lomi nodded. "Glory is a terrible thing to seek. The Sky Sages kept many things for their own glory, treasures from across the world; statues, swords, and a *crown*," her voice darkened at the last word.

"I won't go looking for a crown," Rob shuddered. "Last time I looked for power, I was a monster."

"Are you still that monster? In you, I see a young man who wishes to heal the hurts of the world. You see bullies and you stop them, you see injustice and you stand in its way. That does not sound like a monster."

"Don't tell me you are encouraging me to escape?" His lips curled.

"I would be a very poor warden if I did! But what do you imagine would happen if you went into the world?"

"I'm not sure."

"I did not ask what you were sure of; I asked what you imagine. Tell me, what images go through your mind when you think of the rest of the world?"

"I think about the Sky Sages, about getting a new pendant. I think about my mother, the adventures she had; I think about my crew and everything we did, and I think about Mothar and how much he wants to kill me. I'm afraid. I'm afraid of what my memories will do to me, to my friends, and I'm afraid of what I might become again."

"And do you imagine you can stand up to your fears? Do you imagine your time here has given you the strength to stand in the face of your deepest horrors?"

"Honestly? No. I was defeated; I'm weak."

"It is when we reach our weakest point that we discover where our truest strength lies."

"Do you have a book filled with vaguely uplifting rhetorical nonsense?"

"Several," she chirruped. "You should read them; it might do you some good."

"Or send me round the bend."

"That too is possible." She patted his arm again. "I would advise you to stay, you still have much to learn."

Chapter Eight

Alliance

A BELL RANG, SHUDDERING THROUGH THE CRYSTAL WALLS AND glass pillars. It was hollow and droning, unlike the tinny clang of the hourly tolls, this was a dirge, a mourning sound that haunted the tower. Rob shuddered as the sound went through his bones.

He came to a balcony overlooking the lands about Bron'Halla; he peered towards the forest and beyond the cliff wall into the white wastelands. Shapes were rushing towards the tower, tall sails and wide bows slicing through snow.

"The assembly will no doubt be a spectacle of the usual pengish self-congratulatory tradition," Alya's voice came from behind.

Her dress was wound about her in smooth slashes of white, purple and black with sun-like patterns embroidered into the fabric. She held in one hand what seemed to be a small paint-brush and a mirror in the other, with a snort she set about painting dark blue swirls around her eyelids.

"I'm sure the pengs aren't the only ones who indulge in traditions of self-congratulation," Rob said.

"I don't need traditions to congratulate myself. However, sometimes traditions can send a message."

"What are you talking about? And what's that stuff you're putting on your eyes?"

"It is from my homeland," she lifted the brush and frowned at it. "I have never worn it by choice before."

"Why the change?"

"The pengs wish us to become more like them, to take on *their* civilisation and ideals. They march across Diyngard and ransack cities in the name of their empire. In the Amser Wood, where I grew up, some pengish explorers visited." She marched to the window and stood beside him. "What do you make of the other towers, the ones surrounding this monstrosity?"

He looked over the balcony and scanned the architecture. "The nearer towers were the first to be built. They're the ones with jagged edges, made to resemble Bron'Halla itself. The later structures have smooth edges, domed roofs and stark walls. They were built in defiance of the spiked disorder of the tower. Lomi said they are 'all pengish architecture, all masterpieces of design and ingenuity, and yet, all standing in the shadow of the ancient Spire of Frozen Fire'. A little overdramatic, but it stuck in my memory."

"Those fortresses over there," she pointed. "They're as pengish as my foot. The domed roofs, the blue stone, speckled with gold, the minarets, all stolen."

"They moved a building all the way down here?"

"No," She looked at him with exhaustion. "They stole the plans, my people's ingenuity, and called it their own. Virtually nothing here is pengish."

"If your people were so wonderful," someone said, which made Rob jump, "they would not have allowed us to take their designs. They would not have been conquered."

Kerrok's beady eyes narrowed, a mischievous twist to her cheeks giving Rob an uncomfortable feeling.

"We were not conquered," Anya smiled grimly. "Amser is too close to Draig Cendyl, and your empire is not going to provoke those fire-breathers anytime soon."

Kerrok chuckled. "Keep your eyes on your own affairs, prisoner. It won't affect you either way."

"What do you want, Kerrok?" Rob asked, trying to sound calm.

"A few more manners from you; I was hoping you would join me and the others for the procession, but as you are hiding I have decided to demote you to fetch-and-carry. In two hours you will be in the lower halls collecting blankets."

"You are so kind." He gave a mocking bow.

"And you," she pointed at Alya, "perhaps you should tell Sardan why it is that the warden knew he was planning an ill-fated escape."

Rob gave Alya a glare, which she returned with interest. There was a rage in her eyes that went beyond seeing her people's buildings replicated by the pengs. Her gaze was deep but he could see something burning, a ferocity likely to burst.

Kerrok left, chuckling as she went. Rob looked away, his mind clanging with confused thoughts. He needed to escape; he wanted to get to the Sky Sages. But was that enough? He thought of Mothar, Skagra, and countless dangers.

"Your plan to escape the supply run was foolish," she said. "And it didn't require me to tell her you were thinking of it."

Rob hung his head and gripped the side of the balcony, letting the icy wind sting his face. A considerable amount of stubble had grown there, and he scratched at it absently. Alya was still standing beside him, her posture relaxed and smooth. He glowered at her, but she smirked.

"I need to get out of this place," she said. "I need to get my ship back and, well . . . other things."

"What other things?"

"The pengs imprisoned me to keep me quiet, to stop me from sharing my expertise, they fear what is in my mind and they wish to keep it there."

"Why didn't they just kill you?"

"You have been here for two years and have learned nothing of pengish social customs and traditions. Their laws prohibit death sentences except in cases of a direct threat to the empress. And even then they are not keen. Their honour binds them." She knitted her fingers. "They live on the ice where staying together is essential for survival. Their traditions, laws, and honour are all part of the binding nature of their culture. If a piece of it breaks . . ." she uncoupled her fingers and shrugged.

"How do you know this?" Rob tried to keep how impressed he was out of his voice, but by how much she smirked he supposed he had failed.

"I watch people, and I listen," she leaned closer so that he could see the intricate patterns on her eyelids. "If you keep your attention in the right place, you learn how to direct others' attention."

"I'm not following."

"My people have used kuhl on our eyes for centuries; it is part of our history and part of our identity. You appear surprised."

"I never had you down as someone who would wear face paint."

"It is a tool, a very useful one. If you wish to draw focus to your eyes, say, subtle variations here and there, unwittingly the observer pays attention."

"And what is the point?"

"You of all people should know the impact of eyes; I have seen the glare you give Kerrok, that much hatred forged into one glance must have taken practice. The face is a tool for expressing your emotions; the kuhl sharpens the tool." She grinned. "Also, it makes me feel better."

"How so?"

"In many ways; it is an act of defiance. They wish me to conform to pengish ideals, to forget my home and join their supposedly enlightened ways. I choose to remember my home, my people, and my history. They do not own me, and I will show them. I will take back what they stole, my identity, my freedom, and my ship."

"Sounds honourable." He looked away. "I wish you all the luck in the world."

"You're afraid to escape," she said. "You don't trust my plan."

"Of course I don't," he laughed. "I don't even know your plan. I'll escape somehow."

"And leave the rest of us here? What about my ship? What about Vann? You won't leave without him, will you?"

"I . . ." He put his hands against his head, blood throbbing through his temples. "I don't know what I want."

"I would not blame you for leaving him behind, either way."

"Why do you hate him so much? Why do you have to be so damned antagonistic? It's unnecessary, and you're making me not want to trust you. You're cruel and unkind to everyone; it's like you don't even want people to like you."

"I have no need for people to like me." She looked away, grasping the railing of the balcony. "If you must know, Vann tried to get on my good side while we travelled here. He was too eager, too friendly, and all too interested in who I was and what I could do."

"So? He's friendly; he's done much the same with me."

"Right!" Her brow crinkled. "People who try to get too close too quickly with strangers are rarely acting honestly."

"What, you think he has some ulterior motive? I thought you didn't think he was clever enough."

She laughed. "Yes, I suppose I did. The fact remains, I do not trust him."

"What about me? Do you trust me?"

"I don't trust anyone." Her eyes darkened, and her shoulders sagged. The lines etched on her face suddenly seemed to show relief, and she looked unspeakably weary. "But there are few people I actively *mistrust*, and Vann is one of them."

"But why? So he got a little friendly with you, has it ever

occurred to you that he might just have liked you?"

She regarded him with surprise. Her jaw worked slowly, and she rubbed at her chin. At last, she shook her head, "No, I don't think that can be right."

"I think you're frightened." Rob's mind was racing. The look on her face and the shift in her posture as soon as the topic of trust had reared had given him new thoughts. "I think you're afraid of trusting people, of letting people like you, of letting yourself like others. I think maybe you lost someone you loved? Believe me, Alya, I know what that feels like. It hurts, doesn't it? It hurts every time you think about it, about them, and about what happened. But you don't have to let it turn you sour, you don't have to let it turn you into a bitter, snarling little bottle of poison."

"Are you done?" she yawned. "No, I have not lost anyone. Nobody I loved has died, so far as I know."

"Then what is it, Alya? What reason do you have to treat everyone around you like absolute dirt?"

She stepped dangerously close, her eyes meeting his with fire and venom, but there was sadness there, too. Something moved behind her gaze, and her lip quivered almost imperceptibly.

"There are some things worse than death," she said.

She moved in a way he recognised; three years in the fighting pits of Khamas had taught him those movements. The way the shoulder dips, the change in breath tone, the flexing of the hands followed by the reach. He moved without thinking, pulling out of reach and rolling as the sound of metal rang through the wind.

Alya drew a sword from under the folds of her dress; it was double-edged, straight and long. The guard was a bronze disc decorated with suns and moons. From the pommel spilled a red tassel that fluttered, but she flicked it around her wrist and adjusted her grip so that it was firm.

"Nice isn't it?" she said, beaming. "It is a jian sword from Gesne Nord if I am not mistaken. The branding mark has been scraped off, which suggests a pirate stole it. The blade is in good condition, and the tassel has not frayed."

"Where did you get that?" He backed away, his knees bending into their old stance. It unnerved him how naturally he fell back into fighting positions; they were ingrained in his muscle memory, as well as his mind.

"It was kept in the stores under a pile of bedclothes."

"How did you know it was there?"

She lowered her head but kept her eyes on him, menacingly. "Tell me, with the warden's discovery of *your* escape plan, will you go through with mine?"

"Why should I?"

"The Sky-slayer's pendant," she said. "I like to know the exact intentions of those I conspire with, so I looked into you. All the things you did at sea, and everything you've done since, I have looked at all of the records."

"A little obsessive, isn't it?"

"I have been betrayed in the past. Now, are you going to come with the escape party?"

"Party? How many have you got?"

"Just us," she frowned. "I need you to convince Gorm and Ilma to join. I shall need their skills."

"What skills am I supposed to have, then?"

"First of all, you have a natural instinct for combat. Secondly, you can convince the others. Those you have graced with your presence do trust you. These past few years have made them grow closer to you, even if you have tried to stay away. You will convince them."

"Oh really?" He beamed sardonically.

"And thirdly," she went on, her face stony. "I need to use your reputation."

"My reputation? Do you know what I have done?"

"Yes, but more importantly I know what people *think* you have done, and I know what people *think* you are. That kind of fear will be useful."

"And I am just going to go along with this?"

"Do you want me to threaten you?" She moved closer, pointing the blade at him.

"That would be amusing, go ahead," Rob said.

"So you wish to die laughing? Good choice." She smiled. "I dislike confrontation, but if necessary I will be open to physical persuasion."

"Don't bother, it won't work."

"All right then, what about the trasati?"

"What about them?"

"I had been under the impression that Vann's glorification of the torture and enslavement of the trasati was a source of anger for you. I am offering you the chance to set creatures you claim to care about free. If finding a pendant is not enough for you, that is."

"Anger is not a good motivation," he growled. "I lost too much chasing vengeance and anger; I won't do it again."

"Back then you wished to inflict pain, to kill the Pirate Lord and his people, to destroy them and become a hero. Now you can use your skills to save others, and so set *yourself* free. Or would you rather stay here in chains while others stay in theirs?"

"Don't try to make it sound like you care," he spat and sidestepped her, but she followed and bounded to the door, blocking his exit.

"I *don't* care," she said. "I do not care for your trasati. I do not care for your Sky-slayer's Curse. And I do not care for you. But I *need* you. To get back what was stolen from me. The day I arrived you defended Vann but allowed yourself to be beaten bloody. I could tell you were not putting forward your skills. Your muscles twitched to fight, but you held back. I am giving you the chance to be true, rather than hide. Will you follow your deepest principals or will you rot in that cell?"

"I don't know!" Rob backed away and pulled his hat off, letting his dreadlocks fall around his face. The familiar screams echoed as he thought about taking up arms again. Shivering, he leaned against a wall. "Of course I want to escape. I want to do it for the right reasons. I want a Sky-slayer's pendant, I want the abuse of the trasati to stop; I'm angry, furious and beyond reason. But I don't want to be motivated by anger and fear."

"Anger is fire and lightning in your spine, what matters is how you direct it."

"You just want to use me for your own ends. I will not be manipulated again."

"I am not manipulating you, Rob Sardan. I am being honest with you," she said calmly. "My intentions may not be the same as yours, but we can mutually benefit. Help me escape, help me get my ship back, and you will have your chance to help yourself, and those you say you care for. You do care for them, don't you?"

Rob nodded.

"Stuck here, wallowing in self-pity, you can't help anyone. Escape with me and you will be able to help them."

She stretched out her hand, and he eyed it warily.

"I will need a pendant," he said, taking her hand. "That is my condition. We search for the Sky Sages. Will your ship be able to handle that kind of quest?"

"I expect so," Alya smiled and shook his hand.

Chapter Nine

Frost and Fire

The panopticon was a circular room that spiralled up in coils of glass. Stairs and a mezzanine arched in a spider's web design that vanished into a dazzling ceiling. This was the centre of the tower, a hollow middle that spanned earth to sky. The light, focused by layer upon layer of glass and crystal, made the panopticon almost warm.

In the centre was a plinth of blue stone, atop which was a nest of white marble. So much brightness in one area was giving Rob a headache and he glared at Gorm, who was sitting cross-legged at his feet, hands cupped in her lap.

Her meditations in the panopticon unnerved Rob. She enjoyed it here at the centre of the tower, at the centre of the world. Slowly, she lifted her head, eyes opening to drink in the light that danced across the room. Rob helped her to her feet and she loomed over him, broad shoulders wrapped in layers of cotton. Her dress was fitted to her stature, flowing and with many folds. Rob compared her sash to his own and was pleased that his was in better condition.

A series of pengs marched across a skywalk above their heads, halberds waving and armour clanging. The echoes rang and Rob took it in and then looked back at his own clothes, feeling suddenly vulnerable.

"The pengs carry weapons and wear armour," Gorm said, following his gaze. "The draigs in their home country do not. Have you ever wondered why?"

"I can't say that I have," he replied. "Alya wanted me to talk to you about . . ."

"The great war of Frost and Flame," she said, raising a hand. "It is the oldest tale known to this world, with the exception perhaps of Razal's Shield."

"But Razal's Shield is just another name for the sun." Rob looked through the mesh of crystal above, hoping to catch a glimpse of the white circle that hung in the sky. "Every culture ever has legends about the sun. It's hard to miss."

"Indeed!" She closed her eyes and clasped her hands together. "Do you know how the War ended? Histories tell of ice retreating, melting in Ginnungagap, the pengs were driven to the south while the world warmed. That much is true, but only to a few is it known why the world warmed."

Rob looked around the chamber. Talking about draigs was dangerous in this place and he needed to shift the conversation.

"So, we need to get out of here," he pressed, but she stopped him again.

"Three volcanoes, larger than any others in the world, all of them erupted within a year. It was unprecedented and unexpected; it was deliberate. First, there was Geata, and then there was Helzar, and finally Voltous. Someone set those mountains to blaze, filling the sky with smoke and ash until the ice died. The Gulf of Sumair was created by the flooding, the land of Cath was split, and the wide expanses of Nasgadh sank beneath the waves. Such a cataclysm was not the work of nature."

"Volcanoes erupt naturally, you know," Rob suggested.

"This was different. Legends hidden in the vaults, and whispers spoken beneath the Wymhold, all tell of a secret society that set those mountains to burst. It was to end the war.

To forge a new world, first they burned and drowned the old."

The shiver that went through him was deep and cold. Gorm kept her eyes closed and head bowed. Her expression became pained and she put her hand on his shoulder as if to steady herself.

"You went to the vaults?" Rob realised. "Who told you about them?"

"Alya," she said. "I do not know what she thought I would find, but she knew I wanted knowledge. I believe I found the connection I had been looking for since I was young, the Legend of the Great Ending. I heard it in the Wymhold when I was a girl, and I heard it on the sea, and now I see it written in the pengish records. It really happened, and I tremble to think of what this may mean."

"There's a way you could find out," Rob suddenly perked up. "I hear there are libraries and draigish colonies in Geata. That was one of the volcanoes, wasn't it? You can go and find this connection," he said eagerly. "Come on, Gorm, we need you. Without you, we'd be Gormless."

She laughed and tapped him on the back of the head, knocking his hat off. "It will be a deadly quest."

"I should tell you that Alya has been plotting . . ."

"Yes," Gorm nodded. "She has spoken with me and I have been considering this for some time. I was unsure, but since my readings, and my meditations, my mind has been shifting."

"Yet you never said anything to Alya?"

"No," she sighed. "I do not think she would trust me if I said yes to her. If I say yes to you, however, she will believe. She thinks I trust you more than I trust her."

"I should hope so!" Rob lifted his hat from the floor and dusted it off.

She knelt beside him and put a hand to the ground. "The world is turning, right here. They call this place the Needle of the World."

"And a hundred other names; pengs are good at that."

"If you concentrate you can feel it spinning. It is hurtling around this point, like a top hanging in nothingness."

"You have been speaking too much with Lomi." His face cracked into a smile. She looked at him and his face straightened again. "No, go on, I like it."

"When you killed the Air King the winds of the world moved, returning to their natural state. For some this is good, for others it is not. I have a great fear; there is something in the air and its voice is growing."

Rob folded his arms, remembering crimson air pouring from the hands of Mothar the Pirate Lord.

"Have you heard of a pirate named Skagra?" Gorm asked suddenly.

"Vann's home was taken by her. She's Mothar's second in command."

"Rob, please do not be angered." She breathed slowly and met his gaze. "I need you to understand the urgency of the situation. We must escape and find a ship, soon; a terrible thing is coming. It will rip this world apart."

"What are you talking about?"

"*All shall die in the flame-filled sky.* Those words were Skagra's motto; she repeated them every night and every morning. She made her crew repeat it as they burned ships; she made her victims repeat it as they were tortured."

"What does it . . . hang on? How do you know this?"

"I was on her crew," Gorm's shoulders sank. "I was her first mate."

He stared. She had always been quiet, collected and grim, but he could not see her as a pirate, let alone one of the most dangerous ones to ever sail. Stepping back he took a horrified breath, shaking, denying her words even as they echoed in his mind.

"I was a pirate, perhaps I still am," she smiled. "Rob, I want to get out of here because Skagra needs to be stopped. She will burn the world if she can, and she won't care who she takes with her. She was just as interested in the tales of the Great Ending as I am. I am sure she believes in it. I am sure she is seeking to make it happen again. That is why she went to Geata."

"No, back up." He put his hands on his hips. "When were you on Skagra's crew?"

"Since I was a child. I was born somewhere green, I know that much, but the pirates took me before any true memories could form. I was schooled and disciplined at sea, I was given tasks and I was good at all of them. I rose through the ranks and might have had my own ship if I had not stayed with Skagra.

"When Mothar returned, Skagra brought us the head of Kenna Iron Helm. She ordered us to drink from the skull." She shuddered. "I was sick that night and many nights afterwards. Something was in that drink and half of the crew died. She never told Mothar; he would not have cared. *She* did not care. She threw the bodies into the sea.

"I was in my bunk, screaming, desperate for relief; I begged her to end it, to stick a knife in me. But she wanted to see how long I would last. I begged everyone who came near to end my suffering, but they refused, terrified of Skagra's wrath. I dragged myself out of the bunk, burning from within, hardly able to think. I crawled onto the deck and I threw myself into the sea. I thought I would die. I wanted to die. Oh, how I would have loved to have perished, but I lingered. Then I saw my hands, glowing with silver light."

Rob blinked. "Saagara?"

"Aye, Saagara, the silver body of the Ocean's Eye, god of the sea. I had heard that it granted powers beyond belief. But it was said to be deadly. One in ten thousand might survive a dosage, but I did not feel like I would be one."

Rob knitted his brows. "What happened?"

"Isn't it obvious?" She put her hands on his shoulders. "You happened, Sword-breaker. You destroyed the heart of Saagara's power and the power was ripped from my body. On that day, you killed a god, and you freed me."

He looked up at her eyes, wide and glimmering. For the first time since he had done it, he almost felt as if he had done something good. It was such a strange thought that he could not move. She patted him and broke his trance.

"You should not judge yourself as harshly as you do," she said. "You are not all-powerful; others make their choices as you make yours. Please, do not argue." She lifted a hand to stop him. "I am glad you are escaping, Rob. I believe I can help you, and you can help me. I want Skagra stopped. Not for vengeance, not for malice, but for the good of the world. She will be drawn to your fame, and because of what you represent to pirates. They say you are the only one who can kill the Pirate Lord."

Rob lowered his eyes at last. "I beat him in a sword fight once, but to kill him would be a different thing entirely. He's immortal."

"So was the Air King."

"I had the Sea-Stone Sword."

"The rumour is important, the story has infected minds and they are curious. They believe you can kill him, and that is the issue. Rob, it is your choice. I ask you to help me. It will help your own cause."

"The Sky Sages?"

"Indeed." She gave a solemn nod. "I suspect Skagra will use them to break one of the three great volcanoes and change the world."

"But why? I don't understand why anyone would want that."

"She has always wanted to destroy the powerful, to tear down queens and lords, to make rulers a thing of the past."

"That sounds fine," he laughed. "Does she take it too far or something?"

"No, that is not it. The problem is the incongruence within her. She has ideals, but she also has desires. Calamity!" Gorm frowned. "She embraces calamity and chaos. It is difficult to convey quite how exhilarating our exploits were when we were at sea. We spread fear and destruction, yes, but it filled us with energy and joy to see catastrophe. Walls fell, towers crumbled, and forests burned. And Skagra sang. We relished those days."

"And what about now?" Rob's insides turned sour. "How do you feel about those things now?"

"Conflicted," she admitted. "Much as Skagra has always been. We were close, once. She would agonize over her choices; to tear down power, or to embrace calamity. To seek her joy, or seek her ideals. She has much in common with your own problems, Rob."

Ilma burst into the panopticon before Rob could reply, her hair fluttering wildly. She was clutching a thick cotton bag and looked haggard; with a forced smile, she hopped in front of the pair of them.

"I've just escaped the procession," she said. "They're halfway through the third liturgy, so we've got a good twenty minutes before we'll be disturbed." She reached into her bag and handed Gorm a set of bandages. "How is the arm doing? Any pains in the elbows?"

"Last night I felt some small stinging on my wrist, nothing more. The healing process is going as planned."

"*The healing process is going as planned*," she mimicked. "Yes, very good. I don't want you getting it harmed further; it'll give you some peace."

"I will be at peace when the sea is under my feet," Gorm bowed. "What of your own health?"

"My health is my own business," she snapped, and then turned to Rob. "Oh, Rob, I am glad you're going! Finding the Sky Sages is an excellent idea. No doubt they'll be able to heal your magical problems. Then I can do *my* job. I need a handsome young body like yours to prod and probe; it's all academic, of course, I'm much too old for any of that."

"Thank you for coming, Ilma," he said, nodding.

"Well, those healing scrolls have been on my mind since you mentioned them. If there's one thing I can't stand, its people who hide essential knowledge. But, like you said, there's a whole world out there."

"Your daughter would be proud of you," Rob said, putting an arm around her and squeezing.

"I . . ." Ilma coughed and looked away. "I suppose like you said, I can't live wondering what might have been for the rest of my life."

"Why not just say to Alya that you wanted to go? Why wait for me?"

"Alya's not exactly a friend," she snorted. "Oh, she's smart, but she could never give me that something to make me want to, you know, *go*!"

"And I do?"

"Of course you do." She sighed and slung her bag over her back. "Time is precious at my age. I've been thinking about what you said ever since we talked, and yes, it's been growing. I suppose I always wanted to go. My own mother was stuck in her old ways, and I wanted to impress her by being the same. Maybe that's why I never went anywhere until I was forced."

"This time, you're going of your own choice," Rob encouraged. "Trust me, you can do it."

"I never doubted I could! It's just hard to know who to trust, especially when Alya's around."

"Well, Vann's coming too," Rob grinned. "She'll be so distracted criticising him she won't notice the rest of us."

"It's difficult to trust one who does not seem affected by cruelty," said Gorm. "Rob, I would advise you to speak to Vann on this, rather than avoiding the topic. You care for the trasati, and if you care for Vann, you will help him understand."

"I know I should," Rob squirmed. "I know I should be furious. I feel conflicted." He smiled at Gorm. "Besides, what makes you think he'd listen to me?"

"What indeed?" Ilma grinned, baring her teeth.

"Oh stop it." He nudged her. "Speaking of not trusting people . . ."

Alya was striding towards them with a determined grimace. She stopped in front of them and folded her arms.

"We will escape tonight," she said. "If all goes according to plan."

"Tonight?" asked Rob, startled.

"Everything is in place; it is the perfect time."

"If we're supposed to trust you, then you'd better explain what this plan *is*."

"I don't expect you to trust me." She sidled closer and looked him in the eyes. "You, Sword-breaker, will know what to do when the time comes. Just remember, I want you for your reputation, for your history and fame."

"Thanks, I feel really loved and appreciated," he growled, pushing his face closer to hers in the hopes of intimidating her.

"The procession is on its way here," she said. "Follow my lead. If everything falls into place, we shall have to run to the snow ships." Rob tried to pull her back, but she shrugged him off and led them to the double doors.

Gorm put a hand on Rob's shoulder as they walked. There was warmth in her eyes as she gazed after Alya, who was counting on her fingers and frowning.

"She trusts you," Gorm said. "Though she wishes she did not."

"What makes you say that?" Rob asked.

"I do not think she is as cruel as she would like you to believe. There is a natural drive to seek friendship and closeness within her. She has sought you out, shared deep things with you, but there is also fear. Yes, I sense much hurt within her, fear has moved in where trust should be. And yet, she trusts you."

"She trusts you, too," Rob scoffed.

"Do *you* trust me?" Gorm asked, softly. "Even after I told you what I used to be, and what I wish to do?"

"I . . ." Rob looked into her kindly face, but he could see the lines of concern and anguish that lingered about her eyes. "I do."

"Even with my allegiances, you trust me. There are clouds in Alya's mind, storm clouds of betrayal."

Rob shrugged. "Doesn't give her permission to act like she's a hammer and we're all nails."

Chapter Ten

The Pengish Procession

A stream of pengs in flowing robes carrying banners scattered across the room, one line carrying a tapestry, which showed pengs entangled in battle with worm-like monsters. As they went further, the images turned to scenes of pengs with laurel crowns, some upholding scrolls or quills.

Rob and the other prisoners were directed to stand in a line; commander Kerrok oversaw the arrangements and gave Rob a warning glance. She was dressed in full imperial armour, the gold and pearl plates polished to a shine while her cloak was pinned by red brooches. Reluctantly, Rob admired it.

Trumpets were blaring beyond the room, and shadows moved through the corridors. Standing as still as he could, Rob pushed his mind over the vague plans Alya seemed to have. He disliked not knowing what was going to happen; he disliked being kept in the dark, and he disliked feeling manipulated.

The procession arrived, pengs and prisoners at its head carrying banners and ribbons. Vann was holding a pole with a tassel and looking markedly disgruntled. He caught Rob's eye, and there was panic in his face; this set sweat running down his back and he looked at Alya.

"He's coming with us," Rob insisted.

"Why am I not surprised?" she sighed.

"I still don't understand why you hate him so much."

She shrugged. "He has skills, perhaps. Thieves generally have to have at least a minimal set."

Trumpets and cymbals clashed in an increasingly triumphant symphony that rang through the halls. The glass took the echoes and made them ring louder and clearer. It chimed and sang in cold voices, tangling with whistles as soldiers entered. They came to a halt and split, leaving a path through the crowd. The chiming music was reaching ever higher, humming in their ears. By the time it died, Rob felt his legs numbing from having been stood for so long in the cold.

Vann caught his eye again, and there was even more panic in his face; Rob was about to speak when a group marched down the gap in the crowd. Golden helmed and wearing flowing capes of pearl and silver, new pengs were approaching.

The peng at the head was almost of a height with Lomi, who hobbled beside her. This leader's helmet had plumage of silver and blue strands flecked with snow. An entourage wearing visors while their cloaks were wrapped around their bodies followed her.

"Fleet Admiral Orna," the leader said, stiffly. Lomi was at her side, huffing and leaning on her staff. "We have come to inspect you. The great and noble lore of the pengs has decreed that each prisoner be given the opportunity to become part of our store of knowledge. You have been blessed with the chance to live in the Spire of Frozen Fire and to admire the wonder of our people. We have given you access to the libraries of the pengs, we have allowed you to learn from our wise teachers, and we have given you life where savage cultures would have given you death."

Rob's mind wandered from the speech; he had heard all this. As Orna went on, chirruping and whistling, he let his eyes fall on Vann. The young man was fidgeting and trying to catch

Alya's eye, but she was focused and stony-faced.

The pengs around Orna stood more relaxed than Rob had come to expect of Imperial Pengs. Lomi led her sister to the prisoners, and they looked each of them up and down. When they came to Rob, Orna paused and touched his chest, frowning.

"They told me you were a Sky-slayer," she said.

"My pendant was broken," he replied, trying not to look at Kerrok whose eyes glittered from the crowd.

"How do you sleep?" She looked at Lomi, who shrugged.

"I have offered him dream tea," she said. "The pendant was taken as punishment for disobedience, defiance and causing disorder."

"I see," Orna stiffened. "Sky-slayers are rare, but that will not excuse you. There are pirates in your number, outlaws and delusional dreamers. My mother was one of the few pengs to hold the title, Sky-slayer, and we revere her for it. The pterosaur was old, strong, and threatened the settlement of Bad'Inis. She brought a storm of lightning and horror; desert sands fell on frozen planes, and the screaming wind . . ." she stopped and Lomi patted her back, urging her to move on.

Rob furrowed his brow. Remembering the dreams sent stinging nettle sensations into his skin. The pengs made their way along the line, stopping every so often to question one of the prisoners. Alya stared Orna down with such ferocity that it seemed they were communicating with the power of their minds.

"The feast will begin soon," Lomi announced once the inspection was complete. "Sister, comrades, guests and prisoners, to the mead hall, if you please."

"Are my chambers ready?" Orna asked. "I would change first."

"Indeed, let me show you, I need to talk to you."

"No need, I would prefer to rest, we can talk during the feast."

Lomi looked ready to object, but her sister's entourage closed in, guiding her away. The prisoners gave Lomi a curious glance, but when she turned to them, they averted their eyes.

The new pengs all filed out, slamming the doors and leaving a shudder in the air. The remaining guards exchanged looks, but eventually Lomi clapped and pointed towards the opposite end of the circular chamber. "Come, let us all go to the feast," she said. "I believe it has been prepared, so I hope you all have your appetites."

They made their way out, shuffling and muttering. Rob hung back with Gorm and Ilma. Vann was further down, still trying to catch Rob's eye; Alya went to him and whispered something that made him look terrified.

"I don't like this," Rob said to Ilma. "Something is not right."

"I know," she shuddered and took Gorm's arm. "Maybe we should forgo this plan. You know, it's a bit odd, isn't it, and we're not exactly suffering, are we?"

"I am." He indicated the missing pendant.

Ilma had nursed him back to health after he had been adrift at sea for days. She had guided him to this prison and had never abandoned him. Her skills were superior to any doctor he had met, and she had ideas, so many wonderful ideas.

"Your uncertainty is showing," Gorm told him. "Speak your fears and they shall disperse before your eyes."

"Or become even clearer," he growled. He looked at Ilma and put an arm around her. "I can't help thinking you shouldn't be here. You followed me; you cared for me, and so many others. All those wonderful inventions of yours, all those medicines and remedies; the pengs won't share them, they won't even spread them around the empire. Here, your work will be forgotten, and . . ." he breathed. "Never mind."

"No, tell me." Ilma returned the embrace though she was a head shorter. He rested his chin on her grey hair and closed his eyes.

"You would be so wonderful out in the world. Imagine

what you'll discover, all the cures and healing methods in every corner of Diyngard."

"I am far too old to explore *all* of Diyngard!" she laughed.

"I'm serious; you have all this potential, and it's my fault you're here and not doing things and being amazing."

"I am plenty amazing wherever I am, thank you very much!" She gave an indignant snort.

"Think of all the lore you've never even heard of! It's rumoured that, in the Yalal, they have a desert snake that has healing venom!"

"As fascinating as that sounds, there's more to me than being a doctor, you know? I want to see the towers of the Wymhold, the Golden Mountains, and surf the rapids on the rivers of Lizarn. Alas, these old bones may just about permit me to see it, but little else."

"Don't say that,"

"I know my limitations," she scolded. "Oh, look at me, now you've got me all excited about escaping again."

"Sorry," he grinned.

"No, please, keep saying nice things about me!"

The dining hall was a long room with golden tables along the centre. Steaming food was laid out, some having come from as far as Y Rhwth, according to the chefs. Said chefs were standing across the back wall, hands behind their backs and eyes on the ceiling. Lomi spoke in their various languages, congratulating them on their achievements.

"Rob!" Vann hissed, hurrying towards him. "There's something wrong!"

"Vann, if you speak another word I will skin your face off," Alya shot from behind him, and her face was the embodiment of death.

"I want to hear what he has to say," Rob said, sitting at the table and pulling a plate towards him.

"And I don't want him to say anything," Alya sat next to him.

"Don't I get a say?" Vann squirmed to Rob's other side as if he would be a barrier from Alya's wrath.

"Whisper it."

"Those pengs up there," he gestured to the ceiling. "In the procession, with Lomi's sister. I've seen them before! I'm sure of it."

"Vann, you are not helping," Alya insisted.

"Do you know about this?" Rob turned on her. "You expect us all to trust your escape plan while you withhold vital information from us, is that it?"

"Trust is dangerous. But if you wish to escape then you might try it this once."

"Don't expect me to like it," said Vann.

"Look," Rob said. "Vann, just tell me what's going on."

"I . . ." He bit his lip and fidgeted. "The pengs, I recognised them. It took me a while to work out where I'd seen them before and . . ."

The doors burst open, and Fleet Admiral Orna marched in with her entourage, all of whom were still wearing their cloaks. Lomi looked from the head of the table and then stood, stretching her hands in welcome. Despite the warm gesture, Rob saw her hands twitched.

"Tell me what's going on," Rob whispered to Vann.

Vann pushed his head close to Rob's ear. "Those pengs following Orna are the ones that attacked us on the road! They're renegade pengs!"

Black, beady eyes turned to Vann, glowering from beneath helmets; the pengs stopped and turned to him.

"I warned you," Alya hissed.

Rob put his arm in front of Vann to shield him, but Fleet Admiral Orna raised a hand and strode forward.

"That is a very serious accusation, prisoner," she said. "I am a true peng, a servant of the Empire," Orna's breath caught, and she glanced at Lomi.

“Orna,” Lomi was tapping closer with her staff. “You said you were going to rest, but you look like you’ve been running, and your voice is hoarse.”

“It is no concern of yours, prison master,” said one of the other pengs

“She is my sister, my blood; she *is* my concern.”

“Lomi, leave, go to your chambers and wait,” Orna leaned in close, but her companions pulled her back.

Rob’s eyes went to the pengs who had pulled the Admiral; their wide hands were reaching beneath their cloaks, and their faces were drawn in anger. A blur danced below his eyes and threw one of the pengs backwards so that the armour clattered against the wall.

Kerrok stood and drew a pair of long knives. “I saw that one reaching for a weapon,” she said.

“Yes,” said another peng, pulling a knife on Kerrok. “Your armoury was most kind.”

The soldiers flung back their cloaks to reveal blue and grey armour, the sign of a snowflake with giant antlers emblazoned on their chest plates. The prison guards shouted, and rusty halberds flew this way and that.

Rob dove under the table, dragging Vann with him; they dodged and wound their way to the head to where Lomi had been sitting and then he barrelled out. Vann remained hidden, his eyes wide and his teeth chattering.

“Vann, come on!” Rob insisted. “We have to fight!”

“No way! I’m not getting involved; I’m staying here!”

A flash of blue and Rob ducked under a halberd; the renegade peng whistled high and piercing. Rob reached for the bench and lifted it as a shield to catch the blow. The wood strained in his grip, and he threw it to one side. The halberd was still stuck, and the peng let go as it tumbled. Rob leapt at his attacker, blood raging in his ears.

A horn split the air, making the walls shudder. The sound of clattering steel and breaking dishes died and Rob took his eyes off the peng he was engaged with.

Lomi and Orna were stood on the table, surrounded by renegade pengs, all pointing crossbows at them from the ground. Rob inched closer, but one of them noticed and turned their weapon on him.

"This is a takeover," said one of the renegades, leaping onto the table in a single bound.

Chapter Eleven

The Sword-breaker

"My name is Liadan, leader of the Freedom Fang." The renegade said, taking off her helmet. "Your tower is forfeit. We have come to restore the pengs to their rightful nature. To be free of the oppression of others, to be free of the far flung lands that spawn unholy beings."

"I'm sorry," Orna said, hanging her head. "They forced me. They took our sisters, Lomi! They took my crew, they took my friends; I couldn't stop them."

"Fleet Admiral Orna," Liadan strode close to her. "You and your siblings were acting against the interests of the pengs."

"We uphold the Empire," said Lomi, suddenly defiant.

"You are without honour, you are without pride; you are perverted and grotesque. You collude with enemies of pengs; you have no right to stand in the ice-forged lands."

"We make this world better," Lomi's voice cracked, and she swayed on her staff, Orna caught her and held her. "No, let me stand. These renegades are not going to be the death of me."

"Your life is of no concern," Liadan hissed. "You give our enemies shelter, you give them food, and you give them our secrets. You dare to stand before me and claim to be a peng. You are nothing more than vermin."

Rob tried to get a better look at the leader; her face was lean, her feathers frayed and thin. She had bloodshot eyes and a deep gash along the back of her head. He edged closer, his hand reaching into his pocket; there he found a vial.

"So, I suppose you're setting us all free then?" Vann said as he poked his head out from under the table.

"You!" A renegade pointed at him. "You injured one of us on the road, you and the traitors. I will have you executed as a demonstration that . . ."

The prisoners and guards erupted in shouts. Vann was pulled from the floor, screaming and kicking, but the pengs overwhelmed him. Rob moved, but a halberd tickled the back of his neck; he stood still, blood turning to fire.

Vann was shoved onto the table, his arms tied behind his back as the renegade pengs lined up either side holding halberds and spears while Liadan motioned to one with a crossbow.

"The Empire is an abomination," she cried. "There are things nature set in stone and froze in frost. Pengs are pure, pengs are inimitable, pengs are powerful and indomitable; we alone have the knowledge and wisdom that will save our people. The war with the draigs should have taught us but the Imperialists are fat with pride, fat with greed, and blind with silver."

"It's difficult not to agree," said Alya.

Rob caught her eye and she gave him a nod and then nodded towards the peng with the crossbow. He blinked, and then Alya reached into her own pocket and took out a vial of silver. She blinked hard and then nodded to him once again. Rob grasped the vial in his own pocket. He had taken it from the armoury. It was a smoke pellet, but Lomi had said it was defective, like the weaponry.

He looked at the crossbow, and his mind raced. His eyes shot this way and that, spying every peng, every upturned bench, and every gap in the crowd that would give him an attack path.

"You who are born of warm blood, of bare skin, of flesh mouths and long legs," Liadan was still speaking. "Those of scales, of wings, those who have solid bones, those who lack feathers, all of you are abominations to pengish purity. You Imperialists seek to turn these savages into our shadows; you seek to bring them into the enlightenment of pengish culture. That folly is your great sin."

"The Empire is mighty!" Kerrok spoke from the crowd. "We shall sweep across Diyngard, and you and your backwards ways will be lost in the wind."

"You are blind," Liadan retorted. "Your mind has been corrupted. If you truly loved our people, if you truly believed our people to be superior, you would not allow this regime of integration, of appropriation and mingling. Blood is blood; we are pengs, they are not. Do not bring them into our lands. Kill those that have invaded. Those are our true paths, the only paths."

"The Empire was built to spread pengish ideals," said Lomi, waving her staff. "Our ideals are pure; our ways are perfect, we will show that by spreading our reach into every corner of the world."

"If you believed that, you would not have built those towers of treachery," Liadan gestured wildly. "Buildings stolen from the north lands, pillars from Shen, domes from the Yala, and there are even some of you who speak the languages of foreigners. You dirty your tongues with filth, you take the names of savages, you take their writings, you take their songs, and you forget your pure pengish hearts."

"Yet you are speaking Concaedian," said Rob.

The pengs burst into riotous argument at his words. Imperial or renegade, he was not sure which he hated most.

"Why me?" Vann sobbed as he was pushed onto his knees.

"We need to demonstrate that our cause is pure," Liadan assured him. "That our resolve is firm, and that our justice is absolute."

"Well, why didn't you say so?" He hung his head and muttered insults.

"Speak to me again in that tone and you will suffer torture before your demise, human. Chains bind you in body, but we can break your mind." She stepped closer. "Have you ever seen a caged animal? They die inside, they lose all sense of freedom and become nothing but puppets for their masters."

Vann craned his neck and met Rob's eyes.

"The Pengish Empire has enslaved you," Liadan went on, spreading her hands. "They took you from your wild lands, removing you from your places in the savage world. Where before you would have roamed the world free to forage and frolic, the Imperialists have chained you to civilisation, they have forced you to wear clothes you do not deserve. These monsters have taken away your true nature," she spat and pointed a feathered finger at Lomi. "You should be ashamed, to think you could raise animals to our level! They should all be slaughtered for their own good."

"This is unbridled cruelty," Lomi shouted. "Orna, why did you bring them?"

"They took our family," Orna's voice shook. "They said they would torture them and kill them if I did not lead them here."

"No life is more important than the Empire; you should have let them die."

Rob's eyes widened; Lomi had turned from a graceful pacifist into a raging imperial mouthpiece.

"Perform the execution," Liadan nodded to the crossbow bearer who lowered the weapon.

"This is completely unnecessary," Vann pleaded. "I'll work for you if you want! I can be really helpful. I could carry things, and move things and I could even hold your cloaks for you; this is all a complete misunderstanding. I didn't hurt anyone, I hardly fought at all, ask Alya she'll tell you I'm a coward!"

"Silence him!"

The crossbow was aimed and primed.

Rob swept his way through the gaps in the crowd and leapt.

The crossbow thrummed, its bolt flying towards Vann, its blunt blade reflecting the light.

Rob soared over pengish heads and his hand clasped the bolt in mid-air.

He rolled onto the table, still holding it aloft, head bowed. Breathing hard, he reached into his breast pocket and grasped the smoke pellet before slowly rising. He broke the glass, feeling the wafts against his skin as grey mist rose through his coat and filtered through his sleeves and collar.

"How?" Liadan asked, crouching as if to pounce.

"I'd like to know that, too," said Vann.

"You know who I am," Rob roared.

The pengs shuffled, wide-eyed and twitchy. Many of the prisoners shrank back, their mouths open and their hands clasped. There was a hush as each took in what was happening, the sight of Rob Sardan shrouded in silver mist and fury.

So this is what Alya had meant about his reputation. He smiled his most formidable smile and lifted his hand; the broken glass had cut him, and blood trickled from his closed fist.

"I am Rob Sardan, son of the dread pirate Morven; she who passed the seer's veil and tamed the sea monsters. I destroyed the mines of Kenna Iron Helm. I bested the Pirate Lord in combat. I sailed the forbidden seas and took the Ocean's Eye. I killed the Air King. And I broke the Sea-Stone Sword. They call me King-killer, Sky-slayer, and Sword-breaker."

The pengs looked on. Liadan chattered her beak ever so slightly, but it was enough to catch Rob's attention, so he pressed his advantage.

"Saagara lives in me," he said, forming his face into a menacing grin though his insides recoiled from the lie. "I have the power of the waters of the world, even when it is frozen. If you do not leave, I shall watch your bones turn to dust."

Alya stifled a laugh but controlled her face. She was unused to this kind of melodrama, but the pengs had a greater sense of theatrics that bordered on reverence. From the way they fidgeted, Rob supposed that they had heard of the Sea-Stone Sword, of Saagara, and the Pirate Lord. This kind of show fit the way they recorded their history and speeches, emphasising grandeur, exaggeration and splendour.

Rob flung the crossbow bolt at Liadan's feet before leaning to look her in the eye. White smoke was wafting from his coat giving off a salty smell and making the air taste like the sea.

"Do you smell that?" he asked. "It's the power of the ocean, and you have awoken it, Liadan of the Freedom Fang. You might survive a day or a week, but sooner or later, the Eye will find you. The Ocean's Eye does not forget, and it does not forgive. You may believe the pengs to be mighty, but what are empires and renegades when compared to the power of a god?"

Another crossbow thrummed, but this one Rob caught lazily, just as Lomi had when she had been a child. He hoped they would not fire anymore otherwise they would soon work out that the weapons were defective.

"Leave my people alone," Liadan said though her voice was dry with defeat. "These are not soldiers; they are not killers. They came on my command. If anyone is to be punished, let it be me."

Rob nodded to Liadan. She gave a signal to her people, and they filed out. Their armour clattered once they were beyond the doors and they scrambled over one another to get away. Lomi waved to her imperial pengs, and the doors were closed.

Rob fell to his knees, shaking, almost hysterical. His lungs were vibrating and tapping on his ribs; he kept breathing to stop the nervous laughter that was building.

"So," Liadan cleared her throat. "You are the Sword-breaker?"

"And a Sky-slayer," said Orna. "He killed the Air King!"

"I heard."

Rob locked eyes with Vann, who had fallen backwards and was panting heavily. He then burst into laughter and gave Rob a smile.

"So it's actually true? You killed the Air King?" he sang. "That is amazing!"

"I am not proud of it." Rob tried to get to his feet, but his legs were made of melting snow. His face fell into a sour, wrinkled mess.

"You'll get over it. Besides, the Sea-Stone Sword, eh? I never even knew it was real, and then you broke it? You could have been the new Sea King!"

"Vann, please." Rob put his hands on the sides of his temples. "It hurts to think about . . . I regret it."

"Why?"

"Because of what I became!" He finally stood. "The Sea-Stone Sword turned me into a monster, it took my deepest desires and exaggerated them into horrors beyond imagining. Those things are still inside me; there is still the potential for terrible, terrible . . ." His throat was closing, and his lungs felt as if they were collapsing.

"What is this?" Liadan asked, narrowing her eyes.

"A bluff, you dunderhead," Orna whistled. "You and your gang fell for it."

Rob breathed again. "Fleet Admiral Orna, your crew and your family are still in danger. The renegade pengs will not leave while we have their leader. And Alya, I take it this was all part of the escape plan?"

"My plans are flexible," she said. "You have played your part well enough for now; it will be more of a challenge as we go further."

"An escape plan?" Lomi's voice rose from behind Orna. "I know you want to leave with the supply run, but . . ."

"This is not the same plan," Rob said. "This is Alya's plan."

"Alya . . ." Lomi gulped and looked at her. "I am sworn to maintain this prison. I do not wish to see you all throw your lives away. Please, reconsider." She turned to Rob. "Do you truly think you have matured, that you have changed enough to go into the world?"

Rob looked into her eyes and saw glimmers that might have been tears. "Perhaps."

"How quickly did you slip into this persona?" She pointed at the last remnants of smoke wafting from his coat. "You struck fear into the renegades, and into your friends. I was afraid; I feared for you, Rob Sardan. I fear for what you may become. Stay and you may live a fulfilling life. If you leave, you will suffer."

Alya stepped onto the table and drew her jian. The pengs jumped to attention and pointed their halberds at her.

"Rob," she said. "Don't you think it's strange she never took you off the supply run, even when she knew you wanted to escape?"

"I hadn't thought . . ."

"Under proper guidance," Lomi said, shrilly, "your violent urges can be explored in safety, and you can heal!" Lomi was begging, her hands ringing. "Please, Master Sardan, consider the future, and consider your life."

"Tell me, Lomi Thinlomine," Alya's smile turned sour, and she lowered her jian, making the pengs point their own weapons closer. "What happened to the last prisoner who went on the supply run?"

Lomi's terrified eyes turned from Alya to Rob. The hesitation in her answer struck him like a hurricane; before she could open her beak, Rob lowered his head and balled his hands into fists.

"You were sending me to die," he said, simply.

"Please understand," she said, each word raw. "You insulted Kerrok; you left me no choice. No one can see an end to your problems, your anger is too deep, your pain too bloody. Kerrok demanded recompense for your disrespect."

"I didn't think you cared about such things." He stepped closer to her, and the pengs turned their halberds on him. "You always seemed so wise, so hopeful and determined to heal. Was it a lie?"

"I wanted to believe in you. I argued against it. I tried to talk them out of it, but they were all in agreement; you had to die."

Rob was apoplectic. "You were supposed to be the leader. I thought pengs obeyed orders; I thought your subordinates would never question you."

"The orders came from higher up," said Alya. "I saw the messages that were brought with our escort. To reduce the prison population; starvation was their suggested method, but I believe the warden felt leaving you in the cold would serve a better purpose."

"What would be the point?" Vann asked. "Why not just kill us outright?"

"Because that is not good for their image," Liadan laughed. "The Empire wishes to appear friendly to non-pengs, benevolent saviours to savages. Oh, this is just fantastic! You were telling the world that your mighty prison was a place of healing where no torture took place and criminals became loving members of civilisation. Yet you plotted death and starvation instead. You are just the picture of the Empire, aren't you, Lomi Thinlomine. A fraud and a liar."

"My family will take no insult from a renegade like you!" Orna slapped Liadan. The renegade fell but continued to laugh.

Rob put his hands over his eyes, trying to block out the world. His hand was being forced once again, his choices limited to death or flight. He had seen too much death. He shivered and tried to fight frustrated tears.

"Oh stop that." Alya waved her jian at him lazily. "Self-pity is not of any worth to me, and if you were not worth my time, believe me, we would not be talking."

He looked up, tilting his head curiously. "I do believe you just said something nice."

"I have my moments of weakness," she shrugged. "Now, do as I say and perhaps we shall survive."

"You don't think I'm dangerous, or that you'll be better off without me?"

"I will decide what will make me better off; now you are coming with us?"

"He can't be trusted on his own!" Lomi cried.

"He won't be on his own." Ilma scrambled onto the table and stood beside Alya. "He'll have me, and Gorm and Vann to help."

"Don't I get a say in what I do?" Vann complained.

"No," Ilma gave a smug smile. "What do you say, Gorm?"

"I have no particular investment in the Sword-breaker," she said, nudging pengs aside. "But Rob Sardan, you are a living being, a breathing body of heart and mind. To yourself, you must be true, and on that road I can help you, and in doing so, you will help me. There are many who are suffering. The trasati you love; the people of the Ginnungagap, the victims of Skagra and the Pirate Lord. To live is to suffer, and to be immortal is to suffer most. I believe we can put an end to these things."

Rob looked at them; Alya's stony face, Ilma's beaming smile, Vann's concern, and Gorm's quiet confidence. They were different, but at the same time, they were a group he could be a part of, they were people who cared for him. They were . . .

"A crew." He found that his chest warmed to the idea. The hair on his arms stood up, the skin prickled, and the hopelessness finally slid away.

Chapter Twelve

The Battle of Bron'Halla

The armoury was in turmoil, its weaponry ransacked and the clothes slashed or torn. Rob found the shelves where the smoke pellets had been, and he found them still intact; stuffing as many as he could into his pockets he shot back along the room to where Alya and Ilma were waiting.

"I don't think it will work as well a second time," he said breathlessly.

"You may find other uses for them." Alya pulled a coil of rope from a shelf.

"Why the rope?" Rob asked.

"Ropes have many uses."

"This is true, but it doesn't answer my question."

"What a shame; my heart bleeds for you." She strode away. "I shall meet you at the main gates. You heroic types tend not to work to schedule, but please try."

"As you say, your majesty," Ilma mocked.

"Don't antagonise her too much," Rob warned. "I don't trust her as far as I could spit, but we need her for now."

"For now? You going to dump her off the first chance you get?"

"You make it sound like a bad thing."

"It would be," she nudged him. "She's got a good heart, you know."

"No doubt, I just worry whose heart it is and where she keeps it."

They turned to the door, but Lomi was standing there. She signalled to two other pengs. They lifted a chest into the room and planted it at Rob's feet.

"What's this?" he said.

"My shame . . ." she said.

Within were the golden artefacts, the bracelets and the sword. The light of the higher chamber made the gold gleam though it was dusty and dulled by time. Lomi walked closer, hobbling on her staff.

"I stole these from the Sky Sages," she said. "There were other things they kept in that tower. Dark things I should have destroyed, but I was too afraid. The Crown of Black Glass still lies there, waiting."

"What is this Crown?"

"I have only felt its presence and seen its picture in paintings, but something pulses from the altar, a power that curdles my blood. It was part of the reason I fled, that and my own greed. If I am to fall today, and my tower with me, then I would have these be taken back."

"You might not fall," said Rob, reaching for the sword hilt. "Your people are trained, aren't they?"

"We are outnumbered." She put a feathery hand on one of the bracelets. "Wear these and if the Sages still live, they will let you in. Perhaps, you will find a pendant."

"Thank you," he wasn't sure what else to say.

The bracelet was tight, so he put it on his right wrist, avoiding his stronger hand. The other he gave to Ilma, but Gorm refused the sword.

"It is too cumbersome," she said. "I would rather a short blade."

"It's not designed for fighting," Rob said. "It's a symbol. If it touches blood, it will change colour. Then everyone will know you're dangerous. That's what Lomi told me, anyway."

"I think you should take it," Gorm said. "You who wish to escape the trappings of power would be best served holding a sign that insults that power. To hold a golden blade would, for you, be a tremendous testament to your intentions."

Rob smiled at her strange logic and picked up the weapon, feeling the weight and balancing it in his grip. The twin drakans on the guard had ruby eyes, and their wings were etched with the details of veins.

"You know," he said. "This is the first sword I've held since . . ." he thought and then nodded. "The first one since *the* Sword."

"I must go," Gorm bowed. "There are things I must attend to."

She left, shooting Lomi a glare, which the peng returned before lowering her head. There was a sound like sobbing, and soon Lomi threw her hands over her eyes, and she fell to her knees. Rob stared down at her, pity warring in his heart. She had been willing to send him to his death, but she had been kind before.

"Lomi," Rob put the sword in its scabbard and knelt beside her. "If I can do nothing else on the sea, I'll show you that I deserve to live. I'll put things right."

Leaving the peng crumpled on the floor, he left the room for the last time.

WINDING THROUGH THE catacombs, Rob went through the fragments of the plan; to break the front gate and frighten the renegades with smoke and impressive speeches. Then they would have to fight to the snow ships on top of the cliffs. After that it was a simple matter of sailing through ice and wind to the coast at which point . . .

They had no idea. Alya had said she knew what she was doing, but had kept them in the dark. He wanted to force the information out of her, but she was too skilled for a physical altercation.

A crowd of prisoners were shouting at the pengish guards on the gate. Halberds were waving, fists were flying, and whistles were ringing. Ilma tried to hold Rob back, but he rushed down the staircase into the fray.

"What is going on?" he bellowed, but the fighting continued with only a few looking his way.

A fist knocked him in the side of the head, and he stumbled; a foot was aimed at him, but he dodged. His reflexes were still rusty, and he was jabbed in the stomach by the blunt end of a halberd.

"Let us out!" the prisoners shouted, one after another.

"Nobody is leaving," a peng countered. "Go back to your cells now!"

Rob bounded through the crowd, shouldering people out of the way until he reached the pengs. He towered over them and was about to shout when a halberd pole slammed him in the ribs.

"I have to get out!" Rob managed to say while wheezing.

"Nobody is leaving!" said the peng.

"Why do you think you can escape and we can't?" asked a prisoner, pointing at Rob.

"I didn't plan any of this," he protested, but the crowd was shouting.

"Alya said the rest of us would sit quietly while you go," said the prisoner. "I'm not about to sit on my arse and let you. I'm going too! I've got family, and I've got business with the Pirate Lord. I've as much a right as any of you!"

"You can do what you want," Rob said. "I'm not stopping you."

"We are!" the pengs chimed, lowering their blades to point at them. "Keep back or you will all be impaled."

"So it's true?" Rob turned on them. "You don't care about us; you'd kill us just to protect your image?"

"We protect the Empire."

"So, the renegades were right. As long as people *think* you're great it doesn't matter. You can pretend to be moral, but underneath you're rotten."

"We cannot let anything tarnish our Imperial might," a peng said, but she sounded uncertain. "How dare you lecture us! You savages have no respect! We gave you civilisation; we dragged you out of the mud, and this is how you repay us?"

The argument sprang into wrath and fists hit beaks while halberds slashed. Rob screamed for quiet, but nobody was paying attention. He breathed hard, diving between the rioters and the guards.

Ilma was on the stairs, her hands over her mouth as blood was spilt; one of the prisoners crawled from the fray, and Rob hurried to help her. A slash across her chest was bleeding. They reached the stairs, and Ilma whispered to the prisoner in her own language; they conversed for a while and eventually the doctor ripped strips from her dress to tend the wound.

"What started this?" Rob prompted.

"Alya was talking to us all after you ran off," the prisoner explained. "Saying that we should all go back to our cells and that she and the 'chosen ones' would be getting out; we got angry and decided to take matters into our own hands."

"That seems unnecessarily callous even for her."

"What do you mean?" Ilma asked.

The doors burst open with a roar, shattering crystal raining across the hall in a silver shower. Shouts and screams filled the air, and the renegade pengs rushed through the breach. Gold armour met blue, pearl helms clashed with grey, and halberds clanged off chest plates and chain mail. The renegades pressed their surprise attack and pushed inside; some were on the stairs, and Rob moved back with the injured prisoner.

Rioters were thrown aside as the pengs fought, bitter insults in various languages screeching back and forth. Rob and Ilma backed away, but the violence was intensifying barely three steps away.

Rob's chest was roiling with panic, and his hands scrambled into his pockets, seizing the smoke pellets. With one in each hand, he crushed them and flung the glass away; eyes found him as strings of white and grey erupted, he roared and rushed at the line of pengs, which broke around him. Ilma followed.

Confusion faded, and the ranks closed in. Surrounded, he drew to his full height and wondered if he could fight them all. Three pengs leapt; he ducked under two, but the third struck him on the jaw with a fist. He fell, his skull humming; pengs were coming at them, screeching and whistling so high that he thought his ears would burst.

There was a thunderous boom and the floor shook. Crystal and glass flew, and a cloud of ice soared through the air. Rob was blinded, but Ilma's hand found his, and he was pulled from the mêlée.

Cold hit like a tsunami; he felt as if he would drown as it clawed at his lungs. His eyes cleared, and a shape came rushing towards him; he cringed into a defensive curl, but a cloak fell about his shoulders and arms pulled him into a tight embrace.

"Come, young Sardan." It was Gorm. "The wind is harsh, but the blades are harsher. Let your legs be as wings."

"She means run!" shouted Vann from somewhere close.

He pelted across the boulevard and into the white stretch. The trees were ahead, but he could hear iron feet rushing toward him from behind.

Vann was shouting into the wind; Gorm responded, but Rob could not make out any words. His hand was still clamped around Ilma's, giving him warmth. He pulled her close and held tight, not wanting to lose her, not wanting to lose any of them. He had a purpose; he had people who he wanted to help, and who wanted to help him. He had a crew. He had a purpose. He had a quest.

'The quest is the quest.'

The memory made him trip; cold like knives sliced his skin. He thought he was being cut to ribbons, his flesh a bloody ruin. The others were calling, but his ears were dull with cold. He just ran. He ran and pumped blood into his legs so hard they might have launched him into the sky.

The trees entered his vision, and he collapsed against one of them. A string of needles fell before him, and he took a breath of pine. Steeling his limbs, Rob pushed off the tree and ran through the trail.

"Keep up!" Vann called. "We're almost there!"

"What happened?" Rob asked. "What was that explosion?"

"Alya gave me some explosives," he grinned. "Told me to throw it at the gate if the renegades got through."

"I thought they'd retreated and would bargain for their leader." Rob panted as he spoke.

"They worked out you'd bluffed, I suppose."

"Or somebody told them." He focused on his feet as they ploughed through the snow and into the packed earth beneath the trees.

The white rock face leaned over them with a grim formidability, it was too smooth to scale, and there was no way of telling how far they were from the stairs. Vann and Gorm came close while Ilma bobbed about with her eyes sharp as ever. Rob scanned the clifftop searching for any sign of the Snow Ships.

Vann looked mutinous and pointed at the cliff. "How do we get up?"

Gorm led them along the foot of it at a swift pace. Pengish feet were clamouring behind, and Rob's insides clenched. They kept running until Gorm stopped at the foot of a set of clear stairs cut into the cliff. The edges were hard and fine, the surface slick with fresh snow. Rob took an experimental tap with his feet and found it slippery. He took the next few with caution, but as the sounds of pursuit grew he hurried.

"I don't like heights," Vann complained. "I don't much care for lows, either. A nice warm couch and hot broth, that's what I like. What am I talking about? I'm babbling, aren't I? The cold's getting to me. I think I'm dying."

"You're not dying," Ilma insisted, pushing him up. "Just keep going."

A crossbow bolt hit the wall; it stuck in with force and Rob whipped his head around to see a group of renegade pengs at the foot of the stairs, their weapons pointed at them.

"They fixed the crossbows," Vann said.

"Yes, Vann, thank you for your observation," Rob growled. "Run!"

They ran, bent double to avoid bolts. Pengs were mounting the stairs, more sure-footed on the slippery surface. Rob slammed his chin into the stone; blood splattered and he screamed. Gorm helped him, but a bolt grazed her arm, and she hissed at it.

"We're going to die!" Vann moaned. "They'll catch us, and we'll die."

Rob held his bleeding chin and looked at the approaching pengs, his heart making a desperate attempt to escape his chest. He tightened his fists and pushed past Gorm and Vann, but Ilma stopped him.

"Don't," she said. "You didn't come all this way to die."

"Maybe I did," he said. "I can hold them back while you get away."

"Rob you're coming with us, we want you!"

"But what about what I want?"

He bounded down the stairs, almost falling into the pengs; he thrust three of them into a fourth. Rob snatched a broken halberd and backed away as they recovered. A bolt grazed his head, and he fell, cursing and spluttering. The pengs rose, ready to pounce.

With a thunk, the foremost peng was hit with a vial, which exploded in green powder. Above, Ilma was rummaging through her bag and pulling more vials out. Rob backed towards her and then ran with her up the stairs. She handed him vials, and he hurled them at the pengs, some missing, and some hitting.

"What is this stuff?" he asked.

"Important medical supplies," she replied. "So make each one count!"

They threw more, their backs to the stairs. Rob's sweat was building, his mind clawed by cold fury, he hit a peng between the eyes, another on the beak, a third in the chest. Each time a cloud of powder would rise and choke them.

Snow slammed him in the back; he had fallen onto the top of the stairs, and he rolled from the cliff edge with Ilma at his side. He looked around and before him stood two tall rafts of white wood, in the centre of them was a triangular mast that fluttered in the wind.

He shivered; the wind was punishing, threatening to tear his hair from his skull. With one hand on his hat, he pushed towards the Snow Ships and tried to clamber onto them. A foot slammed beside his fingers and made him jump.

Alya was there, her heavily booted feet leading to her cloaked and robed body, her laughing eyes partially hidden beneath a headscarf of green fabric. She helped him onto the ship and pointed towards the front of the bow where Vann was sat by several ropes.

"He better not weigh us down," she shouted.

Crossbow bolts tore into the sail, and Alya screamed; they could not make out her words, but they guessed the meaning. Rob helped Vann and directed him through hand motions until the sails and the ship moved. Ilma and Gorm took the second ship, and it sped ahead; Rob looked to the cliff and spied three pengs hurrying after them.

They pulled the sails around, but the wind sliced the sides of the ship until it leaned too far to the right. Rob forced Vann away and pointed him towards the smaller sail while Alya struggled with the rudder. More bolts flew past, but the ship would not move in the right direction.

A searing pain bit into Rob's shoulder, he shrieked to the sky and closed his watering eyes. A bolt had grazed him again. Alya was pointing towards the left, a storm cloud was whipping towards them, the wind roaring from its vortex in nightmarish screams.

The ship burst forward, sliding through the snow like water, steering closer to the maddening storm. Rob put one hand on the ropes and another on his hat. He breathed, the icy air a forceful knife in his throat, but he loved it.

Snow thick as mud filled the air; Rob kept a scarf over his mouth and his hood over his hat, but the world was turning white. Wind bellowed, frantic roars like a chorus of giant trasati. Wave upon wave of snow slammed into them, filling his clothes and making every second full of pain and shivering.

He struggled to keep the ship in line while Vann and Alya seemed intent on trying to kill one another with glares of increasing ferocity. Rob tried to ignore them and keep his focus on the ship in front of them. Ilma and Gorm were sailing expertly, darting in and out of whirls of snow.

Lightning scorched the sky as his heart filled with acid and his limbs weakened. Images invaded his mind, a red wind billowing, a screaming pterosaur, the rising tide of the silver sea. It came like a flood. Tears froze as he watched blood spill from the Air King's stomach.

He saw his crew, the captain dead at his feet, the ship torn by the sea, and a blast of crimson horror. His hands clasped around a stone hilt, his arms aching with the weight as he lifted the weapon above his head. Power shone in his arms, silver light pulsing through his veins, pushing the might of the ocean into his limbs.

He hurled the weapon, he hurled it with all of his hatred, with every ounce of regret, with every piercing, gnawing drop of guilt.

The Sea-Stone Sword shattered, its god screaming as it died in the wrath of Rob Sardan. At that moment he had become the Sword-breaker. He had become the King-killer, the god-destroyer, a Sky-slayer, and so much more. He hated those titles. He hated them more than anything.

Then he was holding a crown. A black monstrosity that whispered at him, told him to wear it and take control of the world. He could wear the Crown of Black Glass and become a god once again. He tried to breathe, but his mouth filled with snow.

Snow! He was in the ice. He was fleeing the prison at the end of the world. Storm clouds were growling, white, black and purple. Despite the danger, he breathed easier. The broken sword was in the past, two years in the past; he was not there now. He needed to remember where he was. His hand went to his chest where the Sky-slayer's pendant should have been.

But the Crown? He tried to ignore the thought.

Alya shouted as her arms waved to the right. Rob tugged on the sails, forcing them into the wind. The ship swung through the storm, creaking and groaning under the strain; a torrent of snow slammed into them, but they crested the wave and shot forward at an increasing speed.

Vann screamed, slipping, and Rob grasped his arm as he slid. Their eyes met through the snow, and Rob held all the tighter.

"Don't let go!" Vann shouted. "Don't let go!"

The words sent fire through Rob; he was back in the cell again, watching Niall die of slow poison. '*Don't let me go*' he had said. '*Don't let me go.*' The trauma was ricocheting through his head. Vann's arm was in his hand, and he held tight, clinging to the present, clinging to the living body, it was the only thing he could do.

'I am here in the snow. I am fleeing the prison.'

The ship shrieked with the strain; Rob looked around and gasped. He heaved Vann up and together they clung to the ship, breathing hard.

They had shot out of the storm at an angle, the momentum of the winds thrusting them forward, away from the darkness and into the wastelands. Alya was leaning against the rudder, her eyes on where Gorm and Ilma were sailing in earnest.

White hills rose, and the ships crested each and then slid along with increasing speed. Rob could not help admiring the strength and speed of the pengish ships, but his revelry was broken as a sail whipped him in the face.

Hours passed, and the ships showed no signs of slowing. White hills gave way to white flatlands, and white skies shifted to blue and then back to white.

Vann pointed towards a shape on the horizon to their left. It was a set of mountains with snow-cracked sides and heads hidden in clouds. They turned the sails and weaved their way past Gorm and Ilma.

Darkness appeared ahead, but Alya maintained their course, giving Rob a curt nod as he turned an inquiring glare on her. They crested another line of hills, and the shape became distinct; pointed pines and shivering boughs rocked in the wind as the smell of trees came to their nostrils.

The ships swung under the cover of the pines, and the wind died. Alya gave a call and they let the sails down. The ships groaned their appreciation and the crew disembarked with shaky feet.

Chapter Thirteen

Across the Water

"What in the name of Razal's beard is going on?" Vann slumped against a tree.

"We escaped from the greatest prison on Diyngard," said Ilma, beaming. "I never thought I'd have such an impressive act on my record. It's quite exciting, isn't it? Who knows what will happen next?"

"Who indeed," Rob said, turning his eyes on Alya.

"We are not free yet," she said. "We must reach the coast soon, or the pengs will pick up our trail. The storm hid our tracks, and the momentum carried us quite a way, but the rest of the journey will be on foot."

"Let's have a break first," Vann suggested. "My arms are like rocks, look!" He held them up to Ilma.

"You're fine, stop complaining," she told him.

"I'd like to know a few things," Rob asked, and stepped closer to Alya. "What happened back at the prison? What were you up to?"

"My plans were a success, do you need to know the details?"

"Yes. If we are recaptured, I would like to know exactly what insult you have done to the pengs and the prisoners. Perhaps we can repair some of the damage."

"Unlikely. Renegade or imperial, the pengs will kill us if they find us, and so would the prisoners. We are best on our own."

"What did you do?"

"I see you are intent, and ordinarily I would let you fester, but arguing is tiring," She stretched and leant against a tree. "When I knew the empire would send me to prison, I contacted my associates who have dealings with the renegades. With instructions to find me at the rendezvous point, they followed the imperials through the wastelands.

"They got jumpy and attacked the convoy before we reached the prison. Fortunately, during the scuffle, I was able to give a message to one of them, that Fleet Admiral Orna was their key. She has been visiting her sister for years, and it stood to reason that the next visit would be soon. I informed Lomi of a renegade plot, but not of the escape plan. She had no idea her sister was involved, but I think she may have been suspicious. Her tendency to believe the best of people, especially her own kin, was her downfall. So when the renegade pengs attacked, I relied on them using the tower's armoury, which they did. I had convinced them that the imperial arsenal would be superior to anything they had ever used, and they believed me. Then, I relied on your penchant for reckless stupidity; you did not disappoint."

"Thanks," Rob grumbled. "Glad to be of service."

"Neither groups of pengs would have allowed anyone to leave, so I instigated a riot using the prisoners."

"You're a real nice piece of work," Vann said.

"The riot was a success and while it took place, I went to a balcony and scaled my way down. I informed the renegades that your trick, Sardan, was just a trick. They stormed the gates, and the riot became a battle between pengish factions. In the chaos, we were able to escape to the ships."

"But they chased us," Ilma said. "We got hit with crossbows, and I threw away valuable supplies to keep them back."

"Some stayed in the forest, to watch for escapees," Alya shrugged. "It was a calculated risk."

"Let me see if I understand," Vann said. "You do realise that you double-crossed both the renegade pengs and the imperial pengs at the same time?"

"Yes, I am aware of my own actions and their meanings, perhaps you should try it some time, Vann."

"Now if we ever meet any peng they'll want to kill us," said Rob. "Thanks for that, Alya, you've just made us the enemies of an entire race."

"It was my pleasure; they had already become my enemies."

"Seems petty of you, doesn't it?"

She blinked and then pulled down her scarf. "They stole my ship, my life's work, and my freedom. I am repaying them."

"And you never thought to confide in any of us?" Rob stepped closer. They were the same height, so he met her knife-like gaze with one of his own. He wondered how old she was. She did not seem much older than he was, but he could not be sure. "You thought we were too stupid, was that it? Or you didn't trust us? Gorm seems to think you do, but I don't believe it."

"Oh?" She looked suddenly uncomfortable but quickly regained her composure. "Why would I trust you?"

"You can't withhold important information if you want to work with us; it doesn't work like that."

"What doesn't work like that? What is it that you think this is?" She spread her hands to the group.

"A crew," Rob snapped. "A group of comrades, whatever you want to call us it doesn't matter. If we are to survive then we need to trust one another."

"Do *you* trust *me*?"

The question hung like an icicle, poised above their heads. His eyes went to Ilma, Vann and Gorm; they were watching with rapt attention. Rob cleared his throat. His hesitation had made him nervous, and he could see the others exchanging looks.

"I need to think," he said. "Then you need to explain to us what is going to happen from here. Where is your ship? How are we going to get it? What is your plan and why do you need us?"

"Why should I bow to your orders? You are not in charge."

Alya stepped away from the tree and towards her pack, a canvas bag with ribbons and strips flailing.

A squawk alerted Rob to a ṭrasati-bird who had settled on the ship and had been disrupted by Alya's meddling. Vann peered after it as it flew into the trees, hissing and growling.

"Leave it, Vann," Rob advised.

"But . . ." he sighed as the bird fluttered from branch to branch. "My ma' was so good at training them, but she used a whip."

"If you took a whip to a trasati, I would skin you," Rob warned.

"Oh, sorry," he grumbled, scowling.

"You're talking about whipping a trasati for your own amusement."

"Yeah, I know, I'm sorry," he opened his mouth to say more, but Ilma stopped them by putting her arms around them both.

"Will you two stop talking for a few moments," she huffed. "You're going to upset whatever else is living in this wood."

"I doubt anything does." Vann folded his arms firmly and sulked.

"Yes there is," said Gorm. "I can feel its breath on the wind, I smell its musk in the air, and its feet are shivering through the earth and snow."

They looked at her, but Gorm's eyes were closed, she smiled slightly, her poise relaxed and calm. Rob strained his ears, listening through the rustle of the trees and the whispering of the wind.

"Mammoths used to live here," Alya said. "But the pengs rounded them up and herded them to other lands. They wanted to keep this land free of any creatures other than themselves."

"Let's move on," Rob said at last. "I'd rather not get in the way of a mammoth if any are left. Not while we're tired and cold. Any creatures we meet will likely be frightened of anyone they see."

THE WOODS OFFERED small amounts of food and Ilma managed to scrape a few herbs. She was not satisfied, though, and muttered about her broken vials, giving Rob an angry frown every now and again.

Alya kept her distance, allowing the others to lead and this gave Rob pause, he wondered about her and what she had planned for when they reached the coast. It was barely a day's walk away she claimed, though Vann had pointed out the sun never set in the south, so days were difficult to discern.

They had seen shadows moving among the trees, large shapes disturbing the branches, and the stench of fur had redoubled. Rob had hurried them, but his eyes had always followed the creatures.

"We could find one," Vann suggested. "One of them mammoths. I know you like creatures and monsters."

"I don't think they're monsters," Rob smiled. "But we shouldn't get in their way. I don't like to think of what the pengs have been doing to the poor things."

"Poor things? A mammoth could squash a battalion of pengs in a heartbeat! They got them big tusks and huge feet, you know?"

"I've seen pictures," Rob said.

"If we got us a mammoth, we could use it to fight the pengs. Ride it into battle, and . . ." Vann caught Rob's eye and fell silent.

The woods fell away in a mess of white and black, dead trees flailing through the drifts. Beyond, the land was broken with shattered ice floating in dark, inky waters. There were huts on the shoreline, but they were hollow and had empty windows, the little walls around their perimeter blackened.

"There's a settlement," Rob called back to the others. "It's been abandoned."

"Are the huts burned?" asked Alya.

"Not all of them."

The roots and tangled foliage became a maze that left their trousers and cloaks torn. Rob fought the urge to throw his cloak away as they forced their way through frozen brambles and became entangled in them for some time. However, it did not take as long as he had feared for them to break out of the trees and into the settlement. Gorm strode away and ducked into one of the huts; she took a long breath and put her hand to the floor. Eventually, she beckoned the rest of them in.

"Would it be too much to ask what happened here?" Vann ventured.

"Fear has been here," Gorm said, solemnly. "The people who abandoned this place were afraid of something."

"Can't say I'm particularly comfortable," Rob said, sitting on the dry earthen floor. "What sort of settlement is this, anyway?"

"A fishing village," said Alya. "The pengs pull fish out of the water and devour them. Perhaps the fear Gorm can feel is from the fish; perhaps it is from the pengs. It does not matter."

"Do you think the renegade pengs came here?" he asked.

Alya walked to the entrance and peered at the water. "We shall need to cross. If my calculations are correct, we should be close to the opposite coast, a five-hour journey on a raft, if we could survive it."

"On a what?" Vann demanded.

"We could upturn one of the huts and make a large coracle," Rob suggested. "We'd need paddles. Gorm, do you think you could have a look for some tree branches that might work?"

"I could," she nodded. "Once I have rested. Without rest we become like the stones; we become unfeeling and unhelpful."

"True," he turned to Ilma. "You and Vann should look through the supplies and see what's what. If we've got enough to last the night, I'll be surprised."

"Sounds good to me," Ilma nodded. "Vann, pick your lazy bottom up from the floor and get over here."

"Alya," Rob went on. "You should check the huts and see if you can make any of them into a raft. Perhaps streamline it; the trees might be serviceable in reinforcing the framework. Also, see if you can make a way of steering it."

"Is that all?" she said coldly. "And what should I do with my other hand?"

"I wish I could tell you." He pushed past her into the air and took a breath. "I'll patrol the perimeter in case there are any signs of pursuit; we should take it in turns."

"May I ask why you are in charge?" Alya folded her arms and eyed him.

"I'm not in charge; I'm just suggesting things."

"They sounded like commands."

"Alya, they're good ideas," Ilma said. "Calm down and make yourself useful."

"Make myself useful?" she sounded irate. "I have just got you all out of prison near single-handed."

"*Near* being the operative word," Vann intoned.

Rob left them to their argument and forged his way through the snow and clambered into the woods, heading for a hillock where he could overlook the land. As cold and tired as he was, he felt a desperate need for isolation. He had spent the majority of the past two years alone and had grown accustomed to it.

Crunching footsteps announced Vann's arrival and Rob steadied his emotions as the man came nearer.

"You should stay with the others," Rob advised. "Alya needs your help."

"Nobody needs *my* help," Vann replied, almost spitting.

"Please, just try and keep the peace for a while. I need some time to think."

Vann looked at him and moved closer, his hand reaching out but pulling back again at the last moment.

"I'm scared," Vann said. "Of the pengs, of the pirates on the sea, and of Alya. You're the only one I'm not scared of."

"I'm scared too," Rob said with a small smile.

"What have you got to be scared of? You're the flaming Sword-breaker!"

Rob's mind was a mess of dread. He was not sure what he feared. During the escape, the flashbacks had shaken him and he was still uneasy from the experience. But it had brought up other memories, and other fears.

"The Pirate Lord Mothar made me into target," Rob said slowly. "He manipulated me into taking the Sea-Stone Sword. Mothar had been convinced that I could kill him; quite a feat given that he's supposedly immortal."

"So you can go and kill him!" Vann's hand found Rob's arm and squeezed it. "Come on, that'll be worth a song or two one day!"

Rob shook his head. Locked in the pengish tower he had heard very little about what Mothar had been up to. Gorm and Vann spoke of Skagra and the torment she was spreading. Rob was not sure he wanted a confrontation with such a figure; to be swept back into the world of pirates was not his ideal future.

"You can help people, you know?" Vann pressed. "You helped me."

"Did I?" Rob mused out loud. "I once tried to help a village on the Keeker Isle, but I ended up killing a giant, almost magical tree. I remember putting my hand against its bark, I remember the Sword draining it of its moisture, and I remember the villagers crying in horror. I tried to help my crew by finding the Sea-Stone Sword, but that led them to them being torn apart by the Air-keepers. Even the Pirate Lord was afraid of Thestor the Air King, lord of pterosaurs."

"But you killed him!" Vann tried to sound encouraging.

"But that didn't bring them back; it brought nightmares."

His hand groped for the pendant that wasn't there. With the Air King gone, Mothar the Pirate Lord had taken his place; that had been the plan all along and Rob had walked right into it. He had been so ashamed. Perhaps that was why he had gone so willingly into the prison.

The clouds over the mountains were purpling and growling with snow. Rob gave the wilderness a critical gaze and then turned back to the water; over the waves and ice, shadows were moving, following the sun. Pengish trading ships heading to who knew where; he wondered what they were carrying, whether they had heard about the escape, whether they would be sending reinforcements.

"Go back to the others, Vann," he said at last. "I need to be alone."

Leaving the man behind, he wandered, not really paying attention to where he was going. Vann's shadow vanished after a while and Rob felt his heart beat a little easier again.

He came along the coastline, thick ice solid under his feet though he could see water beneath its clear face. The wind brought moaning sounds that reminded him of the Mourning Hall. It was behind him, and he didn't want to think about it. But the sound grew and became a wail, too rough and warbling to be the wind.

He crested a rise of snow, and peered into a cove of broken wood and shattered stone. In the centre were bodies, bloody and bruised, they were trasati, but not ones he was familiar with. They had flippers instead of feet, long, snake-like necks and thick bodies that ended in winding tails. One lifted its flattened head and screeched at him.

'*Fear*,' was in the voice. '*Blood. Birds. Fear. Death.*'

Rob slid towards the trasati, his insides thunderous; blood was oozing from wounds around chains that clamped them to the stones and the bruises looked to have come from beatings.

Grinding his teeth he raised his hands to the trasati and tried to gather his thoughts.

'Friend,' he said as best he could. '*Help. Friend.*'

The largest of the trasati was blue where the others were white; it lowered its head and snaked towards him with quivering nostrils. Its teeth were barbed, and its maw was wide enough to engulf Rob's upper torso. He retreated a few steps but kept his hands up.

Rob knelt and shuffled towards the chains that bound the flippers, as he passed he spied gills along its neck and found its scales to be smoother than any trasati he had encountered. Over the rubble of whatever had been here previously, the sea was lapping against the ice. He supposed these were water-dwelling trasati, unused to being on land for so long.

Some of them had laid down their heads and were still. Rob hung his head at the sight and tried to offer sympathy by expressing sorrow. One of them nodded and rattled its chains. Rob pulled on them, but they would not budge, he examined the fixtures and came to where they had been bolted to the stone.

With an effort, he pushed the snow away from the bolts and set about unscrewing them. It took him longer than he had anticipated, but soon one of the chains came free. Next he freed two others. The rest were dead or too weak to make it to the water. He expressed sorrow once more.

Rob retreated while the trasati headed for the sea. Once he was at the crest of the hill he waved, but they did not return the gesture. His eyes went back to the wilderness, and his insides were a fire once again.

Why had the pengs chained them? Why keep them out of water? He was more determined than ever to get Alya's ship, anything to annoy the Pengish Empire.

He returned to the others and found that Gorm and Alya had upturned one of the huts and were reinforcing it with beams from other houses. Ilma and Vann were inside another, rubbing their hands together, their eyes glinting in the firelight.

Rob headed to Alya, who was directing Gorm. The raft was taller than she was and showed signs of having been sawn. Her jian hung at her side and he let out a sigh.

"You shouldn't have used a sword for this," he said. "You'll blunt the blade."

"Are you planning on cutting people?" she smirked. "I have a whetstone, besides we had no other blades."

Rob fingered the pommel of his golden sword. He was determined not to unsheathe it, but that had been with regards to killing, not making things. He hummed. "How long will it take?"

"Another hour at this pace."

"What about another pair of hands?"

"Are you volunteering to follow my directions?"

"If it helps, I'll dig in the mud."

"That I would like to see." She smirked.

"Vann, would you patrol for a while?" he asked. Vann appeared mortified.

"What if something happens?" he squeaked. "And something *always* happens!"

"Come and tell us."

"But what if they chase me?"

"Come faster." Rob said, and winked at him as he left.

The rest of them moved branches and fixed them in the framework of the upturned hut. It was taking shape and by the time Vann returned from his patrol, several minutes early, it was almost ready. Ilma offered them all a tonic made from the herbs she had foraged. It was sharp and stung his throat like nettles, but it made Rob feel a little more invigorated. Working as fast as he could, Rob encouraged the others to follow suit.

"I saw some trasati over there," Rob said and pointed. "Sea-dwellers who'd been tortured and chained; I think the pengs abandoned them. It looked like they'd destroyed some sort of habitat."

"Renegade pengs attacked several settlements along this coast," said Alya. "There is a full-scale rebellion going on. Abandoned trasati are nothing out of the ordinary."

"They'd been beaten! They had bruises that were years old. The pengs have been keeping trasati prisoners for Razal-knows how long!"

"Yes, I suspected those trasati were around here."

"Why didn't you say something?"

"It was better you see it for yourself," she shrugged. "I hope it makes you even more willing to go along with my plan, to take my ship and get some vengeance."

The light was fading as the sun was dragged along the horizon. Ilma and Alya walked around the upturned hut while Vann stood awkwardly by Rob's side. Rob looked at him and watched his nose ring bob. It was some kind of traditional garb from Geata, he supposed.

"Vann, is there a volcano in your country?" he asked. "Gorm said something about that."

"What? I don't know, maybe?"

"Have you heard the story about the peng-draig war and how it ended?"

"That? Oh yeah, my ma' and sister got obsessed with that stuff when they joined the Tomb of the Dead God. All that religion talks about is that war and how their god died, and there was stuff about a black crown, but I never paid attention."

"What about the Flame-Filled Sky? You heard of that?"

"No, I've not heard of nothing."

"I find that hard to believe."

"Honestly, I was a bit of a daydreamer. When I got taken by that pengish family, nothing interested me, except their jewels. Expert lock pick, I am, best and most subtle thief there ever were."

"Yeah, you're so subtle that you got caught," Rob teased.

"That had nothing to do with my skill! I was ratted out by a sneak I thought were a mate. Reminds me of someone else." He nodded towards Alya, who was stood atop the raft, her head turned away.

"I'm not sure how to feel," Rob admitted. "She's got five times the brains of any of us, but I would rather trust a crab not to pinch me than her not to betray us as soon as it becomes convenient."

"Yeah, well, if we gang up on her she can't do anything, can she?"

"She outwitted two factions of pengs, a dozen prisoners, and all of us. If it comes to it, I doubt we'd get away with anything."

"So let's dump her, then! Let's get that raft and go off on our own."

"We need her ship. It pains me to say it, but she was right. We need a ship that can outrun pengs, this raft won't get far, and we wouldn't even make it to Bad'Inis, let alone the Ginnungagap."

"She said her ship could be sailed by five. It must be tiny, even if we can't outrun the pengs we wouldn't survive on the seas."

"The ship would survive a hurricane," Alya shouted to them. "I designed it to withstand even the harshest wind attacks."

"Why?" Vann sounded grumpy, and he folded his arms tight.

"Air-keepers have been attacking pengish ships; some think it is vengeance for their king, others that they are following a new master. Whatever the reason, I designed the ship to withstand them. Nothing will breach the hull, wind, earth, or water."

"And what about fire? Wood still burns you know?"

"Then I will thank you for not taking any bonfires aboard."

When Gorm returned, Alya announced that the raft was ready, and the taller woman nodded her head.

"Something is coming through the snow," she said. "I could not see it, but I fear it may be foes."

"Then we had best be quick," Alya said.

They gathered their belongings and pushed the vessel into the icy water; Gorm took a large trunk and sat at the head of the ship.

"We need to break the ice," she explained. "This hull will not hold otherwise. It shall leak and bleed; like the heart, it is fragile when bombarded with cold, hard resistance."

"Is everything an opportunity for poetic waxing?" Vann said.

"To the free mind, all things are open, and all things wax, all time is an opportunity for thought."

"Perhaps you should try it," Alya suggested. "I'm sure you could benefit from spending more time thinking than talking, Vann."

"Watch it, you. I've not ruled out chucking you overboard."

"That would be tremendously ambitious of you."

Rob looked to the coast, and his stomach dropped. Shapes were moving along the ice, light bouncing off armour as cloaks snapped in the wind. He waved to Alya and urged the others to quicken.

"Razal's shield!" Vann cried. "They tracked us!"

"They went the long way around," Alya said. "I had hoped that they would search the forest rather than come straight here."

"Well, you were wrong, how does that feel?"

"I have planned for this," she said, drawing her jian.

"You can't fight them all," Rob objected. "And that sword is blunted."

The snow ships pushed onto the ice, and the pengs screeched triumphantly. Gorm cracked the ice with vigour while Vann and Rob paddled, but the pengs were closing, halberds raised. The snow ships slipped from ice to water while Alya stood, sword in hand and eyes on the pengs.

They came into open water, but the pengs were keeping their distance. They were dressed in the blue and grey armour of the renegades, their halberds were blunt, but some were holding crossbows. A bolt thrummed into the side of the boat, and Rob was shaken, he lurched to the side and stared into the water.

Something moved below; Rob had a suspicion, and a plan formed. He looked at the others for a moment and breathed slowly.

"What are you doing?" asked Vann, panic in his eyes.

"Trust me," he said.

"Oh?" Alya said. "You want us to trust you? After you berated me for the same?"

"Trasati are in the water; I can speak to them."

"Or you'll die in the cold," Alya turned on him. "As hilarious as that might be, it would be most inconvenient for my plans."

"Razal damn your plans." He sprang and smashed through the ice.

Cold like ripping claws sliced him. A torrent of water pummelled his skull, threatening to shatter it like an egg. The world was a blur of white and blue, bubbles assaulting his hair and hat. He spun around and swam towards a deep shadow his eyes streaming. The shadow reached out a long, snaking neck.

Rob's lungs were failing, and he pushed to the surface, gasping for air as he broke through it. His leg was yanked downwards, pressure rising in his ankle. The cold had numbed the limb but streams of blood came from the wound, and he wanted to scream.

The trasati whipped him back and forth, his spine straining as he was flung under the frozen surface. The pressure released, and a reverberating roar slammed his head, vibrating through his body. More trasati were coming, their mouths wide, their barbed teeth ready to tear him to pieces.

Chapter Fourteen

City of Glass

The Air King was looming like a gaunt tree with branches that reached into the sky. Rob cowered and tried to shout apologies, wishing he could take back what he had done, wishing he could end his dreams. But Tethra's wings closed, enveloping him in an embrace of warm dread.

Red eyes blazed and fire turned green, roaring in the eye of a different creature, one that he had seen as a child. A creature of wood and dirt, its eyes the only thing alive; the secret that had earned Rob his exile.

'King-killer. Sky-slayer. Sword-breaker!'

He shivered, clenching his hands into fists. He had killed the Air King. He had broken the Sea-Stone Sword.

'Yes,' *he thought.* 'I am a King-killer. I am a Sky-slayer.'

He stood to his full height, and the world became an emerald inferno. The sky was full of screaming fire, the earth was boiling in gold, and the sea was frothing silver. And through it all, a wolf howled a long, lonely cry.

There at the end of the world, while everything died, he stood. Behind him was the past, all of the death that had made him what he was, and behind him also was the Sword. It had not broken him; he had broken it.

"I am Rob Sardan!" he screamed at the flaming sky. "I am the King-killer! I am a Sky-slayer! I am the Sword-Breaker!"

The gold at his feet burst with song, and a shape emerged from its rippling depths. A figure, dark and streaked with shining veins. Atop her head was a black crown, which housed an amber gem.

He coughed, vomited and his eyes stung in the white light of a low hanging sun. Hands were pulling him out of the vision and into cold reality. Not for the first time, he remembered how sick he was of cold.

Ilma was looking into his eyes holding them open and making him follow her finger. Then she stepped back and nodded to Vann, who drew Rob closer to a campfire that spread heat against his shivering limbs.

"What's going on?" he managed though his throat was raw.

"We're alive; that's what's going on," said Vann.

They were on a white shore, though the snow was light, dusting the wilted grass. Their boat was smashed on the rocks just off the coast, and there was a set of sails that looked to have been torn from a pengish snow ship. Behind them were hillocks and a swathe of flailing trees.

"I am amazed you are not half dead," Ilma said. "Gorm's taken a day to recover, but you were under for a lot longer."

"A day? How long . . . ?"

"Never mind that! Come on, you need to get warm. Keep moving now you're awake, and you'll need to drink some hot tea."

"I'm fine." Rob stood, and Ilma almost screamed her frustration.

"No, you shouldn't be fine!"

"Where are the others?"

Ilma frowned and pointed. Alya and Gorm were further along the coast, their cloaks fluttering. Rob tried to walk after them but he stumbled, his left leg was bound in bandages, and lightning pains stabbed his calves.

"Well, how clever do you feel?" Ilma asked. "You know most people who have their leg chewed don't manage to walk it off, but you're not like most people, are you? And jumping into freezing water! What were you thinking?"

"Oh leave him," Vann said. "I'll help."

Vann gave Rob an arm and they marched after Gorm and Alya.

"Keep moving," Ilma said. "We've dried your clothes, but by Razal it's a close thing that you're still able to move at all!"

"Tell me what happened," Rob said. "It'll take my mind off this stupid leg."

"Your leg shouldn't be the problem," Ilma said, her face strained. "The Inner Cold, we used to call it. Just don't jump into any more freezing water."

"What happened to the trasati?" Rob insisted.

"Well, they started attacking!" Vann said, theatrically. "They were mad about something, especially the pengs. But we got clouted, too. I got this big bruise on my arm!" He rolled up a sleeve to reveal a welt on his bicep. "Alya and Gorm started paddling, and then I spotted you'd resurfaced so Gorm pulled you in. She got attacked by one of them beasties, though, and had to punch it on the nose."

"That's unfortunate." Rob looked at Gorm, she and Alya had crested a hill and were in deep discussion.

"The trasati kept attacking, the pengs tried to stab them but they were retreating, and we just paddled like there was no tomorrow. Alya and Ilma argued about how to get to the coast, and Gorm and I just kept paddling while you were lying in the boat, bleeding and shaking like a stuck fish."

"Not a pleasant image," he shuddered. "We need to get Alya's ship as soon as possible."

"Yeah." Vann shifted his eyes to Gorm and Alya.

Rob's leg was hurting more than ever, but he kept going, grinding his teeth. At the top of the hill Rob turned to talk to Alya, but his eyes stopped on the scene below. A swathe of snowy grass, blotched red, churned with earth and weapons; there were torn standards and a banner fluttering in the sea breeze.

"Look here," said Alya. "The rebellion in all its glory."

"This is horrible," said Rob.

There was blood, feathers and discarded armour, but there were no bodies. Gorm had her eyes closed and was whispering into the wind, a drawn and hollow expression over her face.

"The city of Glasoghear is close," Alya went on. "The city of glass. That is where my ship is hidden, in the harbour beneath the citadel."

"*Beneath* the citadel?" Vann laughed.

"It is a secret harbour, underground; is the concept too much for you?"

"I think you're making it up." Vann shook his head.

"It doesn't matter what you think, so long as you do as I say."

"And why should I? You've led us on a merry dance so far, and I've got no reason to think this isn't more of the same!"

"And what have you offered to this venture, Vann of Geata? Not that I fully believe that you are who you claim to be."

"Here, what are you trying to suggest? You think I'm lying? Why would I bother lying to someone like you?"

"I can think of several reasons, but I have the common decency not to act rashly when I do not have all of the facts."

"So you're just being mean to me for no reason, is that it?"

"You're acting like a child."

"Will you two be quiet, we need a proper plan." Rob shoved between them and limped towards the desolation.

A pengish banner bearing the sign of a snowflake with a laurel crown above it stood in the middle of the bloody scene. Rob plucked it from the ground and ripped it from its wooden pole so he could use it as a walking stick. Hobbling, he waved the others to follow. He was tired of being led.

Alya had been keeping too many secrets, had been keeping them in the dark. It was time he took matters into his *own* hands, and set out by his *own* choice. Vann and Gorm caught up while Ilma and Alya kept their distance. Gorm's eyes were sunken and distant as they passed patches of snow that were a deeper red.

"Cheer up, Gorm," Vann said. "They were only pengs. Good riddance to them, I say."

"You speak with cruelty," she warned. "The cruelty of the voice shall be reflected in the acts of your peers. Speak of dark things and darkness shall follow, for you are bringing it into the world."

"Yeah, well, say what you like, I'm not going to mourn some pengs killing each other. Why should I?"

"Because when death comes, there is a little less love in the world."

"You don't make any sense."

"Yes, she does," Rob said. "Vann, maybe you should listen from time to time. It wouldn't hurt you."

"Is everyone here against me?"

"No," he smiled. Rob offered a hand, and he took it.

Soon the coast climbed through boulders with snow covering their sleek sides. Rob struggled, his bound leg stinging and aching. He looked to the sea, wondering where the trasati were; he should have known not to expect kindness from them.

Humans were as bad as pengs, in Khamas he had seen trasati used for transport and farming, often taken from their families and homelands to work the land. Thankless as it may have been, he still felt good for having rescued them. It ignited the old desire, the flare for adventure, the thrill of doing something positive, and the idea that he was making a difference. He thought of Vann's family's old business and his resolve hardened.

Alya pulled him back as they reached the top of a rise. She put a finger to her lips and crouched, urging the others to do the same; once they were all bent she pointed to the top of the ridge, and they followed her.

Over the rocks they spied a tall city carved into a white cliff. Towers were topped with glass spires, the walls were white and blue marble, the windows were stained white and yellow, and the walkways were twisted silver iron.

Cupolas and balconies reached from the higher towers while the lower levels were a tangle of weed-like houses. There were leaf-shaped roofs, thorny battlements, and a long string of pillared causeways. In the cove that stretched before the city, there were smaller domed houses of white and grey stone, but they seemed dull and fragile compared to the rest of the rising buildings.

There were carts moving down the roads, some scaling the cliff along paths carved into its side. Along the top of the rock face, there was another set of houses and battlements as well as a string of catapults that looked over the inky waters.

"There used to be a river here," Alya said. "Before the pengs hid it underground; this city is away from prying eyes, so it was perfect for them to use as a secret harbour for ships they did not wish others to know about."

"And you're absolutely sure it's here?" asked Rob.

"I oversaw the installation. It will be guarded, and we will need a great deal of stealth in order to get to it."

"Well, good luck," Vann backed away. "I don't fancy a suicide mission."

"Nobody is forcing you to come," said Rob. "But from the looks of things we could use the help."

"Help? Oh yes, you've all been saying how useless I am this whole time, and now suddenly you want my help? Ha!"

"Where will you go?" Alya asked. "Feel free to run back to Bron'Halla, if you like, but don't expect the pengs to be welcoming. They may have been lenient at first, but now the empire is facing a rebellion, anyone who has a past with the renegades will be killed or worse."

"I had nothing to do with the renegades!"

"You told us you worked for a pengish family who turned out to be renegades, are you changing your story?"

"No," he looked furious.

"The family, if they existed, must have brought you here at least once," Alya went on. "You can guide your friends."

"Oh, can I?" Vann seethed and then turned to Gorm for help. "Come on, you must think this is mental, too?"

"Mental?" she glowered at him. "A differing of the mind is not a thing to be hurled lightly. Use your words with caution."

"Right, so you think I am useless, too?"

"You did not listen. I believe all people are worthy of love and respect. To be of use is to deny you your own mind, to deny you your own choices and make you but a tool in my hands. I do not think that way," Gorm said it slowly but kindly.

"Was that an insult or did I miss something?"

"You missed something," Rob said. "Vann, you said you could break into anything. If you put those skills to use, we can all escape. Don't you want that?"

"I'm confused."

"This is simple enough for a newt to understand," Alya sighed. "Stay with us and you will escape; go alone and you will not. Choose wisely."

"Since when have I done that?" He frowned, then sat beside Rob with a grunt.

"Do what you want," Alya moved forward. "I shall meet you at the under-gate before sunrise tomorrow."

"Where's that?"

"Below the citadel. Getting to the entrance will require the soldiers to be distracted long enough for you to get in."

"Is that all?"

"For now," she grinned and set off.

"Don't kill anyone!" Rob called.

She waved and vanished behind a set of boulders. The sound of her feet trudging through the snow faded. Rob whirled his eyes to Gorm, who was still watching her shadow.

"I will go with her," she said.

"Really?" Rob shifted uncertainly. "You *want* to spend time with her?"

"If you wish to forge a crew, finding a way to trust is essential."

Gorm left at a brisk pace, her long legs taking her further and faster than any of the others could. Rob wanted to go after her and stop her, but he held back and lowered his head, letting her have her way. Once she had gone, Ilma and Vann came closer to Rob, and he knelt amongst them.

"Vann, *do* you know anything about this place?" he asked.

"I only came here once when the pengs wanted to meet some highbrow types and rub shoulders with military brass. I didn't go further than the servants' quarter in the lower town."

"Are there humans there?"

"Enough for us to go unnoticed for a bit," he shrugged. "At least, there were when I was here. It was a while ago so things might have changed."

"It's the best we can do."

They clambered down the rocks and through crumbled pathways that wound in and out of snowy boulders. Rob's leg troubled him with every step, but he did not have the energy to complain.

They came to a sweeping road of granite, flattened and smoothed. There were grooves in its surface where carts had been passing for generations, but it still had a shine and a polished look about it. Rob furrowed his brow, uncertain. There should have been traffic around this town, especially as midday was approaching, and the city seemed to be bustling with people.

Pressing on they followed the road, keeping their heads bowed and their collars up. Rob wished he had picked a less conspicuously coloured coat as it stood stark against the snow and stone. Ilma was at his side as they passed a bend in the road. Rob avoided her eyes, but she was concentrating on his leg as he limped along.

"I suppose I shouldn't be walking," he suggested.

"Under ordinary circumstances, of course," she said. "But these circumstances are far from ordinary, in case you hadn't noticed. You need to keep moving, or the cold will take you. Besides, anyone with half a brain could see we can't hang around waiting for a leg. Even Vann saw that."

"You don't like him, either?"

"He's all right." She patted Rob's arm. "A bit dim, though. That nose ring isn't real gold so far as I can tell, and he's left himself open to infection by not keeping it clean. It's from his homeland; all adults have them. But only when they've proved their honour." She looked over her shoulder at Vann, who was humming and keeping his head down. "I suspect he made that ring himself."

"Why would he do that?"

"Not for me to say," she cleared her throat. "Your leg hasn't fallen off yet, which is remarkable, it's strange that you're able to walk at all."

"I heal quickly," Rob shrugged. "And don't try and change the subject."

"What subject's that, then?" Vann asked, coming closer.

"Hush!" Ilma raised a hand.

The path fell in a long, flowing stairway that dove into darker stone. There were huts at the foot, some little more than cloths hung over snow-built walls. As they got closer, the shapes of humans milling around became clearer.

"Servants," Vann said. "They'll be loyal to the empire, most of them."

"What do you remember from last time you were here? Anything that could help us get underground?"

"Give me a minute, I need to get my bearings! I'm not a bleeding wizard!"

"Yes, you are," Rob nudged him.

"Oh, right, am I?" he beamed. "Maybe I'll turn Alya into a frog."

"That would be a spectacle."

"Yes," said Ilma. "A ribbiting tale!"

Chapter Fifteen

Blood Pengs

Night fell like a purple cloak with the stars faint behind thin clouds that frothed from the sea. Ilma and Vann were sitting on the dock walls, looking over the boats below, but they were whispering to one another and Rob caught the occasional word.

He stopped pacing and glowered at the rising cliff face on which the glass city had been built. There were cranes and wooden shafts running to where the tallest towers crested the cliff, he supposed those were for the poorer pengs or servants.

The docks below the city were packed with barrels and crates, some marked with bright red signs in various languages.

"This is a trade port?" he asked.

"No, it's war stuff." Vann said.

"Those barrels down there, any idea what might be in them? I feel like I've seen that writing before."

"How should I know?"

"Looks Cendylic . . ." Even as he said it he couldn't believe it. Cendyl was the homeland of the draigs, and pengs wouldn't be seen dead with anything from there.

Rob strode towards the docks, tired of the inaction of the past few hours. He needed to do something. Perhaps it was the pain in his leg making him irrational, but he didn't care.

"Rob! You'll be seen!" Ilma hissed.

"Only if they're actually looking for us," he said over his shoulder. He wasn't sure he believed it, but he was feeling restless.

Pengs and humans looked at him scathingly but they kept their distance. Once near enough to read the words on the barrels he stopped. All of them implied danger and to keep fire away. He stepped closer but then his muscles froze. Blood was on the air, stronger and more potent than before.

With slow, deliberate movements, he turned to the crowd now staring with dark, beady eyes. All the other humans had shuffled behind the pengs and a regiment of soldiers was approaching from further down the walkway.

Rob raised his hands and looked towards the crates and barrels only to find that pengs had scurried in-between them, leaving him surrounded. The night was closing, cold mist fluttered from the sea and Rob knelt with one fist on the ground, ready to spring.

"Get away from those," said a peng.

"I don't want any trouble," he said softly. "Just curious."

"Curious about Imperial cargo?" the peng retorted, her eyes narrowing. "I should arrest you for being without proper escort at least."

"I was just checking the crates, they looked out of place."

"None of your business, human." The soldiers closed in. "You're the third to try and take a closer look at these crates today."

"It's not every day you see Cendylic writing in pengish lands."

There was a shocked hush. The pengs looked scandalised, some of the non-military folk gave the crates another look while the soldiers turned their weapons on Rob.

"Nothing to see here," said one of them.

"Oi, I know this one," said another. "You look familiar!"

Rob decided it was time to leave. He turned and prepared to run, but one of the soldiers moved forward and swung. Rob caught the pole of the halberd, it stung his palm and it broke his skin, but he controlled his face and twisted it into a threatening grin. The peng fell back, eyes wide and beak open. Rob's hand went to the remaining smoke pellet in his pocket.

"Do you know who I am?" he shouted.

"An escaped prisoner!" shouted one of the pengs.

"More than just a prisoner!" He stood to his full height and felt the smoke rising through his clothes, to pour out from his sleeves. "I am Rob Sardan; I am the . . ."

Something hit him in the small of the back; the pengs swarmed, jabbing and prodding him with their beaks. Putting strength into his legs, Rob leapt but some pengs clung to his arms. He swung, flinging one of them off, but another remained.

Vann rushed to meet him and bowled into the crowd, knocking a few of them over. Rob flung the peng still clinging to his arm, hitting some of the others. But the effort had left him exhausted, his leg screaming at him to stop, yet still the crowd surged, heading straight for him.

He bolted, springing over a peng, but a flash of steel whipped out, clipping the bandages on his leg. He stumbled but managed to break into a sprint. The pain was blinding, his leg feeling as if it were being chewed again. He fell, his chin slamming into stone and salt water. Blood splattered his mouth and he felt a tooth chip, agony blinded him before he heard a scream.

Vann was being held, chains and clamps being pushed onto his limbs. Rob got to his feet, but the pengs were on him, whistling in tones that shook his inner ear. The space between him and Vann was filled with a sea of pengs, the armoured ones waving halberds, those in robes lifting knives from hidden pockets. Retreating Rob's lungs cried for mercy as did every muscle in his body, but he had no chance, no pathway.

He slipped; the whole world twisted and turned upside down, and his spine felt as if it had been whipped back and forth. His head slammed against a wall and then he fell again.

Water shattered in a shower of ice before he was plunged into the inky depths. His ears filled with a roaring, bubbling riot, his skin was assaulted with cold, and his eyes burned with salt. Flailing, he steadied under the ice. He was under a frozen sheet but he could see the hole he had fallen through. Behind were the bows of ships, some with paddles. Ahead there was the wall of marble he had fallen from, below the water it vanished into darkness but he could still see small gratings lining it.

'*Ilma is going to kill me*,' he thought.

Thuds hit the ice above and shadows were moving towards the hole. Panicking, he swam towards one of the gratings his lungs begging him to halt and his leg bleeding less from the cold but still seeping red into the water.

He reached the grating and squeezed through the bars, while pengs were diving in, their sleek bodies flying through the water with ease. Their eyes found him as he pulled through into a narrow pipe.

Air was his desperate need. His body was collapsing as if being squeezed by giant hands. His throat retched, his eyes stung while his leg became an agonised lump, but he kept going, fighting the current, dragging one arm in front of the next again and again.

The pipe had other pipes branching off from all sides, including from above and below. He headed upwards and broke the surface of the water, giving him precious air. Hauling his body out, he found he was in another tunnel, wider and with a sliver of green slime running from above.

Pengs shot by under his feet, soaring further up the pipes, searching. He breathed deep, coughing and choking, but he pressed his back against one wall with his feet against another, keeping himself above the water. Overhead the pipe led straight towards another grating that looked towards the sky.

Something grabbed his leg; it was a feathery hand and Rob screamed the last of the air out of his lungs as he was yanked into the water. He grasped the side of the pipe and clung on, lifting his head out, but the pressure on his leg grew, blood began pouring from the wound.

He kicked the peng against the wall, knocking her unconscious; the body floated and Rob rolled her over so that her beak was not facing down, making sure she could breathe.

Leaving his attacker floating at the bottom of the pipe, he scaled the side, putting as much pressure on his least injured leg as he could. Once he came to the top, he stopped and pushed, but the grating would not yield. With a series of breaths, he grasped the bars but still made no progress. Eventually, he leant against the wall and kept his legs against the other side, suspending his body there at the top.

His insides felt colder than ever. Ilma's warnings came clanging back into his head and he shivered violently. His head was light and his fingers tingled as his wet clothes weighed him down and he felt as if he would fall asleep.

Stars flickered beyond the clouds as the mist clawed in from all sides. The smell of his sweat, the salt of the sea, and the blood from his wound crowded his head. His mind rolled to the sea and he could hear the sigh and pull of the waves.

When he had held the Sea-Stone Sword, the ocean had lived inside him. He had breathed the roaring waves; he had felt the moon, and the rush of the shore, everything the waters had to offer had been inside his tiny body. The power had been so immense that he had lost who he was.

He drummed his fingers on the wall. If he were the Swordbreaker, he would break swords. It was ambitious but given that his previous dreams had been to overturn the Pengish Empire and the Blood King of Ha'Tiryah, not to mention every other tyrant in Diyngard, he felt this was a more modest aim. The thought brought a bemused smile to his face and he tried the grating again.

It moved! He lost his balance and almost fell. Clinging to the grating, he swung, choking back laughter as he hung. Regaining his place, he pushed the grating open and scrambled through.

He was in the middle of an isolated square covered in snowy ivy that crept from pots. There were statues of pengs, some in robes, some in armour, and others were naked but for a laurel crown. A fountain gurgled, its water spilling in spirals that ran towards the drain he had come out of. Rob's eyes passed over the grating, the bolts that had held it had been removed.

Gulping, he sniffed and tasted blood. He straightened and flexed his aching arms. The shadows moved soft and swift; Rob would not win the fight, but he was determined to try either way.

"Come on, then," he said. "I've been around stealthy people long enough to know when I'm being watched."

A peng emerged from behind a statue; she was dressed in what looked like imperial armour, but it was covered in thick, viscous blood. It did not drip or shift as she moved. It was frozen onto the metal, but there was no frost, and it had not cracked as dried blood usually did. Rob's attention was so fixed on this strangeness that he had to double take as she removed her helmet.

"Kerrok!" he said in astonishment.

"Hello, Sardan," she said. "You look damp; perhaps you should change. Where are the others?"

"I won't tell you." He folded his arms. "Take me, if you can, but the others go free. You won't learn anything from me."

"Disappointing," she sighed. "We could kill you, but it looks like you'll die of cold soon enough. Aren't you feeling the bite already?"

"How did you get here so quick?" He put a hand against his chest, wondering why he wasn't feeling as bad as he should have been. He'd seen people die from cold water before. It made his chest tremble with fear. "Last I saw, you were still in Bron'Halla fighting renegades."

"I took a short cut," she spat and signalled to the other pengs who came from various hiding places. All wore similar armour. "Took a leaf out of Jareth's book. My employer gave me a means of outrunning the snow-ships."

"Your employer?" he smiled. "So, you aren't actually imperial pengs, then? You're *Blood Pengs*; mercenaries for hire."

"My employer was very interested in a certain individual," she said.

"Only one?" Rob's curiosity was piqued. "So you don't care about Vann, or Alya, or Gorm, or Ilma? They can go free?"

"Self-centred as always, Sardan. You may have heard of our employer." Kerrok seemed to be enjoying Rob's discomfort and so she pressed on. "It is someone you have met. Though you may not have known it at first."

"Mothar, the Pirate Lord," Rob ground his teeth.

"Close." Kerrok pulled out a golden knife from her belt. "No, it was not Mothar. Look at the inscription on the blade." She held it to the light and he saw letters he recognised.

"Draigs," he said, quietly. "You were hired by draigs."

"We were hired by one who used the Cendylic language," Kerrok sneered. "If you could read it you would know her already."

"I can read a bit of it . . ." Rob scrutinised it but Kerrok clicked her tongue.

"We do not have time for you to riddle it out. Our employer wishes one of you escapees to be brought back to her very soon."

"Her?" Rob knelt so that he could look Kerrok in the eye. "Who is this employer of yours? Some noble draig with a vendetta? Perhaps it is one of the Magma Masters? Whoever they are, they can't be telling you the truth."

"You are very dim, as I have said before. You have met our employer, and I will say no more. We keep our employer's secrets unless you can offer a price greater than what she has offered us."

"Fine, take me back to Bron'Halla if you can."

"You keep saying that as if we were interested in *you*." The Blood Pengs closed in, their hands going each to a golden knife at their belt while Kerrok spoke. "We want Gorm Foulheart. Tell us where she is."

Rob's brain stopped. He boggled at her but then tried to form his face into a passive expression; Kerrok was already chortling as she stepped closer.

"She was travelling with you, and we know she was not with you when you entered this city, so where did she go?"

"I thought you were supposed to be the greatest trackers in the pengish world," Rob sneered. "Why do you need my help?"

Kerrok tilted her head and narrowed her eyes. "You know her past, this should not surprise you. We tracked you, Rob Sardan because you leave the most obvious trail and to get to the strongest link in a chain, you must start at the weakest."

"Is that what I am?"

"You cannot walk properly, you are tired, and you are unfamiliar with the territory. Not to mention your usual method of bringing attention to yourself. As soon as we saw you on the docks we tried to calm the riot before it broke out, but you incited them. As soon as you went into the water, I guessed you would come up for air. We stationed watches at every grating and when I was informed that you were here, I prepared a welcome for you."

"You are so kind."

"I am trying to let you know that you are a noisy creature and that you leave a visible trail. You will not be able to hide, wherever you go."

"I have no intention of hiding."

"I always knew you were an idiot," she snapped her beak and the Blood Pengs lifted their knives. "Tell us where Gorm Foulheart is and what you are planning. We may help you."

He eyed them, turning on the spot, much to the chagrin of his leg, which stung violently. His chest also sung with guilt as images of chains and a swarm of pengs came into his mind; Vann had been taken captive. And now Gorm was being hunted. As for Ilma and Alya, Rob had no idea where they were. He was alone again.

"Okay." He paused, waiting for them to press him, but Kerrok only glowered, impatiently. "She will be heading to the dungeons, to rescue Vann. They were friends."

"Razal's shield," Kerrok swore. "I knew she was sentimental. I always said so. Was she watching your escapade on the docks, then?"

"Yes." Rob hoped his face looked honest enough to get away with this.

"I don't recall seeing them together." Kerrok cocked her head. "If you are trying something funny, Sardan, I will not hesitate to have your skin peeled off."

"You never did pay much attention to Vann or Ilma, did you?"

"A thief and a doctor are of little concern to me."

"Ilma had you figured out from the start. Never thought you were quite right; you always seemed keen on making sure everyone knew you were loyal to the empire. Any other peng would have let it go without saying, but you boasted and shouted about it. That's what gave you away."

"Are you going to chatter all day?" Kerrok hissed.

"Fine," Rob formed his hands into fists. "Let's go and find them."

Chapter Sixteen

A Mammoth Task

THE DUNGEONS WERE AT THE END OF A LABYRINTH THAT Kerrok led Rob through. He was draped in thick grey cloaks, and the Blood Pengs had called him one of their servants whenever questioned. The nearer they got to the citadel the more inquisitive the guards had become.

One of Kerrok's subordinates had confiscated Rob's sword. It looked cumbersome for the little soldier, but she held her head up with dignity. He wasn't sure he would have used it even if he'd kept it.

Rob had convinced them to walk back along the dockside near to where Ilma had been in the hopes that she would see him and follow. There had been no sign, though as they had wound their way through the streets, he thought he had seen suspicious shadows.

They were almost denied entry into the tunnels, as the guards seemed to think something had happened. If not for Kerrok's insatiable appetite for violent rhetoric, Rob doubted they would have got so far.

The walls were curved overhead just high enough for Rob to walk without ducking, but he had to remove his hat. He kept looking over his shoulder, hoping the shadows he had seen following them were what he thought they were.

Glittering patterns made by small shards of glass had been worked into the stone. Yet, despite the white walls, it was dark, the light coming only from a pair of torches held by Kerrok's subordinates. They stopped at a set of doors carved into the shapes of roaring mammoths; their tusks were white wood while the rest was black. Kerrok pushed the doors and shoved Rob through.

"If this place blows, I want you to catch the first of it," she told him.

He groped in the dark and laid hands on a crate. The Blood Pengs followed, and the torches shone onto crates and barrels as high as the ceiling. Each was plastered with red letters and symbols of fire. Rob looked at Kerrok, and she shrugged.

"A weapon for the war," she said.

"Which war?"

"Perhaps this civil war that's been going on for days? You were caught in it, remember?"

"No, that's not possible." He wiped dust off one of the crates. "This stuff has been here for years. Those letters have been painted over Razal-knows how often. What is this stuff?"

"I thought you could read Penguvian," she scolded.

Rob focused on the words. "The letters are Penguvian, but the words don't make sense."

"It's Voltisian," said one of the Blood Pengs.

"Voltisian? Never heard of it."

"It's the language the draigs used during the War of Frost and Flame. The letters are Pengish, but we have translated the sound of the word, not the meaning."

"Why?"

"That is a matter for the Imperial Family," said Kerrok. "All I know is that if we get too friendly with this stuff we could all die. I heard some guards talking about it last night, so get your hands off that crate."

Rob raised his hands and backed away, but his eyes remained on the words.

"It's some kind of explosive," he said.

"Perhaps," Kerrok shrugged. "It is here for security. Pirates have been attacking ships, so transporting this stuff is becoming difficult. We need faster ships, stronger ships."

"I see . . ." Rob thought of Alya. This must have been why they had commissioned her, and why they had imprisoned her. This fire powder was probably able to rip a regular galleon to pieces, so she had constructed something that could withstand assault.

Or so they thought. Alya had made suggestions about not bringing fire onboard. She had made it clear that the ship could withstand winds, rain and rocks, but fire was another matter. Had she deliberately refrained from protecting against fire, just to get at the pengs? He would not have put it past her.

"And you approve?" he asked.

"I am not part of the Empire," Kerrok snarled. "I am a general of the Blood Pengs, my loyalty is mine to give. Do you think I like what the Empire is doing? This is an abomination that destroyed countless pengs. Our people were consumed by a fire that came to life. If I could stop it . . ." she paused for breath. "If I could stop them, don't you think I would?"

He looked at her black eyes locked in a glower of determined anger, a frenzy of hate and pride. They continued through the tunnels, but the pengs were looking at one another with twitchy movements.

Rob slowed; something musky and sour was coming from ahead. Kerrok prodded him, and he moved, the smell getting stronger every step. Soon a sound was there, too, a grunting, groaning sound.

The tunnel ended on a balcony overlooking a bleak hall. Metal doors were scattered, chains were shattered, and splinters were sprinkled like snow. Rob held up a hand, and the pengs stopped, letting him take the stairs that ran from the balcony down into the main area.

He limped over the ruins and scanned the sawdust floor; it stank of musk. Under the balcony there was a tall door that had been burst, its frame bent outwards on rusty hinges. Within, there was a huge shape, hairy and filthy, two giant tusks yellowing in the torchlight.

The Blood Pengs were approaching; Kerrok's eyes scanned the mammoth as it stirred, but Rob put a finger to his lips and turned back to the creature.

'*Friend*,' he intoned. The mammoth raised its shaggy head. It was young, its legs were skinny, and there were patches where the fur had been torn from its flesh. Blood streaked its side, and a crack ran down its left tusk.

'*Hurt*,' the mammoth said. '*Pain. Danger*.'

"What is this thing?" Kerrok asked, disgusted.

"Keep quiet," Rob waved at her. "She's hurt."

"Why is it here? I was labouring under the impression that this was a holding cell for criminals."

"It looks like there was a break-out," Rob glowered. "And don't call her 'it', thank you very much."

"Save your self-righteousness, Sardan," Kerrok stepped closer and looked into the eyes of the mammoth. She whistled and chirruped; the mammoth got to her feet and lowered her head, growling.

"I don't think she liked that," Rob said.

The mammoth roared and charged; Rob dove, his leg burning. He rolled in sawdust and scrambled towards the stairs. The pengs whistled and screeched, darting between smashed cages before leaping over the swinging trunk. The Blood Pengs moved like liquid, flowing with one another in a dance they knew by heart.

Rob clambered up the stairs, breathing hard and realising how tired he was. The last time he had slept had been when he'd been bitten, and it had not been a good rest. He struggled to the top, leaning against the wall, coughing.

The Blood Pengs were throwing chains over the mammoth, moving and twisting with formations that boggled the mind. It was expert work, and it didn't seem to bother them that their opponent was five times bigger than all of them put together. They ducked under tusks, slid from stamping feet, bounded over the mammoth's back and tail, curling their chains until they brought her down.

The mammoth yowled to the ceiling, which shook. Rob's fists tightened, and he backed into the tunnel. Why the pengs had a mammoth here was beyond him, and he ground his teeth in bitterness.

He knocked into a barrel and it toppled, but when he reached to stop it, the weight was far less than he had anticipated and he almost fell over. Once it was steady, he shook it, expecting a rattling that did not come. The barrel was empty.

New questions burst and he dashed from barrels to crates. All empty, but many had remnants still in their bottoms.

He kicked one of them over, and there was a muffled sound from within. Rob stepped back as the barrel moved. Frowning, he approached and pulled the lid off to reveal a head with short, grey hair. Ilma lifted her face and met his, a sheepish grin spreading across her features.

"What in Razal's name are you doing in there?" he asked.

"Hiding," she said, squeezing out of the top. "They said something had escaped down here. Some sort of monster they'd been training."

"Yeah . . ." Rob shuddered, imagining the mammoth tethered to a war chariot.

"Right," Ilma breathed and straightened. "I assume we need to get out of here now that you've got them distracted."

"We need to rescue Vann," Rob insisted.

"Is he down there?"

"I didn't see him, but where else could he be?"

"You don't make a very convincing case," she bit her lip and pointed the way they had first come. "Not that we can go back that way, anyway."

"What? Why not? Is it blocked?"

"Before I came here there was a horn that sounded all over the city; you must have heard it! Then a bunch of soldiers started running around, sealing doors and keeping everyone away from them."

"What is going on up there?"

"I think . . ." she whispered. "I think the city might be under siege." She knocked the barrel and sent it tumbling away.

Rob sprang after it, but the thing hit the stairs and toppled with a series of echoing clangs. A moment later the Blood Pengs were at the foot of the stairs, their keen eyes on Rob and Ilma.

"Well, distraction over," the doctor said.

Kerrok shouldered past her subordinates and mounted the stairs, her eyes simmering, still heated from the struggle with the mammoth. Rob's gaze went to the beast, chained and suppressed; she met his look with one of her own. He approached the pengs and stepped past, knocking one of them aside with his injured shin.

Out of the corner of his eye, he spotted the golden sword discarded on the floor. The peng who had been carrying it was nursing her wrist and Rob tried to avert his gaze, keeping the weapon in mind as he crept closer to the mammoth.

'*Hurt*,' the mammoth moaned. '*Many hurts*.'

He patted her fur and tried to soothe her with a calming tone, but the pengs were hissing. Annoyed, he turned to them and was about to demand the release of the mammoth when he spotted a shadow move in one of the cells.

"Is there another way out?" he asked, making Kerrok focus on him.

"If this place is built to regulations, there should be a shaft leading to the lower tunnels. Perhaps in that mammoth's cell; it was big enough."

The shadow darted towards the cell, but the pengs were too quick. Their feathery hands were on Vann before he had got halfway across the hall, and he got knocked to the ground. Scrambling, he pounded the sawdust and scratched his attackers, but they held him fast. Rob limped and tried to drag one of the pengs off, but a knife was drawn.

"No!" Kerrok shouted. "He's not worth our blades."

The peng returned the golden knife to her belt and rolled from Vann's back, letting him lay on the ground, panting.

"So, the crew is half complete," Kerrok snorted. "Only two missing." She pulled Vann to his feet. "Where is Gorm?"

"I won't tell you nothing!" Vann said, giving Rob a smile.

"Pity." Kerrok punched Vann in the stomach, knocking him off balance. He coughed and groaned, held up by the pengs on his arms.

Ilma hurried down and muttered something about opening wounds and lack of hygiene. The pengs threw Vann to the floor, but Rob picked him up.

"I was going to escape," Vann said. "Managed to pick the lock, didn't I?"

"How?" Ilma asked. "Pengish locks are notoriously complex."

"I said I could open anything," he grinned and tapped his nose ring, which was bent out of shape. "Very useful, it's me pride and joy. Can't go anywhere without it."

"You never used these skills to escape from Bron'Halla," Kerrok said.

"I got out of my cell plenty of times, but that was just a hobby. No way of getting out of the South Pole, I thought. Not till Rob came up with the plan."

"Me? I didn't do anything; it was Alya."

"Yeah, well, I never did trust her. But you made it worthwhile. Gave me ideas, you did. All that talk of saving the trasati. When I saw that beasty, well, I thought I'd set her loose. Make a nice big distraction while I got away."

"You set that thing loose?" Kerrok was apoplectic.

The pengs hissed with fury rather than amusement. They advanced on Vann, some twitching their feathered fingers towards their knives. Rob rushed forward and grasped his sword from the floor. He leapt up and stood in front of Vann, staring into Kerrok's eyes.

"He did the right thing," Rob insisted. "If you want to find Gorm, you will not lay a finger on him!"

"This is *not* a negotiation." Kerrok launched a fist into Rob's stomach, forcing air out of him. He bent, and she punched him in the jaw, knocking him to the ground.

The sword skittered and clanged against the wall, its gold dulled in the torchlight. Coughing, Rob lifted his torso and spat. Kerrok had already advanced on Vann, but Rob got to his feet, slowly and deliberately. She turned to look at him and snapped her beak at her subordinates.

The Blood Pengs head butted, slapped, and pecked him; he was forced against the wall and pummelled by steel-clad arms. They dodged every flailing fist, ducked under his kicks, and struck again, slamming his head into the wall. Ilma called his name but he hit the ground and the dungeon dissolved.

A red sky thundered, rain plastered his face, and wind screamed with a thousand terrified voices. Rob stood on a mountain in the sea, his back aching with the weight of the great Sword strapped to it. He lifted a hand, and the waters rose, he clenched a fist, and the water hardened into a white-hot ball.

Voices screamed inside his skull. He thrashed and tried to shake them off, but they only got louder and harsher. The blood in his ears grew so hot that he thought his head was on fire. He couldn't bear it. He wanted to die. He wanted it all to end.

The hall came back into focus. Air forced its way into his lungs. Rolling onto his front, he lifted his body by the elbows and let his eyes fall on the pengs.

"I have the Sky-slayer's Curse," he told them. "I won't stay unconscious for long. The dreams will wake me."

"I shall put an end to them, then." One of the Blood Pengs sprang towards him, knife upheld. Kerrok shouted, but the peng drove closer; Rob dodged, but another peng slammed a head into his chest.

He stood and knocked one of the pengs aside with a swipe; then he bounded to Vann, who was spread against the wall goggling at him. Rob stood, bleeding and panting with his arms outstretched, forming a barrier between the pengs and Vann.

Kerrok leapt on Rob, her fists assaulting his face; blood splattered the two of them and they fell into the sawdust. She kicked him in the chin and turned her attention back to Vann, drawing her golden knife.

"Stop!" Ilma shouted. "You'll lose your contract!"

The pengs contemplated her, making Ilma shrink and avoid their acidic eyes. She coughed and pointed at the weapon in Kerrok's hand.

"It's a Llafn Gwaed, a Blood Blade, yes? Like Rob's sword. They change colour depending on what kind of blood first touches them."

"Our target is human," said one of the pengs.

"Hush," said Kerrok. "I was getting hasty. It's easy to think a knife is just a knife, but Gorm is no ordinary human. That's why our employer gave us these things." She snapped her beak and put the knife back in her belt.

"Why? What's she got that we don't?" asked Rob.

"You must have heard her story," Kerrok said. "She was poisoned with Saagara. It's a miracle she survived. That stuff leaves a trace in blood. To prove that we killed Gorm, our employer needs to see the right colour on these blades. She wishes to guarantee Gorm's death. Carrying her head would be cumbersome."

Rob struggled to get up but only got as far as his knees. His left eye was swollen, and he tasted blood. He had lost at least one tooth and had bitten the inside of his cheek twice. His legs seemed more reluctant than ever to comply with his wishes.

"I thought you only wanted to capture Gorm," he said, slurred. "Not that I approved of that, though. But I really, really can't let you kill her."

"How nice for you," Kerrok clicked her tongue, and her subordinate pengs gathered around her. "You tried to stop us and look at what happened."

"I don't care what happens to me," he laughed, suddenly.

As he said it, he felt a rush through his blood, remembering what it was like to do something to save another person. He'd done it all his childhood with his sauros friends. He'd defended youngsters in Kenna's mines. He'd even defended the Pirate Lord when he'd thought him nothing more than a fat old man.

"You've been reading too many stories, Sardan." Kerrok dismissed him with a wave. "You cannot stop us from completing our contract. Razal knows, I'm already sick of it. I want it over and done with, so we can all go back to something more comfortable. You know she made me stay in that ridiculous prison for two years?"

"Why not kill her there, then?"

"I wanted to. But the terms of the contract were to observe her. Our employer had regular reports from us, telling of Gorm's state of mind and how she descended into a pitiful pacifist under Lomi's guidance. She was supposed to stay and never leave. Our employer could not let the secret of her experiments get out. Now she is out, she needs to be disposed of."

Rob lowered his head, his fists clenching as his skin burned. "Use your knives on me!" he shouted, his eyes closed with the pain of talking.

"What would be the point? We already explained to you . . ."

"I had Saagara in me," Rob opened his eyes and met hers. "I held the Sea-Stone Sword! I had all the power of the Ocean's Eye inside me. You think that wouldn't make my blood like hers?"

Kerrok considered him, her brow furrowing so that the feathers stuck out.

"Rob, no!" Ilma shouted, but the pengs held her back when she tried to rush forward.

"The crew needs Gorm; she has the experience and the strength. She has a calm mind, a cool head, and wisdom beyond her years. What do I have? A name that some people recognise. That's not enough."

"Don't give me that," she snapped. "You're not just a name; you're a person! You might feel guilty. You feel like you want to do something noble. But there must be a better way. Being brave is one thing, but right now you are being downright thickheaded! Listen to me!"

Rob met her eyes and tried to hold back his tears. Ilma's hair was loose, but some had stuck to her face where sweat and tears were streaking. He looked at Vann, and there was a pleading intensity in his features that melted him; he wanted to embrace him, to give him some reassurance.

"Rob," Vann said. "If they could do me in instead, that'd be better."

"They can't," he shook his head. "It has to be me."

Kerrok walked closer, her hand stroking the handle of her knife. Her cheeks bulged in a pengish smile, and she turned to face her five subordinates.

"I want to go home," she said. "How about the rest of you?" The Blood Pengs exchanged looks and then nodded. "Well, that's that, then."

The knife jammed into his abdomen. Rob collapsed against the wall, his insides an inferno that erupted from the wound. The shapes of pengs hurrying to and from his bleeding body merged into one blurred image. Ilma shouted; Vann cried, and the world was torn into a frothing mass of pain.

Chapter Seventeen

The Bear

HE WAS COLDER THAN HE HAD EVER BEEN. THE SHIVERS WERE violent, and his organs were shifting out of place as he convulsed. Ilma pushed him and growled harsh words into his ear. None of them made it to his brain, all he could hear was a cacophony of furious wind.

The mammoth's fur was warm; as he was settled into it, his muscles melted. He flittered in and out of time; the stone above became red clouds, lightning-strewn seas, and then a sapphire dome deep underwater.

Stuffy, putrid air surrounded him, and he coughed, which made everything hurt even more. The soft movement of the slow breathing of the mammoth was like a melody. Sleep clawed at him, and he fell into a warm embrace, leaving the cold tunnels behind.

He was back in the mines, drenched in blood, screaming bodies all around him. Their faces looked at him with horror and hate. He had done this, he had killed people, he had betrayed them, and he had laughed as he had done it.

'No,' *he thought.* 'No, it was Saagara. The Ocean's Eye possessed me; it took over my mind!'

But other thoughts argued. The power of the sea had looked into his heart and brought out his basest instincts, it had pulled at his deepest desires and made them possible. The Sea-Stone Sword had given him so much power, so much potential, and how had he used it? He had killed a giant tree; he had slaughtered people by the dozens, he had let his friends die.

King-killer. Sky-slayer. Sword-breaker!

He jerked awake, his muscles tensing as if he were going to fight. *Sword-breaker*. The name sang inside his skull, but it no longer hurt.

"Will you lie down?" Ilma snapped. "It's incredible that you're alive, and I don't usually nag about these things, but really!"

Rob pressed a hand against his wound. It had been bandaged, and he could smell herbs coming from beneath the coverings. They were in the tunnels, the mammoth behind taking up almost all of the room. She was sleeping, and they were leaning against her bulk. Vann was snoring, his bent nose ring moving with his breaths. Meanwhile, Ilma rummaged in her pack before pulling out a set of phials.

"Now, choose, red or red." Both phials looked the same.

"The red one, I suppose."

"Really? You sure?" She stuck out her tongue and then opened the glass container before dumping the contents in his mouth. "Swallow."

He did, but the aftertaste made him want to gag. "What is it?"

"Not entirely sure," she said. "But it helped me when I had a headache. It might dull your pain. Now, you need to get warm. Your clothes are wet again! I will be tearing my hair out if you so much as jump in a puddle, young sir!"

Rob leaned into the mammoth's fur and listened to her breathing. It sent his mind into a calming stream of low hums that made him want to sleep, but he kept his eyes open. Sleep would be more painful than full consciousness.

Before he had decided to escape, that thought had depressed him, now he just felt annoyed and angry. Kerrok had smashed his pendant, leaving him open to the curse and making him vulnerable.

"I've been meaning to ask," Ilma said, suddenly. "How much Saagara did you ingest, not counting the influence of the Sea-Stone Sword?"

"I have no idea," Rob shook his head. "When I broke the Sword, all the Saagara around me, and for all I know all around the world, was sucked into the air where it dissipated and died."

"I don't know . . ." Ilma was looking at him in a strange way. "Your body is unusual, I hope you don't mind me saying so."

"I don't mind." He cocked his head. "Mostly because I'm not sure I understand what you mean."

"You heal quickly. Very quickly. And there's other stuff. How old are you?"

"Depends what month it is, I might be nineteen."

"You look older." She lifted his shirt and traced a finger along his chest. "I have never seen muscle build like this. You do not do the right exercises, and you certainly don't actually have the strength of someone who would look like this."

"Thanks." He pulled his shirt down and pouted. "I'm plenty strong. It's just, I don't get any sleep now, and I've hurt my leg, and I've been stabbed."

"I have seen plenty of bodies in my time, and I know my subject. There is something about you that isn't right. Look at your eye."

"How can I look at my own eyes?"

"Funny. Your eye was swollen not ten minutes ago, but now it's open and working fine. Don't you find it strange?"

"I suppose." He shrugged. "But, what about you? Why'd you rescue me?"

"Why would I leave you?" She looked hurt by the question. "I've helped people all my life. It makes me happy. Life is life; even if I save someone who is mean, or cruel, or just rotten, I still feel better because I can bring something good into the world."

Vann yawned and stretched. "Oh, you're awake, good stuff! We off, then?"

Rob and Ilma lingered on one another's eyes for a moment before getting to their feet. Vann helped Rob steady, and then they woke the mammoth from her slumber. Pain was a background hum in Rob's existence, and the knife wound was just another in a long line of scars he would have to show. His chewed leg, however, did not nag him as much as it had done and he could walk on it.

"Where are we?" he asked as he examined the dark stone walls.

"Sewage system below the dungeon," Ilma replied. "The mammoth broke in, and we followed. She seemed to want to see you safe."

"Not like those ungrateful trasati in the water," Vann snorted.

"What about the pengs?" Rob asked. "Why'd they let you go?"

"Something Vann said," Ilma smiled at the smaller man. "They were wondering how to get us out of the city, and back to Bron'Halla, only Vann made such a ruckus and threw such a tantrum that Kerrok said not to bother."

"Doesn't sound like her," Rob said, frowning.

"I wasn't really listening," Ilma said with a guilty look. "I was too busy trying to stop your bleeding. I have to say I was surprised that they left. What did you say, Vann?"

"They was tired," Vann said with a shrug. "I kept telling them about all the different problems we'd have getting out of the city while it's under attack. That's what that alarm thing meant, I think. They seemed to agree."

"Perhaps," Rob strained to stay conscious. "But I doubt this is the last we'll see of Kerrok before we're through. But thank you, Vann."

"Pleasure," Vann winked at him.

Rob shook his head, his long braids swinging against his chin. He kept his eyes on Ilma's back as she led the way; she had tied her hair in a ponytail of grey strands, and the style reminded him of an old friend. Ilma's expertise had kept him alive, but he couldn't help wondering why she had done it. It would have been much easier for her to escape with Vann and leave him to bleed.

"That was sweet of you, by the way," Vann said, making Rob jump. "Ridiculously stupid and completely mad, but it was sweet."

"I'm sure Gorm would chastise you for calling me mad," replied Rob as he put his arm around Vann's shoulder, walking was difficult and it made him feel better. "But you are welcome."

"Yeah, well." He held the golden sword and passed it to Rob. "I saved this, though. Don't suppose that little peng wanted to carry it."

Rob put it in the scabbard at his hip. He felt his wound stinging at the movement, but he hissed away the pain and kept walking.

"Why'd you do it? I mean, you could have let them hurt me and they'd not have done a thing to you. If you'd never said anything they'd not have known the knives would work on you, and, well, it just seemed like you had a death wish."

"I did, once," Rob coughed, his abdomen erupting with cramps and thorny pain. He bent double and almost fell from Vann's grasp.

"How are you alive?" he asked.

"It's only a knife wound," Rob tried to smile. "It's not like I've been eaten by a sea monster or anything."

"You should be dead. I don't *want* you dead, of course. Just, it don't make sense."

"Hush!" Ilma held up a hand.

They were at a junction in the tunnel, the new passageway filling with a stream of grimy water. The stone above was vibrating, dust trickling in a slow shower. Rob shrugged away from Vann and stepped closer to where the passages met. Ilma gave him a look, which strayed to his wound.

A bubbling, rumbling noise grew like an approaching stampede, getting harsher and deeper as it approached. The mammoth stamped and groaned; Vann tried to soothe her but only made her even more terrified. The tunnel shook, water splattered and cracks fractured the stone. Ilma grabbed Rob's arm and pulled him into the next tunnel, Vann and the mammoth following at a run.

Dazed and short of breath, Rob tried to keep up with Ilma, but his wounds and his left arm tingled ominously. By rights he should have been dead; the thought that something beyond his control was keeping him alive was troubling. He was not sure how far to push this, but his fingers rummaged under his shirt until he found the knife wound. It was not as tender as it ought to have been.

The noises grew monstrous, the stones cracked and steamed. The mammoth roared and charged, making the others sprint to keep ahead, despite their starved state.

The tunnel was lightening, the air growing hot, and the noise of falling masonry echoed behind them.

"Ah, you are here," said a breathless but confident voice.

Sliding in the squelching waters, they peered at a torch flickering ahead. Alya came into view, holding the light aloft, a satisfied grin on her face.

"You!" Vann growled. "What have you done?"

"I have done only that which is necessary. Come, the ship is near."

The walls shook again and they heard screaming, high whistles and a string of curses echoed above. Rob's eyes turned in horror to Alya, who was making a quick escape. He broke from Ilma and he went into a reckless sprint.

"How many did you kill?" he demanded.

"None," Alya replied, keeping pace with him.

"It is very difficult to believe you," Rob snarled but carried on alongside her.

At the end of the tunnel, there was a set of stairs down which water was trickling, they followed it and were soon swept into a large chamber.

The subterranean walls were blue and grey, covered with stalagmites and stalactites as sharp as daggers. The water ran into a wide, clear lake, the ripples trailing towards the centre where a ship was moored.

It was less than forty feet in length and its narrow, ellipsoidal frame gave it a pointed shape. It had two tall masts rigged with triangular sails. It had a railing that flowed to the main deck and towards the forecastle. There was a bowsprit that extended five feet, jibs and pulleys running from its nose to the tips of the sails.

Below the bowsprit, the head had been carved into the shape of a creature; it had a high forehead with a crest, a muzzle and rounded ears, the wood had been shaped to suggest that the creature had fur almost everywhere. Its mouth hung open and its cheeks bulged as if it had just finished a very large meal.

"Behold," said Alya. "My ship."

"How long were you waiting to say that?" Vann asked, sounding mildly disgusted. "What's that thing carved on the front?"

"It is a bear, a creature from the folklore of my people. It is a hairy beast that haunts the woods and forests, taking children and eating honey."

"It looks fat. Can I name it Fat Ted?"

"You can try, but every time you do, I will tear a bit of your skin off."

"Well, Fat Ted and I disagree. And anyway, this thing's tiny!"

She scowled at him. "It can be sailed by a small crew, which, in case you hadn't noticed, is what we are. I suppose counting, or anything that involves mental activity, is beyond you."

"Enough of that please," Rob insisted. "Where's Gorm?"

"She is putting the finishing touches to our escape plan."

"Could you see your way to explaining said plan to us?"

"Could you see your way to explaining the mammoth standing behind you?"

"Ah . . ." Rob squirmed. "Yes, it is odd. She was being held captive by the pengs. Without her we would not have gotten this far, so don't go making fun!"

"I wasn't going to," she grinned. "You need to think about what will be done with her. We require speed if we are to escape. Think hard. No good deed goes unpunished." With a wave, she urged them to follow her around the water's edge.

"I stole a considerable amount of the peng's fire powder," Alya explained as they walked. "It burns green, but it is not the true green fire of legend. It is less hot, but it is visually impressive. Gorm was setting the blasting powder at various points around the city while I took some into the nearby forest. I took the shaft over the cliff and marched to the woods and set them alight.

"When the pengs saw this, they believed that the renegades had come to lay siege to the city, so they called their soldiers, who then raced up the shaft and across to the forest. As soon as they had gone, Gorm blasted the tower and the shaft, once as I had climbed down, that is. With no way back for their soldiers other than a ten-mile march, the pengs in the city were stretched thin, fighting the fires and damages."

"This is horrific!" Rob cried.

"I am confident there were no fatal casualties. As I said, the fire is not hot. It is impressive, but not destructive unless concentrated. It is designed to instil fear, and that is what it did. I used their own weapon against them. Quite neat.

"After that, I ran to the catacombs; there were some soldiers here, but not many. The others had evidently been called to fight the fire, and those that were left were in fear for their lives and livelihoods, they paid little attention to my passing."

The roof shook and Rob stopped in his tracks. Sulphurous ash hit his nose and a sudden image of fire filled his mind. He grasped Alya by the shoulder and turned her around. "You said it wasn't destructive!" he bellowed.

"It is not my fault that they have flammable materials in these lower caves." She shrugged out of his grasp. "But trust me, nobody will die."

"You want us to trust you and not give a second thought to the consequences of your actions?"

"You never think of the consequences of yours."

"I have spent the last two years dealing with the consequences of my actions!"

"Oh, you can't sleep, you have nightmares, you've got a few scars, and you lost friends. All very hurtful, I'm sure, but you never dealt with the real cost of what you did. You didn't have to live in a world where the Air King's death tore the coasts to pieces. You didn't have to deal with pirates running rampant, screaming tales of the great Sword-breaker. You never had to watch a city burn in the name of Rob Sardan."

She gave him a cold glower and then moved on. He watched her go, followed by the others, and then the mammoth pushed him forward. The line of the water narrowed to a river that flowed towards a long, black wooden lock, which acted as a bridge. Rob was still reeling, but he crossed.

Nearer the ship they found a walkway that led to it, though the wood was narrow and rickety. Alya stopped them before mounting it and looked at Vann, who squirmed and backed away.

"You said you can open anything, now is your chance to prove it," she said. "The lock needs opening if we are to get out of here. Make yourself useful."

"You always said I was useless," Vann objected. "And why should I do what you want me to, eh?"

"There is no other way out of this cavern; not if we want to take the ship. Besides, would it not give you some perverted sense of satisfaction to prove me wrong about something?"

"Have it your way, but I do it under protest!"

"Duly noted." She watched him head to the lock with a sardonic smile. Rob nudged her and she hurried them onto the walkway and then onto the deck of the ship.

There were two hatches in the centre of the deck with wooden gratings across them and held shut with ropes. Rob strode to the quarterdeck and then to the wheel. Next to it on either side were two great levers and a series of cogs he had never seen on any ship in his life.

"Ilma and I can take these," Alya said, pointing to the strange configurations. "I know what they do and the doctor is more adept at learning."

"Am I? That's good to know." Ilma sidled closer to the levers and examined them with a furrowed brow.

"From here the sails can be lowered and directed," Alya went on, pointing to the rigging. "I developed a system by which the jibs and ropes can be worked either manually or by these controls."

Alya turned some of the cogs and Ilma mirrored her actions. Rob stepped back and peered towards where Vann was working on the lock. The ceiling was shaking and the sounds of panic above were growing, Alya seemed to have noticed this, too, as she pulled the great levers and the masts turned as if thrust by giant hands.

"How does it work?" Rob asked.

"Ordinarily it wouldn't," she said, looking immensely proud. "A series of cogs are entwined with a sort of spring system. On any other ship, the mast would snap the first time the wind got up, but this ship is different. The wood is special. I've never worked with anything like it."

"Where did you say it was from?"

"A great ash tree in the Nasgadh Sea, perhaps you heard of it. The tree of Dun Geili on the Keeker Isle, it is said that *you* killed that tree with the Sea-Stone Sword."

He looked at the grain between his hands and felt a shiver of regret pulse into his chest. The image of the villagers begging him not to kill their tree was one that would haunt him.

"Something about what you did to that tree made this wood almost indestructible," Alya went on. "It bent and twisted only as much as I wished it to, but it will not snap or shatter."

"How did you cut the wood if it's so strong?"

"I used techniques the pengs would not have approved of." She smiled even more broadly, revelling in her cleverness. "I used draigish blades made from a substance called D'haara. It is incredibly expensive and I had to use a confidence trickster to get it. The stuff is found only in the Tomb of the Dead God."

"That's where Vann's family is!" Rob said, widening his gaze. "You never said . . . how can I even believe anything you're saying?"

She shrugged. "Believe what you like."

The ceiling cracked, a stalactite fell, shattering when it hit the water with a crunch. Alya rushed to the railing and waved to Vann, who waved back. There was another explosion and the waters frothed. The mammoth on the bank reared and trumpeted.

"Calm that beast!" Alya ordered.

Rob bounded back to the main deck and called to the mammoth, trying to send soothing messages, but also trying to get her to go to the lock. She would have the strength to open it if Vann failed.

Fire ripped through the ceiling, bursting and sending hot, red light across their faces. Rob hid his eyes but heard the mammoth shrieking and stamping away from them. He tried to call, but his abdomen hurt, and he doubled over in pain.

Voices were echoing, and steel feet thundered closer. Rob squinted through the inferno that was raging across the roof.

The tunnel where they had entered was shifting with shadows, and one was running at full pelt.

Gorm burst out and slid to a stop at the water's edge. Ilma waved to her, but the fire and water was between them. She waved back and made a dash for the lock, but at that moment the mammoth slammed into it, knocking Vann from his place.

The lock cracked and creaked, straining against the sheer weight of water. Vann screamed and clung to the edge, his feet dangling pathetically. Gorm came closer, but soldiers were rushing out of the tunnel in pursuit. Alya was shouting, the roaring fire and the creaking lock drowning her out.

Fire rocketed through the cave, and rocks slammed into the water. Rob jumped from the railing and darted to the stern, past Alya and Ilma, who were struggling with the anchor. Sickly nausea clouded his head, and he threw up, specks of blood accompanying his last meal. Collapsing, he shivered while Ilma shouted. Alya pushed him out of the way and raised the anchor on her own, saying something he could not hear over his pain.

The ship rocked, and Ilma turned the wheel with all of her might. There were shouts and screams, but the fire, the marching feet, and Rob's inner turmoil made it a blurred mess. He struggled to his feet, his hand clasped over his side, which ached as if it had been ripped open.

Gorm was helping Vann, but the mammoth was struggling to comprehend the lock, which was now half open. Its doors were swinging apart, the heavy hinges screaming an unholy chorus that would shatter glass. The pengish soldiers were getting closer, and Gorm was looking at them with her hair flying in a stream.

Rob vomited over the side of the ship, pain and agony becoming like new chains. He looked around wildly and then made a decision.

"Vann! Gorm!" he shouted as loudly as he could. "Get behind the mammoth!"

"The beast's gone mad!" Vann objected.

"Just do it!" Rob turned to Ilma. "Point us at the gate."

"But it's not open yet!" she said.

"We'll go through," Rob said. "Alya thinks this ship's special, let's put it to the test."

"Yes," Alya snarled. "But we need speed to smash through the lock."

"We don't need to smash it, just push it. It will work. It has to."

"And do you have anything at all to back this claim?"

"Trust me."

"No! Prove it, give me something." Alya hissed the words.

The roof cracked, and stones fell into the water, the waves slamming against the ship and making it lean. The lock was still opening, water draining through it faster and faster. Vann and Gorm had dived behind the mammoth, which was screaming and stamping on the wooden gates, splintering the walkway.

The pengs at the other side were holding halberds and shaking. They looked to the mammoth, then the fire, and then at the ship, which was coming at them.

"This is all we've got, Alya! Vann! Gorm! Get ready!" Rob ran to the port side and threw a rope over it. The pengs saw, and some of them dove into the water.

Fire ripped the cavern roof again, and more rocks slammed around them. A stalactite cracked above Rob's head and plummeted; he dove out of the way and it shattered against the ship's deck.

Blinking at this incredible sight, he backed away on his hands and knees. Alya pulled Rob to his feet and shoved him at the railing.

"You want to rescue those two fools, get on with it!" she shouted. "Ilma, hold the lever. Your life depends on it."

The ship swung towards the lock, and Rob gave Vann and Gorm a desperate look. The bear's head was looming over the sheer drop that came after the gate and then the bow hit the wood. Shaken, Rob toppled, and Ilma screamed; more rocks were falling.

Vann had leapt onto the rope and was climbing, but the swarming pengs were getting closer. Some shot onto the shore, the mammoth roared and swung her great tusks, backing onto the bank, away from the water. Gorm gave a shout and tried to move as lock cracked, fracturing.

At that, the lock broke, and the water was forced down, dragging the ship in a frothing torrent. The ship turned and hit the sides of the lock before leaning into the waterfall; Rob clung to the railing and hoped his strength would hold as they fell.

His stomach left his body, and his blood felt light, but the air was harsh and cold, scraping his skin as they plummeted. Gorm was running across the broken lock, and she leapt, pitching towards the ship.

They hit the plunge pool with a deathlike thud. Rob let go of the railing and fell, but Alya pulled him up just as the ship righted. Ilma screamed again, but this time it was for Gorm who slammed into the deck, her body falling limp as she rolled.

Rob broke out of Alya's grasp and went over the Gorm. She was breathing, but unconscious. Her left arm was dislocated, and she was bleeding from a head wound. He waved Ilma over, and she manipulated Gorm's arm into her shoulder. Gorm screamed, waking and sitting straight.

The ship rocked again and slammed against spikes of stone. They were being dragged down into a subterranean tunnel that churned with white rapids.

"Gorm, are you okay?" Rob shouted.

"No time," said Alya, yanking Rob to his feet. "We are not out of it yet."

Chapter Eighteen

Flight From Frost

The underwater river raged with foaming rapids, tearing the ship to the left and right as they slammed into rock after rock. Rob ran to the side where Vann was swinging on the rope. He hauled him up, straining with the weight of the man until he tumbled over the railing and clung to Rob in a panicked embrace.

"I'm dead," Vann said. "I've been killed. Look at me! I'm dead."

"If only," said Alya. "Get on the wheel and make use of your body while you still have it."

Vann staggered to the wheel while Ilma was struggling with her pack, but the thrashing and shaking floor sent her equipment flying. Rob stumbled to the bowsprit and peered into the waters. The level was rising at an alarming rate, eating into the rocks and drowning them.

"Where does this river lead?" he asked.

"There should be an outlet that will spill us onto the docks," Alya replied from Gorm's side. "I need to know if it has gone to plan."

"I don't think it has," Rob pointed into the water. "The water isn't getting out; it's rising."

"Razal's shield!" Alya sprinted to his side and glowered at the river. "We may have only minutes."

"Before what?"

"Either the opening will be blasted, or we will be crushed against the ceiling. A fine choice."

"What do you mean, 'blasted'?"

"Gorm's task was to open the wall blocking this river from the dockyard using the highly concentrated blasting powder I gave her. If she did not succeed, then we may all die."

Gorm was mumbling, blood gushing from the wound on her head while Ilma tried to bandage it. She was thrown as the ship hit another set of rocks, Vann stumbled from the helm, and Rob and Alya clung to one another in the increasing turmoil.

"This plan of yours," Rob said, pulling the both of them away from the bowsprit "Did you have a backup?"

"Just one." She lifted her shirt and revealed that she had a sack of the blasting powder tied to it. "If I cannot have this ship, then nobody will."

"You'll kill the others, too!"

"We either die being crushed under rock, or we die in fire, and I choose fire!"

"But shouldn't the others get a say?"

"They are free to stay or go, but I will not allow my ship to be taken again."

"Why not use that powder to open the wall from this side?"

"The rock is weaker on the outside, so I planted some there; five sacks camouflaged against the stonework. It will only work if something sets them all off." Alya said.

Rob glared at the ceiling and then at the river around them. "How long until we hit this wall?"

The ship slammed into stone, throwing them off their feet. Rob's shoulder hit the deck with the force of a tidal wave and his joint shuddered in the socket. He got to his feet and rushed to the starboard side; the ship had been forced to turn in against the wall, and got jammed there while the water rose.

The ceiling was full of cracks and fissures; he bit his lip and turned to the others. Vann was on the floor next to the helm, shivering and crying into his hands while Ilma and Gorm were by the main mast. Alya ground her teeth and looked at Rob, almost expectantly.

"I don't choose to die like this," he told her. "And when we get out of here, we will have a very long talk about threatening death." He strode to Gorm's side. "Gorm, can you hear me?"

"I hear many things," she said, barely audible over the roaring waters.

"Can you tell me what happened? Why did the plan to blast the walls fail?"

"I was seen and pursued before I could complete the task." She managed to open her eyes though they were blurred and distant. "I entrusted the blasting powder to a trasati-bird."

"What?" Alya stamped her foot and screamed in frustration. "You gave the fire to a bird? What is wrong with you?"

"They seemed perfectly capable of carrying out the task."

"You were wrong then." Alya pulled Rob to his feet and shoved him against the mast. "You filled Gorm's head with these ideas! If you hadn't, we'd all be alive."

"We are still alive." Rob sprang away from her. "And I will make sure we stay that way. I have a plan."

"Care to share?"

"I will blast this wall open." He leapt off the ship and onto the wall, his hands clasping the stone.

He climbed, his bones singing with new strength. He didn't care where it was coming from, he didn't care that his wound was burning hot, and he didn't care that Alya was shouting more insults at him.

The fissures in the ceiling were just large enough for him to clamber into, so he hauled his body through a gap. It wound in spirals that made him bend his back in painful ways, but he kept going. He had climbed through earth before. He set his hands in every hold and dug his fingers into the gritty holes. His feet slipped, and he caught on a protruding stone, but he managed to maintain his place though his heart leapt into his throat.

Light was ahead, but there was a stinking, sulphur taste on the air. Rob forced his way towards the exit, heat rising in a sudden assault.

The fissure ended, and he staggered out onto the side of the cliff. There was a walkway below, and he slid to it though smoke frothed into his eyes and he coughed. Breaking out of the worst, he stopped, his muscles tightening at the sight before him.

The city was above, fire raging from walls and houses. Green and red tongues of flame ripped through the streets and buildings that were engulfed. Pengs screeched, the sky roiled with raging smoke, and the roaring of the fire made the world seem like it was collapsing around him.

He was atop a wall that ran before the dockside. Leaning over it, trying desperately to ignore the noises and heat coming from the city, he peered at the stonework. He swept his vision back and forth over it again and again; there he saw it, a bundle of sacks dangling some ten feet away.

The sky was choked with smog, and the air was so hot that Rob was slick with sweat. His skin screamed at the sudden change in atmosphere, but he tried to keep his pain and discomfort at bay and focus on trying to get to the bundle.

"You!" the voice came from above.

A peng in red armour was glowering at him from a higher level, the wall she was standing on crumbling and coated in smoke. Rob tightened his fist as the Blood Pengs rushed down, screaming in several languages.

Rob whistled and chirruped as loud as he could, directing his voice into the air, hoping it would rise over the noises of destruction. The trasati-birds would be around somewhere, he hoped, they would likely be circling and waiting for carrion to eat when the fire died.

"Sardan, you are supposed to be dead!" It was Kerrok; her bloody armour was dented and coated in smoky dirt as she ran along the walkway.

"Sorry to disappoint," he called back.

She leapt onto him, and his back hit the edge of the wall with a sharp impact. He coughed, but could not regain his balance as she put her feathery hand over his mouth and lifted her knife. Rob panicked and put all his strength into his legs, launching the both of them into the breaking wall that rose above them. Kerrok screamed and dug her beak into his shoulder, biting hard. The pain was blinding, but he threw her off, tearing his coat as he did so.

She whistled, and more pengs in red came hurrying through the smog. Rob slid away, his heart rampaging in his chest, beating his ribs as if to crack them open. The pengs rushed at him, and he ran at them, he leapt and kicked one of them in the face, but the beak caught his shin and he fell, clattering on top of another. The pengs were swarming over him, beaks pecking, knives drawn.

Something whistled and screeched; Kerrok was pecked in the eye and fell back, bawling at the top of her lungs. The Blood Pengs jumped away from Rob in a rage. A flutter of green feathers passed, and the trasati-bird settled on Rob's chest, spreading her wings protectively.

One of the pengs went to help Kerrok, but the others glared at the trasati-bird, their beady eyes meeting hers in an exchange that mirrored the inferno. Rob's innards sang with relief, but his mind flew to the ship below, still waiting to be crushed.

Rob got up, taking the bird in his arms. A pouch was tied to one of her feet, which he removed carefully. Kerrok hissed, bleeding and coughing as smoke reached them and the heat rose. Rob backed to the edge of the wall; the bird still clutched in his arms. The bird struggled and shot out of his grasp, landing on one of the pengs and making her fall, yowling.

The other Blood Pengs tried to attack, but the trasati-bird flew, whistling and chirping as she fluttered onto Rob's shoulder. He glared at the pengs, his feet on the edge of the wall. Glancing down, he saw that he was above the sack Alya had left.

"What are you doing here?" Kerrok demanded. "Why are you alive?"

"Very deep questions!" Rob lifted the pouch and twisted it between his fingers. It grew hot, stinging his hand.

"You did this?" Kerrok's eyes widened. She screeched and ran at him, but Rob dropped the pouch and leapt after it.

He dug his hands into the side of the wall, hoping against all hope that he would hang on. His fingers slid into a crack in the surface just as he felt the explosion. His eyes were shaken in his skull, his bones felt splintered, and a blinding light burst from below. The wall disintegrated, and green flame mingled with red. Alya had added something to this bag of powder, he realised.

Water howled through the hole and the Bear burst forth. Rob let go and plummeted, wind hitting him as fire rushed past. Water sprayed, and rocks clipped his skin, but he hit the deck just behind the wheel, he slid to the railing and slammed into it with a painful crunch.

The ship was carried forward on a ferocious torrent that hurtled through the streets like a stampede of mammoths. Rob struggled and grasped the wheel; Vann was clinging to the bottom of it, his head against the floor. Alya and the others were hanging onto the mast, but Rob waved to them and grinned.

Alya looked at him with eyes so wide he was sure they would fall from her face. She turned away and flung her hands around the mast as water splashed her feet.

Houses and towers passed as the water carried them further and further, the docks getting closer and closer. Rob clung tight to the wheel and turned it with the flow of the water, guiding the ship as best he could, though the sheer force was doing a lot of the work for him.

"Alya!" he shouted. "We need to get the sails up!"

Rob let her pass to the levers where she struggled to lift them and turn the cogs. The ship was straining and groaning in the total madness of the water, which propelled them down, down, and down again, slamming against the sides of buildings, which burst at their touch.

The water poured them over the dock wall, and they leaned over dangerously. Rob's stomach shifted, his throat closed, and the ship crashed, prow first, into the floor of the docks, sending a shockwave through the whole structure.

Screaming pengs fled but the waters continued pouring, thrusting the ship onto the ice, which cracked and shattered under their weight.

"Get up!" Alya screamed at Vann. "This is no time for your incompetence!"

Vann raised his head and met Rob's eyes. There was such deep and hollow fear in his face, a terror he had rarely seen.

"Do as she says," Rob advised. "We're so close!"

Vann peeled away from the wheel, but the ship rocked, water pummelling the back while ice groaned and fractured at their front. Rob looked over his shoulder; there were armed pengs running towards other ships on the docks, some carrying gigantic crossbows. Teams of rower pengs were already stationed on some boats, and the great paddles were moving in seconds.

"Go!" Rob yelled as his lungs turned acidic. "We have to go now!"

"I am aware of this!" Alya spat back.

The ice was breaking, the water was pushing them, but not fast enough. Pengish longships were moving, their giant crossbows turning to face them. Rob shook the wheel as if this would move them any faster.

"We can't fail now," he said. "We can't! We've come so far! We're so close!"

A spear thrummed and soared past his head. The pengs were nearer, the fastest ship closing in as thirty oars moved simultaneously, dragging them through the ice.

Alya gasped; the levers moved, the masts shifted unfurling their sails.

The wind hit and Rob was forced back as the ship tore through the ice. Another spear soared, missing the mainsail by less than an inch. The pengs upped their speed, oars crashing through ice and churning it into slush.

But Alya's ship was flying, smashing through the frozen water until they broke out of its grasp. The pengs did not give up; they broke into a frantic rhythm and more crossbow bolts were hurled. They bounced off the hull, skidded along the deck and plunked into the waters as if they were nothing.

The ship edged further away, the pengish ships falling behind. There was no way they would catch up, Alya's ship was too good. Behind, the white lands fell away, fading into a haze. The land of their imprisonment had no more hold over them.

Rob roared with relief, picked up Vann and kissed him full on the mouth. The smaller man wrapped his arms around Rob and held him tight. The euphoria rushing through the air was bursting forth in sparks, and when they broke apart, they laughed uncontrollably.

Rob sprang onto the railing, waving his hat at the pengs as they sank behind them. "Thank you for this kind gift," he shouted. "We will use it well. Tell your Empress that her prison has been broken. Tell anyone who will listen that we escaped. And tell Mothar the Pirate Lord that Rob Sardan is coming for him. I broke the Sea-Stone Sword, and I will break him!"

The sea stretched before them, an open horizon of endless blue so deep it seemed to go on forever. The wind filled the sails, roaring with triumph. The ship hurtled faster, and the whole world spread before them.

They were free.

Chapter Nineteen

Captains

Rob knelt by the bowsprit, his hat in his hand and his eyes closed. Wind ran through his loose dreadlocks, his skin prickled at the cool sea air, and his muscles twitched at the future springing to life before him.

'*I have returned*,' he thought. '*I am back on the sea, where I belong*.'

The thought made him smile so absolutely that it hurt. But he did not care. He was out, he was free, he was on a ship with a crew, and they were safe. A storm of needles hummed within him, but he ignored them, and he ignored the pain in his abdomen. For now, he just wanted to breathe.

He wondered what had happened to the mammoth. They had taken it from the cells, only for it to be trapped in the collapsing cavern. He had seen it move away from the water, deeper into the shadows, but then he had been distracted. The sounds of the creature's mourning cries shivered in his mind. He took another breath and calmed his heart.

"What in Razal's name were you playing at?" Vann was shouting. Rob looked over to see he was ripping the blasting powder out of Alya's grasp. "You wanted to blow us up? After everything that happened you tried to kill us! If Rob hadn't saved us, you were going to burn us?"

Alya threw the last sack of powder at him and strode away, stopping at the railing and hiding her face from them. Vann stormed to the other side of the ship and tossed the sacks overboard before meeting Rob's eye and smiling, his cheeks darkening before he turned away.

Rob hobbled towards him, but Vann was already climbing up to the quarterdeck to take Ilma's place at the helm. Gorm gave Rob a knowing look and then shook her head before nodding to Alya, who was hunched over the railing and shivering. Rob took the hint and went to her.

"Care to talk?" he said, breathing slowly as the pain in his abdomen spiked. "What you did was *not* okay. All the spite and jibes are one thing, but you threatened to kill us back there."

"I know," she said quietly. Her eyes were bloodshot, and her throat pulsed as she gulped. "I apologise."

"You should . . ."

"What? I should apologise publically to everyone and beg their forgiveness? That will not change the past; it will not make them like me, and it will not make this crew any better than it already is so what would be the point?"

"Alya." Rob tried to put a hand on her shoulder but she flinched, and he stopped. "This ship means a lot to you, doesn't it?"

"More than anything," she said as she ran a hand along the railing. "You have no idea what I sacrificed to make this ship. You have no idea what I lost . . ."

"So you did lose someone?"

"No," she said as she turned to face him, hardening her expression with a great effort. "I was betrayed. I was betrayed by friends I thought I could trust, by people I wanted to be with, and by those I had considered closer than kin."

The sea hissed, and the wind snapped at the sails, but Rob could only focus on Alya as she steadied herself in the rolling waves. He looked back out to sea, letting her decide whether or not she would stay. After a few moments, she leant on the railing, her shoulders heavy and her back bent.

"Understand; this was the culmination of years," she said. "Ever since I was a girl I dream about this ship; the cogs, the levers, even the bear on the front. I drew plans when I was six years old, and I never stopped drawing them, perfecting them. Even when my sister pulled me away to go on her adventures, I just wanted to build my ship. Then, one day, I found myself in Emerald Port, and someone offered me the chance to make it real.

"I promised them a ship to surpass all others. They were eager, they were friendly, and they accepted me without question. That should have been my first clue. They never questioned me, never doubted me, and did everything I said. They complimented me, told me I was perfect. Even when an accident left one of the team without legs."

"What happened?"

"I was careless." She shook her head. "A mistake I swore never to make again. It was a mistake I should have been chastised for, but they never made a move against me. I thought they were just kind. I thought they were my friends."

"But as soon as the ship was complete," Rob sighed. "They turned on you."

"More than that," she seemed to be struggling but kept talking. "They tore down my reputation. Spread lies amongst those I had journeyed from my homeland with, until even they turned on me. People as close as kin treated me like a beast; they chained me, beat me, and tore everything from my life. Then they sent me to Bron'Halla as a fugitive."

Rob wanted to comfort her, but at the same time, he still felt the need to chastise her. He looked at her, the strands of hair sticking out of her scarf, the lids under her eyes, and the bruises just visible on her neck.

"They did terrible things," he said. "I can understand why you find it hard to trust. You act like you don't care, like you hate everyone and everything, but I don't think you do. Deep down, I think you miss your old friendships."

"You lost someone you loved," Alya said. "You look back on the times before he died and you know it was real. You know that it was a true friendship. Perhaps it was something romantic, I do not know; that is your business. But I look back at those friendships and I know that it was a lie. Every good memory is turned to hate because it wasn't true. They were playing me, using me, and they betrayed me. That, Rob Sardan, is worse than if they'd died. You should hope that you never experience betrayal. It would destroy you."

"It didn't destroy you," he pointed out. "You survived, and now you're moving on. Look; you're on the ship, with a crew, with people who helped you."

"As if you had a choice," she snorted.

Rob shook his head, but he felt calmer. There was less malice about her. He wondered who exactly it had been that had betrayed her; the pengish empire, perhaps? That would explain why she was so eager to start a civil war. She mentioned folk from her homeland, but that there were others among them.

"You should say something to . . ." Rob began but his ear was suddenly pulled savagely, and his head jerked with it.

Eyes wide, he squirmed as he was dragged along the deck. Between the stairs that would lead to the quarterdeck, there was a wide door that led into the ship, and he was pushed towards it. Turning he saw his assaulter; it was Ilma looking singularly displeased.

"Sit," she commanded, pointing to the floor before the door. "I want you to sit and not move, or I will do something unpleasant to you."

Unsure of what else he could do, he sat; she pulled her satchel off her shoulder and rummaged through it. She lifted a pair of glass plates, one of which was cracked, the other chipped. Grumbling, she connected them into a brass frame that held them apart from one another. Then she lifted his shirt and pulled the bandages away from his abdomen.

"This helps me look at things," she explained, holding the glass close to his skin. "My eyes are not what they used to be. Well, they're still eyes, I suppose, but they are not as *good* as they used to be."

"I did understand what you meant," he smiled, but she prodded his wound, which made his diaphragm spasm. "What was that for?"

"For making me do things," she scolded. "I am very lazy, you know? And that is why I like people to be safe and not do stupid things. The less stupid things you do, the less work for me! I can spend time appreciating the scenery and imagining wonderful adventures."

He sat back and let her explore his cuts and bruises while his eyes wandered up the rigging. The time for wallowing in memories was long since past, he decided. He fixed his eyes on the sky instead and made them focus on the clouds. The world was ahead, a whole set of possibilities.

Gorm was sitting under the main mast, her eyes closed and her face peaceful. She was bandaged and patched more than Rob was, and this gave him pause. Ilma was spreading some ointment on his wounds, but she kept frowning at the hole the knife had made in his abdomen.

"I have bad news," she said at last. "Please don't panic. I think the knife broke inside you. There may be a fragment in the wound."

Rob's mouth went dry. "Can you remove it?"

"Not without considerable pain." She leaned closer, holding the eyeglass firm. "If we hadn't thrown all the numbing concoctions at the pengs during our escape, I would do it now."

"I can take the pain." He took a breath and closed his eyes.

"No, you can't." She patted his cheek, making him look at her. "Do you want to die, Rob?"

"Not particularly."

"You should have died a dozen times in the last few days. That knife may have missed vital organs, but you should have bled more. I am beginning to wonder if something is seriously wrong with your body."

"The fact that it heals so well is surely a good thing?"

"Pain tells us when something is wrong. The more severe the pain, the less likely we are to try something like that again. Healing is important, it teaches the consequences of actions, and it makes us think about what we are doing. Scars are not trophies to impress people; they are marks of our past to teach our future."

"I know that."

"Your leg doesn't hurt you anymore?" Ilma pressed on it and he barely felt it.

"I suppose I stopped thinking about it," Rob said and shrugged. "I'd almost forgotten about it entirely."

"It looks like it's healed up completely," Ilma said, shaking her head. "People don't heal just because they stop thinking about their injuries. That's not how it works!"

"Of course," Alya said. "Far be it for the great Rob Sardan to face consequences for his actions."

"I know you're angry," he said, shifting and making Ilma scowl at him. "But I want to put things right."

"Using this new power of yours? You'll walk up to the Pirate Lord and kill him, is that it?"

"I tried that method, but it didn't work. I'd like to do something meaningful, something to show people that I'm not just a killer, a breaker, and all that Sky-slayer nonsense. That's not what I want to be."

"Is that why you insisted on searching for the Sky Sages?" Alya said and looked over to Gorm and then back again. "You put a lot of people in danger when you broke the Sea-Stone Sword, you know?"

"What choice did I have?" He sat straighter. "It was either that or let the Air King take it. You know what he would have done? He was going to subjugate the world, kill anyone who spoke against him, and drown island after island."

"How do you know this?"

"Because I see the Air King's mind," Rob tapped his head. "Every night I hear his dying thoughts. He wanted to drown the world and wipe out humanity. Not to mention the pengs, draigs, and saurai!"

"And you're the one to save us all?" she said sadly. "I cannot stand heroes. You broke the Sea-Stone Sword, you killed the Air King, and then you ran and hid in Bron'Halla."

"Well, I'm out of Bron'Halla, and I'm in the world. I'm running back to it, in case you hadn't noticed. I want to put a stop to the Pirate Lord; I want to make a difference, and . . ."

"Yes, there will be rainbows and sunshine across the world, I am sure." She massaged her temples and looked tired. "You'll swing a sword, you will jump off mountains, and nothing will ever harm you, not permanently anyway."

"I'm not magical," Rob said. "I can still die, you know!"

"Care to give us a practical demonstration?" Alya stepped closer.

"I thought you were calming down," Rob muttered. "And while we're at it, I'm not the one who wanted to blow us all up, so think about that next time you want to send a jibe my way."

Alya blinked and looked away for a moment, folding her arms and shivering. "We are on the brink of the Farraige Sea and should decide on a course soon, the longer we stay, the more likely it is that the pengs will come after us."

"So what?" said Vann. "We can outrun them."

"True," Alya conceded following him with suspicious eyes. "But we have few supplies, and most of those we do have are designed for pengs."

"We should head for Ginnungagap," said Rob. "The further north we go the less peng-friendly folk will be."

"I agree," said Alya.

"If we skirt Concaedes," Ilma said, "I can pick up some new supplies either in the wild or at any settlement with a decent set of stores."

"Herebealde would be a good option," Alya intoned. "It's closer, and I know some traders who might be interested in certain items."

"Also, there's Vann's sister," Rob said. "We can visit her at the Tomb of the Dead God."

"Yeah," Vann hummed from above. Rob shuffled further up the ship so that he could see him. Vann was at the helm, hands firmly on the wheel. As Ilma huffed and seethed at Rob, he gave Vann a wink.

"Lomi said the secret of the Sky Sages was something 'only the Dead God knew'," Rob went on. "If there's a tomb for this dead god there, it seems like the place to start. Gorm, what about you?"

Her calm expression became uneven. She rubbed at her shoulder and took deep breaths. "I fear what sails the Ginnungagap. My heart is unsettled, my inner being is riled, and all my thoughts are dark when I regard that place."

"Where would you like to go?"

"My desire is for peace; my hope is for tranquillity. But, to be removed from fear, I must face it."

"Skagra . . ." Rob realised.

"Indeed," she breathed softly. "Now we are at sea my fears are growing. I recall Skagra's skills, I recall her thirst for blood and . . ." she shivered. "Perhaps it is best I stay away from her."

"After all this?" Rob got to his feet and shook Ilma off. He approached Gorm and knelt beside her; she kept her eyes on the ground between her feet, breathing slowly and deliberately. "Somebody paid the Blood Pengs to watch you in Bron'Halla. Kerrok was one of them. She was under a contract to watch and then to kill you. I'm willing to bet it was Skagra."

"Knowledge of such things is not within my power," Gorm said.

Rob stood and put his hat back on. "I have my own course in mind. I need the Sky Sages. Gorm needs to face her fear, and the world needs to be free of Skagra. We should go to the Ginnungagap."

"May I ask who decided Rob Sardan was in charge?" Alya asked, her face becoming a storm.

"I'm not in charge," he objected. "We're discussing options."

"But we should have a captain," Vann said, happily. "I'd vote for Rob."

"Me too," said Ilma.

"Aye," Gorm nodded. "I cannot think of a better candidate among us."

"I can," Alya said.

"And where were you when the pengs captured Vann?" Ilma challenged. "You were running around blowing things up and killing people."

"Nobody died," she insisted.

"Rob saved Vann's life," Ilma went on. "He put himself between Vann and the Blood Pengs. He was willing to die to save us. If that doesn't make him captain material, I don't know what does."

"Leadership skills," Alya said. "Knowledge of the sea, knowledge of the ship, an ability to bring people together. Which of us organised the escape from Bron'Halla? Which of us built this ship? Which of us brought this crew together?"

"Rob brought us together," Vann said.

"Only because I asked him to!"

"He *kept* us together," Vann went on. "I'd have left before we even got out of Bron'Halla if not for him."

"That's only because you fancy him," Ilma said. "But he makes a good point."

"I'm too young." Blood flooded Rob's face in embarrassment though he could not help laughing.

"No you are not," Gorm said. "Eighteen is the generally agreed on age for a young captain."

"Only if they have been personally trained by the former captain." Rob shook his head.

"We have no former captain." Gorm stood, towering over the others. "I have no wish to captain this ship or any ship. My desire is for peace, and I cannot attain that if my fears divide me. Rob Sardan, the one who broke the Sea-Stone Sword and fought the Pirate Lord; who killed the Air King, and spoke with the Ocean's Eye. I vote for you!"

"You led us," said Ilma. "It was Alya's plan, yes, but you led us, you kept us together. I vote for you."

"I . . ." Rob fumbled for words. He felt like he should decline, but he was so swollen with joy that he couldn't bear to reject them. And deep down, he wanted it. "Yes. Okay, I'll do it."

"Excellent!" Vann clapped and whooped.

"Captain Sardan," Ilma said with a dramatic bow. "As stupid as you are, I don't think there's anybody else more likely to do everything they can to protect us."

"You are all forgetting something," Alya said. "A captain should be chosen by the whole crew. I do not think Sardan should lead."

"We disagree," said Ilma. "And you can't bully all of us into doing what you want. Not this time. We've made our choice and you should respect that."

"You need to realise and respect what I have done for this crew!" she seethed and balled her fists. "I took us out of the prison at the end of the world. I outsmarted the imperial and renegade pengs. I built this ship. It was my plan. It was my idea."

"You intimidated us," Gorm said. "I admire your mind. You have a great sense of your foes; you have sharp wits and deep insight. Your trust is at war with your fear, and you must master them. What you lack is the ability to make us feel as though you care for us."

"And Sardan can do that?"

"He took a knife for us," Vann said. "He saved us from the Blood Pengs; he called the trasati to help us, he actually cares if we live or die, or were you not paying attention?"

"It was reckless, suicidal, and irrational," Alya spat.

"It's called caring about people," Vann said. "Not that you'd understand that."

"Am I required to become irrational to prove that I care? Why should I have to prove it at all?"

"How else can we trust you?" Ilma asked. "Trust is earned."

"No," Rob said, catching Gorm's eye. "Alya is right. She does not need to prove anything. She did get us out of Bron'Halla, and she did build this ship. I know it means a lot to her, so we shouldn't . . ."

"Don't try and defend me," Alya turned on him, her eyes threatening to rip him in two. "I built this ship, and now you want to snatch it away from me? I cannot let you do that."

"The crew has spoken," said Rob. "Alya, we are not trying to rob you. We are free, and so are you."

"You want me to leave?"

"I want you to do what you want to do. Why did you escape?"

"You know what I escaped for."

"Yes, we have the ship, now what? What was your plan for after we got away? Just sail around aimlessly?" Rob sneered.

Her face darkened. "And what is *your* plan? To take down the Pirate Lord? To release the trasati? To break the Sky-forged Throne and scale the Golden Mountains? Perhaps you should set course for the moon and bring back one of the stars. Or would you prefer us all to sit around and make songs about you and all your great deeds, oh master of wonders?"

"I want to do something with my life, what do you want?"

"I want to be free."

"You are free, now!"

"Am I free from you? No, not while you masquerade as a captain and drag the others with you. You can fight as many pirates as you like, you can wade through blood up to your ankles, you can destroy a thousand tyrants across the seas, but there will be no end to it! I've tried fighting tyrants, but it never ends, a new one always crops up, or else you become one."

'*There are no heroes, only villains who win*,' Rob's mind echoed the old phrase. He had felt the twist of power in his gut. When he had held the Sea-Stone Sword, he had become the very monster he had wanted to fight.

"This isn't a betrayal, Alya," Rob said gently.

"Isn't it?" She shook with rage, her breathing laboured and furious.

"I will not betray you." Rob put his hand against his chest. "I promise you that, please believe me. I'm not like the people who put you in that prison."

"No? You stand there with your pride and your dreams," Alya said as she stepped closer, only an inch from his face. "You are going to lead all of us to death or worse. King-killer. Sky-slayer. Sword-Breaker."

"Don't throw that in my face," he said. "If you are unhappy with the crew's choice, then you *can* leave our ship."

"*This is* my *ship*!" she screamed into his face.

Her eyes were passionate, resolute, and full of the fire of one who is sure they are right. Somewhere in his mind, he thought she was. They looked at one another, cold fury boiling between them. But Rob could not bring his anger to its full height.

Alya turned and strode to the door under the quarterdeck. She pulled it open and slammed it behind her as she vanished into the depths of the ship. Rob gave a slow breath and closed his eyes. She had a right to be angry, and he could only imagine how he would have felt in her position. He wondered how she had been able to contain her anger so much that she did not hit him.

"How far to the Ginnungagap?" he asked.

"I'm no navigator," said Vann. "But it's probably a few days away."

"I can help," said Gorm. "I navigated on occasion. My guess would be that we are somewhere near Bad'Inis."

"We could stop there for supplies," Vann suggested.

"Pengs will be there," Rob said. "We'll need to make our supplies last a bit longer. I suggest we head for Herebealde like Alya said and stock up."

"Herebealde is five days away at least," Gorm said. "Will we make it?"

"I will put you in charge of the food rations, Vann. Let me know if we can get to Herebealde on what we have, I'll make sure we get a long rest once there."

"Sounds good to me," Vann yawned.

"Thinking of rest, I assume there is somewhere to sleep," Ilma stretched and yawned, too.

"Go look. Gorm, Vann and I will keep the ship going. Alya's design seems to have kept it quite simple. She said it was ideal for seven to sail, but we will make do."

"I do not like our prospects," Gorm admitted. "But rest must come or we shall soon make bigger mistakes."

"Let's get to it, then," Rob dismissed them.

"Aye, Captain!" they all said.

Despite everything, despite his wounds, his fears, and his pain, the sound of that word directed at him made him indescribably happy. He beamed at them and bowed, whipping his hat from his head as he did so.

Chapter Twenty

Sunken Silver

Rob walked into the forecastle. The floor was polished and had a bear painted in the centre, its teeth sharp and its claws pointing to the door. On the right there was a chest with gold edging, locked and bolted. On the left, there was a bunk with blue linens bundled over it, torn from their spot by the turbulence the ship had been through.

He fell into the covers, and his head sank into the pillows, they were softer than any he had felt before. Pulling the covers into place he settled and his limbs tingled, the old pains throbbing in a mild hum.

He and Gorm had been struggling to keep the ship going for hours. The pounding energy that had been in his blood had made him leap into action whenever they'd needed it, but he had tired as the sun had gone down. Now he had to rest while Ilma and Vann helped.

Gorm, meanwhile, had decided to talk to Alya. Rob wondered if her prospects were good, but as they had not had any trouble from the shipbuilder, he hoped some progress had been made. He supposed that if anyone could talk sense or clarity into Alya, it would be Gorm.

A pterosaur soared, glowing red eyes piercing him as she snapped her toothy beak. She screeched so loud that Rob's ears burst and his skull became a fractured ruin. A shock of red wind pummelled him, thrusting him into the rocks before he fell into wrathful waters.

Then he was underground, surrounded by bubbling molten rock. Gold was melting from the ceiling and a lone figure stood in the centre of the chaos. She was crowned with a black crown, an amber gem glimmering as she turned. Her hair was a tangle of flailing dreadlocks, and her skin was even darker than Rob's.

Her face was almost skeletal, her eyes were empty, and she reached a bleeding hand towards him. Rob backed away, but the creature took a step closer, mindless and groaning, driven by some animating power.

The Crown of Black Glass steamed, heat pulsing from its shimmering surface as vicious claws dug into the woman's head. Blood should have come from those wounds, but all was dry and empty. She was like a corpse, moving only because the Crown willed her to.

Pale sunlight was resting on the bunk and he tried to move his head. The dreams still echoed, getting weaker with every rise and fall of the ship. The space around his neck where the Sky-slayer's pendant had once hung felt more naked than ever.

Getting to his feet, he found that he had been bandaged again, and there were new patches on his clothes. Walking was easier than it had been and he congratulated himself on gaining his sea legs so quickly.

Pushing out of his cabin, he shielded his eyes with his hat and took a breath of the salt air. The wind held a chill that buffeted and prickled the skin, so he tightened his coat and buttoned it. As the sunlight became more bearable to his eyes, he realised what was nagging his mind; the ship was hardly moving. The sails were down, and the waves were calm.

"Captain!" Ilma called from the quarterdeck. "We couldn't wake you."

"Why have we stopped?" He approached the railing and leaned over, peering into the clear blue water.

"We couldn't handle it," she said. "This ship, it's small, it's clever, but there were only three of us. If we're going to sail, we need all five of us working on it non-stop. We just can't do it."

"Where are we?"

"Somewhere in the Farraige Sea, north of Bad'Inis."

Rob frowned at the sky. There were clouds on the northern horizon, swirling and purpling with thunderous rain.

"You were out cold," Ilma went on. "Without Alya's help, we'd have been flying blind. You've been unconscious all day, Captain."

A string of ice shivered down his spine, and he closed his eyes. What use was a captain who fell unconscious? Had they all made a terrible mistake in choosing him? His hand clasped his chest, determined to fill the void as soon as possible.

"Your injuries must have kept you out," she said, eyeing his hand as it grasped for the pendant that wasn't there.

"Alya helped, then? I'm amazed she hasn't stabbed me."

"I doubt she would do that. The rest of us would turn on her in a snap if she did. She came up a few hours after you went to sleep and gave a bit of help. Not much, mind. She loves this ship too much, and I think she respects you, in a strange, twisted way."

"How'd you work that out?"

"When you asked her not to kill during the escape, she listened. She took pains to make sure we were not responsible for any bloodshed."

"She helped start a rebellion; I'm supposed to believe nobody died?" Rob said.

“That rebellion had been brewing for years.” Ilma leaned against the railing and blew her grey hair from her face. She gave him a pat on the arm and looked into his eyes. “Anyway, how are you feeling?”

“Are you trying to change the subject?”

“Evidently.” She nudged him with her hip. “Any pain in the right arm, stiffness in the neck, or a bruising of the fingernails?”

“I feel good. You’re good at your job.”

“Not *that* good. Though, I don’t mind praise. Please continue.”

“Did you get the shard out?”

“No,” she frowned. “I hesitate to do anything until I’ve got proper tools. Normally I’d get it at all costs, but normally you would be dead by now, given the things you’ve done the past few days.”

“Days?” He laughed. “Less than a week ago we were all still in Bron’Halla, whiling away the hours of days that never ended.”

He gave Ilma a quick hug and headed for the quarterdeck.

Gorm greeted him with a bow and went back to sweeping her eyes across the horizon. They stood together, listening to the wind, the sea sighing and hissing around them, and the singing trasati-birds.

Breathing softly, Rob looked over the ship. Ilma, Vann, and Gorm, they were his crew, his friends, and this ship was his. He hoped Alya would come to be one of them, too. He felt guilty. She had a mind for planning, for strategies, and for getting to a goal. Despite her sharp words and dismissive demeanour, he suspected that she cared a great deal. She certainly cared about the ship, and he thought he could understand why.

Vann, though, was young and inexperienced. He was cheerful, beautiful, and lively to the point where Rob envied him. There was youthful naivety in him; it reminded him of Niall, the boy Rob had been in love with in Khamas. He remembered the promise he had made. He had promised to make him his first mate. Niall had also promised to make Rob *his* first mate, too. The memory made him laugh quietly.

"I am glad that you have joy," Gorm said, soft and slow.

"I have friends," he said. "It sounds silly and like something from a story. But this is the life I wanted, and it seems to be, actually real. Strange that my real life should now be so dream-like while my dreams are now the horrors of my past. I used to dream of the sea, and to dream about the future. Now I'm here, on a ship, with a crew, heading for Razal-knows-where, I dread sleep."

"Then we must both face our fears," Gorm advised. "I look at that sea, and I see my death coming like a storm. I see my fate clawing at the door of life, and it seems as if I may drown. I know Skagra is out there, and she is waiting. I know that when I face her, she will kill me. I wish to be ready."

"We don't have to let that happen," Rob put his arm around her shoulders though he had to stand on his toes to do so. "Skagra, Mothar, all the people who would do us harm, we can beat them."

"Do you mean 'kill them'?"

Rob let go and grasped the railing. The smooth wood was firm, and he could barely feel the grain. The ocean spray was a concoction of salt and sweat that rushed into his nostrils as he breathed deeper.

"Can we find another way?" he asked. "If we can, we'll take it." Rob looked at her and he envied her apparent ease. "How is Alya doing?"

"Betrayal is raw and it seems to have cut into her like a flaming blade. However, there is a streak of something within her, a desire for friends. If her harsh words were true, she would not have spoken so openly. When she cried out in anger, that was truth and it was her heart made clear. I believe her words tend to be a cloak, a shield to hide behind."

"What's she hiding from, then?"

"I doubt she knows. As I told you, fear has moved in where trust ought to be."

Thunder roared on the horizon and Gorm put the spyglass to her eye. Rob felt exhausted by the conversation. He followed her gaze and saw that she was intent on a dark spot under the clouds.

"What is that?" he asked.

"A ship. It seems to be in some trouble. I am attempting to determine if there are any people onboard."

"Why didn't you say anything?"

"Your concern for Alya was more pressing."

"We need to get closer!" Rob ran to the main deck and skidded to the door into the aftcastle. The stairs were cramped and he had to duck into the cargo deck; there was a lantern swinging above his head and he turned around and headed back along the passage that ran through the middle of the ship. It opened on either side to the crew's quarters. Within, he found Vann and Alya sitting on bunks, their hushed voices stopping mid sentence as he came bustling in.

"There's a ship," Rob said.

"I know," Vann replied, lying back. "We're on it."

"There's *another* ship." He pulled Vann out of the bunk. "It looks stranded, so we're going to investigate. If there's anyone on board we need to get them off before the storm hits and tears them to pieces."

Sighing heavily, Vann brushed his trousers and followed Rob. Footsteps told him that Alya had joined them. He looked at her over his shoulder, but her face was downcast and her arms tightly folded.

"You don't have to come," he said. "I thought you didn't approve of reckless heroics and such."

"I don't," she said. "But this other ship may have supplies. Besides, you'll never get close without my help."

"Good of you to offer."

"I am not overly eager to die of starvation. Or to die at all."

On the main deck, they gathered around the mast and Rob put his hat on, shading his eyes from the sun as it climbed over them. The other ship was dangerously close to the storm and the wind was already picking up.

"Gorm, take the helm," he ordered. "You've got the experience and that's what we need. Vann, Ilma, you take the ropes; Alya and I will keep the sails in order."

"Will we?" Alya tilted her head. "I would be better at the helm, from there I could instruct the rest of you in how to steer."

"But you know how the levers work properly, and I need to learn."

"An emergency is no time for lessons; Gorm should work the cogs as she knows them already from my instructions."

"All right, Alya and Gorm should take the levers while I take the helm."

"I already told you that I . . ."

"And I gave you my orders, are you going to be difficult?"

Alya gave him a cool glare and then shrugged before walking to the quarterdeck and taking a position by the levers. Rob breathed easier and nodded to the others who took their places as he went to the helm.

"Understand this," he said to Alya as he passed her. "You know this ship and I respect that. But this crew chose me, and as long as you are here it would be nice if you didn't show barefaced disrespect in front of them."

"Why? Is your grasp of leadership so feeble that it is destroyed by logical questions?"

"Isn't all leadership?"

She started at his humour and then gave a reluctant smile.

The sails unfurled and the ship groaned into motion as they caught the wind. Waves rose and the howling storm grumbled on the horizon. Rob took the wheel firmly, though it fought him.

"Move with the wind," Alya insisted.

"The wind will blow us off course!"

"No, go with it and then we'll swing around to get them, like we did on the snow ships. This isn't a coastal run, this is the open sea; you can't just point and go."

"This is true," Gorm said, nodding. "The storm is a vortex that swirls about a central point."

"It looks small for a storm." Rob peered at it with scepticism.

"I suspect it is an Air-keeper's storm," Alya said. "They are common since their king was killed."

Fear sank claws into Rob's spine. His hands froze on the wheel, cold nibbling at his fingers as they strained to turn and follow the swirl of the tempest. The wind filled the sails and they shot through the waves, leaping at times as the prow soared.

Rain pelted them in a sudden onslaught, a thunderous roar broke the air, and the sea rose in calamity. Alya shouted to Vann and Ilma to hold the lines in place while she and Gorm turned the levers, which twisted the mast ever so slightly. Rob left them to it, keeping his attention on the storm as it loomed, lashing harsher and harsher with wind and rain.

The world was dark and thick, water above, below, and swirling in a soup of fury. The ship leapt, dove, and was slammed by waves. Vann and Ilma slid on the main deck, tying the jibs and pulling ropes into place as Alya called to them.

Whirls of white gushed over the starboard side, drenching them. A rope whipped out of control and struck Ilma and Vann in the chest, knocking them down. More jibs loosened and the sails slid from their places; Rob yelled at Alya, and she leapt to the wheel while he bounded over the deck and grasped one of the ropes.

Securing the lines, Rob turned back into the fray. Saltwater pummelled his face from the foredeck, which was being assaulted by waves as tall as hills. Rob pulled Ilma up and then went to help Vann.

"We're dead!" he cried. "We should go back; we shouldn't have tried this, what's the point?"

"Trust me," Rob shouted through the screaming wind. "Please, Vann, there could be people in trouble on that ship."

"And there could be nothing on the ship, too! We don't know!"

"We soon will."

Their quarry loomed closer. It was larger than their ship, its hull light grey and ornate, but it was partially burned. The main mast had been snapped and there was a hole in the prow; the more the ship bobbed and moved, the more water flowed into the hull.

"It's sinking," Rob shouted from the bowsprit. "We need to hurry!"

"Thank you for your statement of the blindingly obvious," Alya cried back.

Rob ran to the wheel, leaping up the stairs. Alya backed away with a glower and went back to fixing the lines that ran from the aft to the main mast. Gorm gave the both of them a disappointed frown.

The ship was on their portside, closing as it rose and fell in the storm. Rob turned the wheel, and they heaved and groaned around, the weight of the ship pivoting about the middle. The mast strained, and the sails shot back on themselves.

"Lower the sails!" Rob shouted. "We'll overtake them if we don't!"

Ilma and Vann hauled the sails down while Alya and Gorm tied the jibs behind the aftcastle. The other ship was tumbling closer, the waves crashing against its hull with increasing force. Water gushed over its decks, and a lightning strike showed that it was covered in debris from fallen masts.

Rob let go of the wheel and allowed Alya to take it while he sprinted to the forecastle. He took a length of the strongest rope he could lay his hands on and turned to the sinking ship. He tripped on the slick, wet deck, but recovered quickly enough to see Vann being slammed into the railing as the boat lurched again. The wind was battering them, hurling barrages of waves at their hull and masts with a frequency that made Rob suspicious.

The prow turned, and the bowsprit speared towards the starboard hull of the other ship. Rob clung to his rope, but when the vessels hit, he was flung overboard, his hands slipping on the already soaked line. He got his grip and was hurled against the side of their boat, coughing and heaving air into his lungs.

The sea billowed beneath his feet, stretching to grasp him with straining tentacles. The sky was a war of sound, chaotic clouds flinging their weight against each other. With a squeal, the ship turned against their quarry, a heavy wall of solid wood racing towards him. Rob swung and leapt onto the opposite vessel's hull, clambering as it slid past their own.

Alya's ship was stronger than this new one. It dented the wood of the hull, and he wondered what it would have done at speed. He dug his fingers into the crumbling wood; the burns and gashes in the hull were large and claw-like.

Rising, he breathed harder until he reached the railing. Once he was on the main deck, he was thrown and pummelled by more water as the ship lurched. The clouds broke into screaming wind that shook what was left of the masts until one of them shattered, raining splinters of wood.

Rob fought his way to his feet and turned just in time to see his own ship slam into the hull again. Alya and Gorm were knocked against the railing while Ilma and Vann stumbled against the mast.

Pain shot into Rob's back, and he was thrust against the deck. His arms were pinned behind him, and a rusty knife flashed in front of his eyes. Pressure built as someone put a boot on his neck.

"Come back to finish us off?" the voice was squeaky and panicked, but the force with which he was held down made Rob uneasy.

"Nobody is finishing you off, we're here to help," he tried to say more, but his lungs were being compressed by his assailant who now leaned on him.

Feet hit the deck, and Vann was shouting, but Rob lifted his head just enough to catch his eye and stop him in his tracks. The person holding him slowly pulled him up and turned him around.

She was shorter than Rob, wide and fierce, her hair a tangled mess of braids and dreadlocks. Her velvet jacket was deep red and set over a torn white shirt that had once had frills. She had a set of knives on a belt that hung at her hips.

"No flag," she said, nodding to the ship. "Who are you?"

"My name is Rob Sardan, and that is my ship," he said.

"What's your ship called?"

"I . . ." his mind fell blank.

"It's called Fat Ted," said Vann.

"No, it is not called Fat Ted!" Rob glowered. "It doesn't have a name yet; we only got it two days ago."

"This your first mate?" she gestured to Vann.

"We, well, we don't have a first mate yet."

"Well then, Rob Sardan, Captain of the nameless ship." She scowled, but at that moment they were hit by another rolling wave.

Tumbling, she landed on top of Rob, crushing him into the deck; he pushed her off and leapt up, staggering and shaking off the shock. Red streaks ran through the gaps in the sky, and something with wide, nightmarish wings flew past. A needling cold hit his stomach, his head felt like fire, and his hand went to his chest.

"Get back on the ship!" he ordered. "Take . . . you . . . what's your name?"

"Kari Harshwater," said the woman. "And I am not leaving the Long Silver."

"There's a bloody Air-keeper here, it'll kill all of us as soon as it gets a chance. My ship can still sail, this one is sinking, and you need to go!"

"You're not my Captain!" Kari drew a knife. "Not alone, I won't go without . . ."

"Without who? Where's the rest of the crew?" Rob demanded. "Is there anybody else on board? Please! We can help! Let us help you!"

"You're pirates," she said. "You'll kill us; you'll kill him. Well, you can tell Skagra that we won't join her!"

"Skagra?" Rob let go. "Vann, go below and see if there's anyone there."

"But water's getting in!" he objected.

"Yes, and they might be drowning, so rescue them!"

"No!" Kari ran to the aftcastle and spread her hands before it. "You'll not take him. I won't let you."

"This is getting ridiculous," Alya strode onto the lurching ship and drew her jian. "We are not pirates; we are not mercenaries. We don't even have a name for our ship. But by all means, assume the worst; you can stay on your sinking ship and die that way."

"I'd rather die on the Long Silver with my friend than alone on your nameless ship," Kari wiped at her face, and Rob spotted blood trickling from her hairline.

"What about this other crewmember?" Alya stepped closer. "Do they not want to make their own decision? Let us talk to them."

"No! You'll kill him."

"You're already dead. That pterosaur will tear your ship to pieces."

"Then I die here," she nodded firmly.

"Suit yourself," Alya ducked and clipped Kari's ankle with her foot. She fell, screaming, clutching the injury.

"Razal's beard!" Vann cried.

"I didn't stab her," Alya shrugged.

"Alya, you and I need a word about diplomacy," Rob snarled.

"Yes, because you are so good at it!"

"Vann, go," he snorted. "I will deal with the Air-keeper."

Rob ran to the aftcastle, his head blazing with anger at Alya, raging against her violence. It was almost enough to push aside his crippling fear of the pterosaur. His heart beat faster and his hands twitched to his hip. No, he wouldn't use this blade on the Air-keeper, not if he could help it.

The pterosaur shot past the ship, and a wave of air pummelled the hull, blasting it below the railing. Wood churned in the sea and a screech made Rob cover his ears.

"You!" he shouted. "Air-keeper. Do you know who I am?"

The beast hissed and laughed, skipping another gust to rip what was left of the sails from the Long Silver and worry at those on Rob's ship.

"I am Rob Sardan!" he shouted. "I killed the Air King!"

The glowing eye of the pterosaur came nearer, and it met his stare. The rain eased off, fluttering away from them, momentarily suspended as the Air-keeper hissed past him. Its face turned away, and then it swung a wing at him; Rob dived, rolling across the deck, but a spear of air ripped through the wood.

Splinters and hot wind blasted past him and forced Rob to scramble back onto the main deck. The Air-keeper shot into the clouds and vanished. The storm shivered and broke into a bleeding cascade of red wind that plummeted into the sea, hitting the centre of a whirlpool.

The ship was thrown into the air, Rob clung to the railing and closed his eyes as everything turned red and his skin blazed. With an explosion of bursting timber, they landed. The floor leaned, and he slid, opening his eyes he gasped.

A hole had been blasted in the centre of the deck; water was gurgling in and flooding the ship. Rob leapt back and ran to the door of the aftcastle where Vann was struggling to help an old man up the stairs.

"Who is this?" he asked.

"Don't know," Vann said. "Won't say. Just keeps saying we need to get out."

"Get him on the ship, tell Ilma to help."

"No!" Kari coughed from the port side, her hands clasped around the railing. "Sir, you said we should stay onboard! No surrender!"

"Life," the old man croaked as they came near her. "We can have life."

She stared open-mouthed as Vann helped the old man onto the other ship. Alya was at Rob's side, but she was looking at the sky. The clouds had broken and revealed a dull grey sky with small gaps where blue glinted through.

"The storm's gone," she said.

"Now who's stating the obvious?"

"That Air-keeper was not working alone," she replied, her lip twitching. "If it is not reporting back to somebody, I will be very surprised."

"I have a horrible feeling you're right."

"I usually am."

"Yeah, I noticed."

Chapter Twenty One

Traders' Tales

THE LONG SILVER SANK SLOWLY, GIVING THEM ENOUGH TIME to ransack what was left of its supplies. Much had been burned or lost, but the sacks of grain were a slight encouragement to everyone but Vann, who moaned about a lack of 'good food'.

Rob and Ilma walked the hold of their own ship, tallying the new cargo and calculating how much food they could get out of it and for how long. Ilma had a knack for calculation, and Rob hoped he could learn too. However, the numbers and amounts soon clouded his head, and his temples hurt. But she informed him that they would have enough to get to Herebealde.

Rob headed back to the deck. Alya and Gorm had set the sails, and they were taking the strain of the wind that blew them north. Kari was standing by the starboard rail and watching the Long Silver as it sank.

"How is Jarl?" she asked. "Will he live?"

"Ilma says his injuries are pretty bad," Rob leaned next to her and spoke softly. "Can you tell us what happened? It might help."

"Who are you?" She narrowed her eyes. "A ship without a name or first mate, and a captain who can scare Air-keepers, quite the coincidence you showing up unless you were commanding that pterosaur all along."

"No, I wasn't. I'm a Sky-slayer."

"Seriously?" Her face cracked a reluctant smile. "You're *the* Rob Sardan? The Sword-breaker?"

"That's what they keep calling me." He put his head in his hands. "I don't like it, frankly."

"Well, it's a pretty famous name." She tapped her fingers on the wood, her brow creased. "Why did you come? I want an explanation."

"We happened to see you in the storm," Rob shrugged. "Couldn't leave you. Besides, we were low on supplies."

"Let me see if I understand. You got this ship, no name, no first mate, and no supplies, and then you went into the middle of an Air-keeper's storm to save us? Forgive me for thinking this is a bit hard to believe." She straightened. "How do I know you're not working for Skagra? She's been after these routes for years, and virtually nobody is around to stop her."

"Why not?" Rob asked. "What about the pengs? Don't they patrol these waters? And the traders of Herebealde have their own muscle."

"Two years ago, yeah," she snorted. "Since the Air King died we traders have been bombarded by pterosaurs and pirates nonstop. The pengs don't bother with pirates; they're too busy."

"Not even when they're being attacked? We heard they'd had some blasting powder stolen by pirates."

"If it's true then news isn't getting out."

Rob leant on the railing and let his eyes rove over the ripples and foam that churned around the hull. So Mothar had gained control of the pterosaurs and was using them to increase piracy. He should have expected as much.

"What about the Ginnungagap?" he asked. "That was Mothar's haunt of old, apparently."

Kari eyed him sidelong and drummed her fingers on her belly. "If you are trying to play like you are stupid then it won't work."

"Rob Sardan does not *play* stupid," Alya said from the quarterdeck. "It comes naturally to him."

"Thank you, Alya, that will do," he growled.

She gave him a cool sneer and made her way to the wheel, relieving Gorm, who went to help Vann with the sails. The ship was making good speed, and the wind was steady, carrying them on a smooth course.

Ilma came from the hold, her head bowed and her hands clasped. "Your friend," she said, looking at Kari. "Whatever sickness he has is really, really bad. I mean, most sicknesses are, but this is *very* bad. It's as bad as bad can be, and then add a whole other barrel full of bad."

"I know," Kari said. "Jarl fought with Skagra, herself. I have never seen anyone fight like she does, savage, but precise and surgical."

"That about describes it." Ilma shook her head. "He's been wounded in very specific areas, just above vital organs and arteries. She knew what she was doing, and the blade must have been infected."

"You seem to know a lot about it." Kari leaned closer.

"Your friend needs medical attention," Rob said.

"He's not my friend!" she snapped. "I hated him. He was the first mate on our ship, a bully who didn't like us having a thought of our own. But he was . . . *is* my superior. I am still a member of his crew, and I need to act like it." She rushed into the aftcastle, hardly looking back.

Rob and Alya exchanged a look.

"You had better hope that her misguided loyalty won't lead her to do something stupid," Alya said.

"Such as?"

"Getting us all killed, for example."

"I wouldn't have brought her on board if I thought she'd do something like that, would I?"

"You know as much about her as I do," Alya countered. "Perhaps you ought to learn more, then decide whether or not we're likely to wake up with a knife to our throats."

"It's not her knife I'm worried about." He walked past Alya before she could retort and went after Kari. The light was dull and hazy, but he followed her footsteps until they came to the crew's quarters.

Jarl was on a bunk, his face plastered with sweat while his hands tugged at his beard. With small, awkward movements, Kari settled beside him and whispered something in a language Rob recognised as Cendylic.

"You've been in draigish territory," he said. "You speak Cendylic very well."

"I learn quickly," Kari said. "We've been working for a family in Gwasgar, delivering silk to Cath. Three years we've been on this route, and we've been beaten back time and time again." She snorted bitter laughter. "Perhaps we should be proud it was Skagra who beat us in the end, and not some second rate subordinate."

"That's one way of looking at it," Rob smiled.

"What are you lot doing here?"

"We're looking for the Sky Sages," he lowered his voice and moved closer. "We don't know where they are, but we think there may be a clue in the Tomb of the Dead God. Do you know it?"

"I knew some draigs who worshipped a dead god. Well, worship isn't right. They revere, respect, and adore the dead god."

"Skagra!" Jarl groaned clutching at his covers as sweat beaded on his face. "She poisoned me! Skagra!"

"Hush!" Kari prodded him awkwardly, her face twisted in discomfort. "Skagra is gone; she's not going to hurt you." She looked back at Rob and scowled. "Big, stupid lump that he is I can't bear seeing him suffer."

"Ilma will help," Rob assured her with a pat on her arm, but she threw it off.

"I still don't know if I can trust you. Skagra's witch doctors poisoned our crew; they injected . . . something into them."

"Was it silver?" Rob leaned forward. "Was the substance silver and glowing?"

"No, it was gold."

"Gold?" Rob sat back, astonished.

Gorm had been injected with Saagara in one of Skagra's sick experiments, but now she seemed to have moved on to some other torment. He stood and paced, moving with the rocking of the ship, feeling the rumble of the sea beneath his feet.

"What are you doing?" Kari asked. "Thinking of a way to kill us?" She stood, making the cramped space more claustrophobic. "Perhaps this is all part of the experiment, to see what happens to Jarl, to see if he dies in the most painful manner imaginable. Is that it?"

"We aren't working for Skagra," Rob growled. "Gorm was once one of her crew, but she escaped. Skagra injected her with Saagara, but she got away. You can't imagine the torment it caused her, nor what it caused me."

"Did she inject you, too?" Kari sounded sceptical.

"I held the Sea-Stone Sword. I spoke to Saagara's mind. I held the heart of the Ocean's Eye, and I broke it against the Teeth. I heard the sea god die; I heard it's screaming. I know what it is like to have some god inside you, and I would never, *never* want another person to go through that. Do you understand?"

They looked at one another in the wavering candlelight, Kari's eyes narrowed, and her mouth twitched into a frown.

"If I have any reason to suspect you," she said. "I'll not hesitate to start chopping bodies like Skagra chopped our hull."

"She did what?"

"She rammed our Long Silver with that big galleon of hers. The giant fist of a figurehead smashed right through the wood and burst us apart. They didn't need to do much after that."

"Well, she won't do that to us," Rob said, confidently. "This ship is stronger than any to have ever sailed."

He left, heading back to the main deck as his head developed a dizzying ache. Blinking in the sun, he walked to the main mast where Gorm was tying one of the sails.

"I'd like you to talk to Kari," he told her as she worked. "Jarl seems to have been injected with something like you were."

Gorm froze in the middle of tying a jib. With a sidelong glance at Rob, she bowed and walked towards the cabins, but Rob stopped her.

"It wasn't an order," he said. "If you don't feel able, you don't have to."

"I fear that I may be of little help," she said. "My time with Skagra is a past I wish to leave. But if my Captain asks, I shall do."

"Gorm, you and I have had similar things happen. We have both had Saagara in our veins. I would rather forget it, and I wish I could. But my past is too big to get away from, too much a part of me to ignore. Whatever future I have will be shaped by my past, and so your past will shape your future."

"I wish for a future free of Skagra, free of pain, and free of my past."

"Don't we all? You've given me plenty of advice over the years, and it's time I gave you some. If you run from your past, you are still letting it control you."

She looked at him with her head tilted to the side. After a moment, she laughed and pulled him into a grateful hug. "You are a good student, and a good Captain."

"Yes," he gasped as her grip tightened. "But I would also like to breathe."

She let go, and he coughed but gave her a sheepish grin as she went into the aftcastle. Massaging his arms and chest, Rob went to the bowsprit and peered into the waters that churned around the ship.

His ears filled with the wind. The Air-keepers were still out there, and it seemed that some were under Mothar's command. The Pirate Lord certainly knew about the Sky Sages, and it was unlikely that he would ignore them.

He frowned at the clouds. Though sparse and thin, he had a nagging foreboding sense that grew at the sight. The dreams had never stopped, the screaming and death would follow him every night. He had no choice but to seek the Sages or, at least, to find out what had happened to them.

"Captain!" Ilma shouted from the quarterdeck. "There's a ship approaching."

Rob turned and bounded back up the stairs to where Ilma stood with a spyglass to her eye. She handed it to him and pointed at the shadow that ran along the horizon. It was a galleon, rigged with two dozen sails, a long, black hull, and a figurehead shaped like a fist. Atop the main mast flew a black flag.

"They're coming for us," said Ilma. "What do we do?"

Rob looked at Alya, who was at the wheel, her eyes on him with deep, dark rings under them. "Can we outrun them?" he asked.

"No," she said. "They're a fully rigged ship, designed for speed and long hauls. They will have around a hundred in their crew, so if they meet us, they will outnumber us. They will likely have catapults and crossbows to hurl at us; that will not be so much of a problem, though. My ship can withstand their attacks."

"*Our* ship," Rob corrected. "How long until they get to us?"

"I cannot say for certain," she frowned. "But I can estimate." She paused and creased her forehead. "Twenty minutes."

"Twenty minutes?" Ilma shrieked.

"I suggest we gather the crew," Alya said. "All hands will be needed if we are going to fight."

"We may not need to," Rob said. "I have a plan."

Chapter Twenty Two

The Black Sword

The pirate ship loomed, its dark hull like a wall of starless night, casting them into shadow. Rob swung the wheel to bring them closer; the sails were drawn, and they slowed. The pirates pulled their sails in too, and there was a roar of jeering from above.

Gorm and Kari stood by the main mast, the latter trying to hide, but Gorm was not large enough to be an effective shield. Alya shoved Vann towards the forecastle and settled him near a set of jibs. Meanwhile, Ilma stayed by the bowsprit, her hands on the lines to the sail, but her eyes on the pirates.

A figure stood atop the railing of the pirate ship, her long, black, braided hair fluttering around her dark face. She wore a long coat of tattered cotton, a blood stained shirt that had been unbuttoned to show a chest covered in tattoos and a long necklace of glass vials. Her smile was full of jagged teeth, her eyes flashed with keen amusement, and her nose flared as her crew cheered.

"Ahoy!" she called. "I see you found the traitors of the Long Silver. Are they to your liking?"

Rob let go of the wheel and stood on the railing of the quarterdeck. "I am the Captain of this ship. My name is Rob Sardan. What is your business?"

"Really?" she leered, mockery in her voice. "You know, this is the fifth Rob Sardan this year. Honestly, they're not even trying anymore. If you were Rob Sardan, you'd be at least six inches shorter. I knew Rob Sardan in Khamas; I saw him kill dozens in the mines."

"Believe what you like," Rob shrugged. "Tell us what you want?"

"Jarl," she said. "If he still lives."

"Perhaps," said Ilma. "Tell us who you are and we might tell you more."

"I am under no obligation," she replied. "Sterl, fire at the old one."

Another pirate lifted a crossbow and notched a bolt to it, but as she aimed, Kari leapt forward and screamed.

"Sterl!" she shouted. "Sterl, it's me, Kari, we were shipmates, don't you remember? We were friends!"

"I believe he has betrayed you," said Gorm.

"Oh, my word!" the pirate captain exclaimed, her eyes flicking from Kari to Gorm. "This is a magnificent happening! Gorm Foulheart, as I live and breathe. I had been assured that you were dead." She lifted a knife from her belt and threw it.

With a thud, the blade bounced off the main deck and skittered to Gorm's feet. It was silver, swirling with red ripples where the metal had been folded in forging. The point of the blade was chipped, and Rob's eyes were fixed on it almost hypnotically. It had been gold the last time he had seen it.

The pirate captain crouched on the railing of her ship and then whispered to her subordinates. The pirates looked surprised, but she waved them away and stood, stretching her arms to the sides, giving a few more instructions.

Alya strode to Rob and nodded at some of the lines and then back to the wheel. He shook his head and pointed to the stern and made a circular gesture. She considered and then nodded, but indicated a different angle on the main sail.

Above, the pirate captain was still talking to her crew, many of whom looked disturbed, shifting their feet and letting their eyes roam. Rob wondered if these were new recruits.

"They don't seem to like what she's saying," he said to Alya.

"No," she agreed. "Imagine having a captain with whom you disagree. It hardly bears thinking about."

"Don't start."

With a laugh, the pirate captain strode back to the railing. She took a breath, and with a bend to her knees, she leapt from the ship. Rob gripped the wheel tight in surprise as she plummeted.

She landed with a resounding thud on their deck, the vibrations reaching Rob even though he was several feet away.

"Captain!" some of the pirates shouted.

"It's fine," she said. Standing, she grinned, showing bloody teeth.

Kari growled and pulled a knife; rushing at the pirate she swung hard, but the attack was dodged, and Kari was sent sprawling by a swift punch to her stomach. The pirate sniffed and kept walking as if nothing had happened.

"Hello Gorm," she said.

"Captain Skagra," Gorm said with a nod.

Rob's heart turned to ice. Skagra. Lithe and powerful in every inch of her body, her eyes were sharp as her teeth. He couldn't move; it was as if she radiated intimidation, from the power of her stance to the terror of her voice.

"My, my, you are as tall as ever." Skagra leaned back with her hands on her hips. "And sailing on a very unusual ship, I must say. Where did you get it? I have never seen sails like this, or a design quite so streamlined."

"It's mine," said Alya, drawing her jian. "It was very foolish of you to come alone onto my ship."

"Was it?" Skagra circled Gorm, and as she came close to Alya, she whipped her own sword from beneath her frockcoat. With a lazy flick, she disarmed Alya and kicked her into the railing, pinning her there with her foot.

"Not very good, are you?" Skagra pulled her foot back, leant forward and grasped Alya by the hair before shoving her onto the deck.

Rob jerked, but Skagra had already returned her sword to its scabbard and was back to circling Gorm as if there had been no interruption.

"You live," she said. "Nobody else did. How did you do it?"

"Saagara left my body when the Sea-Stone Sword was broken," Gorm said. Her back was straight, and her hands were behind it. She stood as if she were addressing a superior officer. Rob kept his peace, determined to stick to the plan though Skagra coming onto the ship had been a surprise.

"And what are you doing here?" the pirate went on, waving her crew away as they leaned over to peer at her. "I heard you had been taken to Bron'Halla."

"You know full well what happened," Rob said, attracting her attention at last. "You paid the Blood Pengs to find her and kill her."

"Ah, of course," Skagra laughed. "Yes, I wanted her dead when I discovered a new line of experimentation." She grinned threateningly. "Did you think Saagara was the only power in this world?"

"What about my crew?" Kari said, finally managing to stand and put her weight against the mast. "You tortured us. You took our Captain. You made us . . ." she gulped and tried to speak again. "You made us do things . . ."

"Oh do be quiet," Skagra barked and kicked Kari in the mouth, sending her reeling. "You're making yourself look pitiful."

Rob bounded after Kari and tried to help her, but she pushed him away.

"I knew I shouldn't have trusted you," she hissed.

"Please, I want to get to the bottom of this," Rob tried to reassure her, but she backed away from Skagra, who advanced toward them.

"What exactly are you trying to get to the bottom of?" she asked. "You can't seem to control this crew very well, 'Captain'." She made the word an insult. "My crew chooses to obey me, even when they think they know better."

"You rule by fear, I lead by trust," Rob growled.

"I'm sure that will be a great comfort to you as you watch your crew being devoured," she winked. "The truth is, so-called Captain, there is no *ruling*. No human can lead another. They obey because they choose to." She turned, flourishing her coat-tails. "But now the important matters. Gorm, tell me what happened to you while you had Saagara in your veins. Did it hurt?"

She nodded.

"Yes? And?"

Gorm hung her head, her hands shaking behind her back as sweat flowed down her face.

"You are not her Captain," Rob said. "I am."

"Oh, that changes everything, doesn't it?" Skagra said, sarcastically. "I'll be on my way and abandon my plans." She drew her sword and pointed it at Rob without looking at him. "Bring me Jarl, there's a good boy. I want to see my test subject."

Rob looked at Vann, who then walked back along the ship, heading for the aftcastle. Once he had pushed through the door, Rob gave a hard breath and backed from Skagra's blade.

"There, wasn't that easy?" Skagra said. "Now, Gorm, I want you to give me the information. It is in your best interests."

"You see power and blood as all life has to offer," Gorm said.

"You know this is not true," Skagra's voice deepened. "Power will end. I've seen it. I've seen *the* ending. Remember, Gorm? I told you all about it." She pressed her hand against Gorm's chest and closed her eyes. "I remember the feel of your breathing and the thunder of your heart. Do you remember mine?"

"I remember the horrors we inflicted." Gorm pushed Skagra's hand aside. "I remember that you betrayed me. You think nothing of peace, of compassion, or of anything that might bring light. My mind is clear; my heart has no clouds obscuring it. Your words of hate are like knives in your own belly; when you speak of darkness, you devour your own mind, and become the dark things."

"Well now," Skagra laughed. "You have become a philosopher in exile! You're adorable."

"My appearance is of no importance," Gorm said.

"Sharp, very sharp," Skagra lifted her sword to Gorm's neck. "But see now, Gorm, this is sharper than your tongue."

"Leave her alone!" Ilma shouted, leaping forward.

Skagra barely moved, but she sliced her sword back over her shoulder, swung it at Ilma and then back to Gorm's throat. Ilma screamed loud and piercing; she fell to her knees, clutching her hand, three of her fingers lay in a pool of red, her hand was cradled against her chest, and her face was plastered with tears and sweat. Blood drained from her face, turning it almost beige.

Skagra's smile split her face, and she reached to pick up the severed fingers. "Whoops," she said. "How clumsy I can be. What a shame. But, we cannot let things go to waste, can we?" With a deep sigh, she plunged her teeth into a finger, chewed and swallowed.

Rob fell to his knees, his stomach churning. He vomited, blinded by stinging tears. Alya leapt up the stairs to the quarterdeck before throwing up over the side.

"Always a winner at parties," Skagra went on, waving the remaining fingers at Ilma, who fell to the deck, shivering and breathing hard.

"Pangles . . ." Ilma sobbed.

Skagra froze, bristling and shivering before turning her head slowly to stare at Ilma, wide-eyed. Rob pulled his belt from around his coat and went to Ilma; he tightened it around her hand, and then she tore strips from her skirt to use as bandages. All the while, Skagra went on staring.

Gorm alone seemed unaffected by the events. She stood resolute, her eyes on the sky, her hands firm behind her back. Skagra leered and tossed the remaining fingers away, wiping her own palms on her shirt, adding to the bloodstains.

"Never thought I'd see *you* again," she said to Ilma. "I have nothing to say to you. Go back to being dead."

Ilma burst into tears while clinging to Rob's jacket; she shuddered and heaved in a cacophony of babbles. Rob held her tight, pressing her hair and doing all he could to soothe her. He felt like he had missed something.

"I asked the Blood Pengs to kill you," Skagra said to Gorm. "I didn't want you to tell anyone else about what I did to you. I don't want Mothar hearing about my work. Now all these others know, too. What a shame. I think I will have to sink this ship of traitors. No witnesses."

"No!" Kari rushed at Skagra, but she was kicked in the leg, and fell screaming.

"Stop!" Rob commanded, but Skagra barely glanced at him. "I won't let you harm this crew. Take me hostage, mutilate me, kill me if you like, but leave them!"

"Nobility will get you nowhere," Skagra yawned. "I am not interested in you. Gorm is my quarry, Kari and Jarl my interests. Who are you?"

"I told you; Rob Sardan," he stood and squared his shoulders. "I fought in the mines of Kenna Iron Helm. You went by the name Pangles, didn't you?"

She looked at him, considering, and then smirked.

"You are not my problem," she said at last. "If you are who you say you are, then you are Mothar's concern. You're nothing to me."

"But you're Mothar's second in command," he said, desperately. "I must be worth something to you!"

"No," she shrugged. "He's the one obsessed with you, not me."

"What if I died, then?" Rob leapt onto the ship's railing. "Mothar would be angry if his great set piece were to vanish, wouldn't he? And he'd want to know why you didn't stop me."

"He might," she snorted. "Mothar *is* an idiot."

"He's an Air-keeper," Rob shouted. "He's the only human to master their powers. He's the new Air King. You don't think he could make you do something? I saw him control minds. He made a member of his own crew commit suicide. You don't think he'll do that to you?"

She stepped closer and laid the point of her blade against his chest. "No."

Rob turned cold; his blood ground to a halt, and his head swam. Skagra pressed the sword closer, grinning with uncontrolled glee, pushing him off balance. He tripped but righted himself so that he did not fall. The pirate laughed, and her crew above joined with jeers and spat.

"I will not let this go on," said Gorm, her hand on Skagra's shoulder. "I will give you an end to your experiment if you would spare my Captain and my crew."

"*I* am your Captain!" Skagra shrugged her off and stood to her full height though she reached only as far as Gorm's chin.

"Then we have but one way," Gorm's voice deepened, and her face turned murderous. The change was so staggering that Rob almost fell. She seemed a different person, and the shadow of a pirate was standing before him, terrible and beautiful.

"Oh, good! A duel!" Skagra leapt, spinning her sword before crouching into an arched stance. Her body turned sidelong towards Gorm; her knees bent with her feet parallel to her shoulders while her sword hand was raised and her left hand was behind her back.

"Alya," Gorm called. "May I borrow your jian?"

Alya waved her assent as she got to her feet. She was by the wheel and used it as support while Gorm went to the stairs where the jian had been dropped. Picking it up, she gave Rob a nod and then crouched into a similar stance to Skagra.

Rob got down from the railing. Sweat bubbled on his face and ran down his back, his throat dried, and his stomach clenched, but he stood firm.

Gorm moved forward, her long coat swishing as she whipped it from her back and tossed it aside. Her loose shirt was fastened with frog buttons, the long sleeves ending in a tight cuff. She loosened her silk belt and adjusted her trousers, and then gave Skagra a small bow.

They flew at one another, graceful and smooth. Gorm stepped, squatted into a twist, then drew the jian in a circle, arching her body away from Skagra's lunge, and then spun back. Skagra twisted her sword towards Gorm's belly, but the larger woman stepped forward, slid her arm around her opponent's blade, and spun the pair of them around the mast. Breaking apart, they stared at each other, breathing faster.

Skagra slipped under Gorm's swipe and spun, lifting her sword, but Gorm bent her arms back and around, her shoulders relaxed as her knees curved down. Crouching, she whipped the tassel of the jian in a circle and then sprang from Skagra's strike.

They moved in whirlwinds, diving, crouching, arching and sliding across the deck while the pirates above cheered and hissed. Gorm maintained a steely expression, her chest hardly moving as she breathed, while Skagra laughed and snarled. Neither blade had met, nor had they cut flesh.

Rob inched his way to the stairs to the aftcastle and met Alya's eyes. This was a good enough distraction, he decided. She blinked, and then gave a signal to Ilma, who got to her feet at last.

While the fight went on, Alya, Rob and Ilma took their positions around the ship, hands on jibs and lines. He hadn't counted on Vann being sent to fetch Jarl and the fact that he was taking so long irked him.

Gorm circled away from another attack and slipped the jian around Skagra's sword, but the blades still did not touch. They broke apart and then drove together, dodging, sliding and then breaking away from each other. Both were panting, sweat and tension painted across their faces and backs. Gorm's muscles showed through her damp shirt and Skagra unbuttoned her own as a cool wind picked up.

Rob looked at Alya one more time and then backed towards the aftcastle. The two combatants were so engrossed with their battle that he was at the wheel before either of them noticed. Rob gave Alya a raised finger, and she signalled Ilma.

The sails unfurled, the ship groaned in sudden strain as the mast pulled taut. The pirates on the Black Sword cried out, and two of them leapt, one plunged into the sea, the other slammed into the deck before bouncing off into the water. Skagra stumbled mid-attack and Gorm was able to pirouette around her and knock her sword from her hand.

Rob turned the ship away from the Black Sword, and they swung towards the open ocean. But the pirates were already setting their sails, screaming in harsh voices. Rob gave the wheel a full turn to starboard, and they sped off in a wide arc.

"Do you trust the ship?" he asked Alya.

"With my life," she said.

Skagra struggled as Gorm grasped her from behind and lifted her off the deck, her teeth gnashing at the air as she kicked and writhed. Kari got to her feet, shaking and stumbling, gave Rob a look, and then punched Skagra in the stomach, silencing her.

"I disapprove," Rob shouted though he was grinning.

Kari hobbled to the forecastle to tie a line that was falling loose. Rob nodded approval and glanced at the Black Sword, which was moving behind them. They still had a significant lead, but the wind was turning, filling the sails of the fully rigged galleon and thrusting it through the waters.

Grasping the wheel he urged them further starboard, churning water around them as they turned. Rob tightened his jaw and watched the sails flicker and die momentarily.

Alya and Kari dashed over the deck, turning the sails and moving the main mast into place. Ilma struggled to help, but she was only just able to stay on her feet. Alya eventually whispered to her and she sat, breathing hard.

Rob straightened and turned the wheel a full rotation, pointing them back at the Black Sword. Skagra stopped squirming as they moved, rocketing towards her ship. She gave a pained scream and fought Gorm with all her might.

"Hold her," Rob commanded.

"I am endeavouring to do so," Gorm replied through gritted teeth.

"You're going to kill us all!" Skagra cried, but then she laughed.

They gained speed, ploughing closer, the bowsprit gleaming in the sunlight, rising over the waves. Rob leant over the wheel, holding it firm. They were seconds away. Alya held the ropes to the main sail, Kari and Ilma another.

The Black Sword's crew shouted, their sails turned, but Rob roared his defiance, and their ship slammed into the pirate's hull.

He was thrown from the wheel and slammed into the deck, his head screaming in sudden pain, but he lifted his eyes, dizzy. Alya leapt over him and turned the wheel, making them scrape the hull of the Black Sword, tearing wood and ripping into the ship as a knife into flesh.

With a tremendous crack, they broke free and rushed from the aft of the Black Sword. Rob sprang to the nearest jib and loosened it, gave Kari a nod, and she grasped another, making the mainsail twist. Ilma tried to pull another line, but she collapsed, coughing and wheezing.

Rob ran to her and lifted her off the deck; she was shaking, her face becoming more bronze by the second. Sweat flowed over her in rivers.

"My ship!" Skagra screamed. "My ship!"

The Black Sword was leaning, its crew sliding from the deck, some toppling over the side as water rushed into the breached hull. Rob gave Alya a smile of approval and then held Ilma close. He had hoped for a euphoric celebration at the sinking of Mothar's second ship, but all he felt was poisonous grief.

Skagra broke Gorm's grasp and fell to all fours. She coughed, laughed, and clawed at her throat, tears sliding from her eyes. Rob looked at her with utter hatred, the blood around her mouth still shining, reminding him of what she had done to Ilma.

As they drifted further from the Black Sword, he got to his feet, helping the doctor do the same though she wavered and groaned like a dying person.

"Alya, do we have a brig?" he asked.

"The cargo hold can be locked," she replied, spitting.

Rob kept hold of Ilma. "Come on," he whispered. "You looked after me countless times. Now it's my turn. I learned a bit of healing, you know?"

"You hate it," she managed to say. "You told me so, you little scamp."

"I know, but I'll do it for you." He pushed her grey hair from her face before turning back to Alya. "We sail north!"

"Aye," she replied.

"And, Alya," he added with a twisted smile. "Thank you."

She returned the grudging smile and then looked away. Rob thought this was the best he could hope for. He lifted Ilma against his shoulder and brought her to his cabin in the forecastle.

Kari followed, eyes downcast. She shuffled her feet and then leaned on a chest that was bolted to the floor. Her eyes were blackened and her nose was bleeding, so Rob reached into his pocket and handed her a handkerchief.

"Cheers," she said, sniffing and dabbing her nose. "Is she going to be okay?"

Rob laid Ilma on the bunk and pulled the covers over her. He put her hand on the top and unwound the cloth that held it. The cuts were clean, almost surgical. He shivered and tried to push his stomach down as it rose to his mouth.

"Captain," Ilma murmured. "Don't kill her."

"Nobody is killing anyone," he said, smoothing her hair back. "Listen, we are not pirates. We are better than that. I want to know what she knows about Mothar's plans. I want to know what is going on with the Air-keepers. She can tell us."

"I can't stand it," she sobbed. "I just can't."

"I'll go and see if the others are okay," Kari said, moving awkwardly.

"No, go to the quarters and find Ilma's bag. She'll have supplies I can use."

"Aye-aye," she said and left.

Rob watched her go as he realised she had just taken one of his orders as if he were her captain. Shaking the thought away, he tightened the belt around Ilma's arm and she hissed.

"You're doing it wrong," she moaned. "You shouldn't have taken the cloth off until you had new dressings."

"Oh, yes," Rob frowned. "I should have thought of that."

"Doesn't matter," she sighed, settling into the pillow. "I'm dead already."

"No, you are not," he patted her. "You're more alive than the rest of us. You'll see. Ilma three fingers, greatest healer there ever was. That's what they'll all be saying one day; you mark my words."

She looked at him, the haze in her eyes clearing momentarily. "Rob, it's her. It's Skagra . . ." she gulped and wet her lips before going on. "She didn't recognise me at first. It's been so long. So, so very long."

"Why? Were you and Gorm with her ship? Did she attack you in the past?"

"No," she struggled and locked eyes with him. "She's my daughter."

Chapter Twenty Three

Skagra

Vann and Jarl were sat in the crew's cabin, laughing and prodding one another. Rob gave them both a terrifying glare and they fell quiet.

"Sorry," Vann said. "I meant to do what you said. But by the time I got him up the stairs, she was fighting Gorm, and we thought we best stay out of the way."

"We needed you on the lines," Rob said. "The plan could have failed."

"It worked out, though, didn't it?" the man put in. "Sorry, I'm Jarl, by the way. Jarl Steer-eye."

"Odd name," Rob said, sitting next to them. "Doesn't matter. Vann, please, in future do as I say."

"Didn't see you chastising Alya," he snorted. "Some people get special treatment." He winked at Jarl, who grinned with childish laughter.

"She hasn't accepted me as captain, but you have. She's helped this crew, even though she's contradicted me every chance she's had. When she has chosen to do something I said, it has been for the good of all of us. You need to do the same."

"On my ship, you obeyed the captain, no question. I was first mate, you know? I had the responsibility of making sure every word of the captain's orders was carried out, no second guessing," Jarl said, sitting in his bunk.

"What happened when the pirates attacked your ship?" Rob leaned closer, the cramped quarters making it almost unnecessary. "How many did Skagra kill?"

"None," Jarl shrugged. "Offered us a chance to join her. Said she could give us all the wonders of the world. Our trade has been slow for years. The Khamasi have been upping the levy, the Ginnungagap's full of ships under the Blood King demanding tribute to fund his war, and then there's Mothar. Hard to turn down that sort of offer."

"*You* turned from it," Vann said. "Honourable, I say. We should keep him."

"Aye, I kept my place on the Long Silver," Jarl patted Vann. Rob twitched but tried to maintain his attention. "It were a hard choice and no mistake! Skagra said she'd sink it, said she'd make me watch. But I told her I'd rather be on its deck. I loved that ship, loved it more than my own family. I saw it built, paid for half of it out of my own pocket. Sold my pockets to pay for it!" he laughed, and Vann joined in. "I weren't going to leave it."

"What happened to the captain?"

"She went with Skagra," Jarl sighed heavily. "She was in it for the money, for the adventure and the thrill. The ship was a means to an end, so getting on a bigger, more exciting ship, was what she needed. Couldn't hold that against her."

"She's joined Mothar," Rob said, frowning. "I'd hold that against her."

"What? Nay, she joined Skagra. She's twice the pirate Mothar will ever be."

Rob leaned back, surveying the older man with curiosity. "It sounds like you admire her. Do you know what she did?"

"She's a true pirate and no mistake. Mothar's a king, and proper pirates don't like kings."

"Skagra is Mothar's second in command; she's his first mate."

"No she isn't! She's his admiral; if pirates even have such things. Mothar's not got no first mate. A bit like you, Master Sardan."

"*Captain* Sardan." Rob stood and pulled Vann with him. "Skagra is our prisoner. I'll choose a first mate when I'm ready. Vann, we've got a pirate to talk to."

He marched into the corridor, and Vann trotted along grumbling and shuffling his feet. Rob tried to breathe easier, but the cramped passageway did not lend itself to this. As they squeezed towards the cargo hold, he stopped and leaned against the door, giving Vann a curious look.

The lantern glimmered against his nose-ring and made his dark skin shine with sweat. Rob's hands twitched, and he wanted to take Vann's arms, to draw him close, but he pushed the urge aside.

"Sorry," Vann said and looked at his feet. "I know you're angry. I should have done what you said; shouldn't have stayed below when you wanted me to take Jarl up."

"Don't dwell on it," Rob said. "Just, please listen to me in future."

"I will, I'll do everything you say! I'll never miss another command. You want me to stand on the edge of the bowsprit or dangle from the end; I'll do it. I just . . ." he hiccupped and wiped his eyes. "I was too scared."

"What?" Rob stepped closer and put his hands on Vann's shoulders. "What are you talking about?"

"Skagra, you know? She's vicious. I didn't want her clocking eyes on me and doing something unnatural to me. I can't bear it. Not after what she did to my home."

"She's human," Rob said, drawing Vann into a hug and resting his chin on his shoulder. "You'll see that. I need you there to watch my back while I interrogate her."

"I'll do it," he said, breaking the embrace. "I will, you watch me. I'll do everything you say."

Rob turned to the door. Even the short time spent in Vann's arms had warmed him. The dread that had grown at the sight of Vann and Jarl laughing together was dissipating and his skin prickled. Vann needed protecting, teaching, and guiding; Rob felt a thrill at being able to do that. The man's eyes were wide and full of anxiety, but Rob felt more than ready to face Skagra, to put her through the mill and see what came out.

In the centre of the room the main mast's stem was fixed like a great, gnarled tree, branches leaping from its boughs digging into the ceiling. Chained to the bottom with long, steel links lay Skagra, her hands cushioning her head as she snored softly. Vann slammed the door, but the pirate barely moved.

Rob kept back, letting Vann step closer, unhooking a lantern from the wall and shining it into Skagra's face. She opened her eyes and gave them both a bored glower.

"I would like you to tell me what Mothar is planning," said Rob. "What has he done with the Sky Sages?"

She shuffled and drummed her fingers along the floor, the clinking of her chains echoing dully. Vann looked sidelong at her while cracking his knuckles.

"What is this ship made of?" Skagra asked. "I thought you were all suicidal when you rammed my Black Sword, but no, you sank it. Such a thing should not happen. I should like to own this ship."

"You won't own any teeth by the time I'm done with you," Vann said.

Rob gave him a slow stare and then turned back to the pirate. "I want you to answer my questions."

"For a small vessel to break the hull of a galleon," she sucked air through her teeth. "A captain with this ship would be invincible. What do you call it?"

"Fat Ted," said Vann. "The bear on the front looks like a 'Ted', and he's fat."

"The ship is *not* called 'Fat Ted'," Rob scolded. "It doesn't have a name yet."

"Ah, well, I might call it Ship Breaker, perhaps," she grinned. "Hand Eater, would be a good name."

"It would work for you." Rob sat, crossing his legs. "Your ship was The Black Sword, so, how about we call our ship, The Sword-breaker."

"I thought that was your title, Sardan," she yawned and tugged on the chains. "I'm used to chains, you know? Been in them many times, do you think that I won't escape?"

"Perhaps. Nevertheless, you will answer my questions."

"I have no interest in your questions; they're boring. Mothar, Sky Sages, Air-keepers, none of them matter. You heroes and villains can stand around crying about immortality all you like; it's nothing to me."

"What *is* important to you, then?"

She turned her head from side to side, a smile creeping across her features, making her eyes brighten in the gloom. With a clink of chains, she crawled closer until the bonds pulled taut about her hands and chest. She was inches away from Rob, her bloody breath wafting over him as she opened her mouth.

"*I* am important to me," she said. "My life is the only thing important to me."

"Does your crew know this?" he asked, snorting.

"We are pirates; we are free. Queens, lords, barons, and armies, they can all go and burn in Razal's shield for all I care. We are free. We have adventure, treasure, blood and sweat, love and hatred; everything that one could want in life, with no restrictions. Whatever you may wish."

"I see the appeal," said Vann, though he was frowning. "But you kill people."

"As does your captain; I saw him kill dozens in Khamas. Not to mention those he slaughtered on the Keeker Isle, and the Air King, of course."

"I learned from my mistakes," Rob said. "That's the difference between you and me. I hate what I did; I never want to kill again."

She turned her head slowly towards Vann. "What function do you serve? Navigation, no, I don't think so. Cook? You don't have the hands or the stench. Shipwright? Certainly not with that body. Perhaps you're just that, a body. You're just a boy to warm the captain's bed."

"Shut it!" Vann cried, stepping forward and raising a fist.

Rob held Vann back with a hand. "She's trying to hurt your feelings."

"I have not lied," she said. "I don't need to." She winked and then looked at Rob. "Mothar will hunt you. He'll have everyone on this crew killed, and then he'll end you. Is that what you wanted to hear? Or should I make it more theatrical?"

"Plenty of people have tried to kill me," Rob's voice deepened as he said it. "The Blood Pengs you hired stabbed me and yet I lived."

"I did not say he would kill you. He will end you." Her grin widened until it became obscene. "There are things worse than death; betrayal, heartbreak, vengeance, a life without love, sooner or later, you will wish you could die."

"I've already been there," he said, darkly.

"Well, isn't that fantastic for you?" she laughed and lay back against the mast. "Perhaps I *will* kill you in the end, who knows? You've nothing to offer me, and I've no reason to keep you alive, let alone tell you anything."

"What about an exchange?" Rob stood, his head almost reaching the ceiling. "I want you to tell me about the Sky Sages; where they are and how to get there? Also, what is Mothar planning with the Air-keepers? In exchange, I will let you talk to Jarl and complete your experiment."

"Rob, no!" Vann cried.

"*Captain*," he said, sternly. "Skagra, what do you say?"

She gave him a twisted smile. "Not a fair trade. I'll tell you about the Sky Sages, perhaps. But Mothar's plans are worth more."

"Is it worth your freedom?"

"You cannot give me what I shall win for myself," she said as she tapped the chains. "We shall see what Jarl has to offer. May I take some of his blood when I leave?"

Rob shrugged. "I can't compel him."

Skagra fingered the vials that hung about her neck, clinking them as she tilted her head one way and then the other. "Blood is interesting, isn't it? The Sky Sages say that it carries our breath. They had tomes and scrolls that spoke of the breath of Vaata the air god permeating every inch of flesh and taking control of the mind."

"What's this got to do with anything?" Vann asked impatiently. "Talk proper for a change."

"Mothar uses the red wind. He has the power the Air-keepers discovered and kept to themselves. He uses it to reach into people's breath, to slip into the mind and thoughts. There was only ever one person he could not hear, well, two people now, and he was so, so frightened." She beamed at Rob. "First there was your mother, Morven. Perhaps it is because she passed the Seer's Veil, or saw the Shattering City. Not even Mothar knows for certain. And then you. When Saagara was in you he could not hear your mind. When you held the Sea-Stone Sword, he was deaf to every move you made."

"I suppose that's why he was so happy that I broke it," Rob grumbled.

"Partly. Mothar's plans are really boring, though. I can tell you about the Sky Sages; they're nothing important."

"Where are they?"

"What makes you think I know?"

"Mothar wants them, and you're his second in command, or his admiral, or whatever title you chose."

"I'm flattered." She gurgled and spat. "But I do not know where they are. I have ideas, though. The nuns who keep the Tomb of the Dead God are connected to them. I have interrogated them. They sent me on a false trail through the pass of Dilwen to the Chambers of Olwyn Whitefoot. After I tortured them, one young girl with a ring in her nose told me that there is a pass through an underground river full of rocks and foaming rapids. Beyond there it would be impossible. There is magma. If a ship did get to the pass, the fire would consume it in moments."

"I have full confidence in our ship," Rob nodded. "Now tell me; what happened to the Sky Sages?"

"I don't know," she frowned. "And I don't care. They were never friends to the Air King, but now that Mothar rules, perhaps they are more accommodating." She spread her hands. "That's all you'll get from me."

"Thank you," Rob stood.

"Don't thank her!" Vann objected. "After what she did to Ilma!"

Skagra's head jerked, but she looked away instantly. Rob gave Vann a nod and then turned back to the door.

"Why do you do it, Sardan?" Skagra asked suddenly. "This obsession you have with being a hero, with what you think is 'the right thing'. Where did it come from?"

"Why do you care?"

"You remind me of Mothar. He has his reasons; I would like to know yours. I would like to know just how misguided you are."

He eyed her and frowned. "Heroes are remembered; that was what I thought. The things they did were told and retold all over the world, and then other people would be inspired. If people hear stories of tyrants being overthrown, they might start to believe that they can do it."

"*And* you want your name to echo through history, is that it?" She met his eyes. "Of course. Don't try and paint over your true motives, Sardan. I can see you for what you are. Let me ask, do you know how the War of Frost and Flame was ended?"

"Volcanic eruptions," he said at once. "Someone set off three giant volcanoes and destroyed the air, making the ice melt."

"Do you know who it was that set the volcanoes off?"

"No," he shrugged. "Nobody does."

"Isn't that interesting?" she grinned. "The greatest act in history, the deed that ended three generations of war; the thing that changed the world forever, and nobody knows the names of the ones who did it."

"They must have been lost," Vann said. "People must have written them down, but it's been ages since it happened."

"Precisely. Their names and their glory lasted a few years, but their deeds lived on. Glory is like a circle in the water, which never ceases to enlarge itself, till, by broad spreading, it disperses to naught."

"What does that mean?"

"You're the captain; you have power over these people. I thought you wanted to avoid power, but here you are seeking it out all over again. You're looking for glory, just like before. Already you've made yourself captain over these people."

"They chose me as their captain."

"Chosen or imposed; power is the same."

"You're a captain, too," Rob smiled, feeling suddenly triumphant. "Doesn't that make you a bit of a hypocrite?"

She opened her mouth but closed it again, thinking. At last, she growled and said, "Power will be dismantled, it must be for the sake of making our lives worth living. It is a cruel irony that to destroy power, one must first attain power."

"Is that how you justify it to yourself?"

"Mock me and you will regret it," she said as she narrowed her eyes. "You once held power, and then the power held you. It eats at your consciousness. It itches, and you want to scratch at it, to hold power again. Perhaps you will soon wear a crown. The Crown of Black Glass would suit you well. I should like to see what it does to you. I should like to watch you become the monster."

"You're trying to intimidate me. It won't work."

"Do you remember Faolan?" Skagra asked. "She was on your old crew, wasn't she? Do you remember what happened to her? She lost a hand, remember?"

"The pirates wanted to drown her," Rob recalled.

"Indeed. Who do you think took her hand?" She licked her lips. "It tasted delicious. Her name will be forgotten, but what I did to her will haunt you, Sardan. The price of your freedom would seem to be the hands of your friends. Perhaps let them know that in the future." She leaned forward, her sharpened teeth glinting. "My ship will be paid for. I will *take* payment."

Closing the door behind him, Rob took a breath and let his chest recover from the tense, brittle stresses he hadn't realised had been building up within. Peeling away, he led Vann through the ship, his mind overflowing with thoughts. Vann dawdled by the crew's quarters but eventually chose to follow Rob.

"What do you think?" he asked, catching up.

"She seemed to confirm what I suspected," Rob hummed. "Find the Tomb of the Dead God, which means we're heading to your homeland. Excited?"

"Yeah." He frowned and pushed his hands under his armpits. "I suppose."

They mounted the stairs onto the main deck and let the cool breeze hit them. Ilma was standing at the door to Rob's cabin, her bandaged arm in a sling and her face still drained and drawn. He felt sick inside at the sight and went to her.

"I want to talk to her," she said. "I know you'll probably think it's stupid of me, but I'm used to being stupid. I've been stupid my whole life."

"Not that I've ever seen," he said. "You joined this crew, after all, and that was pretty clever."

"Yeah, I'm doing really well out of it." She raised her hand and gave a small smile. "She's my daughter. I never came to terms with that."

"You told me your daughter was dead, I thought you said you hated people keeping vital information hidden!" Rob pushed his way into his cabin, and she followed. Vann started to, but he stopped him. "Vann, please give us a moment."

"What should I do?" he asked.

"Find Alya, she'll put you to work." He closed the door and drew Ilma onto the bunk and sat next to her. The old woman breathed heavily, her wrinkled hand grasping at her frayed skirt and pulling threads. Her face was so pained that he worried she might faint.

"You told me that your daughter died," he said. "You told me she was an adventurer, and . . ." he sighed. "You admired her. But now you tell me she's Skagra? She's Mothar's admiral, and she did this to you!"

"I know what she is, Captain," Ilma said, defiantly. "Don't you think I've heard the stories? Don't you think it breaks me inside every time I hear that name and all the things she's done? She hardly recognises me; it's been that long." Her tears fell, but she kept speaking. "She went away, she chose to go to sea, and I let her . . ."

"You couldn't keep her locked up," Rob said. "That would be cruel."

She looked at him sceptically. "And what have we done now?"

"Ah, fair point," he shifted and frowned. "But it's not your fault."

"It doesn't matter whose fault it is." She balled her hand, clasping her skirt. "I miss her. I miss her so much. I miss the girl I used to tell stories to all day, I miss the girl who helped me stock the shelves and clean the bathtubs. I miss her . . ."

Rob knew what it was like to suffer a loss. Skagra was alive, and Ilma could go to her, but she wasn't the daughter she remembered. He also knew what it was like to have people spill platitudes at his feet, words that didn't mean anything, words that didn't help. Sometimes it was good just to have someone to listen.

He put an arm around her and drew her close. She put her head on his shoulder and coughed, her tears dripping onto his coat. They felt the rise and fall of the ship, and they heard the sea and the wind. Those noises brought back so many memories, but Rob ignored them and focused on Ilma.

"I lied to you," she said. "Because I liked it. I liked to think, just for a while, that she had never become Skagra. I liked to pretend that she was always and forever the child I had known. My Pangles died, and Skagra took her skin."

Rob kissed the top of her head and held her tight. "It's okay," he whispered.

"Perhaps that's why I hate people hiding things so much," she hiccupped. "Because it's what I've been doing all this time. Ancient healing scrolls indeed!" she snorted. "I came out to sea because *she* was here."

"If you want to talk to her, you can. But don't do it until you are ready. If you feel like it will hurt too much, if it will compromise you, don't do it. Do *you* think you can face her?"

Chapter Twenty Four

Dreams of the Sea

The ship was anchored off the coast of Herebealde and Rob sat on the beach, waiting for the other crewmembers to conceal the little gig in an overhanging grove. Behind them, a set of mountains rose with white heads and grey bodies flowing into grassy hills, which plummeted into the beach.

His eyes lingered on Gorm as she worked with a peaceful expression. She had offered to show him some sort of meditation technique during their time ashore. He had had a hard time not mirroring Alya's sceptical noises when the subject had arisen.

Gorm and Alya finished tying the gig and tramped towards him. He stood and they all clambered up the rising sand towards a plane of long grass that led north.

"I do not agree with your decision," Alya said.

"You never do." Rob put his hands in his pockets and let her carry on with her argument. He urged Gorm to catch up, but she lagged behind, deep in thought.

"Ilma I understand, but we know next to nothing about Kari and Jarl. The doctor is maimed; if they decide to take the ship we won't have any way of stopping them."

"Vann is with them. And he has Skagra's sword. Ilma would have yours if you'd have lent it to her."

"On an outing we need at least one armed person," she sniffed, glowering at the sword he would not use. "And Vann is another problem."

"Oh, here we go." Rob turned on her, walking backwards. "Look, you've done nothing but complain about Vann."

"He has some skills; I do not contest that. However, he is a thief, and thieves are by their nature unlikely to respect ideas of ownership. If anyone were willing to steal a ship, or let it be stolen, it would be him."

"You could have killed him at any point, but you didn't."

"I didn't anticipate him surviving this long. He can open locks, yes, he can get out of a set of chains, and this may be useful. But he has displayed a blatant disregard for orders, has complained non-stop and is lazy."

"Apart from that last one, you could be describing yourself."

"Perhaps, but my objections have been based on facts. Vann has refused work, has bungled basic tasks and has been a drain on your crew. I do not trust him."

"Why not?" Rob asked.

"I wasn't sure at first." She put her hands under her armpits and furrowed her brow. "When we were being taken to Bron'Halla we were attacked by renegade pengs, as you know. Vann shouted something. I didn't think much of it at the time, but now it haunts me. He said, 'Don't hurt me, *she'll* kill them if I don't get there.'"

Rob glared. "You're making it up."

"Give me some credit," she scoffed. "If I were making it up I'd be much more creative. I think he was sent to that prison for a reason."

"You're just looking for any excuse."

"Listen to me, for once in your life," she pressed. "You may be blinded by your affections; you want your old friend back, the one you lost in the mines. You want to have your romance and live it out in reality. But that boy is dead, Sardan. He is dead and you are alive. Vann is not Niall. For the sake of the crew, for the sake of the ship, be wary of Vann."

"And I shouldn't be wary of you," he snarled. "You with your sarcasm and your scorn, you seem just like the person I should blindly trust."

"I would never ask that." She looked furious all of a sudden. "Where am I wrong? Where is my reasoning misplaced? Vann got close to you immediately, got very friendly and has always been on your side."

"Except in the matter of the trasati," Rob pointed out.

"Even there he seems willing to compromise," she countered. "I've met people from that trade and rarely do they let go. Either he is acting or he is a bigger fool than I imagined."

"What do you want me to do? Throw him overboard?"

"That would be nice. But my suspicions are not, alas, founded on any *solid* proof. If you test his loyalty, though, it will break."

"And if it doesn't? What if I test his loyalty and he stays true?"

"Then I will admit to being wrong," she smiled. "But if I'm right and he turns, then I think you should step down as captain."

"I'll take that bet." He quickened his pace, making space between them.

Loath as he was to admit it, Alya had been able to see problems and solutions beyond him. The fact that she did not trust Vann gave him pause. Try as he might, he could not see a way around her objections. He had struggled with some of Vann's dismissive attitudes and lack of empathy towards the trasati, but he thought the man had a good heart. Rob glanced back at Alya as she slipped a small knife from her belt and tossed it from one hand to the other, absently.

"Where did you get that?" he asked.

"From Kari," she said. "Must I report all of my actions to you or can I live without your watchful eye every second of the day?"

"Are you planning to trade it for something?"

"No." She gave the sky a look. "This is Herebealde, and they have a market town. They did not sign the Ginnungagap Traders Truce, so there may be pirates. It would be best if we did not make boast of our prisoner."

"We don't know if all pirates are under Mothar." Rob also gave an uneasy glance at the sky. "Who knows? There might be some on our side."

"I doubt it. Before I was taken to prison, I heard about Skagra. Most regard her more favourably than Mothar, she is, as they say, a 'true' pirate where he is a self-proclaimed king. To some, Skagra is a liberator, to others a monstrous destroyer."

"The same is true of Rob," Gorm said catching up at last. "To have broken the Sea-Stone Sword has made you both great and terrible. Indeed, Skagra has desired to remove the powers of the world and once had her sights on killing the Air King. She has many of your desires."

"I don't want to eat flesh, though," Rob gagged. "And I'm not a pirate."

"We do not fly the flag of any power," Gorm went on. "We are not sworn to any government. We sail free and so, to many people, we are pirates."

"We don't steal stuff or kill people, though!"

"We stole the ship, and you are named King-killer. What do you imagine that makes you?"

Rob wanted to argue, but he couldn't. What constituted a pirate was becoming less clear to him. More than anything he wanted to put distance between himself and the label, but instead he kept coming back to it. It made his chest ache and his head was suddenly light. He desperately wanted to get away, so he quickened his pace.

"If it is of any consolation," Alya said with a sly smile. "Perhaps we did not *steal* the ship so much as reclaimed it."

"*You* could say that," he allowed. "Not sure about the rest of us."

They came to the woods above the sand dunes and Gorm took deep, sighing breaths. The trees were spaced at regular intervals and were far too uniform for Rob to mistake them as a usual growth pattern. The path that wound amongst them was made of stone rising and falling with the rolling land. Looking at the spacing of the trees reminded him of the woods at Bron'Halla.

Already the prison seemed a cold and distant memory, but there were older memories that stung harder and harsher. His hand went to his chest and he frowned. Finding the Sky Sages was more important than Skagra, he decided.

"What do you think we will find when we go to the Sky Sages?" he asked the others, changing the subject.

"I suspect Mothar has either recruited them or killed them," Gorm said, solemnly. "He has never been one to suffer opposition. Where he could not win by stealth, he has always destroyed. Where he could not destroy, he deceived."

"What about Skagra, did he deceive her?"

"Skagra is dangerous in ways Mothar could never be. Where Mothar desires a throne, she seeks blood and fire. *All shall die,* she said, *in the Flame-Filled Sky*."

Rob grimaced. "Alya, what do you think about the Sky Sages?"

She looked at him and folded her arms. "From my brief conversation with Skagra, I gauged that she is aware of why we are seeking them. She has been aware of many things."

"How?"

"Kerrok," Alya fingered her jian. "Skagra let slip that she would have 'further words with the Blood Peng'. It is my guess that she has reported to Skagra recently."

"That's impossible, how would she get there so quick? I thought your ship was supposed to be the fastest ever!"

"For its size," she snarled. "I told you we couldn't outrun a galleon. Or an Air-keeper. My suspicions were raised when that storm appeared over the Long Silver. Kerrok was able to overtake us at Glasoghear. I suspect the Air-keepers do Skagra's bidding as they do Mothar's."

Rob stopped. "Why didn't you say any of this before?"

"You did not ask," she shrugged. "You are not my captain, and I had no reason to say words I did not think you would listen to."

"Why wouldn't I listen? This is important information!"

"As important as the fact that Ilma is Skagra's mother?" her lip curled. "Yes, I worked it out. The last thing we need is for those two to talk. Skagra is very good at planting chaos, and the fewer opportunities she is granted, the better."

"I trust Ilma." Rob turned and stomped along the path, angry and confused.

They came to a clearing encircling a single fig tree. Its branches were spread in extensive patterns, reaching in every direction. There were puddles of clear water streaked beyond the reaches of the tree's shadow, leaves resting on top and gliding in the reflected sky.

Gorm strode ahead and bent under the lowest branches and put her palm against the bough. The tree creaked and swayed, small trasati-birds twittered and squawked overhead.

"This tree has known time," Gorm said at long last. "Ages of time beyond count. It has known hurt at the hands of humans, and draigs, and saurai. And yet still it stands, and still it gives breath to the air, still it gives shade to the traveller." She sat and cupped her hands in her lap.

"I suppose this is where we do that meditation thing?" Rob said.

"We can't waste time," Alya said. "We have supplies to buy."

"I'll join you later," Rob snapped. "It's important I find a way of dealing with the curse in some way. I'd rather try this stuff on solid ground first before we get back on the ship."

"So you want me to trade everything on my own?" she smiled grimly.

"I trust you know what you are doing," Rob snapped.

"I do, actually, better than either of you, apparently."

Alya slid away and vanished into the trees, hoisting her pack higher on her back as she went.

Gorm crossed her legs as if she were meditating, her hands in her lap. Rob mirrored the motion and breathed slowly as Alya's footsteps became distant and finally faded.

"She has a hard time trusting us," he said after a moment. "I want her on our side, but she won't be, so long as she thinks we're about to betray her. She already thinks we did so by making me the captain."

"Fear has taken root where once trust bloomed," Gorm said. "I sense, however, that there is much love within her, though, she may express it in strange ways. Honesty and caring are indicators of affection more so than embraces or intimacy may be."

"I suppose," he frowned. "But I can't let her keep insulting the crew and injecting poison into every conversation."

"She feels twisted inside," Gorm sounded sad. "Hurt and betrayed, lost and alone; these feelings can push us away from those with whom we would be friends. It is a defence we employ when we are in pain, to distance ourselves from the source of anguish. For her, the source is friendship. She pushes us away because she fears being hurt by us."

"What can I do?"

"To give trust, we often must first receive it," she closed her eyes and breathed deep. "We have given you our trust, Captain Sardan. If you show Alya that you trust her, she will, in time, come to trust you in return. Think, perhaps, of what she can do for you; why would you want her on this crew?"

"In a strange way, her being so negative is comforting. It reminds me that I'm not perfect."

"Do you require reminding of this?"

"Apparently," he laughed. "I've done terrible things. By rights, I should have spent the rest of time in that prison. But that wouldn't have helped anyone."

"Alya can help you if you let her."

"I know," Rob sighed. "I think I'm still trying to come to terms with you accepting me as captain."

Gorm smiled and reached into her pack, pulling out a pouch. "You and I struggle against fear. Are you afraid of Mothar? Or of Skagra?"

"No."

"What do you fear, Captain?"

He drummed his fingers and met her eyes. "I'm afraid of what I've done, what I could do, and every violent urge in my mind. I became the Monster of the Mists; I killed, and I broke the Sea-Stone Sword. Breaking, killing, being a monster, those are the things I am capable of. I don't want to be like that, but I know they are hidden inside me."

"When you were young you wanted to bring down the oppressors of the world. The Blood King of Ha'Tiyrah, the Pengish Empire, the Pirate Lord; all of them were doomed in your hands."

"They hurt people," Rob ground his teeth. "I grew up surrounded by bullies who took advantage of weaker people. When I was little, I wanted to be strong enough to stop them."

"To have power in order to stop the powerful," Gorm drew a deep breath. "That sounds an awful lot like Skagra, Captain."

He stared at her and fidgeted.

"But I don't *want* to be powerful," he protested. "Not just for its own sake. That's the difference. I want to change; I want to be a better person. She wants to be worse!"

"I do not think so," Gorm said and she shook her head slowly. "What did you learn from her when you spoke? Did she tell you anything about her mind?"

"Not that I recall."

Gorm reached down and picked up a stone from the floor. Holding it up she turned it in her fingers and then tossed it into one of the nearby puddles. It sank with a plunk and the ripples agitated the surface.

"Glory is like a circle in the water," Gorm said, but Rob interrupted.

"Which never ceaseth to enlarge itself till by broad spreading it disperse to nought. Yeah, I heard."

"Consider the meaning; that glory dissipates even as it spreads to its greatest length. Great deeds, the names of those who do them, they are lost, and the water seems unchanged."

"Right," Rob kept his eyes on the water, his brow furrowed.

"Skagra keeps those words close, almost as close as those speaking of the Flame Filled Sky. You saw the stone, yes? But you cannot see it now, it is below the surface, it is lost in time. Yet it is still there. Imperceptibly, perhaps in your eyes, that puddle has been changed by its presence. Though the glory passes, the act remains fixed, and it changes all around it, for good or for ill."

"I think I understand." Rob took a breath. "Like the ending of the war of Frost and Flame? Whoever did it didn't do it for fame. Fame wasn't the point; it was the act itself that changed the world."

"Every decision creates ripples in history," Gorm said softly. "Like a stone cast into the lake. The ripples merge and rebound in patters unpredictable until they are gone. Yet every stone changes the lake, though it may not seem so to the eye of one on the bank."

Gorm breathed slowly and emptied her pouch into her hand.

"Ayumu Flowers," she said. "When brewed, they can be used for deep meditation. You dropped them when you fell in the water with the trasati. I kept them safe. Would you like to drink?"

"What will it do?"

"The thing you fear, this monstrosity you imagine to be your true self, you must face it, look it in the eye and overcome it. You must be the master of your destiny. To know fear, know darkness, and know that you can defeat it. Only then will you be truly immune to the schemes of the Pirate Lord."

She set up a pile of twigs and rubbed them until they caught fire. Rob watched her as the flames licked higher. The things inside his head were not mysteries he was eager to explore. He did not want to fight them; he wanted them gone.

Gorm pulled a bowl from her pack and filled it with water from her flask. Holding it over the fire, she brought it to a simmer and scattered the leaves in it. The aroma was like perfume slicked with the musk of mammoths and a hint of fish. He wondered if that was something Lomi had added.

"What do you think is going to happen?" Rob asked, sceptically. "I've seen real magic, you know? Drugs and hallucinations aren't going to impress me."

"It is not about being impressed," she said. "I am already impressed, Captain. You risked your life for us many times. Tell me why you did that?"

The muscles in his back became as rigid as a mountainside. He felt like he could crumble to pieces. The risks he had taken; throwing his body in front of the pengs to save Vann, diving into the water to save the rest of them, and clambering through the cavern to blast a path for the ship.

All of it seemed like the acts of a reckless child seeking recognition. But, what had his mind been filled with? All was buzzing fear, a calamity of anxiety that forced him to keep these people alive.

"Guilt," he said at last. "I saved you because I felt guilty. About my old crew, about the people I've hurt, and I worry about having a future that is just like my past."

"We all have a world of our own terrors," Gorm nodded. "Mine is chained on the ship; yours is chained in your own mind."

"If I face it . . ." Rob picked up the bowl of simmering tea and eyed it to hide his struggle. "What if it defeats me?"

"What would you like to happen?"

"I would rather die. To become that thing again would kill me. It would kill anything I would recognise as 'me', leaving a hollow shell to house a creature of violence and destruction."

"Melodrama is a strong point of yours," Gorm said, sagely.

"Very funny." He frowned and lifted the tea to his lips.

The taste was different to the smell, so much so that he took several sips to make sure he was not imagining it. It reminded him of hot ale, spiked with nettles and mint. As he gulped, his throat convulsed, but he kept the drink down and gasped.

"How long will it take?" he asked.

"For some it takes hours," Gorm said. "Others, days. For now, we will meditate and clear our minds of . . ."

The tree vanished, disappearing into the sky with a rush of wind. Gorm's words faded as the air turned red, white, and silver. He tried to call to her, but his throat closed and choked him. Mist clouded in a torrent of steaming vapour that clung to his skin. He flailed and waved his hat at the stuff, but it closed again and again.

A shape loomed in the mist, a deep shadow that lurched, black against the ashen sky. The closer Rob got, the more substance it gained, the mist falling away from its body to reveal a torn tower of black stone. Its walls were fragments, bridges spilling from its body and ending in mid-air.

He skidded to a stop as a precipice gaped before his feet, making his chest tighten. Breathing hard he twisted back and forth, but nothing else came from the fog. The land beneath the precipice opened, revealing a valley of bones, armour, and a stench of salt. Rob scrambled towards the scene, his hands grappling loose stones as he clambered, pulling some free. His arms ached but he made it to the valley.

A figure stood in the middle of the carnage. He was tall, broad, and extremely muscular. He was naked except for the tattered remains of a blue coat. He had long, dripping dreadlocks that fell almost to his knees. His dark skin was lined with silver that followed his veins and arteries, creating a criss-cross of white on his brown body.

The man lifted his head and the eyes glowed silver, mist pouring from his mouth as he snarled. The face was a cracked and dehydrated mess, dried blood snapping in the pores and contours as it moved.

"Who are you?" Rob asked. "What in Razal's name is going on?"

"I am the Ocean's Eye," the mouth gaped, the voice ringing through the throat without moving the lips. "I am that which thou wouldst have been."

On his back, the creature wore a sword of stone, its shell pommel rising above his head while the rectangular guard followed his shoulders. The Ocean's Eye laughed with a voice like roaring waves, though the body it occupied barely moved. Blackened and bloody teeth hung in the limp mouth and a cold, dead moan came from the throat with each word.

"Armun, Jareth, Bran, Faolan, Huisdean, Melon, and Luag," it listed the names with glee. "Dead by thy hand!"

"That wasn't me." Rob moved back from the thing that inhabited his body double. "It was the Air King!"

"He came because of thee," the Ocean's Eye gloated and raised the puppet body's hands. As if following orders, blood from the victims at his feet rose and roped around Rob's feet and hands, shackling him. "You found the Sea-Stone Sword. You took it and used it. Thus, you called the Air King. Thus, you called their deaths."

"You are not me," Rob said, struggling against the bonds. "You're just some god, some powerless god. Your heart was trapped in a stone sword, what sort of power is that? Am I supposed to be impressed?"

The Ocean's Eye shot forward and slammed a hand into Rob's throat. He lifted him off the ground and they soared over the valley floor. Rocks broke around Rob's body as he was slammed into the wall of a falling tower. Cracking and smouldering ruins rumbled, filling his ears as his bones shook.

"I am the god of water," the Ocean's Eye shouted. The face was so close to Rob that he could see every gap in the skin, every stretched pore, every crack and bleeding wound. "I am the sea. There is no power that can destroy me!"

"A spike of rock seemed to do the trick," Rob sneered as the grip tightened. "I smashed your Sword to pieces." He pushed the hand and fell. Air slammed into him but he twisted and rolled onto the dusty valley floor.

Above, the Ocean's Eye hovered, wind making his dreadlocks flutter like a coat. Rob's real coat was stained with blotches of mud, but he brushed them off and stood to his full height.

"I am Rob Sardan," he said. "I defeated the Pirate Lord in single combat. I destroyed the mines of Kenna Iron Helm. I sailed the forbidden sea. I killed the Air King in the red storm. I broke the Sea-Stone Sword. I am not a servant of gods; I will make gods tremble."

The Ocean's Eye screamed in fury and flew at him, but Rob leapt aside letting the creature smash the ground to pieces as it landed. The impact sent Rob stumbling, but he steadied and then faced the creature.

"Thou art mine," it leered at him. "Thou desirest to be remembered. Those dreams never left. These grand deeds thou speaks of are but violence and murder. That is what thou art, Rob Sardan. Thou art a tyrant, thou art a bully. Thou art mine own reflection!"

The creature spread its arms and silver light burst from the veins and eyes in a hellish display. Rob fell, horrified beyond measure. His mind was an inferno erupting with fear.

He was this thing. He had not escaped it when he broke the Sea-Stone Sword. If anything, he had truly become the creature that now stalked closer, grinning through a body it did not own.

Rob ran. He stretched his legs as far as they would go and he ran. He kept running, pumping blood into his limbs as he closed his eyes and put his hands over his ringing ears. The laughter of the Ocean's Eye came, cracking into his skull piercingly like a lance.

His lungs closed. His insides were a war of bile and blood. Hate and anger surged, then fear and guilt, and then deep, dark foreboding. Dread deeper than the abyss opened in his head.

A branch slammed into his forehead, knocking him over. The silver-strewn sky turned blue; the clouds went from red to white, and the roaring laughter was replaced by the hiss of wavering trees and someone's heavy breathing.

"Kindly do not do that again," Alya said leaning over him with a scowl.

Chapter Twenty Five

First Mate

Rob sat in his cabin, head full of spiralling thoughts that would not come to order. His bunk was of little comfort, so he had opted for sitting on the chest, which he had still not opened. It was sealed beyond his strength, tight with bolts and locks.

Gorm had told him that during his hallucinations he had run about the woods, shouting, screaming and punching trees for hours. The hours might have explained why his legs ached so much. Alya had stopped him when he'd run towards a cliff that would have thrown him into the sea. The stick had been carved with a bear's head on the handle. If she had traded some of their supplies for it, he would have very strong words to say to her.

But she had sat with him while he had recovered. She had been scathing and critical, but she had stayed. If he had not been in a spiral of mental chaos at the time, her criticisms would have grated on him to the point of distraction. As it was, they kept him grounded. Wanting to respond had stopped him from slipping back into the dream world and its horrors.

She had finally left after almost a day of watching over him. She'd spoken to Ilma and given instructions to the rest of the crew. By the time Rob had regained enough consciousness to give orders he was missing Alya. Her reports on what she'd got from the market, what the crew were up to, and how she would run the ship if she were in charge, had all kept him in check.

The door creaked open, and he expected her to be back again, but Vann peered in, his nose ring a little more bent than usual and his face even more sheepish.

"Captain," he said. "You said you wanted us all on deck; if you're ready."

"Thank you, Vann," Rob croaked.

Vann nodded and turned to leave, but Rob stopped him.

"Do you think I'm a good captain?" he said.

"Yeah," Vann said and shut the door as he came in. "Best I've ever had. But I've never had a captain before, so I'm not the one to ask."

The hollowness in Rob's chest grew, so he stood and tried to shake some feeling into his limbs.

"What should we do with Skagra?" he said, frowning. "I need to find the Sky Sages, but with her in our cargo hold, we can't. What if she gets loose when we find them? Who knows what she'd do!"

"Maybe we can dump her on some island."

"Perhaps we could find somewhere on Geata to lock her up."

Vann squirmed and averted his gaze. "Is everything okay, Captain? Alya and Gorm seemed quiet. I don't mind Alya being quiet; she can stay like that forever, she's useless!"

"She got us the supplies from Herebealde."

"I'm expecting them all to explode any moment."

"She did well," Rob said. "Almost too well. I find it hard to believe she traded all that grain for what she got; a crate of dried foods, a barrel of wine, a star chart and a South-Point Needle."

"What's one of them?"

"It's a needle that always points south."

"Ah, clue's in the name, I suppose. But why would we want that? I thought we were heading away from the south?"

"We go in the opposite direction," Rob grinned. "Come on, Vann, you *are* intelligent."

"I'm used to listening to other people's thoughts, frankly," he smiled. "Following orders, you know? Any order. Jarl said that he was asked to do all kinds of things as first mate, see: running about, telling everyone what the captain needed, and basically being in charge, but not really because he didn't have to think about it, just do what the captain said, and well, I thought to myself, I could do that, I'm very good at that . . ." he trailed off, looking at his feet with darkening cheeks.

Rob thought back to the moment of their escape. When they'd been sailing away from the pengs, he'd been so overjoyed. His eyes went to Vann's lips, and then he touched his own with a finger, remembering the kiss. Was that what he needed in a first mate?

It was what the old Rob had wanted. The boy who'd loved stories of heroics, the boy who'd wanted nothing more than to swing a sword at anyone he met, and the boy who'd loved Niall. What did *this* Rob want? Here, and now, on this ship, what did he need?

Rob put his hands on Vann's shoulders and made him look into his eyes. Vann's were light blue, a dazzling display in his dark face. "Will you follow every order I give, without question?"

"Yes!"

"Will you always believe in me? Never doubt me; never second guess what I do, no matter what it is?"

"Of course, you know I will!"

"If I make a choice, and you think it's wrong or think it might hurt your feelings, will you defy me?"

"Never, no!"

"That's all I needed to hear." Rob let go and strode to the door; his mind settled and firm in at least one direction. He wanted to say one more word to him, but the look in Vann's eyes made it die on his lips.

Gorm was at the wheel while Ilma and Kari tied jibs and lines, adjusting the sails and fill them with wind. Rob waved to them, and all but Gorm hopped onto the main deck. Alya was standing by the door to the aftcastle, arms behind her head and eyes averted. Jarl was leaning against the railing but seemed to be paying attention.

"First of all," Rob said. "Kari, Jarl, you know this sea, you know the routes. If you are willing, and if you feel able, I would like to ask you to join our crew as navigators. Kari, I have seen you at the wheel, and you seem a natural."

"Really?" said Vann from behind Rob. "I just thought she'd be the cook."

"Why?" Kari raised her eyebrows.

"Well, you look like an expert on food, is all."

"Don't insult her like that, or at all," Rob snapped. "Please, Vann, you're better than that. Kari, Jarl, what do you say?"

"I have no objections," said Jarl, waving and grinning as if dazed. "I'll take you as captain."

"Well," – Kari put her hands on her hips and walked to Vann, making him back away – ". . . so long as *he* keeps his mouth shut, I'll help you."

"One more thing," Rob went on, stepping between her and Vann. "You should know that things are likely to get dangerous. We are looking for the Sky Sages. But the path is full of strange and probably deadly things. We may meet pirates or Air-keepers on the way."

"I've met pirates," Jarl said. "I can handle them."

"Obviously," said Alya with sarcasm.

"She has a point," Kari said. "We're not exactly pirate-fighting experts."

"None of us are," said Rob. "But we bested Skagra, and that is no mean feat. We couldn't have done it without you, Kari."

"Oh, well," she smiled, genuinely. "Thank you, *Captain*."

Rob put his hands on her shoulders and then pulled her into a quick embrace. She returned the squeeze and then broke off. Next, Rob looked to Gorm and walked towards the stairs.

"Gorm, I hadn't decided on whether to give you the position of cook or shipwright, I give you a choice of them."

"To cook is to provide life," she replied.

"I will take that as an acceptance." Rob gave her a bow, which she returned. "Now, Ilma, how does shipwright sound to you?"

"Oh, excellent," she grinned, "if only this hand were better!"

"In that case, I'll make you the ship's doctor." They shared a wink. "Now," Rob drew a deep breath. "I need a first mate."

Vann could not conceal the smug grin that was splitting his face almost in two. But Rob turned towards the aftcastle.

"Alya," he said. "I would like you to be my first mate."

"No!" Vann shouted.

"Are you sure?" Jarl asked airily. "On our ship, the first mate obeyed without question and never spoke against a decision. It was my job to do what the captain said and never, ever say a word that wasn't in line with her wishes."

"*This* is your ship now," Rob told him. "And *I* am your captain. I decide what kind of first mate I need, and it is not somebody who will blindly follow me no matter what. Sorry, Vann, but it's just not healthy."

"But . . ." Vann's mouth was hanging open. "But I thought you and I were . . ."

"This is my decision." Rob said sternly. This was harder than expected. "You all accepted me. And I thank you for that, and I love you all. Alya questioned me, she called me out when I said or did something wrong. I need her in order to make this crew work. Alya." He turned to look at her. "With your help, I think we can make the right decisions."

She had not moved from her place, but her lips had curled into a grim smile. Slowly, she unfolded her arms and with deliberate movements, she walked closer and looked Rob in the eyes.

"I never doubted your intentions," she said. "I do not think you are a liar, Rob Sardan, but I think you withhold the whole truth."

"What's your point?"

"You want to defeat Mothar, yes? You want an end to his reign, you want an end to the pirates, you want to avenge your mother and stop the Sky-slayer's Curse. But, there should be an ending, you need to promise me that. At some point you will be done, you will have finished."

"There will be," he nodded.

"After that," she paused and narrowed her gaze. "After Mothar is defeated and the Sky-slayer's curse is gone, I want the ship."

The wind blew into the sails, and the hull crashed through waves. Rob's feet kept their place on the deck as it moved up and down. His eyes stayed on Alya's, but all around he could hear the intakes of breath, the fretful shifting of feet, and he could feel the pressure of their gazes on him.

"Agreed," he said. "But it will be up to the crew to follow you. If they all accept you, or reject me, then you will be captain. Otherwise, we will find another ship, and if you chose to stay on this one, that's your choice."

"Well then," Alya smiled. "Onwards, Captain."

Rob held out a hand and she paused before she shook it. Vann stormed away, vanishing into the aftcastle, slamming the door. Rob felt the pain inside his chest, but he tried to maintain a level expression on his face. Jarl heaved a heavy sigh and looked at Rob.

"I'll go and talk to him," he said.

The rest of the crew regarded Rob with curious looks, but he walked to the quarterdeck. He signalled to Kari, and she followed, relieving Gorm of the wheel.

"Take us to Geata," he said. "You know the best route?"

"If we are where I think we are, then yes," she said.

"His home town might put Vann in a better mood." Rob closed his eyes, his heart still stinging.

"We'll stop off in Leoht." Kari licked her lips and tilted her head into the wind. "In seven days if the wind is with us."

"Less," Alya corrected. "The ship will outpace anything your Long Silver could have dared dream of."

Rob smiled and hopped to the main deck urging Alya to follow. "Carry on, everyone." He waved, and they set about adjusting the sails and lines to Kari's instructions.

Alya closed the door once they were in the cabin and she leaned against it. Rob went to the chest and picked at the lock with his little finger. Eventually, Alya went over and pressed a latch under the left side, then slid three cogs on the back, making the lid pop open.

Within were several bottles of wine, a pair of goblets, and a wooden box, inside which, Rob found carved figures. One was a bear much like the one that adorned the prow. Another was a snake; its body curled inwards so that its long head rested on its coils. The third was a wolf, sitting on its back legs and howling. The final figure was a lion with its paws raised as if to strike.

"Where did you get these?" he asked.

"I made them." She snatched the box and slammed it shut. "They are the figures of the Four Shapes of Nature. Godlike creatures that are sacred to my people; I learned to carve when I was five."

"That stick you hit me with back in the forest . . ."

". . . was of my own making, yes. I gave it to Kari in payment for the wound I inflicted on her leg. That she refuses to use it moults no feather of mine. I consider my debt paid in that matter."

"Did you carve other things to trade at the market?"

"Is this an interrogation? I thought you had decided to trust me and listen to me, not nag me to death."

"I think you are remarkably talented, that's all."

"Flattery is of no use to me." She put the box back in the chest and lifted the wine. "This is what you wanted?"

They poured it into the goblets and stood facing one another. Rob was about to raise it but stopped, an old memory searing his consciousness like a branding fire.

"Someone told me to raise a cup to him the first night I was a captain of a full crew," Rob said slowly. "I suppose now that you are part of the crew that would be tonight more than any other night."

"Raise your goblet then, it's nothing to me."

"You don't understand." He closed his eyes and put the drink down. "That man betrayed me. He killed the boy I loved, and he did *things* to me . . ."

Alya lowered her goblet. "This is not my area of expertise. I suggest you talk to Ilma; she has knowledge of such things. She has a child. I have never had a desire for carnal matters, or romantic ones, for that matter."

"Oh, it's not like that." He shook his head. "He put Saagara in my body, like Skagra did to Gorm, and tried to turn me into a monster. I think he succeeded. When I was hallucinating, I saw that monster. The creature I would have become had I not broken the Sea-Stone Sword."

"But you broke it, so what is the problem?"

"Those things are still inside me." He sat on the bunk, drumming his fingers on the goblet. "The violence, the desire for fame and all the worst things of heroism. Even while I've been with this crew, I've succumbed to those desires. I put my life at risk to save yours, not because it was the right thing to do, but because I was afraid of what would happen if you died. I didn't want the guilt on my shoulders. I didn't want more death on my hands."

She sipped the wine and considered him carefully over the rim. "Let us examine the facts. The Sea-Stone Sword is gone. The desires you speak of are in many people, but you exercise self-control because you care about the world. We each have only one life, so we seek to make the most of it. To be weighed down by guilt is to make a misery of life.

"You have the desire for life, and you need to realise that others have that desire, too. To disregard it is to become that monster. Whatever your actions, do not put others at risk for selfish reasons. That is my stance on the matter. If you ever do anything to put this crew at risk, I will not forgive you. However, it is my belief that you will put your own life at risk before theirs."

"Is this a good thing?" he asked.

"To me, it is the best thing," she grinned. "I would get my ship sooner."

"You are not inspiring me to trust you."

"This is my ship. You are the captain of the crew."

Rob lifted the goblet. "I'll drink to the crew, then. Tethra can go and boil his head." He drained the cup, hardly taking in the balmy, nutty taste. The name, Tethra, stirred his mind. It had been a disguise, a false name to hide the truth. "It's time I forgot the past."

"Remembering the past is useful," Alya said. "I wear the headscarf of my people so that I remember them. To my sisters and brothers it was a sign of reverence, respect, submission or worship. For me, it is a memory." She slipped the scarf off and held it up. "A childhood I ran from. But I remember them. I still want to."

"Why did you run away?"

"It was boring," she smiled sadly. "They had too many rules and too much reverence for old ways. The scarf was part of that, yes. But I like its feel, I like to recall the land of my ancestors, I like to remember my family."

"It's nice to find someone who does not have a childhood filled with pain for once," Rob laughed. "How did you come to be a shipbuilder anyway?"

"I travelled on many ships after I left Amser. I asked shipwrights about how they worked and spent time in ports with shipbuilders. Years of working out what ships worked best for what tasks followed. I've built five ships, but this is the best."

"How old are you?" he looked at her, amazed.

"Twenty-five," she said.

"And you've already built five ships?"

"I am good at what I do." She tapped a beam that held the ceiling.

"Indeed," Rob patted the wood of the bunk. "What do you think of '*The Sword-breaker*'?"

"My opinion of you is irrelevant."

"I mean as a name for the ship? We broke Skagra's ship, the Black Sword. Besides, people already know the name. I'd prefer it to be the name of the ship than my own, frankly."

She shrugged. "As long as you don't call it Fat Ted, I shall be pleased."

"We can agree on that at least."

"Yes," she said and replaced her scarf. "What exactly are you planning? To head to Geata, and then what? Find this secret passage and this lake of fire?"

"I'd like to talk to the nuns of the Dead God. Do you have any better suggestions?"

"I have not criticised this as a method for finding the Sages."

"So, you are happy to go along with my quest?"

"Happy? No," she smiled bitterly. "The truth of the stories is a curiosity, perhaps. But I am concerned about putting the ship at risk."

"This ship can survive anything; you said so."

"Skagra said there was a river of fire. The ship can survive rocks, storms, and even hurricanes. Fire is another matter."

"There must be a way through," Rob insisted. "How would anyone get there?"

"I wonder if anyone is *supposed* to get there."

Chapter Twenty Six

The Fire of Suspicion

They reached Leoht in four days, much to Kari's surprise. Tensions had been high since Alya had been named first mate and while Gorm had accepted her, the rest had been hesitant. At mealtime on the second day, Rob had spoken to each crewmember, in turn, to talk them round.

He wasn't sure how successful he had been. Vann had barely responded to his words and had stared out to sea the whole time. The man hadn't eaten much either, and his work had been sluggish. Rob had not wanted to push him, but work needed doing, and they had to evade any chance of meeting ships with black flags.

Leoht had risen on the horizon before Kari and Ilma had confided in Rob that they thought Alya the best choice.

"Looking at how Vann reacted, I don't think he'd have been good," Kari said. "Besides, Alya's got a good head."

"She didn't exactly act graciously when they named me captain," Rob snorted.

"But she got helping within a day," Ilma said. "Vann's been sulking for three."

"She *is* older." Rob nodded his head. "I think I needed a mature mind."

"Alya hasn't been too hard on us," Kari continued. "She's actually quite sweet when you look past her poison. She knows how to get things done, never minces words, and well, she's just really good."

"Do you want to chew her food for her as well?" Ilma nudged Kari. "Keep your trousers on for now."

"What?" Kari spluttered.

"Calm down, you two," Rob laughed. "We need to drop anchor."

Rob sent Alya, Ilma and Kari ashore for supplies while the rest prepared for the next leg of their journey. Jarl joined Rob on deck to look over the charts.

"We could reach Geata in a couple of days," Jarl said. "I suggest we circle to the west and skim Concaedes. There are pirates around Gold Port, the currents are violent, and many ships get caught on the rocks. We have a crew of seven, so if we keep to a tight schedule, we could sail all the way without a single stop."

"Sounds good." Rob rolled the charts and strode to the aftcastle. He shuffled to the crew's quarters where he found Gorm on a bunk, her eyes focused on the candle in her lantern. Rob cleared his throat to get her attention, and she sat up.

"How are you?" he asked. "With Skagra so close, it must be difficult for you."

"There are many things I have meditated on since we left Bron'Halla," she said. "While locked in the ice prison, facing Skagra seemed the easiest thing in the world, it seemed the key to closing the past out of my mind. But fear is ever near my heart now that she is so close."

"If you need to get away for a while . . ." Rob tried to say more, but Gorm raised a hand.

"Captain, I want to talk to her." She breathed and stood. "I will keep my silence as best I can so as to avoid speaking rashly.

The fear and anger she inspired in me is too great to ignore. Yes, I would speak with her."

"Are you sure?"

"To hide from my fear would be unwise. We must face them head on if we are to defeat them, you and I. Captain Sardan, you fear your own mind, and yet you live with it at all times. I fear Skagra and what she may do to me, and what she has done to me. I will take your example, and I will endure and overcome."

"Right . . ." He shifted uncomfortably.

"I have been meditating for hours in preparation. To focus the mind and clear it of distractions is to bring inner perception as well as outer insight."

They walked through the cramped corridor to the cargo hold, and Rob pushed the door open.

The room stank. Rob recoiled while Gorm held a lantern to spread light into the place. Skagra stood in the middle, her sweaty clothes torn and bloody while around her feet, filth festered. She looked haunted, and her eyes were brimming.

"Get her on deck," Rob ordered, and Gorm hurried into the room.

They kept Skagra's chains, but she collapsed into Gorm's arms as they detached them from the mast. Fury rang through Rob as he grasped Skagra's legs and helped Gorm carry her. The stench followed them through the ship, and the pirate seemed to have soiled her clothing so thoroughly that even putting his hands to it had made Rob feel ill.

"What on earth did she do?" Rob asked.

"I cannot fathom . . ." Gorm gulped and coughed.

On the main deck, they let Skagra down before securing the chains again. Gorm tripped and stumbled away from the pirate who was getting to her feet. Rob tried to push her down, but she sunk her teeth into his arm.

Screaming, Rob sprang, kicking Skagra in the stomach to make her let go. Blood trickled down his bicep where she had dug her teeth through his coat and into his flesh. She had not gone deep, but the stinging made him twitch.

Skagra bounded away, the chains coming loose. Rob cursed that he had not secured them properly. She whipped the chains at him, the ring of each impact threatening serious injury.

"Tell me, Rob Sardan," Skagra said. "What do you expect to find in the Sky Sage's Tower? Another sword for you to break? A crown, perhaps?"

"What are you talking about?" he demanded, keeping his distance as Gorm circled behind her.

"Come now, Sword-breaker, don't pretend you didn't believe the tales of the Tomb of the Dead God. There is a power there that would rival the Sea-Stone Sword." Skagra grinned, her bloody teeth dripping. "Somebody on your crew has been talking. There is a traitor in your midst."

"Who was it?" Rob shouted.

"Why would I tell you?" she laughed. "It's much more fun for you to try and find out, isn't it? Oh, you'll tear this crew to pieces, won't you?"

"Why are you doing this?"

"I will not let you have the power of the dead god's crown."

"Power is not my goal," Rob insisted. "I had a god's power once, I don't want another."

"Don't lie to me! Why else would you seek the Tower?"

"I have the Sky-slayer's Curse! I need to be cured and the Sages are the only ones who can help."

"And it is simply a coincidence that the Crown of Black Glass happens to be in the same place?" She spat. "I will not believe you, Sword-Breaker."

"If there is such a thing there," – Rob tightened his fist and raised it – "I would break it like I broke the Sea-Stone Sword."

"And you would leave this world to suffer. You would watch as tyrants, queens, and lords stripped this world bare. What kind of hero would that make you? One who cosies up to the powerful and lets them live in peace while people suffer under their feet?"

"I wouldn't . . ." His heart strained. The words had a familiar ring to them; he had thought the same of another once, long ago. His own father had been a man so obsessed with the powerful in his country that he had exiled Rob rather than betray the king's secrets.

"Skagra, please!" Rob reached out a hand. "Perhaps we can help you . . ."

She arched her back and took a deep, rattling breath. Then she cried out, voice ringing high and piercing, words in a different language spilling out, as it got louder. Gorm jumped and slammed her palm over her mouth, but Skagra bit. Blood splattered and Gorm screamed.

"It was Spillish," she said, gasping for breath. "It's the language of the Spill Mountains, home of the pterosaurs."

"She's calling an Air-keeper," Rob realised.

Skagra whipped the chains back and thrust a fist into Rob's cheek, pain exploded across his head and he reeled. Skagra burst into fits of hysterical laughter. Gorm's hand was bleeding and Rob wanted to help, but Skagra was bearing down, chains ready to whip. He rolled from the first strike and leapt over the second, but the third knocked him into the mast.

His whole head echoed with pain. Gorm had got to her feet and was racing at Skagra, but Rob's eyes blurred and the whole world turned red.

The wind howled and shook the ship as the water rose in white fury. Crimson clouds circled and Rob felt the breath go out of his lungs. Struggling to stand, he coughed and tried to force his body to move, but his head hurt and his chest stung.

The pterosaur landed on the prow, its great head-crest glimmering with diamonds that had been encrusted into it. With a leer, it opened its maw of teeth and leant forwards.

"You should know, Rob Sardan," Skagra said as she sauntered towards the Air-keeper. "*All shall die in the Flame-Filled Sky.*"

"What *is* that?" Rob demanded.

"The great fire," she said, looking him in the eyes. "You've seen it. The green tongues of living flame. The fire is the end of the world."

"This is wrong!" Rob stepped closer, but the pterosaur snapped at him and his eyes filled with red clouds. Screaming and dying sounds punched his ears and he collapsed to his knees.

"Wrong?" Skagra spat. "Tell my mother that everything she did was wrong. Tell her I did her a favour by maiming her. Tell her coming to nag me was not a productive use of her time."

Rob crawled after her, but she kicked him in the nose. He rolled on the deck, gasping for breath. The pterosaur snapped and spread its wings, darkening the ship. Gorm shouted but Rob was so consumed with hurt that all he heard was a dull drone.

"What's going on?" Vann asked, coming from the aftcastle.

Rob tried to speak, but his throat closed. The pterosaur shrieked and Vann was blasted down the stairs. Rob sprang after him, despite the pain that filled his body. Another blast of red wind hurled Rob off his feet, and he was smashed against the stairs to the quarterdeck. Jarl, who had been cowering behind the wheel, squeaked and crawled to the railing.

"I will have vengeance for my Black Sword," Skagra said. "This Air-keeper shall tear your ship to splinters."

"On whose orders?" the voice came from the Air-keeper, but its mouth barely moved, except to hang open as the words echoed.

"No orders," Skagra said as she hopped onto its back. "But this is Rob Sardan, the King-killer. I leave the decision to you."

Rob was struggling to get to his feet and breathe at the same time. The pterosaur rose and let out a hellish scream that shook the timbers. It flapped its mighty wings and took off, the shock tearing the sails from the mast and flinging them into the sea. Rob clung to the railing, his lungs aching as the ship shook hard and violently. His eyes followed the creature as it hovered, gathering red air about its tattooed body.

Rob looked at Gorm and then at Jarl. Their eyes were wide, their mouths open. The pit of Rob's stomach opened to engulf him. It was happening again. His crew, his friends, his ship, all were about to be destroyed by an Air-keeper.

The blast hit the deck, knocking Rob into the stairs, blistering his skin. The ship was tossed from the water, weight dragging Rob's legs as they soared and then pressing on him as they plummeted. Foam splashed onto the deck, drenching them in salty brine. The pterosaur dove, beak open. Rob braced his legs and jumped just as it hit the ship; the pterosaur smashed against the wood. The beak broke, but the wood didn't even vibrate at the impact.

A tangle of wings and beak scrambled and bit, teeth the size of Rob's arms struck at him, but he dove and rolled away. Skagra was still nestled on top of the Air-keeper, but her hair was flying in a mane of disorder.

"This ship will not break," Rob said. "No Air-keeper can breach its hull. Tell your comrades that Rob Sardan captains the ship that defeats the sky. Tell the pirates that if they see *The Sword-Breaker*, they should flee."

The pterosaur shrieked, but Rob hopped out of reach and spat on the thing's beak. It snarled and took flight, the beat of its wings leaving a red scar across the air. The fog clouded, pressing on Rob's eyes until he closed them and clung to the mast. A high screaming thundered in his ears, and he hunched down as the pressure grew.

It released, and he gasped, blinking at the ship. It was intact, trails of dirt scattered from where Skagra had been dragged from below. He stared at the storm above, watching the bulbous shapes merge and then tear. It dissipated until the blue skies were untarnished.

He could barely keep his lungs going as they pushed air in and out of his chest. His head was echoing with the screams and sounds of death. There was an urge to touch the empty space the pendant had occupied.

At last, he collapsed, his eyes falling shut with exhaustion and his hands shaking. Skagra has escaped. It had been such an obvious ploy, too. If Alya had been there, she would have seen it. Even Vann might have thought twice.

Rob was burnt on the inside, still raw at Vann's disappointment and anger. That thought forced him to sit up and crawl painfully towards the stern. Peering down the stairs, he met Vann's eyes as he, too, was crawling. The man glanced over his shoulder and gulped before looking back.

"I'm sorry," Rob said. "Please forgive me."

"Aye, Captain," he said with a smile. "You're becoming quite the expert at fighting Air-keepers."

Rob forced his lips to curl, but the amusement was false. He could feel his mind slipping, his grip on consciousness failing. The dreams were going to take him again. He was so tired, so utterly tired. But they were like tentacles pulling him into the depths to drown in torment.

Vann helped Rob to sit against the door, but he could scarcely focus on his face. The nose ring glinted and Vann's eyes shone, reminding Rob of another old friend he had lost long ago. Long, long ago.

A CROWD HAD seen them off from Leoht, a day later. Many had marvelled at how the ship had survived the Air-keeper. Rob waved as they pulled away, the repaired sails billowing.

"They'll spread the story," Alya observed. She hadn't spoken up about the attack until now, preferring to listen to the others as they had voiced their concerns. Rob wondered if she was going to take advantage of his slipping hold over the crew.

"But which one?" Rob asked. "The ship that survived against all odds, or the fact that Skagra escaped. I was so stupid."

"Yes," Alya nodded. "But Skagra knew just how to play you. I can't think of how else you would have reacted to what she did. I suppose I should have seen it coming, as should you."

"Don't you think I'm . . . ?" Rob stopped and shook his head. "It doesn't matter. We need to move on."

"We need to learn," Alya added before moving off to help the crew.

Rob stayed where he was, nursing the bandages about his chest and arms. Ilma had done the best she could with her good hand, but Rob had helped tie them. He had not been able to say much, partly due to fatigue, and partly due to the clouds of suspicion.

The crew was ushering the ship northwards, but Rob took up a vigil at the prow, one foot on the bowsprit. He kept his hat on with one hand while the other was in his pocket. The hallucinations he had suffered thanks to Lomi's tea were still haunting him. The attack of the Air-keeper had blasted a hole in his confidence, and the growing suspicion of an informer in their ranks had left him feeling deflated.

Vann was loyal and good-natured, but disgruntled by Rob's decision not to make him first mate. He had argued, and the man had become increasingly sulky. However, he had been willing to fight the Air-keeper and had seemed genuinely surprised when Skagra had escaped.

Ilma was skilled and bright, but her relationship with Skagra was not something he could push aside. Whatever their history, it caused him worry. Was Ilma willing to compromise the crew to make things up with her daughter? He could not see her doing that. Ilma had had several chances to botch Rob's treatments let alone the other members of the crew.

Gorm had not spoken to Skagra before the escape, so far as he knew. She had fought her, she had imprisoned her, and she had kept her word to stay with Rob. However, during their duel, their swords had not even touched, Alya had commented on how her jian was not scratched after the affair. Perhaps there was some lingering respect for Skagra within Gorm's heart.

Kari was mellowing, or, at least, appeared to be. She had been much more involved than he had expected when it came to navigation. There had been storms that she had avoided at a moment's notice, and she had been able to pinpoint their position on the charts to within a mile. However, knowing so little about her left him uneasy.

Jarl was an even bigger mystery. The man was dazed and confused most of the time. His lucid moments were filled with rambling explanations of how things were on his old ship and how his old captain had done things. It irritated Rob, but he could not bring himself to get rid of Jarl. Firstly, he felt that Kari would likely leave, and secondly he pitied him. Whatever Skagra had done to him had affected his mind.

Then there was Alya.

The first mate was giving Vann and Jarl a series of instructions on how to streamline the sails. Her knowledge was impressive, but her attitude grated. She made Vann feel bad, and that made Rob feel even guiltier. Trusting Alya was a risk. She had double-crossed the imperial and renegade pengs in order to escape Bron'Halla. She had been against almost every decision they had made. Rob itched to be able to say for certain if she was on his side, but he couldn't even trust his own mind.

"Captain," Kari's voice broke his thoughts.

Night was setting in; he hadn't realised how long he had been standing there, glowering into the sea, wrapped in suspicion.

"Are we holding course?" he asked, massaging his stiff legs.

"We are," she said, adjusting her belt and frowning at it. "That's the thing. We haven't even gone an inch off course. The wind has been in our sails the whole time, and we've faced virtually no major tidal changes."

"How long until we reach Geata?"

"At this pace, another day or two," she guessed. "But . . ." she bit her lip and then went on. "It's just *too* good. There's nothing going wrong. It's as if we're being guided."

The sky was streaked with clouds, grey and white with some edged red. In the purpling twilight, it was difficult to tell if this was a trick of the light or not. Rob drew a breath and stepped onto the main deck, Kari following with a frustrated huff.

"I don't like this," she said. "Listen to me!"

"I am listening. We've already had one Air-keeper attack us, and I know they'd like nothing better than to get revenge for their king. But I also know we are heading in the right direction; we are going to get to the Sky Sages."

"*I* have no reason to go," she said. "Jarl and I have nothing. I don't want some dead god's power, nor do I want gold."

"What do you want?"

"To be free." She drew herself up and straightened her back. "I want to sail without worrying about pirates or magical flying monsters. I just want to have a good time. Is that really too much to ask?"

"No," he answered and put a hand on her shoulder.

"I'm sick of doing what's expected," she went on. "I came to sea to get away from powerful folk. Now we've got Skagra on our tail, how could you let her loose?"

"We couldn't keep her here forever," Rob said. "The pirates would have come for her sooner or later, no doubt. I don't know if we would have got away with the same trick again if another galleon had crossed us. If anything, this might have been the best outcome for us."

"But now all the Air-keepers and pirates there ever were are after us!"

"They'd come after you no matter what," Rob said.

"Why? What makes me so important?"

"You and Jarl were targeted, and Skagra will want to finish the job. You saw what she was like."

"I did." Kari bit her lip and looked away. "I can't be important, though. I'm nothing special; I'm of no value."

He shook his head and gripped her shoulder. "You sailed

this ship with barely any training. You fought my crew single-handed, and you defended the Long Silver as it sank. You're amazing, Kari. If you don't believe that, then call me a liar."

"You are!" She failed to stop the smile from creasing her face.

"Go, get some rest," he advised. "And please use the stick Alya made for you. It was a nice gesture, and she struggles with emotional displays."

"I like the stick," she muttered. "But if she thinks I will forgive her for smashing my ankle to bits she's got another thing coming."

"I understand. Just be a little less hostile to her, that's all."

"I'm not the hostile one."

"True enough," he allowed.

Chapter Twenty Seven

Tomb of the Dead God

Alya stood at the prow with her headscarf around her neck and her hair billowing. Rob approached and stood next to her while Vann and Ilma were behind.

"Welcome home, Vann," Rob said, gesturing to the green sward ahead.

"I feel sick," Vann said, holding his stomach. "I think I might be ill. Maybe we should just keep sailing. There must be other places we could visit."

"What's brought this on?" Rob stared at him.

"Come on, Rob, I don't want to go home, that's boring . . ." He fidgeted with his nose ring, sweating.

Kari dropped anchor and they drew the sails in, letting the ship bob in the shallows off the coast. The rocky beach ahead was narrow, crested by long grass and beyond, a rising hillside of trees. Rob marched to the gig and gestured to Gorm and Vann to follow him.

"Alya, you have the ship," he told her. "Keep an eye out for signs of pirates."

"Yes, that was my plan."

Rob nodded and led Vann into the gig.

"Here, you can't seriously be trusting her, can you?" he said. "What if she nicks the ship and we never see them again?"

"We'll hunt her down and take it back," Rob shrugged. "For what it's worth, I think she likes the crew."

"Likes you, maybe," Vann spat as they lifted the gig and lowered it via ropes.

Once they were in the water, they steadied and set about paddling, waving at the others as they went. Gorm set a swift pace while Rob stood at the prow watching the water as it became shallower, shale and pebbles thickening as they got closer to the shore.

Landing, they dragged the gig inland before carrying it to the tall grass and covering it with as much as they could find. It was a quick job, but it seemed good enough and Rob took off as swiftly as he dared.

"Vann, what's the quickest way to the Tomb of the Dead God?" he asked.

"Not sure," Vann sighed. "Let's keep walking. Didn't your best mate back there tell you all about it in intricate detail since she seems to know everything about everything?"

"No," Rob nudged him. "Alya, doesn't *like* me, not in the way you mean."

"Oh? She spends a lot of time with you." Vann kicked at the pebbles.

"She's first mate, I have to talk with her and get our plans right. Come on, Vann, you must realise she's intelligent."

"Yeah, too clever by half. Too clever to be mixed up with us is the problem. How can we out-think her if she's three steps ahead of us all the time?"

"You want to betray her?"

"I'm saying we should plan for it. Have a backup. We've not had much of that since we escaped. It's just running and hoping with nothing except a horrible, painful death to look forward to if we don't. I don't like horrible deaths, especially if it's mine! And she's been bleeding horrible to me since we first met."

"We are approaching a settlement," Gorm said, making the two of them jump.

A town of thatched houses was nestled in a dell, the houses were clumped together and slid gradually towards a crumbling windmill. The sails were deep beige and turned as a gust caught them.

"Know the place?" Rob asked.

"Might be Woollenhome," Vann suggested. "I think they've got a mill."

The village was deserted. Doors hung open; the stench of rotten food made Rob hold his breath as they passed. Coughing, Gorm strode ahead and gestured to the windmill's smashed doors.

Rob knelt inside the threshold. Words had been painted in thick, brown muck. It stank of bodily fluids and Rob was reminded of Skagra's state when she'd soiled her prison. It had taken him and Vann most of the journey to clean it.

If this was the same excrement, he could understand why nobody had *volunteered* to clean it. One word had been written over and over again in the muck before him. It made Rob pause and narrow his eyes.

Liberator

"Skagra?" Rob suggested, stepping out of the mill.

"Most likely," Gorm nodded.

"Why 'liberator'?"

"That is what she believes she is, perhaps." Gorm frowned. "It was the name of the first ship she captained. That was where we first met."

They walked away, Rob trying to block out the stench. Vann was glowering at Gorm, but the tall woman was deep in thought, her eyes flicking back to the mill even as it vanished behind them.

"When we sailed on the Liberator," Gorm said at last, "Skagra was younger, she was full of eager energy and wished for nothing but freedom. Together, we traced the paths of Sayyida, the old pirate queen from decades ago. Ah, those day were like bliss."

"What changed?" Rob asked.

"The Liberator was destroyed," Gorm said sadly. "While we camped, our ship was burned and many of the crew with it. I watched as Skagra laughed in her grief. She laughed and I never understood why."

"Did the grief turn her into this lover of chaos?"

"It is hard to say." Gorm shook her head. "She had believed in throwing down queens, lords and all rulers ever since I met her. The fire lit her desire for action, perhaps. I recall she said that she had been too idle, but now she would act."

"And who was it that destroyed the Liberator?"

"Who else?" Gorm sighed. "It was Mothar. That was how he recruited her."

THEY SCALED THE hills and a smell permeated the air. Rob put his sleeve over his mouth and nose, choking as they passed a third village showing signs of similar decimation. Most of it looked to be at least six months gone by Gorm's reckoning.

At the top of the hills, they were presented with a wide bowl of land, the crater stretched for two miles in circumference at least. The sweeping grasslands dove into it, leading to a tower in the centre; it was a grey stone obelisk surrounded by a series of rising walls and bastions. There was a moat of filthy water coated in algae and dead grass, and finally another, smaller wall of black stone.

"There were stories," Vann said, his voice weak. "That this is where a volcano erupted a long time ago. Used to be farmland when I was a kid. All the nuns used to plough and grow stuff."

"Looks like it's been left for a while," Rob said.

The sky trembled with thunder. Clouds were churning like hot soup, purpling with rain. A patter fell and Rob pulled his collars up before setting off into the crater. Intensifying, the rain lashed them until they were struggling through mud up to their ankles. Gorm moved ahead, her larger body acting as a barrier for the others, but it wasn't much. Rob hunkered down and sped up, spreading each stride as wide as he could. Vann tripped and splattered into the muck, yowling with disgust.

As he helped him, Rob caught Vann's eye. The young man snatched his hand back before storming past towards the moat. After a moment's hesitation, Rob followed, and soon they were crossing a splintered and rotting bridge. It rocked under their weight and Gorm's foot punctured a wooden beam, knocking her off balance.

Once they were under the first wall that ringed the obelisk, Rob gave Vann a boost and he clambered onto the top. Gorm then lifted Rob before they helped her alongside them. Leaping onto the soggy ground, they trudged closer to the obelisk, pillars and roofs scattered in its shadow.

"Who comes here?" the voice rang over the grass, magnified and shaking. Rob could taste the fear in the words, so he waved as disarmingly as he could.

"My name is Rob Sardan," he shouted. "We're looking for the Tomb of the Dead God."

"Rob Sardan?" the voice inquired.

A figure appeared between two of the pillars that circled the obelisk. She wore a long hood, which hid her face, and a cloak that coated her body. But on her back were two folded wings, covered by an embroidered cloth that glinted with diamonds that had been sewn into its pattern.

"We would be honoured to speak with you," the draig said.

Vann shrank behind Rob, his head shaking and his throat whimpering. Gorm regarded the man with a kind smile and put her hand on his arm.

"Let not your fear be . . ."

"Oh, shut it for one minute, Gorm," Vann snapped.

"Is there something wrong?" Rob asked. "Vann, please tell me."

"It's nothing . . ." He shuddered. "Just let me sit this one out. Maybe I could stay on lookout here? Draigs give me the creeps, have done ever since I was little."

Rob frowned, unconvinced. After a moment he waved a hand and let Vann stay, urging Gorm to follow to where the draig was standing, rain splattering off her hood and cloaks.

"Hello," Rob said. "Is this the Tomb of the Dead God?"

"In a manner," she bowed. "Come, we shall speak within. Is your friend going to stand in that manure all day?"

Vann jerked his foot out of the pile he had been in and scrambled away, kicking and spluttering while flapping his arms. Rob let his shoulders sag and he shook his wet hair around his head before following the draig under the pillared roof and towards a doorway set in the obelisk.

Within, the floor was a mosaic of draigs, their lithe bodies naked and polished, with each gender shown upholding crowns and helmets. Some had their wings spread, others were folded, and they all encircled a golden creature with a screaming face.

The mosaic was made from various kinds of stone, but the centrepiece of the room captured Rob's attention. A great tombstone, its face carved into the features of the screaming figure beneath their feet.

"The Dead God," said another draig who approached from a set of stairs that branched off from behind the stone. "They called her D'haara, sister to Saagara, Vaata, and the nameless one."

Rob and Gorm exchanged a look and then stepped closer to the new draig. She was dressed in long gold gowns, flowing ribbons of red and yellow were attached here and there and her veil was silver. It all fluttered and golden trinkets clattered around her body.

"We greet you, Sword-breaker," she bowed. "I am Hafwen, priestess of the Tomb. I knew the Sky Sages before their silence."

"Silence?" Rob inquired. The draig nodded, frowning and closing her eyes. "Was it pirates? Our friend outside used to live here. He said his family were in this tomb place. His name is Vann."

"Vann Øster?" Hafwen looked surprised. "This is unusual indeed. Signy Øster was taken by Skagra last year and we do not know what happened to her. She was old, and she had many sins."

"Vann told me about her trasati circus." Rob felt the spark of anger return for a moment. "And what about the younger one, Vann's sister?"

"Sister? There was no younger Øster. Signy came alone with a tale of her lost family, saying that her child, Vann had been taken by the pirates and she had fled, seeking refuge."

Rob stroked his chin and paced. He looked at Gorm and then nodded to the door. She took his meaning and marched out into the storm. A shiver of cold made Rob's skin prickle and he pulled his coat tighter.

"Come," Hafwen said, leading him to a stair. "You are the Sword-breaker and it is time you learnt what that meant."

"Sorry, but can it wait? I need the Sages. I am a Sky-slayer; I need a pendant."

"The Sages have not been heard since Mothar came," Hafwen said, sadly. "I see that you wear the gold of the Sages, though. You must have been there before."

"No, not me." Rob stroked the pommel of the gold sword and the gold bracelet on his right hand. "A peng named Lomi gave them to me to return to the tower. She used to be one of them but she left."

"Ah," she smiled knowingly. "What more could be expected of a peng?"

He followed the priestess into the higher chambers of the Tomb. The rooms were airy, open to the rain. Rob suddenly felt a rumble beneath their feet but it faded. He could smell sulphur, and coughed as a jet of steam leapt from below.

"This land is sacred," Hafwen said. "It is said to be the place where D'haara met her great defeat."

"A dead god doesn't seem like one worth worshiping," said Rob, feeling this was the sort of thing Alya would say.

"There is some truth in that." Hafwen clapped her hands and another draig approached, dressed in red robes and a head-scarf, offering them drinks.

"What happened?" Rob asked, declining the goblet. "What did Skagra do?"

"She swept through here a year ago," said Hafwen taking a goblet from her subordinate. "This was after Mothar had already silenced the Sages. When she attacked, there were casualties, but, alas, far more decided to join her."

"I understand. Fighting Skagra would be difficult, especially if she had her crew behind her. Fear makes us do the worst things."

"This was not fear." Hafwen dismissed the other draig and sipped from her goblet. "Skagra drew people to her cause. She tore down the lords of Geata, threw them into the stocks, and had the people tell her what crimes they had committed. Theft of land, betrayal of trust, the ruling of the rich, all of it came out and the lords were driven into the sea, quite literally."

"Skagra's been recruiting," Rob said. "We came across a ship she'd attacked. She took the crew. What's she doing? Building an army? What for?"

"Who can say? She does not lead as a general or an officer, she has her direction and she allows her crew to follow."

"Is anyone left on the island?" Rob asked.

"A few scattered settlements remain, but they are poor and ill. We have requested aid from the Cendyl, but have yet to hear back."

"Surely the Cendyl will help their own kind?"

"Not as many draigs are here as you think," Hafwen sighed and put her goblet down. "The ruling classes have become ever more reverent of the old ways. They worship their ancestors, they stick to ancient traditions and shun any who have left the homeland."

"I met some draigs in Fort Ewin once," Rob recalled. "They even used their wings and flame breath. I didn't think draigs did that anymore."

"Fort Ewin is a cauldron of debauchery," Hafwen snarled. "To use the flame breath is not . . ." she coughed. "It is not appropriate. Only the savages use it, but we civilised draigs are above beastly behaviour."

"Beastly behaviour?" Rob shook his head.

"Humans can produce water in their mouths," Hafwen sounded angry. "Why do you not spit into one another's cups and drink it?"

"That would be disgusting!"

"Precisely! We are draigs, not drakans. We walk on two feet, we think with high minds, and we speak with language. Drakans, animals, and trasati are all beasts with no such skills."

"I beg to differ," Rob could not help contradicting. "Trasati do have a kind of language, but it is one of feelings and impressions. You can't lie to a trasati. I suspect the same was true of the drakans."

"Did you come here to criticise my people?" Hafwen huffed.

"No, sorry." Rob lifted his hands. "I came for answers, but now I have more questions. I wanted Vann to meet his people; I wanted to help find his family. Signy Øster was taken by Skagra? So, she might still be alive."

"Probably," Hafwen nodded, still disgruntled. "Skagra may be bloodthirsty, but she is not as willing to kill as Mothar."

"Mothar is immortal," Rob glowered at the ceiling. "I bet it's easy to dismiss life when you have so much of it."

She eyed him, and then looked at one of the sisters who was walking by carrying a box. Signalling to her, she ordered the box brought closer.

Within were scrolls and parchments, which she sniffed at. At last, she pulled out a tight bundle and handed it to Rob. It was sealed with wax, set with the sign of a pterosaur skeleton.

"This is the same symbol that was on my Sky-slayer's pendant!"

"It is the Sage's sign," Hafwen nodded. "That scroll was left here many years ago along with these others. If you go looking for the tower, it may be of some help."

Rob broke the seal and unrolled a map. It showed an interlocking labyrinth of tunnels and passages, some drawn with blue ink, others with red. In the centre was a ziggurat, within which was a black crown.

"A crown . . ." Rob touched it. "Skagra mentioned a crown."

"The Crown of Black Glass," Hafwen nodded. "It is the heart of D'haara's power, so they say. Much like the Sea-Stone Sword was the heart of Saagara."

"That's it!" Rob's eyes widened. "Mothar must have been looking for it. After I broke the Sea-Stone Sword, they must have gone looking for other powers. Of course! But why now? It seems a lot more accessible than the Sword ever was."

"What part of '*Dead* God' is difficult for you?" Hafwen sighed. "D'haara is dead, her power diminished and divided. Her mind was destroyed in the great battle."

"So, the Crown won't work?"

"We do not know. The Sky Sages forbade anyone to hold it or even look at it."

"What happened to the Sages, then? Where are they?"

"Mothar silenced them," it was another voice, a younger draig with red robes. She stepped into the candlelight and held a bloodstained banner. It showed the familiar golden pterosaur skeleton on a red field.

"Dylis," Hafwen snapped. "Be silent yourself. We used to have many dealings with them, but then they stopped coming."

"Have none of you gone to investigate?"

"They used secret tunnels and passages to get here, and out of respect, we never sought them. Then, from the sea it is impossible to get to them. We cannot cross the magma. The only channel into their chamber is blocked by a flow of molten rock."

"So, this *was* a volcano . . ." Rob mused, but then he shook the thought away. "Didn't you look for their secret tunnels after they went silent?"

"We respected their wishes. We lived in mutual respect, for we both hold the Dead God in awe. They are closer to the body than we. We keep the stories, the tombstone, and the respect while they keep the corpse."

"The Dead God has a corpse?" Rob said, incredulous.

"So they say."

"Let me see if I understand," Rob continued. "The tower is somewhere underground; it is blocked off by lava . . ."

"Magma," Dylis corrected.

"Right. Is there anywhere the magma is at its lowest level?"

"Not that we know," Hafwen said, apologetically. "If you wish to stay I will have the sisters bring you food. We have roasted vegetables and cooked breads."

Rob paced again, but his eyes went to the mosaic on the floor, which showed draigs, humans, pengs and saurai all gathered around the golden figure.

"It is the scene of great shaping," Dylis said, standing next to him. "D'haara was the god of earth, of gold, but also of shapes and forms. Just as Saagara was the god of water, mist, and emotion. D'haara could reshape the world whether it was the mountains, or the creatures living within it."

"I see," Rob tapped a draig at his feet. "She made the draigs, did she?"

"The drakans were here first," she said. "D'haara loved the drakans but wished to speak with them. She wished to walk with them and to make them more like her. So she gave them throats that could open and close with speech. She let them stand on two legs, and she gave them a spine that would hold them up."

"This reminds me of the legends of the Concaedians," Rob said. "Except, they claim that the earth spirits shaped human forms."

"Ah, humans are often *close* to the truth, but distant at the same time. D'haara made the draigs and set them in the Cendyl to tend the land and to love her work. But the mammals saw the draigs and were jealous, so they came to D'haara and asked to be made like the draigs. They tried to stand on two feet, and they tried to wear cloaks and capes to act as wings."

"You make us sound ridiculous!"

"Well, you are," she laughed. "D'haara granted the beasts their wish and they became the first humans. Then she went to the desert lands and found the trasati. There were some that wished to be like the draigs, but by now, D'haara was weary, her powers spent on her previous work. She did what she could for the trasati, but they were imperfect specimens."

Rob scowled. "This explains why your people and the saurai have such a cold relationship. I'm sure they think that *you're* the imperfect specimens."

"They would be wrong," she insisted.

"I am not here to argue," he turned. "D'haara died. I don't see how it matters."

"Do you know how she died?" Dylis tugged on his arm. "She was killed by another god. By the nameless one. The god of fire, who lives in emerald tongues, burning the world from the inside out . . ."

Rob froze. His childhood had brought him face-to-face with a creature whose eyes had burned green. It had haunted him, but the memory had been buried by so many other horrors. Yet it had the power to send dread into his marrow at a mention.

The floor shook and shivered as a hollow boom rippled outside. Rob sprinted to the window. A gaping, gasping vent had opened in the earth, puking black smoke and filling all with a sulphurous stench.

"Vann!" Rob called, but there was no reply.

Ignoring all the voices that rose, he darted down the stairs and kicked his way out of the door. Splashing through the rain swept grass, he sloshed to the wall and dug his hands into the brick, climbing with all his strength. He slipped and tried again, setting his teeth on edge as he reached the summit.

A draigish priestess was lying at the foot of the other side, her head bleeding and her hand pressed against it. "Vann and Gorm?" Rob shook the draig. "What happened to them?"

"They fell," she said. "The earth opened, and they fell."

Chapter Twenty Eight

Fire and Water

His head was still ringing as he clambered back on board the ship. Once he was on deck, he fell against the mast, his bleeding hands grasping the wood as rain pelted. Alya stood close, but her arms were folded tightly as Rob shuddered and sobbed.

"They . . ." he tried to speak. "Vann and Gorm. They fell underground. I tried to save them, but I couldn't."

The crew stood, eyes focused on their captain. He had failed. He had let two of them die and for what? For some half-baked information from draigs who worshipped a dead god. What was any of that worth? Why hadn't he stayed with Vann? Why hadn't he listened when he had been so uneasy and suspicious?

"How do we get them back?" said Alya. "That is your plan, isn't it? Foolhardy heroism. Or do you want to carry on with your mission into the Sky Sage's Tower?"

"Both," Rob said.

"We could visit the draig city of Gwasgar," Jarl suggested from the wheel. "It's not far from here, and we could get some food."

"Weren't you listening?" Rob goggled at him. "We need to rescue them!"

"All I heard is you don't know where the Sages are, so we should probably be moving on, I reckon."

"Jarl, do not test me." He strode close. "I am your captain. We are going to find our friends, and we will find the Sages. Then we will defeat the pirates, and Mothar."

"Why is it our problem?"

"We are part of this world. If not for your own sake then think of the world."

"Oh, very noble, sir," he sniffed. "I'm sure you'll be remembered for years to come, for defeating the terrible Skagra."

"You can try your luck on your own, but the pirates will come for you, especially after we sank the Black Sword, and especially after we kept Skagra prisoner. Don't think that leaving me will make you immune."

"I don't doubt it," he grinned. "But maybe somebody else should be making the decisions, someone with experience, and not some fresh-faced boy who's spent two years in a pengish prison."

"Someone like you, I take it?"

"I am entitled to be the captain." Jarl stood straighter and let go of the wheel. Rob stopped it from spinning out of control with one hand.

"You were dying on the Long Silver. Ilma healed you; Vann rescued you, and you agreed to join my crew. Vann, who you want to abandon! Gorm gave you food, and now you want her to die."

"Are you going to throw me off?" Jarl snarled. "I'm twice the man you are, boy. Twice the skill and twice the age. I can - AH!" He was pulled off his feet and thrown across the deck.

Kari had pounced from behind Jarl and knocked him unconscious with her walking stick. Rob gave her a surprised look and then frowned.

"I thought you were loyal to Jarl?" he said.

"I was," she shrugged. "But I am not loyal to stupidity."

"That wasn't the wisest decision." Rob knelt by Jarl and propped him against the railing. "He'll be even angrier when he wakes."

"Then he can deal with me, Captain. I need to give him a piece of my mind."

"A rare display of intelligence on this ship," Alya said from behind them. "I feel honoured to have witnessed it."

Rob drew a long, heavy breath and kept his eyes on Kari. "You know Jarl better than any of us. Do you think you could talk him round? I need everyone on my side. We need each member of the crew to be on the same footing."

"I can try," she sounded uncomfortable. "But he hardly gave me a second glance all the time we were on the Long Silver. He only cared about the ship, I think. Probably because he thought he'd be captain one day. Now he feels he's been demoted, it's not really a surprise he turned on you. But, yeah, I'll try talking to him."

"You don't have to," Rob nodded. "I can get Alya to talk to him if you prefer."

"By which you mean she'll have his skin peeled and fed to the sea serpents?"

"Give me a little credit," Alya yawned. "I can get far more creative than that."

"Care to teach me?" Kari's smile was wide.

Rob left them, his heart hammering.

The night deepened and the stars winked between pale clouds as he steered the ship along the coast. They passed the shoreline and a cliff face rose, dark and stark. They went at a snail's pace.

Ilma came to join him on the quarterdeck. She cradled her bandaged hand against her chest and sat on the railing behind him, her drawn features silhouetted by the lantern light. Ilma was prone to fidgeting when frustrated, but Rob left her to it. In the gloom, he preferred simply to listen to the sea. The sea was freedom, it was his route away from prison, and it was his path to Mothar.

He hoped it was not an all-consuming obsession and that if he accomplished it, he wouldn't be left with nothing. He had the crew. These friends had their ambitions, all kinds of dreams and skills that he could help fulfil. That was better than vengeance, and fighting, and struggling.

"Captain!" Ilma called. "Over there, look!"

Over the waters, a mile down the cliff face, there was a waving shape, a snake-like neck rising from a thick body. Rob gave the orders, and the ship swung towards the thing, inching closer and closer.

"What do you think it is?" he asked Alya as she came to the quarterdeck.

"A trasati," she said.

The creature bobbed its head at Rob, the glimmering, shimmering skin still dripping. Turning, it led them along the cliff, winding in and out of the shallows, flippers scattering foam.

"Is it one of the trasati you rescued?" Ilma asked.

"I have no idea."

Alya leaned over the railing to get a better look at the creature while Rob looked at the cliffs. They kept their course and the creature in sight until it stopped suddenly and turned.

Rob's eyes were drawn to the deeper shadows behind it that formed a slim cave entrance that opened in front of them. It was almost triangular, but with imperfections and a strange angle to it. Had they not been looking, it could easily have blended into the cliff face.

They dropped anchor and gathered on the main deck, all eyes on Rob as he stroked his chin thoughtfully. His heart had sung at the sight of the cave, the sudden hope dancing like new fire, but he turned to Alya for some reassurance.

"What do you think?" he said.

"Somebody wants our attention," Alya observed. "Somebody sent that trasati."

"This cave, do you think it could be . . ." He rummaged inside his coat pockets and pulled out the scroll the priestesses had given him. "This belonged to the Sky Sages, I had a quick look at it, and I think it's a map."

Kneeling, he and Kari spread it on the deck and pored over it as Alya brought a light. The patterns were confusing, twisting and turning in ever increasing circles, or else ploughing forward relentlessly.

"It's a labyrinth," Alya said after a few moments. "Following the traditional Cendylic cipher pattern."

"You think it refers to *this* cave, though?" Rob asked desperately

"There," Kari pointed at the edge of the labyrinth. "It says 'open to the sea, the Black Door'. Well, this cliff looks pretty black, and this looks like a door."

"If the map is to be believed," Alya said. "This is a passage of rocks and narrow turns."

"You don't think the ship will make it?" Rob asked.

Alya kept her eyes on the map, following various courses with her finger, tracing and retracing it until she smiled victoriously. "Oh the ship will make it," she said. "I'm not so sure about us."

"Why?"

"If this map is to lead us to this central place, this golden ziggurat, then we have lava to traverse."

"Magma," Rob corrected.

"Quite." Alya smirked. "The fumes will likely be noxious, so we will have to cover our mouths and noses the closer we get."

"I say we go." Rob stood sharply. "It might not be the Sky Sages in the end, but I suspect it is. However, it leads beneath the island, and that's where Vann and Gorm are."

"Somebody sent that trasati," Alya said. "Somebody wants us here. They'll be waiting."

"Let them try it." He tightened his hands into fists. "Let anyone try. We are a crew, we are going to find Gorm, and we are going to find Vann."

"We are going to get killed."

"Then think of something clever, Alya, isn't that what you do?"

She held his gaze for a long moment, and then nodded, going back to the map and examining it closely. Glowers and smiles punctuated her scrutiny, as she seemed to be working something out with it.

Rob leaned over the railing, and the trasati lifted its head. There were whip marks across its face and bruises along its neck. As he reached out a hand, the creature flinched and dove. He watched its shadow vanish, and his heart hardened.

"Raise the anchor," Rob ordered.

Karri complied and soon they were in motion again. The ship bumped as it crossed the threshold, squeezing between the walls before they were plunged into inky darkness.

The lanterns hanging around the ship squeaked as they swung; the cave drew in a lot of wind, and they were propelled rapidly through the waters. Alya took the wheel, guiding them along the river. The ship shuddered and lurched downwards, the forecastle tilting as water gushed over it, and they were thrown off their feet. Rob bounced off the railing and clung there, as they were hurled left and then right. The cave twisted, the water frothing and churning as if it were angry at their presence.

The mast scraped stone, screaming in tones that echoed louder as they sped through rapids. The crew clung on for their lives as Alya struggled with the wheel.

"Get the sails drawn!" she said. "They're pushing us too fast!"

Rob staggered from his place, desperately trying to maintain his balance. Ilma rushed and propped him up as they headed onto the main deck. Another impact threw them; Rob rolled as he landed, but Ilma crashed against the mast and fell.

Kari struggled with the lines holding the sail while Rob came to Ilma's aid and helped her to the forecastle. They were an inch away when rocks slammed into the side, forcing the ship to twist and lean to the starboard side.

Sliding across the deck, Rob grasped Ilma's good hand and then pulled the both of them onto the forecastle. As the ship fell to port, he jumped and grasped the line holding the mainsail and clung with all his strength, Ilma still holding his hand.

The ship righted, and Alya gave a shout of frustration. Ilma let go and fumbled with the lines. They were jerked left then right; Rob ducked under a stalactite that loomed in the darkness and scraped the deck, breaking as it met impenetrable wood.

With shouts the crew pulled the sails down and they soared past another low stalactite as the passage opened. Alya's control increased, and she gave Rob an approving nod.

At last, they were spat into a wide lake. The cavern was lofty, vanishing into an unseen void above. The lanterns that had not been smashed during the journey showed little of what surrounded them.

"This is one of the turning points," Alya said, breathlessly. "There are a number of them. It appears to be a crossroads of sorts."

"I can see a few gates over there," Kari said, pointing.

"Yes," Alya said, nodding. "One of them will lead us back out to sea, the other will take us to the golden tower."

"Which one?" Rob asked, but before Alya could respond, a jet of fire spouted ahead.

Light burst from an island in the centre of the lake. Figures were standing on it, some with torches or lanterns, and others were moving large barrels and crates.

"Who are they?" asked Kari.

"Smugglers?" Ilma suggested. "We can't be the only ones who've ever got through here."

"I fear the worst," Alya said.

"Don't you always?" Rob chided.

He pulled his hat out of his pocket and put it on, frowning at the structure ahead. He stepped back onto the main deck and ordered Kari to lower the anchor, which she did with a worried frown.

A grappling hook leapt onto the deck and clanged against the railing. Others joined it, and low voices snapped across the cavern wall. Rob drew his sword as did Alya, and they ran to the middle of the deck, joining Kari and Ilma, who they kept behind them.

Six torches fell onto the deck followed by six pirates, all dressed in black coats, and all with red vials hanging from necklaces. One of the pirates swaggered forward and nudged a torch with her foot. Her shaved head glistened in the light, and the tattoos on her neck were beautifully realised flowers and lightning strikes.

"Now then, Rob Sardan," she said, grinning. "I don't suppose you anticipated seeing any of us again?"

"Can't say that I did," he admitted. "Who in Razal's fiery name are you?"

"We are the crew of the Black Sword," she said. "We have come for only a small thing." The other pirates laughed. Rob spotted draigs, saurai and even a peng in their ranks. "We've come for your blood."

"Very intimidating," Alya said, sounding bored. "Perhaps you should work on being more original with your threats."

"How about you and me spend a little quality time together, miss? I bet you'd be a great little goer."

"I'm not interested," she smiled. "But your flattery is noted."

The pirates sniggered, and some nudged the one who seemed to be their leader, but she roared at them for silence.

"This is not an invitation," she said. "This is piracy. We'll be taking the ship. Seems fair, since you broke ours."

"Nice of you to ask." Rob narrowed his eyes. "I'm afraid we have to decline. You see, we need the Sky Sages. Their Air-keeper-defeating-know-how could be useful against Mothar."

"I doubt it," the pirates laughed. "Mothar's got more power than you and all the pretty little priests he burned. Speaking of which, burning seems like the best punishment for you and your crew."

Alya stamped a foot and then shoved Rob with both hands. He stumbled back and looked at her in confusion. She was shaking with rage, her eyes narrowed and her eyebrows arched.

"This is what you've led us to," she hissed. "I told you there was danger here, and you would not listen!"

"Alya, what . . ."

"No, you don't get to talk." She shoved him again. "I told you if you ever put the ship or the crew in danger I wouldn't forgive you, remember?"

"I remember, but . . ."

"But nothing! You brought us here, you ill-minded, foul-hearted, ash-mouth!"

"Stop your arguing," laughed a pirate. "Told you Rob Sardan could never hold a crew together, didn't I?"

"We should drown them with the Sage's Tower," said another. "Who needs it, anyway? Mothar's had his way with it."

"But they'll have gold," Alya said. "Nobody said Mothar ransacked the place. Surely the riches will still be there?" The pirates turned their eyes on her, and she strode forward, putting her jian back in its scabbard. "Tell me, pirate, what would you do with that kind of treasure? I hear there's a whole tower made of gold, not to mention a crown."

"Nobody can get to it, though," the pirate leader snapped.

"I can," she grinned. "I will make you a deal, take me as part of your crew and I will lead you to the treasure."

"You're making it up," she snarled. "Why would you do that?"

"Seems the logical thing to do," she shrugged. "Take me with you and I can make the ship sail faster than any other. I built it; I know it."

"Alya!" Kari shouted.

"You can't," Rob scowled. "I trusted you!"

"That was foolish of you," she said.

"Is this some ploy?" the lead pirate asked.

"I have never been a friend to Rob Sardan," she said. "But this is the only way I can save our ship."

Her eyes met Rob's for a fraction of a second. *Our* ship. His stomach lurched, and a trickle of warmth flowed from his chest into his arms and head. He gave Alya a small, almost imperceptible nod.

Rob and Kari stood back to back while the pirates closed in, still eyeing Alya with suspicion. He did not blame them; he would have reacted the same way. The leader was giving her the most curious look.

"Wait," she said. "Why should we believe you're willing to betray Sardan and the crew?"

"I built the ship, and I will sail with whoever commands it. To get the ship, I will throw aside someone as useless as this so-called Sword-breaker. He wanted to name the ship 'Fat Ted'. An insult to the craftwork!"

"I can vouch for her," said a high and horribly familiar voice.

The peng stepped forward, and Rob frowned harder. It was Kerrok, the Blood Peng, still in her red armour, but now with a black coat hanging from her shoulders.

"Vouch for her?" the pirate leader said. "What do you know about this, Bloody? I don't remember asking you for your overly expensive opinion."

"I was in Bron'Halla with them," Kerrok snarled. "Alya betrayed both the Imperial and Renegade Pengs. She and Sardan never saw eye-to-eye, and she only ever used him when it was to her advantage."

The leader grinned at Alya. "I know you! Alya Kadir! Didn't you used to be with old Captain Le'ah? Heck of a pirate, that one."

Rob looked at Alya again, his insides straining with sudden violence. Alya nodded to the pirates, and they jeered at her, but

Rob was a lightning storm inside. Yet another member of his crew was a pirate and she had never even mentioned it.

"I'm no fool," she said. "I know a lost cause when I see one. To leave the ship in the command of Sardan would require a level of stupidity beyond my capabilities."

"You're too modest, Alya," Rob said. "But Kerrok, as a peng, it must really hurt to have to come here, so close to draigish territory."

"I am a Blood Peng," Kerrok replied. "I am loyal to nobody besides my contract, and my contract will not expire until Gorm is dead."

"And how is that going?" the pirates jeered. "Little birdy let the big girl get away, didn't she? Thought you could trick us with Sardan's blood on the blade?"

"It fooled most of you," Kerrok hissed. "I was almost away before that Air-keeper ruined everything."

"Of course," Alya said, grinning. "I knew the moment I saw the Air-keeper that Kerrok had failed. It was my own little revenge to make sure the pirates would keep chasing us. I knew I couldn't defeat this crew all on my own, so I needed something to keep them distracted."

She's thinking fast, Rob thought.

"I thought we could trust her," Kari said as the pirates laughed. "I thought . . ."

"Don't worry," Rob said. "We'll find a way. Gorm's still alive, and Vann is, too. I'm sure of it."

"We're outnumbered, and we've just lost Alya!"

"Take us out," the pirate leader commanded. "We don't want to be around when this place goes up."

"Goes up?" Rob glanced over at the barrels and his head thundered. "Blasting powder? The pengs said pirates had been stealing it, what's it doing here? What are you trying to do?"

"Our captain's plan," the pirate laughed. "Skagra had a backup for if she couldn't get to the Sky Sage's Tower. You see, this is where the war was ended."

One of the draig pirates licked her lips at Kerrok, who shuddered at the sight. Rob glanced at the other pirates, many were leaning on the railing, or else looking towards the gates.

"What was it Skagra used to say?" the draig said. "It was something about how the end of the War of Frost and Flame had plunged the world into chaos. Yeah, that was it. No lords, no queens, just people. The war ended with this volcano blowing its lid, so that's what we're here to do."

"Why?" Rob demanded. "You'll be killed!"

"No, we won't," the pirate leader said. "We'll set it up so that it only goes off well after we're away from here."

"Listen, it won't matter how far you go if this volcano blows then the whole world will die! Isn't that what Skagra kept saying? *All shall die* in the Flame-Filled Sky! Wasn't that a clue?"

"How are you going to get out?" Kari pressed. "The water flows one way."

"There are other tunnels," Alya informed them, holding out the map. "I believe this shows them quite clearly. The gates can be operated easily. I suggest the left gate." She pointed at one.

"How do you know?" the draig objected, looking at the map. "Are you trying to betray us, little human?"

"My size is of no importance," Alya grinned. "However, the size of the ship is important. By my reckoning, the main mast will not fit under the right gate, but it will fit through the left. Have you measured the ship recently?"

The pirates laughed, throwing insults at the draig until she backed away, scowling at Alya. As the sounds rose, Rob took Kari's hand and tried to reassure her through touch. But the noise and the threat of steel were looming, he felt unsure of what was going on, of who to trust, or what to do.

"We've been trapped here for too long," said one of the pirates, grasping the leader's shoulder. "You said just last night you don't know how to get us out."

"Quiet!" the leader protested, but other voices rose.

"This place stinks of fish," said another. "Come on, let's get out! I'm sick of this filthy, flaming cave!"

"Yes, yes," the leader conceded. "The traitor can guide us out, but after that, we can do what we like with her and the others, what do you say?"

The pirates cheered and jeered, but consented to being ordered around the ship. Alya pointed the pirates around to various points to set the sails. Rob and the others were tied to the mast with thick rope that chafed. Ilma and the unconscious Jarl were either side of him while Kari was further along.

The pirates milled about, bringing the ship to a crawl as they headed for the gate. It was a tall, metal thing that swung on two hinges, which creaked and screamed as they tried to hold back the water that was forcing them open. Rob wanted to hold his ears against the sound, but he was forced to let it stab into his skull, getting so loud he thought it would burst.

"Alya," Kari cried. "You'll regret this. You think pirates will help you? When they don't need you, they'll toss you overboard in a second!"

"Be quiet." Alya pulled one of her scarves off and tied it around Kari's nose and mouth. "You're making too much noise."

"We can all make noise," Ilma said, shock ringing in every syllable. "Alya, I treated you, I helped with all of your issues, and this is what you do?"

"I advise we keep them all quiet," Alya said with a yawn.

"Agreed," the pirate leader said.

Soon, Rob, Jarl and Ilma had cloths covering their mouths. Alya's eyes caught Rob's for a second and then she turned back to the pirates.

"The tunnels wind and each turn must be taken with care," she said.

"I thought this ship would survive being bashed about," the leader growled.

"It can, but your crew can't. You want to get out in one piece, don't you? Follow the course, left, right, straight, straight, three lefts and five rights, and we will reach the open sea again."

"Left, right, hang on . . ." the leader blinked.

"I will shout instructions." Alya hopped onto the quarterdeck.

The gate opened and they were sucked through it, the main mast barely missing the stone ceiling as they were plunged into darkness. The pirates were uneasy, but pulled at the sails and tugged them into place as instructed.

They swung, the hull slamming into the walls with reckless abandon. Rob was jolted again and again. Alya was berating the pirate at the helm.

"Despite the structural integrity of the ship," she shouted. "I insist you at least *try* and avoid the walls!"

"*You* try it, you stuck up little creature," the draig's mouth frothed red.

They shot through the caverns at increasing speeds, the tilt making the forecastle plunge into the water. The river gushed over the deck and coated everyone, but they kept going. Some of the pirates coughed and gagged, but their leader ordered them to continue.

"We need to get out," she shouted. "Keep on the . . ." she coughed violently. "Keep the . . ." Her breath came in gasps and then she threw up against the railing.

Alya shoved the draig from the helm and pulled her scarf over her mouth and nose. The draig fell, retching streams of something that Rob did not care to identify.

Kerrok was still upright though her feathers were ruffled and her face coated with soot. Suddenly light burst around her, and she screamed; the draig was flailing, fire spewing from her mouth and Kerrok was almost caught in it. Alya let go of the wheel, pounced on the draig and clamped her mouth shut.

The ship spun and groaned, slamming into a wall before being pummelled on the port side by the raging river. They were tipping, but Alya kept her hands on the draig's mouth.

Higher and higher, the starboard side rose in reaction to the force of the river. Unconscious pirates slid from the deck and the water devoured them. Kerrok leapt on the wheel, turning it until the ship righted itself and was forced down the tunnel once again.

"Hard to port!" Alya screamed, high and desperate. "Now!"

Kerrok obeyed and moved her broad, feathery hands across the thing, making it slide seamlessly. Alya was thrown by the pirate draig who stood to her full height and retched. Then she lifted her eyes to Alya and ran at her.

Rob struggled against his bonds, but they were firm. He tried to scream encouragement to Alya, but the scarf around his mouth prevented him from giving more than a muffled shout.

The draig wrestled Alya, and they rolled against the railing. She wrapped her hands around the pirate's neck as fire built in her mouth. Shrieking, Alya headbutted her, and they both rolled, holding their injuries. Alya almost pulled the jian from her scabbard, but seemed to reconsider, giving Rob a quick look.

With the scarf still around her mouth, Alya wavered and leaned against the railing while Kerrok eyed her with fury. The ship was still moving fast, rising and falling along the rapids.

The draig pounced on Alya, but she fought back, clasping her hands around the throat of her attacker, squeezing with all her might.

"I did work for Le'ah," she hissed. "She betrayed me. She ruined me. She sent me to Bron'Halla. Did you really think I'd *ever* help pirates again?"

The draig choked and fell unconscious as Alya shuddered and fell to her knees. With a lurch and a heaving of her shoulders, she shoved the pirate overboard and then collapsed against the railing, trying hard to breathe.

Rob's lungs were hot, and the air was stuffy, close and humid. Steam was rising, and light was building against the cave ceiling. Struggling, he tried to get up, but he slipped again.

Alya managed to get to her feet and made her way to the main deck, drawing her jian. Her eyes were bloodshot, her brow was covered in sweat, and blood trickled above her eye. She cut Rob and the others free before she collapsed. Kari caught her and lifted her gingerly. Alya's eyes seemed to smile.

"We're here," she said as the light turned red on the ceiling.

Rob headed to the forecastle and leapt onto the bowsprit. Ahead, the river was falling into a vast cavern that boiled with red and yellow light. A colossal lake of molten rock divided them from another gate.

The ship was heading for the magma with increasing speed, and the heat was more oppressive than the cold of the South Pole had been. Rob backed from the bowsprit and fell to the main deck.

"Can we make it?" he asked.

"We have only one way to find out," Alya croaked. "The magma isn't very thick, but we'll be higher in it than we would be in the water."

"What a comfort!" Ilma snapped.

"You are beyond reason!" Kerrok shouted from the wheel. "There must be some other way around!"

"No." Alya stood, shaking with Kari holding her weight. "I trust the ship."

They hit the magma, sparks shot onto the deck and danced. Rob spun from a shining red droplet beside his foot. They took places at the sail lines and Alya gave hesitant instructions, all while holding the scarf against her mouth. Kerrok, meanwhile, had pulled her cloak up about her beak and was coughing into it.

"Keep going!" Rob urged.

The ship groaned, and fire licked the side. One of the lines snapped, making the mainsail droop. Ilma and Kari dove to save the remaining lines. The hull screamed and shook, throwing them around the deck. Rob leaned over the railing and saw blackened dents in the wood as magma chewed into their hull. Columns of smoke rose on their port side, but Alya told them to ignore them.

"The ship isn't going to make it," Kerrok said. "The magma's going to get in; we're going to burn."

"Ship!" Alya grasped the railing as the hull screamed. "My ship! Our ship! Just a little further!"

The railing splintered in her grasp, and she stumbled. Kari went to her, but Alya waved her away and stood. She ran to the forecastle and pointed towards the gate at the other end of the lake of fire. Silhouetted against the red devastation, she looked back at Rob, teary eyed.

"We have to make it," she said. "Just a little more. We have to. I have to prove it; this ship was worth it. I have to know if it was worth everything I did. I have to know it was worth all the pain!"

Rob kept his hands on the lines, pulled the sail around and the ship sped, magma bubbling around them as the hull breached. Timbers sparked, lines broke, the windows of Rob's cabin smashed, and the main mast bent.

The gate was so close. The fire was rising. Rob could hardly breathe; sweat ran down his back and chest in rivers that would not stop. Wood groaned, and the ship twisted, its prow heading straight for the opening.

Closer and closer. Hotter and hotter. The ship stretched to its very limits. Rob planted his feet firmly apart, feeling every strain of the deck, the bubbling magma beneath their feet.

"Ship," he whispered. "Sword-breaker, Fat Ted, whatever we decide to call you. Alya's ship. Our ship."

They shot into the gate, but magma was still all around in a long stream that ran into a hopeless drop. The crew clung to the ship. Rob hung onto a line, dangling as they plummeted, but swung around and regained his balance quickly.

The magma fall ended, and the ship hit rock. The jolt smashed the hull, and they went skidding along a rocky outcrop. Rob fell yet again and then clung to the railing as the ship spun. The spinning and the impact were battering him inside and out, and he felt the shard in his abdomen shift.

The screech of wood on stone came to a stop, and they shuddered to a halt.

Still breathing hard, Rob opened his eyes and let go of the railing. The ship was lying almost on its side. He had to crawl and climb in order to get to where Alya was hanging from the guidelines. She dropped and slid along the deck, almost kicking him in the face as she went past. When she came to the railing, she hopped over it and leapt to the ground.

Lying back on the deck, Rob tried to catch his breath and process what had happened. Alya had double-crossed the pirates, and as expected, had guided them through the underground tunnels, as well as proving their ship could sail on fire.

He laughed. He could not stop it from bursting out of his mouth. It came in deep, rattling breaths that rang off the ceiling and joined other voices that were shouting and cursing.

"You killed them!" someone was shouting. "I know they were pirates, but you killed them!"

"I did no such thing." That was Alya. "I let them fall at a point where I knew that the river would lead them to open water. Once they were at water level, the gases from the magma were no longer as potent. If they are smart, they will have gone with the flow. Within a few minutes, they will be in fresh air."

"Which is more than can be said for us," it was Kerrok who was arguing. "How did you know all of this?"

"I studied the map," she said dismissively. "It is not my problem if nobody else saw the pattern. Getting the pirates to open that particular gate was essential. They did not know the dimensions of our ship, so it was easy to deceive them."

"What about my contract?"

"What *about* your contract?"

Rob shook his head as the argument sprang into incoherence. He made his way from the ship and onto the ground. It was a large, circular chamber lit by the magma that flowed to a plunge pool, which divided into streams that ran left and right. Above, there were three gates that could hold more water or fire, and there was a fourth directly opposite the magma fall.

He turned back to the ship, and his heart clenched hard, cold spreading into his chest and neck. The hull was severely burned with holes running in streaks. Patching them would take hours and without the special wood, it would never be as good.

"You see it, too?" Kari said, coming to his side. "The ship did us proud, though. Good old Fat Ted."

"The ship is *not* called Fat Ted!" he insisted. "Flame Hull might be the best name I can think of right now."

"Hull of holes, more like," Ilma said as she struggled from the ship. "Pirates won't want it now I wager."

"Pirates . . ." Rob turned to Alya and approached, the thunderstorm in his chest resurfacing and threatening to break. "You were a pirate?"

"No," she frowned deeply. "I worked for one. Le'ah the Unbound. She betrayed me."

"Is that all you'll say?"

"For now," she looked away. "We have more important things to do."

She was looking over the damage and seemed to give no more thought to Rob and what he had said. He took a breath and turned away to see Kari, but her eyes were on Alya as she began an argument with the peng.

Kari shook her head. "I should have gone with my old captain, shouldn't I? Then all I'd have to worry about is swimming through these caves. I saw a few of my of crew fall into the water. I would have been one of them if I hadn't stayed."

"We want you here," Rob embraced her sympathetically. "Come on, we have work to do. Alya, Kerrok, can you put aside your shouting for a few minutes?"

"Fine," Alya pulled her scarf from her mouth and revealed a crooked smile. "We have a ship to fix."

"Start with the biggest holes," said Kerrok. "That one right there. Do it."

"I know how to fix my own ship," Alya said.

Ilma was pointing at a hole in the hull.

"Not that one," Alya snorted.

"No, look . . ." Ilma covered her mouth with a hand and shrank back.

Smoke was issuing from it, and a shape was moving in the veil. Alya turned and drew her jian. Rob put his own body between the ship and the crew, glaring into the smoke, lifting the golden blade from his belt.

"Who's there?" he demanded. "Vann, is it you?"

Laughter, cold, reckless and vicious erupted like a volcanic explosion. Hope went out. The figure emerged from the breached hull, clanking with glass vials that hung around her neck.

Skagra stepped from the ship and spread her hands. "Thank you, Rob Sardan," she said. "Thank you for bringing me to the doorstep."

Chapter Twenty Nine

The Tower of the Sky Sages

A knife twisted in Rob's mind as he tried to comprehend. Skagra was striding towards him, fingering the blood vials around her neck as she laughed, high and terrible.

She had never left the ship. The Air-keeper had been a distraction, it had driven them to the cliffs, and now that they had come through the dangers and catacombs, Skagra had left her hiding place. They would never have come here if they had known she was still there; she must have worked that out.

Alya bent and raised her jian, but Skagra hardly gave her a glance as she stepped closer to Kerrok. The Blood Peng lifted her head and looked ready to spring, her feathers rising.

"The contract is not completed," Skagra said. "Where is Gorm?"

"She and Vann were lost on Geata," Rob glowered. "She's dead."

"Oh, you'd like me to believe that, wouldn't you?"

She licked her teeth before lunging and kicking Rob's legs from under him. The dust rose, and he coughed, looking up to see Skagra's foot coming at his face. He blocked it with an arm and his gold armband clanged against her boot. He tried to pull his sword out, but Skagra flicked it away with a foot.

Getting to his feet, he regained his balance and eyed the pirate with all the hostility he could muster. His face fell into the scowl of uttermost fury that he had used so often, the expression he was sure had injected horror into the Pirate Lord. But Skagra smiled, picking up Rob's golden sword.

"You wish to die?" she said. "I rarely spill blood, believe it or not. Only on special occasions." She stroked the vials that hung about her neck. "You see these? Each has the blood of a test subject. This first was a young draig who survived Saagara for three days. Next, a human who lasted a week. This one is a peng, took a month, brave soul. Draigs, humans, pengs, saurai, nobody can survive the effect for long, not unless they have a will so strong, so indomitable that nothing can take your mind."

"I agree," Alya said, lifting her jian. "Why don't we put *your* blood in a vial?"

"Ambitious." Skagra turned and levelled the gold sword at Alya.

The pirate ducked and sidestepped as Alya lunged. With a whirl and a whip of her dreadlocked hair, Skagra twisted her sword and pressed it into Alya's hip. Blood splattered from the small wound, but she kept her feet and pressed a counter-attack.

Rob crept closer as Skagra laughed, twirling her sword with a swagger. He met Alya's eye and then lunged, his arms grasping the pirate's neck. But Skagra jerked and bit, ripping into his coat sleeve as Alya shot forward, jian point soaring.

Skagra slipped and spun, Rob and Alya's eyes met again as pain shot through his abdomen. The jian had been aimed at Skagra's belly, but she had got free, and the blade had stabbed into Rob and against the shard that was still lodged inside him.

The agony was terrifying.

Rob fell, his throat opening to let out a scream that was cut short when he hit the ground. Skagra laughed and danced, waving the sword above her head, but Alya stood over Rob, eyes wide and arm shaking.

A rush of cold spread in a spider's web from Rob's wound. His head weighed a thousand times more than usual; his arms were clamped to the earth, and his eyes darkened with clouds. Voices shouted; feet trampled left and right, and then all turned to droning noise.

Dead things lay at his feet. They were pterosaurs and humans, pengs, saurai, and draigs. One sauros stood from the pile. It turned, and the light caught it, the skin was made of wood and dirt. The sauros opened its horrible eyes, and green fire licked out of its skull as a hollow voice screamed in uttermost pain.

Rob tried to run, but his feet tangled, making him fall into a pit. Darkness swallowed him, but the screaming remained, getting louder, vibrating in his bones and tearing his flesh.

"Rob!" Ilma shook him, and he opened his eyes.

She was sweating and covered in dirt, her injured hand against her chest while her other was pressed over his wound. He breathed, collecting ashen air and sulphurous fumes. Alya was still where she had been, her eyes closed and her sword limp at her side.

"Where's Skagra?" Rob said. "You need to go after her. Stop her from doing whatever she's doing."

"I can't," Ilma said. "Not while you're bleeding. Besides, the reason we came here was for you."

"The Sky Sages healing scrolls . . ."

"I can get ancient healing scrolls anywhere, you know? Ancient scrolls are just lying about everywhere these days. But you're unique. We need to keep you alive."

"I bet you say that to everyone."

"It's still true," she sniffled. "Skagra is my daughter. I should never have put her on that ship and let her go all those years ago; this is my fault."

"No," Alya said. "No, it isn't. Skagra is to blame for her actions, don't try and take that from her." She lifted her jian and watched Rob's blood trickle down the gutter. "You are responsible for healing the crew. I am responsible for the ship."

"I suppose this is what you wanted." Rob struggled to sit, but Ilma pushed him. "You can be the captain at last."

"I did," she said, but looked hurt by his words. "But now I am not sure."

Rob managed to push Ilma away and got to his feet. "If I don't come back, then you can take the ship. Take the crew and get out of here. Go and live your lives on the sea and make our ship the best ship Diyngard has ever known."

"Don't be so predictably sanctimonious," Alya scolded. "Self-sacrifice is the act of one obsessed with fame and pointless heroism. I thought you wanted to get away from that."

"I can't just let them go!" He tried to walk but was stopped.

"Rob!" Ilma objected. "Your wound is . . ."

She had pulled open his coat and lifted his shirt, under the blood there was only a pale scar on his dark skin. Her eyes narrowed as she tried to comprehend what she was seeing, but Rob felt his insides glowing with new strength.

"It's healed," he said. "I don't care how or why at this point, but I think this gives me an advantage."

"Rob, this makes no sense, I . . ." Ilma struggled to get her words. "You don't know how this works. You don't recover at a consistent rate, you don't know how you recover, and you can't rely on it in a fight!"

"What if she cuts your head off?" Alya mused.

"Ilma," he turned to her. "I'd do this even if I couldn't heal. I'll stop Skagra. I'll find the Sky Sages. You'll all be safe."

"How noble of you," Alya said sardonically, as she put her jian in its scabbard. "I cannot say I understand you, but I respect your choice, reluctantly."

"I wouldn't want it any other way, Alya," he said. "Can the ship be salvaged?

"I believe so." She looked at the hull. "It will never be the same. That wood was unique. Any patches will be substandard and won't survive another Air-keeper."

"How many Air-keepers will attack us from underwater?"

"As soon as we know we are vulnerable they will find a way. I would. This ship has been our best defence; now it is compromised."

Jarl waved from the deck, and Rob scowled at him. "Ahoy, Captain!" he cried. "What a wonderful place this is! Is it magic?"

"I think he's in need of help," Ilma sighed.

"Jarl," Rob called. "If you're up, you and Alya should fix the ship. Then you need to refloat it."

"You sure you can trust him?" Alya asked.

"We don't have a lot of options," Rob insisted. "There are gates up there in the cliff. Some will hold water. They'll probably solidify that magma and get the ship floating. Alya, do you know the way to get back to the open sea from here?"

"I believe so," she said.

Rob turned away and looked around. The only path seemed to be ahead, where another gate stood. Taking a breath, he set off, the muscles in his legs tensing as he imagined the coming confrontation. He wanted to intimidate Skagra; he wanted to make a show of being powerful enough to challenge her. He was sick of her dismissing him as an irrelevance.

The gate was closed, its vast face a complex array of cogs and gears that interlocked in tight circles. It was steel and iron and reached thirty feet high and twenty across. He traced along until he came to the side where he found a crack in the wall. The scuffmarks told him that Skagra and Kerrok had come this way.

The passage was tight and the heat oppressive. His coat snagged on rocks and tore, he cursed and apologised to its previous owner. A noise made him look back, and he saw Ilma stumbling along behind. She looked at him in defiance; her hand clasped at her side while her bandaged one was against her chest. She was wearing the gold armband Lomi had given them.

"If I don't confront Skagra I will never die in peace," she said.

"It may guarantee you die in agony," he warned. "Why the gold band?"

"Lomi wanted it returned, didn't she?"

"Fair enough," he shrugged. "Will you retreat if things get too hazardous?"

"Captain," she stepped closer. "I will go back when my tasks are done. When I have said my piece to my daughter. If I have to die for this, then I will."

He met her eyes, and his hand went to the scar on his abdomen. He had so often put his life in her hands, and now she was risking her own. How many times had he done the same? He nodded and led her through the passage.

They struggled through the tangle of meandering rock, twisting back and then forward before dropping in a set of winding stairs. Rob held Ilma's hand as they went on; horror bubbling in his stomach as the air grew cleaner. Light built at the bottom of the stairs, and they slowed. Rob gave Ilma a silent nod, and they stepped together, breathing softly as they crossed into another cavern.

Before them was a gigantic ziggurat of gold, built upside down with the wide base attached to the ceiling and the point hanging a few feet from the bowl-like cavern floor. The structure had whirling shapes carved on its face, lanterns along its slopes and immense pillars in each of its corners that reached to the floor.

Rob stepped forward, his head buzzing with harrowing awe. So much gold in one place seemed inconceivable, but there it was before his eyes. Hopeless wonder took over as he breathed the dazzlingly pure air that filled the cavern.

Ilma tugged his arm and pointed at the cavern walls. There were more gates like the one that had been in the chamber where they had left the ship. From each ran a long guttering that would carry the water to a moat surrounding the ziggurat.

Rob's eyes found the point of the tower and a ladder with two figures clambering it. One vanished into a door at the top, followed shortly after by the other.

"We made it," Ilma said. "If they get the ship floating we could open one of the gates and the others could ride down here, too."

"A little extreme, perhaps," Rob laughed. He could not help breathing deeper. "I think Skagra and Kerrok are already inside."

"But . . ." She waved at the Tower. "Just look at it!"

"We will have plenty of time to look at it later."

Rob walked down the path towards the bowl below the Tower. Ilma followed with eyes on the glittering gold. The lanterns that dangled from the sloping walls were baubles that remained still. Rob tried to guess what was lighting them.

"I can't hear anything," Ilma said. "Do you think the Sages might be dead?"

"Mothar has a tendency to leave at least one survivor," he said. "His intention is to make people remember him. If he came here, there should be at least one left."

"Yes, yes," she looked worried. "So we shouldn't let Skagra get to them first."

They came to the ladder, unsure if it would support both of their weights, Rob allowed Ilma to go first and then followed. The point of the ziggurat was twenty feet from the ground, but the ladder continued through a porthole.

Within, the tower was bright gold and the walls glowed, as if lit by a warm fire. They climbed, and Rob's arms ached with each rung he took. At last, they came to a platform that opened onto a square room with a tiled floor. There were statues, humans, draigs, pengs and saurai, all gold, and all in some prostration of terror or pain. Rob approached one of them and leaned in close; the draig he inspected was naked, her wings folded tight and her chest covered in scars. The gold was so thick that he could not see the scales of her flesh, and the image sent horror into his mind. They weren't statues.

"They were sealed in gold while they were still alive," he said. "I think these people were Sky Sages."

"Do you think they're still alive?" Ilma asked. "Something like this should kill, but they wouldn't be in these poses. Even if the gold were poured on quickly, they would have collapsed under the weight. Their skeletons could not have held it long enough for it to set."

Someone screamed; a long, whistling cry that both of them knew too well. A pengish scream. They ran to the nearest door; the noise was still rising, and something scraped against hard metal. They rounded a corridor and raced up a set of stairs that doubled back to an archway that brought them into a well-lit chamber.

They skidded on a thick red carpet and stared at the ornate paintings that decorated the walls; more Sages, surrounded by images of things that made Rob shiver with fear. Behind one was the black crown, behind another was a red throne, then there was a shadow, and finally a sword made of stone.

Rob approached this painting and looked at the figure that was in front of the image of the Sea-Stone Sword. It was a peng who wore a crown made of tealeaves. It was Lomi Thinlomine, younger and bright eyed. He wasn't sure what to feel as his eyes slipped from the peng to the Sword again and again.

"It's gone," he whispered to himself. "I broke the Sword, it's gone."

But the memory of the final battle on the Teeth was rising, red mist collecting on the edges of his vision. Ilma grasped his hand and turned him away from the painting and shook him.

"Focus, Captain!" she hissed. "Can't you see who's here?"

In the centre of the room was an open fireplace with a cauldron over it. Kerrok was beside it, clutching her chest as she screamed once again. Ilma ran to her, but the peng leapt, flapping and squawking.

Rob circled the fire, trying to ignore the hisses and whistles from Kerrok. The cauldron bubbled with molten gold and the floor around it seemed soft and unstable.

"Be quiet," snapped a voice. It was Skagra, entering from the next room; she held a long, silver needle and blood was pouring from a wound in her arm. "You?" She looked at Rob, confused, and stumbled. "How?"

"I told you!" Kerrok cried through tears. "I killed him and he came back!"

Skagra crouched defensively, her needle twitching towards the gold sword in her belt. "Was Mothar onto something? Are you like him?"

"I'm stronger than him!" Rob shouted, fury rising so ferociously that his eyes grew hot. Skagra looked even more amazed; her mouth hung open. Composing herself, she stood straight and took her hand away from the wound on her arm, letting it bleed.

"That's going to kill you," Ilma said.

"I won't die, mother," Skagra said. "I do enjoy disappointing you, after all."

"Don't let her!" Kerrok shouted. "She put it in me!" she screamed, blood foaming in her beak. "The contract is revoked! The contract is revoked!"

"You have not killed Gorm yet," Skagra said. "The contract stays."

"You attempted to kill me; I have the right to take back the agreement."

"Oh, but I'm not killing you. No, no, I'm giving you immortality!"

Skagra reached her bleeding hand into the bubbling cauldron. She screamed so loud and with such agony that Rob leapt away. The steam and stench of burning flesh slammed his nose and he wanted to retch, but Skagra kept her hand in the gold.

Ilma ran at her, but Kerrok held her back, shaking. "It's too late!"

Skagra collapsed to her knees, breathing hard and fast. Her braids came loose and fell around her face, sticking to her sweat and blood. Rob got slowly to his feet and did a double take as he looked into the cauldron. It was empty.

"What is this?" he asked.

"The Dead God's power," Skagra laughed. "D'haara's mind was destroyed but her power remained, bound into the gold. That same gold used to make the pendants. It made the sword I hold. It made the blade that Kerrok used to stab you, Sardan."

"This is just like the Saagara they used as a drug," Rob said, gaping wide-eyed at the metal that glowed in the wound. "It will kill you like it killed your experiments."

"No," she coughed, smoke spluttering from her mouth. "I will find the Crown now the gold lives in me. With it, I'll be able to control the power. It won't kill me."

"This Crown, it's like the Sea-Stone Sword? The heart of this god is trapped in stone; the power is still in the element, but uncontrollable."

"You learn slowly," Skagra cackled. "You should have realised sooner. The Sea-Stone Sword was but one of many."

"Make her stop!" Kerrok screamed.

"Now," Skagra said, laughing. "A demonstration of what I can do."

Kerrok's hands clasped around her own throat, squeezing tighter and tighter. Ilma tried to force the feathery fingers apart, but couldn't.

"Stop this! Pangles, stop this!" Ilma shouted at the top of her lungs.

"Do not call me that!" Skagra roared. "I am Skagra. I . . ." She turned her face to the ceiling and laughed. "*I am Skagra*! My mind is stronger than you, Mothar! You can't hear my thoughts now; you worm! I am free! The world shall be free."

She opened her eyes and they glowed with a hellish, golden light. The same light bled into the veins around the sockets, oozing through her face until she seemed a patchwork of black skin and gold contours.

"*I am Skagra,*" she said, her voice distorted and inhuman. "*I will destroy the Pirate Lord. I will destroy the queens of Diyngard. I will bring the end of the world!*" Her hair flew as heat and power radiated from her body. "*All shall die in the Flame-Filled Sky*!"

Chapter Thirty

God of Gold

KERROK FELL, CHOKING AND COUGHING, BUT HER HANDS HAD been released. Skagra stood over her and put her foot on the peng's chest. Rob inched towards Ilma and took her hand for comfort; she squeezed his in return, and they tried to back away from the golden pirate, but her glowing eyes found them.

"The gold is useless solid," she said. "Until I find the Crown, I have to melt it to unleash its power. It is unstable until it gains affinity with my mind. It has to stay liquid long enough for me to combine my thoughts with it, and then it belongs to me."

"Why are you telling me this?" Rob demanded, and she spat, molten gold shooting from her lips.

"These are the lengths I will go to," she said. "Don't you see? I have known these powers longer than you, and I know them deeper than you ever will. You are nothing before my knowledge."

Skagra lifted her hand, and Kerrok broke into fits of howling and convulsed before her body was lifted off the floor. Blood spurted from the wound on Skagra's arm and she grinned, showing her jagged teeth. She licked her lips and walked towards Rob, spreading her hands.

"This tower is made from D'haara's body," she said. "It is the core of her ancient power. Without her mind to control it, it will stay in this form until I make it otherwise."

"How will you do that?" He and Ilma retreated further as she advanced, light glowing in her veins.

"The gold must become liquid, of course." She tilted her head.

Rob ran, pulling Ilma after him. The doctor cried in shock as she was tugged through the room, but Skagra only sighed. They burst through a door, and Rob bounded up the first set of stairs, and then they swung into another chamber.

Breathless, he slammed the door and pulled a bolt across it. Ilma was sweating almost as much as he was and she grasped her good hand to her chest.

"This Crown," Rob said. "It must still be in the Tower, otherwise, she would have found it. That's why she told us about it; she wants me to find it for her."

"You think she's that transparent?" Ilma coughed and tried to hold back a series of sobs, but they overtook her, and she fell to her knees.

"If it's here, why didn't Mothar take it?" Rob wondered out loud.

"Why didn't he take the Sea-Stone Sword?"

He hummed and scratched his stubble. "He already has one god's power, but he said two would break him. Perhaps he just wanted to prevent anyone else from getting the Crown?"

"I suppose," Ilma shivered. "Maybe there used to be another way in here, and he broke it! I doubt he imagined a ship could sail on fire."

"Exactly!" Rob sank beside her, his own eyes burning. "Come on, we can keep going, can't we?"

He put a hand on her arm. Ilma's daughter was turning into a creature of horror. He had been such a thing once, in a time that felt a million years ago. The hallucination on Herebealde had brought him face to face with the monster he might have become, and now it was almost like facing it once more.

"I won't do it," he shivered with raging breaths. "I won't become that thing again. Crowns, Swords, I won't have anything to do with them!"

"Rob, it's okay, I believe you." She patted his shoulder.

"I'm so sorry, Ilma. Your daughter, your family, this must be so . . ." His words caught in his throat, but he continued. "To have had that kind of monstrosity live inside you, it's such a burden, such a nightmare. I can't bring myself to wish it on Skagra. No matter what she's done, this is too horrific. We have to save her." Ilma looked faint, her eyes flickering as she slid on his shoulder. "Ilma, are you still here?"

"I . . ." She was shaking, her good hand clawing at the bracelet. "I think I am."

"We need to stand up and get out."

"Yes, I know, I'm trying." She stiffened and stood.

"Rob?" the voice came from ahead, and they both looked round.

A figure was staggering towards them, limping. She had bloody hair and ripped clothes, but Gorm looked whole. Rob leapt to his feet and ran to her. They embraced with such force that he worried he might squeeze the life out of her before she did the same to him.

"What in Razal's name are you doing here?" he asked as they released one another. "I thought you'd been lost or worse!"

"Vann . . ." she coughed and stumbled. "We were in the grass, and he kept stamping around, said he was looking for something. I tried to get him to come back to the priestesses. Rob . . ." Her eyes widened with fear. "There's a . . . *thing* up there."

"A *thing*?" His heart became an inferno, roaring within his chest. "What are you talking about?"

"I do not know, it was sealed in an altar." She shook her head and sat on the ground, her exhaustion showing in her sooty face. "Vann wanted to open it."

"Wait," Ilma scrambled closer. "What happened? You fell into the ground, right?"

"The earth swallowed us," Gorm nodded. "Vann had a pouch of blasting powder. He threw it at a gap in the grass and the earth devoured us. We fell, surrounded by smoke and fire until we came into a cavern. Then, Vann brought us to the top of this tower."

"Where is Vann?" Rob asked.

"Above." Gorm gestured in the direction she had come from. "He was afraid. I followed the sound of screaming."

"Why?" Ilma asked. "Most people run away from screaming sounds."

"Perhaps being with Rob Sardan has taught me to wish for heroism," she smiled. "I felt the desire to come and help . . ."

The door was blown off its hinges as a feathery figure was flung through the debris. Kerrok rolled, sobbing as Skagra strode into the room. The walls glowed, the gold shining in response to her presence. Slowly, she turned her eyes on Gorm.

"You are here," she said. "At last, Kerrok, a chance to fulfil your contract."

"I won't do it," the peng said, getting to her feet. "You're torturing me!"

"*Do as you wish*," Skagra said, her voice becoming even more distorted, grinding like churned earth. "*But thou willst know devastation before I am done*."

"Pangles!" Ilma shouted. "That voice isn't yours! You're being controlled!"

"I . . ." Skagra closed her eyes and her voice normalised. "I will not be controlled. I have never been controlled! Mother, do you recall what happened on the island of Kaede, the day you sent me away?"

"You tried to kill the queen," Ilma said.

Rob stared at Ilma, but Skagra's laughter made him tense, and he turned his attention back to her. The pirate glowed even brighter, her eyes like embers.

"Before that." Skagra stepped, making the ground shudder. "*The mountains slid, broken by an earthquake. The sheer power of the earth moving with barely a thought to the lives of humans, pengs, or saurai; it was glorious. They were all swept under that cataclysm. Remember how we ran?*"

"It was supposed to be a holiday." Ilma's head lowered, and she let her tears fall. "We were meant to see the country in its glory."

"*We saw glory that day, Mother. We saw the glory of the earth as it destroyed the rulers, the queens, and the lords. They were all torn, thrown to their graves. I watched their towers and their palaces collapse, and all of their lies with them. All except the queen and her children.*"

"So you tried to kill them," Ilma finished. "Why, Pangles? What had I ever said to you to make you think that was okay?"

"It was not your doing, it was *mine*," Skagra's anger brought her old voice back. "I saw Ramas, our home, and I saw its pretensions of freedom. But it was all a lie, which I learned when I tried to find us enough food to live on. That farm we worked was dying, and you only survived because of me! But when they caught me, they tortured me. So much for their ideals!"

Skagra's rage was boiling into the floor, making it shimmer, bricks cracking and steaming as her feet moved. Rob dragged Ilma away from the heat as it spread and he took hold of Gorm, trying to pull her along, too.

"We saw Kaede and its fall," Skagra went on. "I never ruled my crew; I won their freedom. True freedom is the destruction of rulers. No queens, and no lords."

"What about Mothar?" Rob said. "You want to bring him down from the inside, is that it?"

"Mothar." Skagra lifted her glowing and bleeding hand. "He has always tried to enter my mind, but I have eluded him. At great cost to my health. This is better. This power will grant me the ability to dismantle the world to its core."

"You . . ." Rob found it difficult to speak. "But how many people will die?"

"Many," she beamed. "Humans, draigs, pengs, saurai, they are *all vermin. The true power of this world* is *this world. All shall die.*"

"Skagra," Gorm spoke up. "You never wanted to kill. Your dream was for blood, but not death. I see your mind has been clouded and corrupted."

"*The end is coming,*" Skagra shouted. "*All shall die in the Flame-Filled Sky! Why should a few years matter?*"

"That is the thing." Gorm stood and hobbled closer. "You said those years would be the most precious. That is why you were so intent on freeing people from their oppression. You saw an end to the world, and so those few short years would be the most valuable of any we would ever live."

"I . . ." Skagra's hands went to her head, and she stumbled. "*The fire . . . Burn. Purge. All darkness, all death . . .*"

"Remember when the Liberator burned?" Gorm pressed, making Skagra step back. "You can't want that for the whole world?"

"*The fire* . . . burning . . . *ending* . . . I can see . . . *the world* . . ." Skagra wavered, her voice falling in and out of the terrible distortion.

"It's the gods, Skagra." Rob's mind was racing. "I felt it when I held the Sea-Stone Sword. They take your deepest desires and exaggerate them, distort them and twist them until they destroy you and everyone around you. Let it go!"

"*You cannot command me!*" she screamed.

The words hung in the air, and Skagra let Kerrok fall to the ground, where she coughed and vomited. Meanwhile, Ilma strode closer to her daughter.

"Remember the farm where we used to work?" she said. "You were a little girl, and you liked using the scythe. I used to give you lessons, and you used to spend hours chopping barley. You said you wanted to do it forever."

"I grew up," Skagra replied. But her eyes had dimmed, and a little of the gold in her veins was retracting.

"You got angry when Aino told you that you couldn't use the scythe anymore. She tried to stop you; she tried to control you. You told me she hurt you. I let it go on for too long, and now look what happened! You *became* Aino, didn't you? You turned into the thing you rebelled against. That's what Rob's telling you! Listen!"

"*No*, I'm . . ." Skagra lowered her face, discomfort showing in all of her features. Her lips twisted, and her cheeks darkened. "No more chains. That is the pirate life. No queens, no lords, no barons, and no laws. It should have been . . ." She stepped closer, her eyes dimming.

"So you want to take down Mothar?" Rob hoped he did not sound too eager. "We can help! We want him dead, too!"

"Mothar is weak," she snarled. "He is nothing in the grand plan. He wanted to control me, but my mind was too strong. I had to block him every day. I had to maintain my freedom. *Now that I have the power of D'haara, I don't need to block him. He cannot approach me. Mothar is nothing. I am everything.*"

"Pangles." Ilma stepped right up to her and put her hand on Skagra's shoulder. "You *are* everything. You are everything to me. My first-born. I always knew you would do something great with your life, but this . . ." She gestured at her body. "You don't need some god's power. You don't need to drink blood, and frighten people."

"But I want to," she grinned. "I want to drink blood. I want to frighten people. The world is full of people who will live their lives without risk, without even thinking of moving. But fear motivates people to change."

"You sound just like Mothar," Rob observed.

"*No*!" she screamed; gold flaring. "He sounds like me! He learned my words; he stole them and used them for his own ends. My life, my beliefs, everything!"

"I don't understand," Kerrok said, getting to her feet. "Why are you doing this to *me*?"

"Because you signed a contract." Skagra kicked Kerrok, and she slid across the floor. "You failed me and must be punished. I do enjoy punishment."

"We're losing her," Ilma said. "Pangles, ignore the peng! Focus on me!" Ilma stood in front of her, spreading her arms. Skagra tilted her head threateningly, and the gold grew brighter. The doctor stood firm. Rob wanted to go to her, but the sight and sound of Skagra was turning his body to stone.

The sword in Skagra's hand was glowing with the heat. The shard inside Rob's abdomen felt hot; the pain was mounting, and he grabbed Gorm's arm for support.

"I need to get out of here," he gasped. "The shard . . . I can't . . ."

"Captain, you should find Vann," she said. "I can distract Skagra."

"*Distract me*?" the pirate snarled. "*Why would I let you*?"

Gorm pushed Rob towards the exit, but Skagra leapt, hurling Ilma out of her way and pounding across the floor with tremendous speed. She shot past Rob and thundered into the door, breaking it into splinters. Her eyes glowed in the debris, and her vicious smile dripped with saliva.

Rob gulped and knelt into the fighting stance he had seen Gorm use against Skagra. The pirate leered and crept closer with suspicion in her eyes. Racked with fear and dread, Rob tried talking to her one last time.

"The power, it's good, isn't it?" he said. "You feel like everything you ever wanted is within your reach. But they're not *your* wishes, they're not *your* desires. It's the power itself. All it wants is to perpetuate itself, and it will use you as a vessel."

"*You are weak, Rob Sardan,*" she said. "*The Sea-Stone Sword was too much for you, and so you broke it, like a coward.*"

"I broke it to save the world!"

"*Nothing can save this world,*" she screamed with hysterical laughter. "*The fire is coming! The endless flames that will eat the world. Death! Death is coming. Fire, living fire. All shall die . . .*"

"In the flame filled sky, yes," Rob growled. "I'm sick of hearing about it! If you want to kill me, do it."

Her fist smashed his face, hurling him against a wall. His nose exploded in a fountain of blood, and his skull cracked into the golden bricks. The world turned red, and the ringing of Skagra's laughter became the screaming of pterosaurs.

Clouds reared but lasted mere seconds before the gold room came back into view. Gorm was looking at him. He winked and felt his skull knitting back together. It was a strange sensation, punctuated by jolts of pain that made him want to scream his lungs to shreds.

Skagra and Ilma were facing one another at the other end of the room. The doctor was screaming words he could barely hear over the throbbing in his head, but he pulled Gorm closer.

"Keep them distracted," he whispered. "I'll find Vann. I have a plan."

Gorm looked shocked, but she nodded and let Rob lie back before she ran to confront the pirate. He listened to the scuffing of feet, the grunts and shouts as they dodged Skagra's superhuman assaults. Risking a little glance, he opened his eyes a fraction and saw that Skagra had her back to him.

The glimmering sword was still in her belt, and he suddenly found his eye mesmerized by it. He slowly got to his feet as Ilma and Gorm argued with her.

"You betrayed me," Gorm was saying. "We stood on that ship together. We lived together, we laughed together, and we slept together, you and me. But you left me for dead, you put poison in me, and you watched me writhe in pain."

"I was giving you immortality," Skagra spat. "Don't you think it hurt me to see you like that?"

"Your ways are strange," Gorm replied. "Perhaps even then you were corrupted by desire and power. Perhaps that is why you sent the peng after me; you did not want to admit to any kind of vulnerability. You wanted to appear heartless, so you wanted me dead. Ever since you gained authority in Mothar's fleet, you have been turning more into a shadow of power. You are no longer Skagra; you are a conduit for power."

"Gorm!" Skagra took a step. "How can you believe that of me? All these years and . . ." She fell to one knee, screaming as her voice distorted and cracked. "*You mock power, but you do not understand it. Always you have fled from it and ignored it. I have a god under my power. Soon, all the gold of this tower shall be under my control. I will become a god in truth. I alone will stand as the world burns.*"

"What about your friends?" Ilma said. "Your crew? Will you let them all die? What about me, Pangles?"

"*That is not my name*!" she screamed. "*I am Skagra*!"

Rob reached for the pommel in her belt and gripped it as hard as he could. He jerked it free, slicing through Skagra's belt. She whipped around, and her face became an inferno of golden light. Rob pulled the sword back as if to strike her, but he met her eyes and his own blood ran cold.

She was his reflection in that moment. He saw the pain and wonder of the god living inside her and he remembered the feeling. The sword felt heavy and he hesitated a moment too long. Skagra was already dodging out of his reach, her face a mess of confusion and pain. He looked at her with pity, his heart tight in his chest. Rob spun and then broke into a run.

"Thank you for the gift!" he called over his shoulder.

Skagra's pursuit sounded like an earthquake. The walls trembled and as Rob flew through the doors and turned up a flight of stairs he felt the floors crack. Shouts and screams echoed after him, but he kept running.

His friends were risking their lives for him. He had set an example, and they were following it, but they were not like him; they weren't going to heal and get up later. They would be hurt permanently. His sacrifices were meaningless, but theirs were not. He had left Ilma and Gorm to die. How could he have done this? Kari, Jarl and Alya would soon follow. There was nothing he could do. He had no real plan. That had been another lie to give them hope, to give them a reason to fight while he ran.

With a gasp he fell into another room and put his hands on the floor, breathing hard. Hatred boiled in his stomach, and he wanted to slip into that hallucination once more, but, this time, he would let the creature destroy him. It was no more than he deserved. He had become the monster, even without the Sword.

'*No*,' he thought. '*I refuse to become that thing*.'

Slowly, he got to his feet and turned his face towards the stairs. Smoke and shouts were coming after him. Vengeance rang in his bones. Reckless heroism, Alya would have called it. But that didn't matter.

"Hello, Captain," the voice rose from the other end of the room and startled him from his thought.

There were gold figures all around, frozen in expressions of pain and fear. One had been crawling along the floor; hand stretched towards a plain stone altar that stood beneath a statue. It was a horrifying face worked in gold, with amber gems in the eyes and a twisted crown on its head.

Standing beside the altar, his hands clasping the seal, was Vann.

Chapter Thirty One

The Crown of Black Glass

Rob's heart leapt and he felt as if all his limbs had become little more than wisps of smoke. He sprinted, his face breaking into a broad grin. His legs sprang with desperate bounds, thrusting him nearer and nearer until he met his lost crewmate. His arms wrapped around Vann tightly.

"Oh, Vann!" he cried, pressing his nose into the man's short hair and taking in his scent. "I thought you'd . . ." He was crying. Rob couldn't stop. His tears came with ferocity, and he let them fall.

"Yeah, I missed you, too," Vann said, pulling away and smiling. "Having Gorm for company was boring, I can tell you. All that 'wisdom' drives me bonkers."

Rob smiled. "She has good things to say occasionally."

"Yeah, and hallucinogenic drugs, too."

"That was an accident." He looked around the room and furrowed his brow. "Where are we? How did you get here? Gorm said you blasted the ground with some of that powder."

"Yeah, nicked it off Alya," he grinned. "Knew there was something under the Tomb. They was always connected to the

Sky Sages; Dylis said so. I used to know her before she got into religion. She dragged my family into it, too."

"The priestesses said you didn't have a sister," Rob frowned. "Only a mother."

"She joined the pirates," Vann smiled. "Thought you'd not like that part of the story. She was good at training trasati, even the sea-swimmers. Long neck beasties take a lot of whipping."

"Someone sent a trasati to lead us into the cave," Rob whispered. "Was your mother on Skagra's crew?"

Vann ignored this and put his hands on the altar. "You want to see something? Open this!"

"Vann, what's going on?"

"You should open this altar, it'll explain everything, I promise."

He looked at it, the image reflecting in his deepest memories, something that hid behind a wall of time and pain. The stone was plain and dusty as if hands hadn't touched it for centuries. He couldn't imagine the Sages leaving it without good reason.

The heat was growing, and he loosened his collar before opening his coat. Vann eyed him and then went back to the altar, his shoulders heaving.

"Alya had you pegged," he said. "You can't see things for what they are, can you?"

"What are you talking about?" Rob said.

"I've been thinking about you and me. What are we, Rob? Do you love me?"

"I . . ." Rob fumbled for words, his tongue struggling to form sounds.

"That boy you lost in Kenna's mines," Vann went on. "Niall. You told me he was the first one you ever loved, and that's fine. But he's dead, Rob. I'm standing here, breathing. I'm alive, and he's dead. You can't be in love with the dead for the rest of your life while I'm standing right in front of you."

"Vann, this is . . ." He looked over his shoulder at the passage behind. It was quiet, and the smoke was lower than he had expected. "This isn't the time."

"It never is," he sighed. "Just my luck. I thought you was this great hero, and when you defended me against the pengs, I just wanted to impress you."

"I know," Rob tried to make it sound light, but it was painful and he wasn't sure why.

"I couldn't help looking at you like you were this legend," Vann went on. "I heard the stories, of course I did. Didn't think they were real until I saw you. And then I couldn't stop looking. You were *just like* the stories. You were a hero!"

"Heroes are more than just stories . . ." Rob wanted to go on but Vann shook his head, laughing lightly.

"I should have known that." He gave a small smile and grasped the altar. "Do us a favour and grab that end, would you?"

"What's in here? What's going on, Vann?" Rob touched his shoulder. "Please tell me what's happening."

"I promise everything will make sense."

"All right," Rob said, slowly.

Gradually, he lifted his hand and put it on the altar, his heart thundering like an alarm. Every part of him cried out a warning, but he could not put his clouded thoughts into order. Against his better judgement, he grasped the lid and lifted it, the stone squealing high and piercing.

Dust clouded, and Rob wafted it away, the movement horribly familiar as an old memory resurfaced. He had done this before, but when? The dust clawed at him like mist, as if the tendrils were alive, as if it were all guided by some distant will. His memory flared and he recalled the temple beneath the forbidden ocean, he recalled the blue child, and he recalled the Sea-Stone Sword.

Looking into the altar he held his breath. Placed in a niche was a crown. It was made of black, volcanic glass, twisted into rugged points, and shaped with a line of claws along the base. In the centre of the face, staring at him was an amber jewel set in a grey stone circle. The gem burned brilliantly, pressing against his memories.

"This is the Crown of Black Glass," said Vann. "She said it'd be in the altar."

"Who?" Rob asked.

"I always wanted to wear it," Vann said, ignoring Rob. "But I could never open the altar, nobody could. Not unless they'd touched one of the gods. How else do you think you were able to get at the Sea-Stone Sword? How else would you have been able to open *this* altar?"

"We can't let Skagra get it," Rob said, his eyes darting to the door, ears straining to hear following footsteps.

"No, we can't," Vann laughed, and Rob looked back.

The man was holding the Crown, eyes drinking every detail of its craggy surface. Rob didn't want the suspicions that were growing to take root, so he reached out a hand, but Vann stepped away and lifted the Crown as if he were going to wear it.

"Vann, stop!" Rob shouted. "You don't know what that thing will do to you!"

"What are you so scared for, eh?" Vann chortled. "You got to hold the Sea-Stone Sword, you got to be a hero, and now it's my turn."

"Why are you doing this?"

"I didn't want to, but this is all I have left, Rob." He raised his head, and he was scowling. "I was nothing to you, wasn't I?"

"That's not true." Rob stepped closer. "You made me feel like my old self again. You looked at me like I was the hero from the stories."

"I made you feel better?" Vann spat. "Was that it? I looked at you and made all your fantasies come true? That's all you wanted, isn't it? Is that what Niall did? Did he make all those dreams come true before you got him killed? The real world isn't a dream, Rob!"

"I know that, better than most. I thought I'd die protecting you. Did you think I did that just to make the stories come true? I was going to die for you!"

"But why? I was just a snivelling coward, a stupid boy who couldn't do anything. Everything I ever did was criticised!"

"That was Alya!"

"And you did nothing to stop her," he shouted. "And worse, you made her your first mate! What about me? I thought you loved me! Turns out I was wrong again, wasn't I? Stupid Vann, can't put one and one together, can he? I bet you spent all night laughing about how stupid I was, didn't you?"

"No! We argued about damn near everything! I needed someone who would challenge me."

"And *I* needed someone who would love me!" He was in tears. "All my life people have looked down on me, my people ignored me and rejected me. I never even earned my nose ring. I had to fake it. I had to fake everything."

"But you were good at opening things," Rob was pulling thoughts out at random. "You got here, didn't you? You got us out of the pengish city, didn't you?"

"And what thanks did I get? I got put in charge of nothing on the ship, I was everybody's laughing stock, I was the whipping boy and nobody took any notice of me. Least of all you, Rob bloody Sardan. Sword-breaker, King-killer, Sky-slayer and all the other titles you want, they're nothing compared to what you really are. A liar!"

"Vann, I never lied to you, I never would!"

"How can I believe you? Everything was turned against me, every criticism made valid, and every time I criticised someone else, you told me off!"

"It wasn't deliberate." Rob desperately tried to think of an example of when this had happened, but his mind was a mangle of confusion.

"I don't know if that makes it better or worse," Vann laughed bitterly. "But *this* is my decision. I choose to leave you here with Skagra. Her crew is looking for a new captain, and they will accept me because I have her blessing. Look!" He lifted his shirt and showed a burn mark on his chest. It was the shape of a jagged smiling face, its square teeth formed around his abdomen.

"The Pirate Lord's mark," Rob said, realisation crawling over his skin.

"He'll make me the new second in command."

"Skagra . . ." Rob suddenly realised everything. "She took *you*! She turned you into her own, didn't she? That's why you were in Bron'Halla, wasn't it?"

"She took me from my home and made me feel like I was important," Vann shouted. "I got to go thieving, I got to feel good about myself. Until the pengs caught me, but old Skagra said she'd make use of me if I got chucked in Bron'Halla. Wanted Gorm, didn't she? You were just a bonus."

"Why didn't you kill me on the sea, then? Or back in the prison?"

"I nearly turned to your side," Vann said, lowering the Crown to his head.

"Don't!" Rob snapped his hands around Vann's wrists, stopping him from putting the thing on. "Is this what you want? To hurt me?"

"Yes," he said it instantly, and Rob was taken aback. "I want you to hurt, Rob. I hate you. I hate what you did to me. You made me feel loved, and then you took that away from me. How could you?" Vann's tears fell in streams, and Rob could only stare. "I thought we'd be together; I thought you'd help me. But all I got was grief. All I got was rejection. Nobody wanted me. So I'm going somewhere that they do want me. I'll *make* them want me!"

"Vann, please!"

"What? What are you going to do?"

The claws in the Crown's base undulated and moved as the gem glowed hot. There was a bloom of red light above them, and Rob looked at the ceiling as it churned like boiling clouds.

"The magma," Vann said. "I released it before coming here. I'm going to drown you and Skagra, and everyone else. If you die in here with her, it'll make the world a safer place. No more Sword-breaker. No more Skagra. Just a normal world. Mothar's not so bad when you're out of the picture, I bet."

"Please," Rob begged. "Don't do this. I do love you . . ."

"No, you don't." Vann kicked him in the groin, and Rob crumbled, lightning pain striking through his body at the impact. "You just wanted someone who looked at you like you were a hero. If you did feel something for me, you would have made me your first mate."

Vann placed the Crown on his head, his eyes turning gold the moment the stone touched his flesh. His skin seared and glowed, heat rising in steam as his flesh tightened against his bones. Hollow laughter burst from his mouth in a sound like a landslide. He lifted his hands and grinned as the gold bricks around him ripped from the floor, twisted and rose. Then he formed a fist, and a brick fell from above.

Thick, sulphurous magma flowed as the ceiling cracked. Rob dodged and weaved as the boiling rock spat at him from above. The floor melted, the gold running thick and sizzling at his feet. He kept moving back, further and further as it flowed like a red waterfall, the unfathomable heat making him hang on to his consciousness.

With a hiss and a gasp, the magma split into two streams, opening like a curtain of fire, and there was now a blistering gap dividing him from Vann, who was kneeling, his head bowed, and his fists balled.

"Vann!" Rob shouted, coughing as poisonous fumes filled the chamber.

"*Don't call me that*," the figure across the divide called, eyes glowing. "*I am the god of the golden ground*."

"Vann!" Rob screamed. "It's Skagra! She's controlling you! The gold, see? She uses the gold to control people; I saw her do it to Kerrok. Just take the nose ring out and you'll be fine."

"Rob," Vann called through the fire and tapped his nose ring. "It isn't real gold, weren't you listening? I chose the Crown; I choose to take control."

Vann turned into the gathering smoke. Yellow clouds were rising, and Rob just stood, glaring into the growing gloom. He gritted his teeth, bared them and then snarled.

"You traitorous, evil son of filth!" Rob screamed. "You think I'm the Sword-breaker, the King-killer, and the Sky-slayer? You think I'm this monstrous creature of legend? Then so be it."

He took a step back, and then pelted forward, leaping over the gorge of magma in a single bound. He slammed into Vann as he landed and they rolled together, wrestling and punching. Rob tried to grip the Crown, but Vann bit at his hands and shrieked in a voice that would shatter glass.

Rob formed his face into the most nightmarish scowl of hatred that he could manage. The gold light in Vann's eyes flickered and died for a moment and Rob got his hands on the Crown. He pulled at it and Vann shrieked, striking Rob in the throat and mouth, but he kept a tight hold.

The Crown's claws dug into Vann's skull, blood gushing from the puncture wounds. The cracking of bones echoed over the bubbling molten rock. Vann kicked Rob, and he stumbled, losing his grip.

They looked at each other again, breathing the stinging air. Rob's hand went to his scabbard, painful decisions forming in him. Drawing his sword, Rob lunged, but the blade glanced off Vann's arm as if he were made of metal. Spinning, Rob caught his breath, but the putrid air climbed into his throat, and he almost collapsed again.

"*The god is inside you, Sword-breaker,*" Vann said, voice distorted and inhuman. "*That shard the pengs put in you. It is part of this power, and as long as you have it, you will be susceptible to it. Even if you take the Crown from me, you will wear it and become a god again. You will defeat Skagra, perhaps, but then you will* become *Skagra.*"

"I won't!" Rob stepped to the altar and steadied against it, putting his sword back in its sheath. "I never want to . . ."

"*This isn't a question of wanting,*" Vann laughed. "*It will happen. I know it.*"

Rob pounced, pinning Vann to the statue, which was melting and about to topple. Rob grasped the Crown and pulled again, the snap of bones and the spurts of blood, making him feel sick. Vann's pained scream was more horrifying than anything Rob had experienced in his dreams.

"I won't let it take you, Vann!" Rob yelled at the top of his lungs. "I won't let it take anyone ever again!"

The claws ripped through Vann's head and then the Crown came free. Vann tumbled, shrieking and kicking at the ground, spewing blood and pressing his hands against as many of the wounds as he could.

"Why?" Vann howled. "I wanted to be something! You won't let anyone be special except yourself!"

"No, Vann," Rob snarled. "I'm sorry this happened. I wish . . ."

"I don't care what you wish!" Vann slammed a fist into the floor as his face was washed with red. "You betrayed me. You tricked me into thinking I was loved. Then you threw it away. You should know how dangerous that makes someone, to take love away from them."

"Yes," Rob lowered his head, gripping the Crown hard. "I know. When I lost Niall, I went on a rampage. But it was wrong."

"*You* are wrong! Everything you do is wrong. One day you'll betray that filthy crew. One day, they'll find out what you are, and they'll leave you like they always should have. You'll wish for death before the end."

Vann sprang at him with his mouth wide as if to bite his face. Rob ducked and swung a left hook, smashing his fist into Vann's head with such force he thought the man would die. Instead, Vann fell and cradled his injury with one hand, but his other reached out to grasp Rob's foot as the magma came closer and closer.

Rob turned away and sprinted back, jumping over the chasm, his heart a monstrous thing in his chest, injecting hatred into every vein of his body. He landed and then struggled to stand. Looking back, he spotted Vann glaring across the divide.

"Put it on, Rob," Vann called through his tears. "Go on! It's what you want, isn't it? To be powerful and mighty again, yeah? Do it."

"No."

"Then everyone will die," Vann spat. "The magma will eat you all, won't it? I wish I could watch it, but I'm going to get out of here."

Vann turned and clambered over the melting statue.

"Vann!" Rob called. "I'll find you again, I promise you that!"

"If you find me," Vann shouted, bitterness dripping from every syllable. "I will break your whole life, Sword-breaker."

He stumbled, bleeding and hurt, but then turned away, vanishing into a passage behind. Rob stepped forward, intending to follow, but the ceiling shattered, and more flaming stones fell, bursting against the floor in a wrathful tidal wave.

"Vann!" Rob shrieked through the chaos. "Come back here!"

Tears were already on Rob's cheeks, swelling in his eyes as his throat choked with pain. The trembles of betrayal branched from his chest, grasping every inch of his body until he thought he would die.

He looked up as a hollow voice rang, metallic and pained. The golden figures were melting all around him, their hands and faces becoming visible. He didn't want to see the tortured remains of the former Sky-sages, so he retreated from the deadly fumes clogging the air. His eyes blurred with tears. His chest was exploding with loathing and fear, and he wanted it all to stop.

He had been betrayed.

Chapter Thirty Two

The Sky-Slayer's Pendant

THE TOWER WAS COLLAPSING. HEAT FILLED THE ATMOSPHERE and scorched his skin as he ran, shooting through clouds and debris. Rob broke into the chamber where he had left Skagra and found it empty. The floor shifted and he slipped. The gold was turning to liquid and the walls were oozing like blood.

He buckled and his fists balled, one hand tight on the Crown of Black Glass. Vann's face flashed before his mind and his teeth gritted in sheer fury. The monster that he had seen in his hallucination seemed to rise within, clawing at his eyes, begging to rampage.

Everything was falling apart; the tower, his plans, his whole life. As the toxic fumes came for him once again, he could hear the Air King's breath seeking him out, reaching ever closer, threatening to grasp him and pull him into that drowning dream. His hand slipped under his own shirt and there was nothing but flesh and sweat there.

Even the quest had failed. This wasn't like the quest for the Sea-Stone Sword; this quest was about Rob's own fate. It was about his life, it was about his dreams, and it was about his nightmares. He punched the melting floor in a rage.

Alya had been right; he had been so selfish, so blind. He had walked right into Skagra's trap. The dreams tugged at him, threatening to plunge him once more into those never-ending death visions.

What could he do? How could he make this right? If he came out of this, how could he face the others? If he had a pendant, perhaps then, at least, it would not have been completely pointless, at least, they'd know he could follow through on his promises. If he could get a pendant, he could rest, he could think, and he could survive long enough to take down Mothar.

All the pain, all the narrow escapes, all the risks, it had to lead somewhere. He had to get a pendant, and this was his very last chance. He had to do it. He had to fulfil the quest. Even if it stretched him to his very limits, he had to do it.

There was a cold, shivering anger building in his chest, a frosty rage that had been born in the ice prison. The anger gave him a burst of strength and he ran on, speeding through chambers and leaping down stairs. The air was hot and bricks the size of his body fell around him, their mortar melted and broken.

Skagra, Gorm, Ilma and Kerrok were nowhere to be seen. He plunged down stairs and past the cauldron as it toppled into the opening floor. Sprinting even faster, he barely thought of anything besides his feet.

He skidded into the room where the Sky Sages stood like statues. The gold was cracking and one of the draigs arms moved. Rob caught the motion in the corner of his eye and spun to see that all of the statues were moving. One of the humans lifted their head and then their mouth opened, spitting gold as a scream escaped her.

Rob picked at the gold, which was chipping off her skin. She screamed louder and louder, but the more she moved, the more the gold fell away. At last, her head was free and she was breathing. He pulled plates of gold from her chest and released her lungs, but strips of skin came with it and the Sage yelled in pain.

Soon all five statues were moving, shouting their agony to the collapsing ceiling. Rob helped them to stand, chipping gold from their knees as they shook with terror.

"How did this . . . ?" Rob began, but as the floor shook again, he put his questions aside. "We have to escape. Don't ask questions. No time for clothes." He added as the draig Sage tried to cover her wings.

The Sages struggled, some attempting to speak but their throats were clogged with gold and they coughed it up, spewing the floor with bloody vomit. The room was collapsing fast, the floor sloping in a droop of melted metal.

Rob spotted a door in the corner of the room. It was plain except for a plaque on the face, which bore a golden pterodactyl skeleton. Every muscle froze. Ice tore into his brain and he felt as light as air. His heart beat louder and louder in his ears.

"A pendant!" he shouted. He leapt toward the nearest Sage, a sauros with burned grey scales and a long, snake-like face. "I need a Sky-slayer's pendant!"

"Sorry," the Sage said. "I'm sorry." She bolted to the ladder and descended.

The other Sages were following with limping and staggering movements. Rob stood in the centre, his eyes flitting from the ladder to the door.

It was what he had come for, he had escaped from Bron'Halla, he had stolen a ship, forged a crew, sailed the Ginnungagap and come through magma. It had all been for this.

"Are the pendants in there?" he asked as the last Sage headed for the ladder. "Tell me! Are the pendants in there? I need one!"

The Sage looked at him, tears in his eyes, and then vanished. Rob bit his lip and clenched his fists harder. The room was still falling to pieces; the air was boiling and the world was warping and changing into a corrupted confusion.

He kicked the door in, the frame already deformed beyond use. His foot ached but he ran through a barrage of collapsing bricks as the floor softened with every step. The corridor led him to a corner room; fire was raging through it and smoke billowed off a flame-eaten rug.

Covering his mouth with his collar, he struggled into the chamber. There was a cabinet against the far wall; its glass smashed leaving shards across the carpet. He crunched towards it, but the floor was melting. His balance went from his feet and he was thrown onto his side as the bricks slumped down.

The wall was ripped open. Rob tried to get to his feet, but the acute angle of the ground was getting worse and the smoke was choking him. Panic soared. The floor was slipping. The cabinet glinted with circles of gold and Rob's breath caught as his heart turned to a hollow fire that sent embers throughout his body.

The cabinet was slipping. He inched closer, leaning. His hand stretched towards the thing, the pendants waving in the heat and gravity. Several were smashed, the glass faces broken to sand, but there were still two intact.

His stomach dropped away and his feet were in the air before he knew what was happening. The floor had melted, disintegrating and collapsing from the ziggurat.

He hit the cabinet as it landed in the pool of molten gold beneath the Tower. It cracked and buckled under his weight, but he stood and balanced. The wood was burning, fire spreading. A slab of gold fell, splashing molten metal at him. He ducked under the spray, but his movement put him off balance.

The wood was being devoured. With a desperate effort, he leapt onto a golden slab. Its shape was still intact, but it was softening. More blocks fell and he crouched, sailing past the cabinet. He stretched his hand but missed the pendants.

Springing from the slab, he landed on another, but it was melting even quicker and he was forced to jump onto a third as it appeared in front of him. Breathing hard, he felt sweat pouring all over his body and his legs were full of pain.

The cabinet was sinking, but he leant into the gold brick, hoping against hope, to push it closer. He sprawled on his stomach, his arm outstretched.

A Sky-slayer's pendant was lying on the wood; its chain dipped in the molten pool. He stretched. The dreams would be gone, the screaming would stop, and he would have achieved something. His quest wouldn't have been a disaster. The quest would mean something. He needed it. He *needed* it.

Pain bit into his arm and he held back a scream. The Crown of Black Glass was digging its claws into him, the gem in its crest glowing. Being so close to the body of its god was not a good idea, he thought. He put the feeling out of his mind, allowing the healing process to fight it.

The pendant was almost in his fingers. His skin brushed it, his mind raced, and he tried to hold his breath.

One more second; that was all he needed. Just one more stretch of his arm and . . .

A golden brick smashed into the cabinet. Rob recoiled as boiling metal splashed. Tears of pain were on his face as his arm burned. He flicked the stuff off his coat and then everything stopped.

The pendant, the last pendant, was in the molten pool. The pterodactyl on the face faded, the disc spread and vanished. Red wisps trickled from its core and then it was gone completely.

Rob could not breathe. The Tower of the Sky Sages was destroyed. The last pendant had melted. Everything had failed. There was nothing left, no hope of escaping the curse. His heart constricted, tightening as if it were collapsing. His future opened like a gaping chasm, into inescapable fear and dismay.

He dropped to his knees as the gold burned all around and the tower collapsed, flinging more bricks into the growing pool. The Crown seemed to laugh in his hand, relishing his pain and trickling thoughts of power back into his blood.

Bitter hatred burned under his skin, spreading from some deep seed within the pit of his chest and growing to a forest throughout his body. He spotted the figures of the Sky Sages, struggling from one floating brick to another, making their way to the shore of the golden pool.

They made the pendants. He stood as realisation hit. Wiping his eyes, he focused on his determination, put his effort into making his legs move, and sprinted. Leaping from brick to brick, he used them as stepping-stones to make his way across. More blocks fell, splashing gold, but every burn healed almost instantly. His mind was a furnace of determined, singular focus. He stretched each leap as long as he could and bounded again and again.

Skidding along the rim of one half melted brick, he backed away from a surge of falling masonry. Wooden doors were on fire, magma was still pouring from the roof, and the ever-present stench assaulted his nose.

Fire exploded around him, but he ran on, jumping to another platform, sending a splatter of gold onto his coat. He shook it off and carried on, eventually slamming a bloody hand onto the rocks that marked the edge of the bowl surrounding the Tower.

Climbing, he blew dust from his face, pressed his arms one ahead of the other, lifting his weight with all of his strength. He was soon on the path that he and Ilma had taken.

Ahead, he spied figures running back and forth, one of them glowing gold, the others fleeing from it. He scanned the path and saw the Sky Sages hiding beneath one of the canals that ran from the gate above.

Running to them, he made them flinch. He must have looked a sight, he realised. His deranged face was cracked into fury and terror, his clothes were ruined, and his hair was flying wild.

“I need a pendant,” he hissed.

"We don't have any," said one of the human Sages. "The Pirate Lord took most of them and broke them, the rest will have fallen in *that*." She gestured at the cataclysm behind them.

"But you must know how to make them!" He was desperate.

"I'm sorry," she said, bowing. "We don't know how. It would take great skill to make one from scratch, especially for you, King-killer."

He looked at her, his face turning into a storm of desperate desire for help. His eyes were welling, his throat closed and he fell to his knees. "Please! Please try! I can't stand the dreams. I need them to go!"

"We are not able to do it," the sauros Sage said. She had a set of small vein-filled plates that ran down her back and they glistened in the fire and magma. "A Sky- slayer's pendant must be made of purified gold from the body of D'haara. The tower is made of ordinary gold with only small parts of the Dead God's power within each brick. It would take hours to purify enough to make a pendant."

"But you could still do it?" he said, excitedly. "You could, at least, make something that would help me?"

The draig stood. Her red scales were more burned than the others had been and it looked as if she had been attacked before being sealed in gold.

"When the Pirate Lord trapped us, he thought we would die, but the gold kept us alive, even through the pain of it melting. D'haara was the master of shapes, as well as earth; her power is said to allow one to control their own body morphology. As such, it can create a block that will stop the Curse from reaching the mind."

"So yes, then?" Rob pressed. "The god's power is in the gold?"

"But the spells required," another Sage objected. "Only the Abbot knows them."

"The Abbot?" Rob looked around. "Which one of you is the Abbot?"

"None of us," the draig replied. "And they aren't 'spells', Keilo. It is the mental and physical binding of an idea into the structure of the Dead God's power."

"Sounds like a spell to me," the one called Keilo said sullenly.

"We will not have this argument again," the draig snapped. "Not now."

"What happened to the Abbot?" Rob demanded.

"She had her tongue ripped out," she said. "Mothar did not want her making more pendants, so she was silenced, and her hands were removed, too."

"Where is she now?"

"We do not know, perhaps she escaped."

"I could try and find her."

"Even if you did, she would not be able to make you a pendant. I'm sorry."

Rob looked into her eyes. They were dark, green baubles that swam with pain. With a long, slow breath, he turned away from the Sky Sages and pulled the golden sword from his belt.

"Then there is only one quest left for me," he said, lifting the Crown of Black Glass. "I'll kill Skagra. I'll kill Mothar. And then there will be nothing left."

Chapter Thirty Three

The Many Coloured Blade

THE PATH WAS CRACKED, SMOKING AND BREAKING AS HE stepped across it towards where Skagra was engaging his friends. Doom rang in his ears. He had no idea how he was going to fight.

Stones were blasted by the malevolent bombardment of Skagra's new powers and the breathless retreat of his companions echoed loud. Yet, it was all a blur of faraway nonsense to Rob. Vann's betrayal, the loss of the pendant, the pain in his body, and the Crown digging into his hand; it had all served to leave him feeling like an empty husk of his former self.

Then, something rose, it was rage, it was fear, and it was boiling desperation. He wanted it to end, he wanted Skagra gone, he wanted Mothar dead, and he wanted to stop struggling.

He still had the Crown of Black Glass in his hand. Its claws had dug into his palm, and his blood was running in rivers. He felt faint, but kept the thing close, his eyes closing and streaming.

The memories of when he had held the Sea-Stone Sword were filling him as his mouth congealed with the throb of blood and the taste of ashes. He remembered standing atop the spike of rock in the middle of the ocean, holding the Sword above his head and hurling it. He remembered the thing shattering from point to hilt, the sapphire gem in the guard dying as Saagara was broken once and for all.

'Chosen or imposed; power is the same.'

He forced his eyes to rest on the boulder in front of him and lifted the Crown. Pushing his strength into his arms, he hurled it against the rock. There was a clang, but the Crown barely shuddered. He hit it again, and again, hammering the boulder with all his power, tears bursting as the fangs bit his hands, drawing blood.

He collapsed, gasping for breath, the Crown still intact. A horrible thought loomed inside him. He'd had to use the Sea-Stone Sword's own power when he had destroyed it. If he couldn't break the Crown now, would he *have* to wear it?

"I have lived in fear of you," Gorm shouted, snapping Rob back to the present. "It is time that fear was ended."

"Speak like a normal person, Gorm," Skagra replied. "You used to have a foul mouth. You used to stand at my side watching villages burn, and you would laugh. Remember? You call me a monster, you accuse me of atrocities, but you stood by me the whole time."

"I looked up to you," Gorm said. "You were my idol; you were the one who encouraged me to find adventure. But I discovered another life."

"With Rob Sardan?" she scoffed. "He is every bit as merciless and brainless as Mothar! If you follow that boy, you'll kill more people than I ever did."

"Stop this! Please stop this!" Ilma cried.

Rob peered around to see Skagra dig her arms into the earth up to her elbows, sending a shockwave through the stone. Gorm and Ilma were knocked off their feet, and steam rose from Skagra's body.

"I won't ask you to join me, Gorm," Skagra growled. "I won't insult your freedom. But at least, admit that I'm right.

That hate; that desire to see pain and to watch people burn that is who you are. It still lives inside you."

"I died," Gorm said, getting to her feet. She was bleeding and lurched towards Skagra with determination. "I died when you injected me. I saw those desires; I saw what I would become if the power took over me, and I said 'no more'!"

She leapt onto Skagra and wrapped her hands around her throat, but the pirate threw her off and roared, light exploding from her eyes. Her strength ripped the earth at her feet, and she foamed at the mouth.

Gorm ran at Skagra again and punched her in the face, but she doubled over, holding her hand in pain. The pirate snarled and kicked Gorm in the stomach, knocking her towards the gold that was bubbling in the pit. They wrestled, but Skagra's strength was devastating.

Rob pelted from his hiding place and stormed up the path. He reached Ilma and helped her stand, she was bleeding from wounds and burns, but when she felt Rob's touch, she flung her arms around him.

"I thought you'd died!" she said. "But I suppose I shouldn't be surprised at this point. Oh, Captain, what are going to do?"

"We'll work something out," he said.

Gorm was hurled again and landed with a crunch. She screamed, her sweat plastering her clothes to her body, but she got up again and ran at Skagra.

"She's suicidal," Rob realised. "Ilma, you need to distract Skagra. I have to save Gorm before she kills herself."

"What? How are you going to . . . ? How am I going to . . . ?"

"You're intelligent!"

"Rob!" Ilma looked at him and gasped. "That Crown, is it . . . ?"

"I think so," Rob nodded.

"Don't wear it!"

"Trust me, I know what I'm doing."

She hesitated and then nodded. She got to her feet and walked towards Skagra just as Gorm was knocked to the ground once again, a steaming wound on her back.

Rob crouched behind a rock and looked at the Crown. It was light, humming to his touch and making his flesh crawl. The amber gem in its face drew his eye, and he was soon falling into its glare.

The power of the ocean had almost destroyed him; he had seen this crown eat into Vann's head and break his skull, he could see what this new god's power was doing to Skagra. And yet he burned to put it on. It was like hunger, bubbling under his chest, yearning and pulling the Crown closer to his head.

No, it would destroy him, and his friends.

But the power was in his hands. He could save them. He could save Skagra and save his crew. Using the Crown he could become the hero again.

"Pangles!" Ilma shouted. "Listen to me, please!"

"I have nothing to say to you," Skagra said, knocking Gorm aside lazily as she attacked again. "And stop calling me Pangles! It is a child's name."

"And you are my child."

"I am nobody's child. I don't belong to you."

Rob crawled to where Gorm was trying desperately to get to her feet. He put his arm around her and helped her sit and then looked into her face. The pull of the Crown was still on his mind, but he closed his eyes and sucked air through his teeth.

"The Sky Sages," he said. "They need our help."

"Skagra is . . ."

"She is not you," Rob said. "You are Gorm. You are the kind, wise woman who helped us. People change, Gorm. I believe that. I have to."

"But she's right, I did enjoy those things. I have a monster inside of me, and one day it will come out."

"No, it won't," he assured her. "You are stronger than that. You can inject peace into any situation. Letting violence be your guide is going to encourage that monster. Don't let it. Be who you want to be, not who *she* thinks you are. Do you trust me?"

She stood, stumbling into his arms on a twisted ankle. "The one who trusts is sure of peace in their mind."

"That's the Gorm I know," he grinned. "The Sky Sages are by that boulder. I need you to take them through that crack there, up the stairs and to the ship. It's a little stuck at the moment, but you'll find Alya and the others with it."

"Skagra will hurt you," she said. "If you still had the Sea-Stone Sword . . ."

"I've held power," Rob showed his teeth as he glowered. "It is the most poisonous thing in the world. It is better left broken."

"But she must be stopped." Her gaze rested on the Crown in his hand. The gem blazed at the stare of her eyes and she snatched it from his grasp, shoving Rob away and standing at her full height.

"Gorm! No!" Rob cried.

"Skagra will bring the Flame-Filled Sky," Gorm said, drawing Skagra's attention. "I will not let that happen. I will not stand by if I can stop it."

Gorm lifted the Crown, daring Skagra to advance. Even as the earth rumbled with strain, as the tower collapsed behind them and the ceiling cracked, the two of them stood absolutely still.

Ice trickled down Rob's spine and he had to wet his dry throat. His fists ached with the effort to keep them still but they trembled. Gorm raised the Crown above her head, closing her eyes in an almost meditative and peaceful manner.

"Tell me, Sword-breaker," she said. "How did it feel? When you stood atop the Teeth and held the Sea-Stone Sword aloft? What did you feel?"

He looked around helpless. The Sky Sages were running along the path, but nobody was paying them any attention.

Rob's heart boiled like the magma and he wanted to help, but the eyes of Gorm and Skagra trapped him.

"It was like having all of the power in the world," he said. "It was the worst feeling I have ever experienced. I wanted it to stop so much. It destroyed me, Gorm."

"So you destroyed *it*," she grinned at him. "Trust me, Sword-breaker."

"Gorm, don't! Please don't! I can't let it happen again! Not to another!"

Gorm pulled the Crown onto her head and she shrieked. Blood trickled from her forehead where the claws plunged into her flesh. Her eyes flashed and her skin hissed with steam. The ground shivered and the walls cracked. The molten gold churned and whirled with new life.

Skagra sped forwards, her feet thundering against the earth as if she weighed tonnes. She made her way towards Gorm and they collided with a brilliant shower of light. They ducked and spun around one another, earthen boulders splintering all over the cavern as their titanic powers met.

Gorm roared, her voice distorted and cracked. Smoke came from her mouth. Skagra was forced back and she almost fell; Gorm lifted a hand and golden light wrapped her like raging clouds in a storm. The two of them clashed, shouting, ducking and sliding along the broken ground, churning solid rocks into slush.

The fight seemed to go on forever, each blow that landed on either opponent seemed also to hurt Rob. Gorm's face was like a volcanic eruption of fury; Skagra's was an inferno. Every time Gorm struck her former captain, Rob thought she fell a little further away from him, and each time Skagra struck back, he feared for Gorm's safety.

He couldn't keep watching, he had to stop it, he had to intervene, and he had to do something!

The pirate tried to run at Gorm again, but Rob leapt and kicked her in the stomach. It was like kicking a mountainside.

His foot sparked with pain as if it had shattered like glass; he fell but so did Skagra. She made a dent in the earth, landing with a clang that resounded about the chamber.

Gorm stepped forward to attack, but suddenly she screamed in pain as the Crown dug its claw into her head with fresh vigour. She put her hands against the sides of the Crown as her eyes bled.

Meanwhile, Rob got up, his leg cracking back into place with sickening sounds. His abdomen burned like wildfire and he could feel the knife shard vibrating against his bones.

Earth exploded and smoke poured from opened vents. Ilma stumbled over and leapt on Skagra, to keep her down. The pirate yelled incoherently and threw Ilma off before standing and glaring at Rob.

"Sardan, you live," she grinned and licked her lips. "You are getting quite good at that."

"It's a skill," he said. "You've done enough to hurt Ilma, leave her alone!"

"You are not my captain. I have no captain. I command the golden power. *I am the god of earth*." She raised her hand and the veins glowed yellow.

"Gorm wears the Crown," Rob gestured towards his crewmate, who was on her knees, bloody hands clasped against the thing on her head. "That rather trumps your claims, I think."

"That is my Crown," Skagra shouted. "*That is my power*!"

"Chosen or imposed, power is the same. Didn't you say that?"

Skagra faltered. The conflict in her mind was turning, but the pulsing light still rampaged in her skin. She reached down and lifted Ilma by the arm. The doctor screamed; the bracelet on her injured hand was burning red, searing into her flesh with a horrifying stench. She was thrown at Rob's feet and Skagra cackled.

"There, take her if you want her," she said.

Rob swung a right hook, but Skagra caught his arm. Her grip tightened on Lomi's bracelet.

"It's gold," she said. "The same flows in my veins."

The band turned hot. Rob doubled over, the pain like having his hand cut off. Skagra laughed, making the temperature rise further before shoving him to the ground next to Ilma, who was rolling on her back, sobbing. Rob felt his tears flowing, but he struggled to his feet.

"You have no way of fighting me," Skagra laughed. "Gorm cannot control the Crown. *I am the master.* Where is your glory now, Sword-breaker?"

"You were right," Rob hissed. He wanted to look at Gorm, but he forced the urge away and kept his focus on Skagra. "Glory fades and dissipates. It's worthless."

"Are you surrendering?" she leered.

"You were right in another way," he pressed, keeping her eyes on him. "It doesn't matter if nobody remembers this, but I will do the right thing. I will stop you. This is my quest; to stop you."

"Useless words," she scoffed. "You, Sword-breaker, what use are you? In this state, you cannot even *use* a sword." She gestured to his burning wrist.

"Is that so?" he managed to grin. He had refrained from using the sword for so long but now he grasped the hilt and took a breath. This was the moment he had to choose what kind of captain he was going to be. He was going to be the kind that gave up everything for his crew. "The power must be affecting your memory." He pulled the sword out of his belt. "I use my left hand."

Skagra's eyes went wide as realisation flared. Rob pressed his surprise and swung at her; she stumbled, tripping as she struggled. He spun and jabbed, but she ducked, her eyes looking desperately for an opening. But she was off balance, unused to fighting from the left, and in the sudden onslaught she was pushed further and further back. The weight of the gold inside her was stopping her from settling into one of her familiar stances. She growled and stamped a weighty foot into rock, shattering it but Rob kept attacking, kept pushing.

She leaned back, trying to avoid him as he slashed at her chest, but the sword cut through the vials of blood smashing them and ripping through her flesh in one swipe. Blood gushed over the blade and Skagra fell backwards, shock on her face as she blinked at him. Rob sidestepped and twirled the golden sword, flicking drops of red onto the ground.

"Captain!" Gorm screeched in an unholy, unnatural voice.

Rob turned and almost dropped the sword. Gorm was standing, gold rushing through her arms and burning out of her eyes like a firestorm.

Her hands were clasped over the Crown on either side, the amber gem shaking as if it were trying to escape.

The power ran through her arms, she tensed, closed her eyes, and pulled all the harder.

"I will not be swayed!" Gorm shouted. "I am Gorm! I am not a god!"

All sound stopped.

The shaking of the earth stopped.

The sound of water pounding beyond the gates was dulled.

Gorm broke the Crown of Black Glass, ripping it in two.

It flew from her hands, twisting in the air. With a thud, both halves landed and the earth trembled. The amber gem cracked and the light within it died. There was a roar like wind, but more robust. The sound battered Rob's flesh and grew. The gold in the pool blasted towards the ceiling, directly over where Gorm stood.

Skagra was pulled upwards, she was lifted from the ground and her mouth opened in a nightmare of sound. Gold was ripped out of her body, flowing from her mouth and the slash Rob had made on her chest.

The sword in Rob's hand jerked and the gold fell away from it, turning to mist and rising off the blade, leaving a brass hilt and a blade that shimmered with every colour he had ever imagined. The folds of the metal turned white, and the flowing rivers of light transformed into a spectrum. It was like oil on water, the colours spread and changed, glimmering as it took over the blade.

Above, a face appeared in the gold, like the one that had been carved into the statues, and on the tombstone. It was a motionless face, gaping eyes, a mouth that opened into a void; it was like a skull. The light faded and the gold trickled down the walls, lifeless and dead.

"The Dead God's power," Skagra breathed tears and blood. "Gone . . ."

Chapter Thirty Four

The Dead God

Rob opened his mouth to speak, but Skagra was looking past him, apoplectic fury painted across her face. He twisted and followed her gaze. The Sky Sages were running towards the crack in the wall. Water was trickling from the stairs, and as the first Sage splashed into the darkness, Skagra gave a howl.

"They survived!" she said. "They were encased in gold, but they survived. Perhaps that is the key . . ." She looked over her shoulder as gold seeped back into the pit below what had once been the Tower of the Sky Sages.

"Pangles, don't!" Ilma came running. "That god is dead; you saw it die!"

"I will bring it to life," she struggled, staggering towards the pool.

Not all of it had risen in the death of the god's heart, and magma was still gushing into it. The gold frothed and churned as Skagra approached, her hand on the wound Rob had given her. Then, she looked at Rob and lifted a hand to him.

The shard burned hot and he screamed in pain, clutching his abdomen as he fell beside Ilma. He gasped and closed his eyes.

"It's dead," Rob said, lifting the sword. "You can't control it."

"It is only a small shard," she said, her face screwed in concentration. "With enough effort . . ."

Rob burned, agony spiking. Skagra backed away from him, her eyes getting brighter. Rob's tears were hopeless as Ilma came to his side.

"Yes," Skagra said. "The Crown is the conduit for the mind to connect to the body. But if I were to become the body and the mind, I won't need one . . ."

Skagra walked to the lake of molten gold, trembling and swaying.

"Please, don't do this," Ilma begged. "You'll die."

"I cannot die," she replied. "I have sworn to see the Flame-Filled Sky. I will watch it happen. I will *make* it happen!"

"Skagra." It was Gorm, still on her knees and staring at the ground. "Within you is a war between your principles. You desired freedom, but you also desired blood. You wanted to tear down power but became power. Do you see how this incongruence has turned you sour?"

"I have to be true to something," Skagra screamed as tears coated her face and bloody chest. "If there is one thing I shall be true to, let it be this."

"Listen to me!" Gorm roared, her face was in more pain than Rob could have thought imaginable. "Skagra, you are more than the gods, you are a pirate and have no need for that power. Trust me!"

"I can't . . ." Skagra was wavering. "I can't trust anything. I can't trust anyone. My crew, they were in Mothar's pocket. My own mother abandoned me, as did you."

"I am trying to help you." Gorm looked ready to pass out, her hands grasping the earth as sweat poured across her bloody face.

"How do I know?" Skagra's voice weakened, and she was almost whispering.

"We can help," Rob said, trying to stand. "We are going to find Mothar and take him down. Join us!"

"Join you?" Skagra's rage returned. "Sword-breaker? And the Crown-breaker? What would I be but a shadow behind your legends? Because that's all you care about, isn't it? You and Mothar, you're just children playing at stories."

"Stories can change worlds," said Gorm. "The story of the Dead God, the story of the Sea-Stone Sword, and the story of the Crown of Black Glass. They changed you, Skagra. If you had not heard them, you would not have come here, you would not now be standing on the brink of boiling gold, prepared to die."

"I will not die," Skagra's voice rose in terrible, tearful wroth. "I will not give in! I will not cower! I will not die!"

She stepped into the lake and shrieked; fire snaked up her body, consuming her clothes and hair. Ilma let go of Rob and ran to her daughter, calling her names, but Skagra turned and snarled, baring her jagged teeth. With an unholy bellow, Skagra walked into the molten gold and sank.

Her voice faced in the hissing and groaning gold, her head vanishing under a bulbous wave that bubbled over her.

Rob felt the pain fade, and he breathed. But he was uneasy, something was not right. The Sky Sages *had* survived; this much was true. But now that the dead god's heart was destroyed, what would happen? Would it still work?

"She's gone," Ilma said.

"I'm sorry," Rob said. "We tried to help her."

"I know," Ilma shuddered, her shoulders heaving.

"We should get back to the ship."

Using the many-coloured blade to take his weight, he got up. Ilma looked at him, utterly devastated. He put his arm around her shoulders, and together they walked the path, away from the pit of gold.

"Gorm," he called. "We need to get to the ship. Can you do it?"

She got to her feet, wavering and balancing against a broken boulder. Her face was a ruin of red, the wounds on her forehead spilling like waterfalls. Ilma padded over and tore bandages from her dress before tying them over the gashes.

"I need to be alone," Gorm said. "I have done something this day. I am like you, Rob Sardan. Am I now the Crown-breaker as she said?"

"If you want to be," Rob laughed.

Gorm made her way to him, and he could see the full fury of the injuries she had sustained. Blackened eyes, a broken nose, and so many punctures in her head; all were difficult to look at. Rob gulped and watched as Ilma bandaged her.

"Permission to return to the ship," Gorm breathed. "Captain."

"Granted," Rob hugged her tightly as soon as Ilma was done. "Better hurry, though. Looks like they've got the water flowing."

"What about you?"

"I want to make absolutely sure about Skagra," he said.

Gorm bowed as she released him and she walked away, head lofty even as she limped. Rob watched her, awe and admiration glowing in his chest. She had heard his story and had done what he had done. Rob had been the Sword-breaker, he had killed a god, and someone else had thought they could do the same. And they had. This was it; this was what he had wanted from the start. To inspire.

As Gorm vanished into the crack in the wall, he lifted the many-coloured blade and watched the colours mix and shift in the light from the glowing gold behind.

"What will the world think?" he said. "That sword has touched every kind of blood. People will think I've killed everyone you've ever met!"

"Rob . . ." Ilma was still crying, looking towards the molten gold. "My daughter, she's just . . ."

He put his arm around her again and she shivered. He wanted to say something to calm her and help her, but all he could feel was relief that Skagra was gone. But when he felt Ilma heave another great sob, guilt flowed into his blood.

"It isn't your fault," he managed.

"Please, don't," Ilma said softly. "I know what she had become. I know what the god's power was doing to her. I can't pretend anymore. I can't pretend that she wasn't this pirate. I can't pretend she wasn't Skagra." She lowered her voice. "That was her real name, I suppose. Pangles was what I called her, but Skagra was her choice. I wish I could have told her how sorry I am . . ."

Fire flared in Rob's body; he doubled over, his hands clutching his abdomen. The pain was so fierce and so complete that he blacked out. He saw red wind for a second, but he forced it away by sheer will.

The golden pool was boiling over the spot where Skagra had vanished. Steam rose and glowed with sparks. Rob's breath fell short as a shape rose from the pit. Skagra was bald, and coated from head to foot in gold. Her body was writhing and screaming with metallic scrapes. Skagra raised her hands, and the gold rose with her ever so slightly.

"Skagra," Ilma said, standing as more tears fell. "You're still . . ."

"The gold still works," Rob realised. "And it's starting to obey her."

"She's still alive . . ." Ilma looked ready to faint, but Rob put his hand on her shoulder even as the pain within him mounted.

"Your daughter is gone," he said. "I don't know what this thing is, but it . . ."

"It isn't her," Ilma said, wiping her mouth. "Keep her distracted, Captain. I'm going to bring something."

"What?"

"The ship. I'm going to bring the ship."

Ilma ran up the path, wiping tears from her eyes, and then she clambered away from the crack in the wall. Her feet flew, her breathing laboured and terrified. Rob could not blame her.

Rob wanted to go to her and help, but the pain was a mountain. It was as if he was being pulled towards Skagra, her will driving the shard inside to join the rest of the gold.

He twisted and ripped his shirt open; the wound was glowing with golden light. His eyes met Skagra's as she lifted her hands to him and pulled her torso out of the pool. The pain increased, and she gurgled in pleasure as he screamed.

"*No more*," Skagra's mouth was open, but the voice was not hers. "*No more queens or lords. No more people. All shall die. All shall die.*"

"Why are you doing this?" Rob shouted through his tears. He could barely stay conscious and red mist was clawing his mind. "What do you gain from this?"

"*No gains, no loss, no glory*!" Skagra laughed and raised her hands. "*Nothing shall remain. Nothing shall live.*"

The power was taking over. Everything that had been Skagra, or Pangles, was being eaten by what was left of this god's body. Its mind and power may have been destroyed, but the body was having the same effect that Saagara's had had on Rob.

"Skagra," he shouted. "You're dying. D'haara's body is taking over you. You can fight it; you can break its influence. I did. You can break the god!"

"*Why break the god? You fool, Rob Sardan. I* am *the god. D'haara has no mind but my mind, no heart but my heart, all that remains is the power of the god's flesh, and I shall make it mine.*"

She tried to walk but her legs were still stuck in the molten metal. She twisted, spraying gold from her smooth head. She pulled further and further until she was up to her waist, but then she sank again. Rob started to back away, but she stretched a hand and his abdomen blazed.

An invisible force dragged his body, slowly and painfully, towards the pit. Heat rose and his boots smoked. Panicking, he scrambled to hold onto a boulder. The pressure mounted and Skagra was rising from the gold, pulling the shard.

If he let go, he would be dragged into the pit, but if he held on, Skagra would rise. Looking at the bubbling gold, he held his breath, wondering what it would feel like to be eaten by molten metal. The dreams would be gone, the danger would be defeated, and he would have saved his crew, sacrificing his own life.

He was so close to letting go, to letting death claim him. He had broken the Sea-Stone Sword, he had killed the Air King, and he had escaped from the ice prison, south of south. That was enough for a story, wasn't it? He tried to release his grasp on the boulder.

But there was still Mothar, the Pirate Lord; the man who had killed Niall, killed his mother, and plunged his life into chaos. There was so much left in the world to see. There was his crew. They had lives, and he wanted to see them live.

His heart was beating faster than it had ever beaten in his life; he drew the many-coloured blade and turned its point towards his scar.

He took a long, gulping breath and met Skagra's eye for a second and then plunged the sword into the wound.

Screaming piercingly high, he felt sick, faint, and his eyes blurred into red dreams. With all the effort of will, he pulled his mind to reality and let the sword drop at his side. He reached his hand to the wound and dug his fingers inside. He retched, his body trying with all its might to force him to stop this.

Above, he spied Ilma almost at the gate, her arm hanging at one side while her good hand clung to the rocks. He gulped and hoped.

Skagra was out to her knees now, her face twisted in concentration as she tightened her hand into a fist. The shard burst into horrendous heat, stabbing deeper into his body, but pulling Skagra further from the pit.

Sweating and on the edge of fainting, Rob dug his fingers in deeper, gritting his teeth to stop himself from screaming.

The noise would distract Ilma. Skagra laughed and moved her hand. The gold band on Rob's right wrist glowed.

His grip was slipping, his hand wanted to let go, but he tried to use the healing power of the shard while he still had it, and directed it into his hand. Skagra made a gravelly, unnatural noise and struggled to lift one foot out of the gold and take a step on the surface of the pool.

"*There are other powers*," she hissed. "*The Sword, the Crown, the Throne, and the unknown. Don't you want to know what they are? Don't you want to know what your mother was really up to all those years?*"

Rob's finger touched the shard and he felt a surge of new pain, but he drove another finger in to get a grip on it. The world was fading, his arm was burning, his abdomen was bleeding so much that he wasn't sure what would kill him first, the blood loss or the shock.

He tugged on the shard, but it was stuck, driven right into his bone by Alya's jian strike. Yelling with all of his strength, Rob pulled and pulled again. His bone shuddered and his spine flared. He was going to die; he could feel it. He'd die; he'd fall into a pit of nothingness. At least, there would be no dreams there.

"If there are other powers," Rob said through tears. "I will break them, too!"

The shard was dislodged and he pulled it out with a gasping, sucking noise. He let go of the rock and yanked the gold band off his hand. Pressing the wound, he held both the glowing shard and the band in his left hand and met Skagra's eyes. The pirate was sinking again, but she was almost at the shore.

One of her hands touched the earth and it shuddered. Cracks appeared along the path; fissures opened and Skagra's eyes billowed with gold. Rob threw the band and the shard; they hit her head and bounced into the golden pool. He raised the many-coloured blade and pointed it at her.

"*Kill me, Rob Sardan*," she said, with horrific bitterness. "*Kill another god. Is that what you want to be? One who breaks, one who kills, one whose sword is so stained with blood that it shines with every colour. That is what you will be.*"

"If I have to be," he said and looked into her eyes. "King-killer. Sky-slayer. Sword-breaker. God-killer."

His ears caught the sound of rumbling and a turning of metal cogs. Relief and a surge of joy went through him and he looked up at the gate. Ilma was turning the wheels atop it and the thing was opening. Water spurted from top to bottom and then burst in a white torrent. Foaming fury charged down the canal, overflowing and sending a flood towards where Rob was standing.

With a tremendous effort, he leapt on top of the boulder and turned to see Skagra screaming with her hand stretched towards him.

"*The fire is inside you, Rob Sardan*," she shouted. "*Your mother put it there. You are not human anymore*!"

Water slammed into her and steamed. Her gold-covered limbs hissed and froze, the water rose, foaming around her body, cooling the gold and solidifying it. The last thing to stop was her face, which contorted into a harrowing expression of uttermost fear and loathing.

The water continued to burst through the gate, heavy and overpowering. The canal cracked under the weight and pillars fell, crumbling under the force. Rob held tight to the boulder; his right hand clasped over the wound as blood oozed from it.

It wasn't healing. He could feel all the wounds, from the small scars on his legs to the giant wound he was holding. It should have frightened him, but he laughed. Whatever Skagra might have said, he was human, and he was dying. He rested on his knees and watched as the water poured in, taking these last few breaths before the darkness would set in.

A chubby bear's face broke through the gate, shattering the hinges as the ship was forced through. The canal collapsed and water gushed over everything. The gold pools hissed as the cooling liquid settled over them and vapour rose over the last remnants of the melted tower.

The stream of magma had abated and all that was left now was a pool of filthy water, rising to take Rob's boulder. But the ship bumped along the shattered pathway, closer and closer, voices shouting from the deck as he waved his free hand at them.

Soon, the water lifted him and he lay back in it, floating like flotsam. He fell, his mind closing on the horrible finality. Red mist clouded his eyes and the old, piercing scream ripped through his head for what he hoped was the last time.

Chapter Thirty Five

Trust

THE SHIP BOBBED IN CALM WATERS, BLUE SKIES OVERHEAD AND a cool wind fluttering in the drawn sails. White gulls called, circling on the far horizon as the hush and hiss of the ocean soothed the air.

The bear on the front of the ship was scratched, burned and dented, but it still looked out over the sea, defiant. On the deck, a woman in a headscarf marched from the prow to the forecastle, listening to the wind. She took her time, breathing the salt air and taking in the world around her.

At last, she pushed her way through a door and closed it gently behind her. The rest of the crew carried on with their work, quiet, yet content. The fear and dread that had been their constant companions for so long were as distant as the gull cries.

Within the forecastle, Rob was lying on the bunk. Eyes were looking at him. He tried to sit but was pushed back down as somebody laughed.

"Don't even think about it," Ilma said. She dabbed his forehead with a wet cloth. "You're certainly not healing like you used to."

"I know," he croaked. "Hello to you too."

"Welcome back to the land of the living," she smiled pleasantly for a moment. "And you've got me to thank for that, so I expect extra rations and a big song and dance made in my honour!"

"Gladly," Rob tried to laugh but it was painful. "I'll need to get used to regular healing times now, I suppose."

"What happened? What changed?"

"I'm not entirely sure." Rob coughed, pain shooting through his abdomen. "But I can guess. The knife the pengs used, it had the body of D'haara, and that god had the ability to change shapes. I was using that without knowing. I had an idea about what shape I was supposed to be, and it kept going for that."

"So, you *are* human?" said Alya from somewhere else in the room.

Rob turned his head on the pillow and saw her leaning against the door of the cabin; her head was bandaged, and she had a hand in a sling, but she was smiling sardonically. He returned the expression and let his head sink into the pillow.

"I'm still alive," he said. "Maybe there's still some of that power left."

"Hardly!" Ilma said.

"Your decision to cut into your own body was suicidal," Alya said. "What's the matter? Living too complicated?"

"Isn't it always?"

"Do you know what I had to do to keep you from dying?" Ilma slapped his arm. "Loads! And what thanks do I get?"

"All the gold you can carry," Rob said.

"That is not funny," she said.

"I'm sorry." He put a hand on her arm. "I really am, Ilma. You did a good thing, you know?"

"I did a terrible thing," she said, ". . . do you think she's dead?"

"No," Rob shook his head. "The Sky Sages survived being encased in the gold. She will, too. My guess is that the god's power will keep her alive."

"A living statue," Alya said. "A fate worse than death, if you ask me."

"Well, nobody did ask you!" Ilma snapped.

"No, they did not," Alya agreed. "Doctor, may I have a moment with the Captain now that he is awake?"

"Fine." She stood and marched from the cabin, hiding her tears.

Alya hung her head and rubbed at her eyes. She sagged against the door, weariness seeming to pile on her shoulders. Rob managed to sit up, but he could feel his wound stinging with stitches.

"You've been out for a week," Alya explained. "We could have used an extra hand while getting out of those caves."

"Sorry," he smiled. "What about the explosives the pirates set? Did you manage to defuse them?"

"I did not," she smiled. "They exploded."

"And this is good?" Rob almost leapt at her. "What about the volcano?"

"Your memory's not too good, is it? They were using the peng's blasting powder. I told you it wasn't destructive, only visually impressive. All it did was fill the cavern with smoke and collapse some of the tunnels. I doubt anyone will be able to get to what is left of Skagra now."

"I see." Rob sunk back down and closed his eyes for a moment. "Where are we?"

"Just outside the cave," she said. "We've been moored here while we've been healing. Kari's pretty bad, and it's my fault."

"What happened?"

"After you and Ilma went, we tried to get the holes patched in the ship. Kari and Jarl said they could do it. My impression of Jarl has always been that he is given to violent outbursts against those he thinks he can control. However, I put it down to panic and allowed them to work while I went to the gates, to refloat the ship.

"After a few hours, I heard a cry; I saw Jarl attacking Kari. There was nothing I could do. The priority was the ship. I opened one of the gates, so the water flowed slowly. Even so, by the time I got back, she was beaten badly. Jarl was beyond control.

"Gold glowed in his eyes, and he attacked me. I chipped my jian when I struck him, and he didn't seem to feel it. The water was rising, but not fast enough. It was steaming against the magma, and in the mist, I managed to dumbfound Jarl long enough to hide Kari in the ship.

"As fortune would have it, a group of naked Sages arrived. I pride myself on being difficult to astonish, but this did leave me somewhat wrong-footed. With their help, we were able to subdue Jarl. Then he started screaming; his veins were burning, and we thought he'd die.

"Something happened, the gold was sucked out of him, and he fainted. We chained him to the mast in the cargo hold while we finished the repairs. It was a tight job as the water was rising. We managed to get it done just before Ilma opened the entrance to the Tower. It was a struggle to get you onboard. Ilma was inconsolable. Despite everything Skagra had done, she still maintained affection for her."

Rob nodded and looked at Alya; her eyes were on the floor, and her forehead was knitted. Her injured arm was tight against her chest while her other was loose at her side.

"You did well," he said.

"If I required compliments I would ask for them," she said. "I miscalculated, and I allowed a member of our crew to be hurt. I should have guessed that Jarl would still have been under Skagra's influence."

Rob strained and swung his legs off the bed with an agonized grunt. "You hold yourself to a high standard."

"I hold myself accountable for my actions," she said. "It is how we realise our mistakes and so improve."

"You need to improve, Alya?" he smirked.

"I haven't needed to for a long time," she smiled. "You are a bad influence."

"I've heard that before," he laughed, painfully. "You'll be a hero if you're not careful."

"What a depressing thought!"

"Where's Jarl now?"

"In the hold." She looked unhappy. "The Sages examined him and believed him no longer under the influence. I am not convinced, and so he is being watched." Alya strode over and helped him steady his weight as he stood.

"We can't let the crew fall apart. Not after everything that's happened."

"What has happened? What have we achieved? So far as I can tell, the Sky Sage's Tower is destroyed, along with all of its secrets. There are no pendants. The ship is damaged, and we have nowhere to go."

"Skagra is done," Rob said. "Gorm is avenged. Another god's power is destroyed. Ilma has closure. You have proof of your ship's integrity. And we have a crew that will stick together no matter what. That's more than most people have."

"It's not much of what we set out for."

"Bright ray of sunshine you are."

"You didn't make me your first mate so I could agree with you."

"No I didn't," he said as he took some tentative steps. "But we have plenty to think about now. The Sword, the Crown, the Throne, and the unknown."

"What are you talking about?"

"Something Skagra said," Rob said with a sigh. "Another mystery, another quest, or another dead end, who knows?"

Alya pushed the door, and they stepped onto the main deck.

Gorm and the Sky Sages were meditating around the main mast. They were dressed in some spare clothes they had traded for on Herebealde. Kari was standing at the wheel, her arms were bandaged as was her head, but she smiled at Alya. There was a slump to her stride, and Rob tried to tighten his grip on his first mate.

"Anything I should know about?" he asked.

"She has strange ideas," Alya said. "I do not wish to cause unnecessary upset, so I am maintaining a pleasant attitude."

"That's very unlike you."

"I have been known to take other people's feelings into account when trying to decipher my position in a group. It is useful."

"As you say," he shrugged. "Gorm, can you help me while Alya gathers the rest of the crew?"

The larger woman stood and bowed to the Sages before taking over from Alya in guiding her captain along the deck. They stopped about halfway along, and Rob leaned against the railing.

"How are you?" Rob asked. "I suppose you had your vengeance."

"I did not need vengeance," she said. "It was peace I needed. Now that Skagra is done, I need not fear. All my fears were for my own heart, it seems. These are troubles I can face; these are battles I can win. We shall have peace when we can be fulfilled within our own mind and not be at war with our own selves."

"Well said," Rob nodded though he was not sure he understood.

"And what of you, Captain? Your fears may still lie ahead of you. The Pirate Lord Mothar still lives, and no doubt his eye will seek you out if it has not already done so. He hates you and your mother with a bitter, unending hatred."

"I have a feeling that I will have bigger things to worry about," Rob said with a hushed tone. "What was my mother up to all those years? What did she do to me? Or was Skagra just saying things to mess with my mind?"

"I cannot answer these questions," Gorm bowed her head as she spoke. "Your mother was a hero to many, a villain to others.

You may follow in her footsteps, or you may make your own circles in these waters."

"Circles in the water." Rob hummed and looked out across the sea. "We changed the world back there, Gorm. Perhaps the ripples we caused will fade, but the stone we dropped will last forever."

"Even stones weather with time," Gorm said, sagely.

"Let's not stretch the metaphor too far. Even if I never got the pendant, that wasn't the point of this quest, not really. We did something good, we made a difference, we put things right, and we built a crew, a real crew; and isn't that what the quest was for?"

"Perhaps," Gorm did not sound convinced. "You broke the Sea-Stone Sword, and I broke the Crown of Black Glass. Wasn't that the point of the quest?"

"No," Rob smiled and looked at the rest of the crew who were now gathering around him. "The point wasn't to break the Crown, it wasn't to defeat Skagra, nor even to find a pendant; the quest is not the quarry. The *quest* is the quest."

The crew regarded him as he raised his voice. Jarl was under the watchful eyes of Alya and Kari, and his hands were tied. Rob heaved a heavy breath and hoped that one day they would be able to trust the man. He seemed dazed as he blinked in the sunlight, but he smiled. The sight unnerved Rob but he shifted his focus onto Ilma, who was damp eyed and her good hand was rubbing at her other.

Kerrok the peng appeared at the door, and Rob met her eyes. She approached and bowed. "I owe you apologies, on behalf of the Blood Pengs. We should never have taken a contract with Skagra."

"None of this would have happened if you hadn't smashed my pendant." Rob shrugged.

"Yes," Kerrok looked unhappy, her beak chattering. "I never believed in its power. I thought it was a folk tale or a comfort charm. I truly believed that you would recover and that there was no curse."

"I probably would have thought the same," Rob said. "I forgive you."

"I do not require forgiveness, only understanding."

"Well, you've got that then," he pouted.

He gave them all an account of what had happened in the Tower of the Sky Sages. He came to the moment where he fled from Skagra with the golden sword and skipped right to the Tower being destroyed by magma; Gorm raised a hand.

"What happened to Vann?" she asked.

Everyone turned his or her eyes fully on Rob. They had forgotten him, he realised. Some of Vann's words came back, hitting hard and sharp. Had any of them realised? What could he tell them? He looked at Alya. What could he say? That Vann had betrayed them? That the crew had already fallen apart?

"He . . ." Rob said. "I couldn't save him. I tried, but the Tower was falling, and he was lost under the gold. I don't think he suffered."

The lie hung in the air, the crew seeming unable to digest it. Gorm sat and closed her eyes, whispering. Ilma put a hand over her mouth.

"I don't know what to say," Rob went on. "He was brave. He helped us escape and get the ship. He helped Kari and Jarl off the Long Silver, and . . ." Rob gulped. "He was loved. I wish we had been kinder to him."

Alya lowered her gaze and seemed deep in thought. At last, she lifted her face and met Rob's eyes.

"It seems I misjudged him," she said. "I was wrong."

Inside, Rob was screaming. '*No, Alya, you were right. I should have trusted you . . .* 'but he could not voice the thoughts.

As the others mourned, he struggled to justify his choice. Vann had said he was going to join Mothar, but he doubted he would be accommodating. If he were lucky, he'd be imprisoned and tortured, if things got worse than that, Rob's lie would become true.

"We must keep going," he said. "Vann died saving us. We're all safe; from Skagra at least. We have a ship. We have the sea, and we have the world ahead."

Rob stepped away from the railing, trying to stand using his own strength. He put his arms on Kari's shoulders and kissed her forehead.

"You belong here," he said, and he moved to Ilma and did the same. "You are valuable, and we need you." He went to Gorm. "With your wisdom, we will never lose sight of what is important." To Jarl, he gave a small bow. "We will learn to help you, and you will learn to help us. I trust you." He turned to Alya and approached her slowly. "I have always trusted you. From the very beginning."

"That's a lie," she said.

"Yeah, it is," he grinned. "But you liked it."

"Ordinarily I would not."

He approached, arms outstretched for an embrace, but she shrank back and offered a hand instead. He shook it and she was trying very hard to smile, but it looked as if she were about to be sick, so he stepped back. With a cough, he looked at Kerrok and the Sky Sages.

"You are all free to stay with us as long as you wish," he said. "If you have any destination in mind, let us know, and we will try and accommodate you."

"Concaedes," said the draigish Sage. "There is a temple in Perge that we may visit. The people of Razal are very accommodating to the Sky Sages."

"We can take you to the coast," Rob nodded to Kari, who returned it confidently. "And you, peng?"

"My Blood Pengs are captured," Kerrok said. "They were taken by the pirates as punishment for failing to fulfil the contract. I will save them if I can."

"Then our paths lie together," said Rob. "It is my aim to bring down Mothar, the Pirate Lord. If they're anywhere, he'll know."

"Very well," she nodded.

"There is only one question yet to answer. What do we call this ship?"

"I thought it was Fat Ted," said Kari. "In memory of Vann, I think we should honour his choice."

"No," said Alya. "Even if he's dead, Fat Ted is still a ridiculous name."

"I agree," Rob said. "I can't tell people I'm the captain of Fat Ted."

"Well, whatever you call it," Jarl said. "I hope it's a happy name."

They looked at him, and he beamed. Gorm looked pleased with this statement, but the others were visibly unnerved.

"A compromise," Rob offered. "You can call the figurehead Fat Ted if you like. The little chubby bear has that name about him. But the ship needs a name that the pirates will fear."

"I don't know about you," said Jarl. "But if the pirates start to tremble at the name Fat Ted, then we will have truly changed the world."

Rob could not help but laugh. Gorm stepped forward and put a hand on Alya's shoulder before giving Rob an appraising look.

"I favour a simpler name," she said. "*The Trygve*, it means *Trust* in the language of Geata, Vann's homeland."

"Very sentimental," Alya said, but she smiled.

"*Trust*?" Rob nodded. "Yes, that could work."

The others hummed agreement as he waved a dismissal and they set about putting the sails into order while Kari went to the wheel, and Gorm raised the anchor. Soon, *The Trygve* was moving, wind filling the canvas and waves foaming about the hull. Ilma came to Rob's side.

"Did we do the right thing?" she asked. "About Skagra? She was my child. What if the same tendencies are inside me, too?"

"You, Gorm and I should form a club." He pulled Ilma into a soft embrace. "We'll carry on because we can. Because we must. We'll watch one another and look after one another. If I ever see you eating hands, I will let you know."

Ilma tried to smile, but she failed.

Chapter Thirty Six

The Unknown

After three days they anchored off the coast of Concaedes, walls of trees rising above a sward of grass. Rob stood on deck and steadied his breathing as cool, pine air wafted from the shore. Despite the safety, despite the trust of everyone, and despite the fact that they still had their ship, he felt he had failed. It dug into his chest like a drill, twisting and wailing in a voice that reminded him of the tower of Bron'Halla.

On the shore, Alya was ordering the others to collect wood so that she could begin more substantial repairs to the ship. The patches they had made in the caverns had sprung so many leaks that it had taken all of the Sky Sages alongside the crew to keep them from sinking. Rob had thankfully been confined to his cabin.

His hand strayed to the bandages on his abdomen. The wound was healing slowly. Skagra's words rang in his memory. '*You're not human anymore . . .*'

Ilma walked from the aftcastle and spotted him. "Bed! Now!" she ordered.

"I just wanted some air," he moaned. "A few minutes, please?"

"Five, and then back on that bunk. Razal's shield, Rob, you'll be in a wheelchair before long. You don't heal the same."

"I'm healing more than I should, though," he said, looking at his hand. There were scars along his palm from where the Crown had bitten him. "I used to heal quickly *before* I got that shard. Perhaps it's . . ." He looked away and frowned.

"Perhaps you're just special," she suggested.

He shook his head. "Skagra said that my mother had done something to me. I wonder if that has anything to do with it. My mother did a lot of things I'd like answers for."

"Maybe you should ask her . . ." she clamped her mouth closed and looked away before going on. "I'm sorry, I forgot."

"I forget sometimes," he shrugged. "Sometimes I like to pretend she's still out there. But then I remember Mothar, I remember Kenna Iron Helm, I remember everything that's happened."

Ilma put her head on his shoulder, and they stood together on the deck, listening to the waves and the muffled sound of Alya shouting creative insults at Jarl, who did not seem to understand them.

Rob wondered how long it would take for him to sleep again. He was still screaming. He was still trapped in the Curse. The idea of finding some special tea, like the one Lomi had offered, wandered before his mind. But he dismissed it, recalling what had happened when he'd actually drunk it.

Webbed feet pattered, and he looked over his shoulder to see Kerrok, her hand clutching a pouch. She looked disgruntled and reluctant.

"Need something?" he asked.

"This." She held out the pouch. "I thought you should have it. I want to pay my way. I'm a passenger, not a crewmate. So, this is my payment. Hurts to give it up, but I feel I owe you. I thought it'd be worth a lot . . ."

He took the pouch, and it jangled with metallic noises. Emptying the contents onto his palm, his eyes opened wide, and all the blood left his face. Golden pieces lay there, the remnants of the Sky-slayer's pendant Kerrok had broken.

"This is . . ." he tried to speak. "You had this all along?"

"I did," she shrugged. "I thought of it as a bit of side payment for spending all that time in that flaming prison. Thought it might be valuable if I got it fixed, but nobody will even try. Thought of asking them Sages, but couldn't bring myself to do it under your nose."

"How thoughtful." He narrowed his eyes and looked onto the shore. The Sky Sages were packing their belongings, preparing for their pilgrimage but Rob waved to them. They waved back and turned away.

"No!" he shouted, but the effort pained him.

"Oi! Sages!" Ilma called, standing on the railing. "Come back!"

Rob went to his knees; his chest weakened with sudden hope. The pendant was in his hands; the pendant he had thought lost, and had spent so much time and effort trying to replace . . .

There was a rustle and a shout, but Rob could hardly move. Kerrok jumped back, her hands on her hips. The draigish Sage was stood on the railing, her wings quickly folding against her back as she stepped down.

"Please, tell nobody I did that," she said. "But you sounded desperate."

"The pendant," Rob held it. "This is a Sky-slayer's pendant. Can it be repaired? Please! Can it be repaired?"

The draig knelt and looked at the pieces, her head tilting one way and then the other. Meanwhile, Kerrok was muttering and grumbling louder until some of her insults became audible. ". . . if one of the intelligent ones were to come instead of this ash-mouth . . ."

"Excuse me?" The draig sprang to her feet. "I am Sage Eurwen, I am an abbot in training, and I am more than capable of this task, peng."

"Must be a simple task, then."

"Please be quiet," Rob said. "Kerrok, go and make yourself useful."

"I'd rather stay, just in case things get dangerous around here."

"If you stay, be quiet."

"You're not in charge of me!"

"Sage Eurwen, feel free to ignore everything Kerrok says."

Eurwen nodded and took the pieces of the pendant. She clutched it to her chest and looked uncomfortable. "If you wouldn't mind averting your eyes."

"Of course," Rob said, looking away as the sound of her unfolding wings snapped like wind.

Hours passed. The Sages had set up a fire on the shore and were heating a pot over it, chanting and dancing in complex circular motions. Ilma led Rob back to his cabin while they worked.

He lay on the bunk and fidgeted. Sleep was not an option. He wanted to keep it at bay until he had the pendant back; if it would work. That thought stabbed. If the repairs were not effective; if he was left back in his old despair, could he handle it? Would he be able to face his future with no hope?

The only other option he had was to find another Sky-slayer and take their pendant. But knowing the torture that would cause made him dismiss the idea. What about a dead Slayer? What would have happened to their pendant?

There was a knock on the door and Alya marched in. She now only had a small bandage on her arm and patches on her forehead. He envied her mobility.

"Everything in order?" he asked.

"Mostly," she sniffed. "Kari wants to help with the repairs, but I am not sure. She is eager because of her misguided feelings."

"She can't help feelings." Rob sat up and frowned.

"She can help her actions, though, and they are not productive." She shook her head. "I am not equipped for such situations. I recommend she have a discussion with you in which you explain to her that I have no romantic feelings. At all."

"You tell her," he said. "You can't be scared."

"I have told her on multiple occasions; I don't think she understands."

"Well," Rob sighed. "She will move on in time, I suppose."

"You never did," Alya gave him a glower. "I can hear your screaming, you know? The whole ship can. Niall, the boy who died. How long has it been?"

"More than two years." Rob looked at the floor and tried to keep his lip from quivering. "I wish I could forget. Don't you wish you could forget things?"

"Sometimes," she frowned. "As you discovered, I worked for the pirate Le'ah before coming to Bron'Halla. Her people helped me cross the sea on many adventures. I was so convinced she was a friend that I didn't stop to think about her allegiances. Now, perhaps, I am beginning to question them again."

"What do you mean?"

She took a breath and looked at him with a deep curiosity, tilting her head from side to side. "Le'ah knew your mother, of course. She and Morven Sardan were close. Very, very close by all accounts."

Rob furrowed his brow and then his eyes widened. "You think she knew I was in Bron'Halla? Perhaps she sent you there because she thought you'd get me out?"

"The thought had occurred to me. It seems an unlikely outcome, though. Such a plan would leave far too much to chance and blind luck."

"Seemed to work, though."

The door was hammered, and Eurwen entered.

"Captain Sardan," she said bowing. "We are ready for you."

"Can you walk?" Alya asked. "If you can't you'll have to answer to Ilma."

"Let *them* answer to Ilma," he grinned and stood. Alya helped him and together they went into the cool, twilight air.

The Sky Sages were gathered about the main mast, the tall sauros a little apart from them, a box in hand. Eurwen called for silence.

"There is a tradition," she said and cleared her throat. "Slayer of the Skies, holder of the Curse; you have done a deed that has marked you. Vaata has sought to drive you into death. Pray, take you now this pendant and be whole for a time."

The box was opened, and there lay the pendant. Its face was gold with the skeletal pterodactyl etched in black. The thing glittered and seemed to glow as the sunlight fell to the horizon.

Rob picked up the pendant and let it dangle before his eyes; it turned on the chain until the back was visible. He saw words in the Spillish language. "Rob Sardan," he guessed.

"Indeed," Eurwen nodded. "This pendant was your uncle Bein'Seior's, but now it belongs to you. We have reforged it and put as much of our power into it as we could. It is not as good as it would have been if a true abbot had made it, but with all of us working together, we believe it will hold back the Curse."

"Thank you." Rob just about managed to speak without breaking down.

"You are a Sky-slayer, Rob Sardan. But you are also the King-killer. That is why the pendant is gold. It is the only one of its kind."

Rob pulled the chain over his head and let it rest against his chest. His skin burst into a clamour of needles; his hands tingled and his eyes watered with overwhelming relief. Gorm, Ilma, Karri, Jarl and Kerrok stood behind the Sages, their eyes on him. He grinned at them and beckoned them closer.

"Now," he said. "We have our chance. We can go and do something amazing. There are other pirates, besides Skagra."

"To free the Ginnungagap would be appropriate penance for me," said Gorm.

"If I could see Ramas one last time, that would be good," Ilma said.

"To honour my lost friends, and to give the Long Silver a better legacy, I'll go with you," said Karri. "Let's kick them into the sea!"

"I like the sea," Jarl said, dreamily. "I like fish."

Alya stepped away and sighed. "I suppose it is my turn to talk?"

"Only if you want to," Rob said.

"Well then," she smiled. "Where are we heading, Captain?"

"To the unknown," he said.

Acknowledgements

This world was born out of those countless years of telling stories about dinosaurs, dragons, penguins and bears to my siblings. So, to Josh, Jonny, Levi and Matt, you all may pat yourselves on the back. And I repeat my message from the previous novel; no, you cannot have my royalties. Stop asking.

For my beta readers, Maria Talvela, Katherine Woodruff and Hanni Halonen, the original Lomi Thinlomine. Thank you for reading my book, telling me how to make it better, and for making me drink more tea than was medically advisable. You and the whole Barrow Downs family are some of the best people I have ever known.

To the Tolkien Society for being a terrific group of wonderful people, always ready to offer constructive criticism and debate. Without you excellent and admirable Hobbits, I would never have reached eleventy-one pages, let alone however-many pages this book turns out to be!

To my oldest and most powerful friend, Gemma Hammond, for always being supportive and ridiculous throughout the entire process of writing this book and others. You're one of the most important people I've ever met. Thank you for being my translation consultant for certain parts. It was all Greek to me. I'm hilarious.

My thanks also to Francesca T Barbini, Jay Johnstone and the whole team at Sci-fi Fantasy Network for giving me plenty of support, encouragement, and amazing opportunities.

Last of all, to Sammy Smith, Zoë Harris, Joanne Hall, and all the wonderful people of Kristell Ink and Grimbold Books for deciding that my book was worth their time and effort.

The Môr Sea
Mores
Y Tywyllwch
Wynhold
Voltous
The Yâlal
The Bôhû Desert
Ty Tan
Draid Cendyl
Gwasrat
The Tôhû Desert
Twyn Dinas
Y Rhwth
The Anser Woods
Y Mor Aral
Findabar
Dhvana
Draig Traeth
Lizarn Minor
Lizarn Major
Fort Ewin
Helzar
Felin Maes
Naug
Digro
Daingean
Bunchnoic
Ubhar Mountains
Cathair
Bua Woods
Emerald Port
Broad Mullach
Nasgadh Sea
Hira
The Sea of Yam
Gloine
Bronze Port
Ennis Rossin
Keeker Isle
Dun Geill
The Teeth
Crossing Sea
Isles of Cath
Khamas
Red Docks
Iron Mines
Har Yam
Concaedes
Aldaron
Dun Coille
Perge
Fior
Gaeleo
Deata
Leoht
Ginnungagap
Herebealde
Gold Port
Shên
Tsayad
Ha' Tiyrah
Galot
Dry Forest
Yabiyn
Tabbach
The Bohu Mountains
Yitskhaq
Lake of Zyph
The Mabow Woods
Mountains of Uine
Woods of Zerem
Eyn Dor
Llygad
Yesh
Wymosh
Spill
Thuris
Kallao
Meggaleios
Luchnia
Xenia
Carn
Carpad Forest
Farraige Sea
Pearl Port
Woods of Paolchu
Sioc
Diamond Port
Bad Inas
Mountains of Cumhacht
Penguve

About the Author

Joel Cornah is a writer and journalist from Lancashire in the north of England. He has written for a number of online publications, focusing on fantasy and science fiction, feminism, and asexuality.

Kristell Ink published his first novel, The Sea-Stone Sword, in 2014, followed closely by a series of novellas, including The Spire of Frozen Fire (2014) and The Silent Helm (2015). He has since been a regular contributor to Sci-Fi Fantasy Network, where he is now the editor of all things Doctor Who. Moreover, he has been involved with the Tolkien Society, giving talks and more at the annual Oxonmoot meetings.

He is open about his dyslexia and the challenges it causes writers, and has talked at schools and universities about the subject. He is also a frequent contributor to the Pack of Aces blog, focussing on issues of asexuality in media, specialising in sci-fi and fantasy.

Besides writing, he also runs an independent café and bookshop in Parbold Village, linked to The Tom Church Foundation, a charity that specialises in helping young people who use prosthetics.

A Selection of Other Titles from Kristell Ink

Fight Like A Girl edited by Joanne Hall & Roz Clarke

What do you get when some of the best women writers of genre fiction come together to tell tales of female strength? A powerful collection of science fiction and fantasy ranging from space operas and near-future factional conflict to medieval warfare and urban fantasy. These are not pinup girls fighting in heels; these warriors mean business. Whether keen combatants or reluctant fighters, each and every one of these characters was born and bred to Fight Like A Girl.

Featuring stories by Roz Clarke, Kelda Crich, K T Davies, Dolly Garland, K R Green, Joanne Hall, Julia Knight, Kim Lakin-Smith, Juliet McKenna, Lou Morgan, Gaie Sebold, Sophie E Tallis, Fran Terminiello Danie Ware, Nadine West.

Spark & Carousel by Joanne Hall

Spark is a wanted man. On the run after causing the death of his mentor and wild with untamed magic, he arrives in Cape Carey where his latent talents make him the target of rival gangs. It is there that Carousel, a wire-walker and thief, takes him under her wing to guide him through the intrigues of the criminal underworld.

But when Spark's magic cracks the world and releases demons from the hells beneath, two mages of his former order make it their mission to prevent his magic from spiralling out of control. They must find him before he falls into the clutches of those who would exploit his raw talent for their own gain, forcing Spark to confront a power he is not ready to handle.

Meanwhile, a wealthy debutante learning magic in secret has her own plans for Spark and Carousel. But the sudden arrival of the mages throws her carefully laid plans into disarray and she unleashes a terrible evil onto the streets of the unsuspecting city—an evil only Spark's magic can control.

Everyone wants a piece of Spark, but all Spark wants is to rid himself of his talents forever.

Green Sky & Sparks by Kate Coe

In a world of magic, wind, and electricity, Catter Jeck is offered the chance to explore a myth. Travelling from city to city, his search for the centre of the magic catches others in its coils. When the Lord Heir of Meton offers to continue the search in his flying machine, the consequences of their crash—and Toru's accidental link to a dying Healer—suddenly become of central importance to all of their lives.

www.kristell-ink.com

Lightning Source UK Ltd.
Milton Keynes UK
UKOW02f1034190117
292328UK00002B/6/P

9 781911 497103